FIELD OF HONOUR

She had realised what was happening right from the beginning. For a while, she wanted to die. Then she wanted to strike back, to hurt both of them for what they had done to her. She gave no sign of it to James, although it seared her heart every time she helped him pack to leave New Mexico for another trip to San Francisco, to *her*. Linda was a wise woman, but she was a woman first and wise second. She hated Catherine Priestman as she had never hated anyone in all her life. The hate lay like black vomit in the pit of her stomach.

Why? Why, why, why?

FIELD OF HONOUR

Danielle Rockfern

Gainsborough Press

This edition published in 1996 by Gainsborough Press
An imprint of Leopard
20 Vauxhall Bridge Road, London SW1V 2SA

London Melbourne Sydney Auckland
Johannesburg and agencies throughout
the world

First published in Great Britain 1985 by Hamlyn Paperbacks
© Danielle Rockfern 1985

Set in Linotron Bembo by
Book Economy Services (UK), Lindfield, Sussex

Printed and bound in Great Britain by
Cox & Wyman Ltd, Reading, Berkshire

ISBN 0 752 90407 8

For
Richard and Nancy
with love

BOOK ONE

LOVE

1

He was burning, burning.

It was as if his throat was going to close tight and never open again. He sensed a formless *something* trying to blank out his mind, and he was afraid, because he knew instinctively that it was Death. He fought hard to free himself, the way a bound man thrown into water would fight. He did not know that he was thrashing on the soaked bed like a gaffed shark, or that he was shouting wordlessly as he did. Then soft, sweet coolness bathed his burning body, and he felt the touch of tender hands, a fragrance he could not identify.

He slept.

When he awoke, Catherine was there.

'Well,' she smiled. 'You've come back to us.'

He started to sit up and found that he could not. His arms felt as limp as string.

'How long . . . ?' he began.

'You've had a fever,' Catherine said. 'Four days.'

'Fever,' he said, thinking about that with what seemed a ponderously slow stretching of the memory. It began to come back to him, details sliding into his mind like spilled treacle. Leaving home in New Mexico. The train trip across country to San Francisco. He'd gone up to Sacramento on some legal business, decided to take the boat back rather than the train. Then . . the chills that started in the hansom that brought him to the Priestman house.

Then . . . ?'

'Here,' Catherine said, and brought a cup to his lips. It tasted like nectar and he asked her what it was. 'Lime-flower tea,' she said. 'It will do you good.'

The fragrance that he remembered touched his senses. He realised that it was hers. He looked at her lovely eyes. She smiled, and he felt his heart move, as if it had suddenly contracted and then as suddenly expanded. There was something he wanted to tell her, but he fell asleep before he could say it.

Three days later he was well enough to get up.

'I want to take you to lunch,' he told her. 'Somewhere grand. How about the Cliff House?'

'You darling,' she said. 'There's no need for that.'

'My way of thanking you,' he explained. 'For taking care of me.'

'No need to thank us, James,' she said. 'You're family.'

'You,' he said. 'You did it. You alone.'

'The Florence Nightingale of San Francisco,' she said, with a deprecatory gesture. 'Worshipped in the ranks, she woz.'

'What is the name of that perfume you wear?' he said, abruptly. Catherine looked up quickly, and he saw surprise in her eyes, and behind that, something else. He cursed his clumsiness but it was too late to pull back.

'I never wear perfume,' she said. Her fine grey eyes held his. Again he felt that strange, unexpected pulse of his heart.

'Catherine?' he said. The entire house was silent except for the measured tick of the grandfather clock in the hall. Catherine neither moved nor spoke.

'How can I have known you all these years, yet never have seen you until now?' he said, softly.

'Please, James,' she said. 'You mustn't . . .'

'I think I have been in love with you for a long time,' he said. 'And only realised it a moment ago.'

'No,' she whispered. But it was not a command. It was disbelief.

'Yes,' he said, and there was wonder in his voice at what he was saying. All these years . . . all this time. He had never looked at her properly, locked in as he was on his own image of himself, a one-armed Civil War veteran, no longer young, not rich and successful like her husband. It had simply been outside his imagination to think of loving her. Yet now he knew it, and saw no refusal in her eyes.

Lust roared in his ears. He pulled her to her feet and kissed her almost savagely. Images of things he had never done with any woman flickered through his mind. His hand found the comb holding up her hair and he plucked it out, so that her hair cascaded to her waist like a golden-brown torrent. She kissed him now, her lips moving. Her arms were strong, her body eager. He plucked at the buttons of her blouse, tearing the flimsy fabric. The room was filled with the sound of their breathing, the silken rasp of hands moving on bared skin. He felt the soft firmness of her breasts against his chest, her hands on his back. He pulled her down to the floor. They knelt on the carpet and he kissed her breasts, her neck, her mouth. Her nipples were erect and hard; he bit them gently, tugging. She moaned and pulled his mouth hard against her body. He rolled her sideways on to the rich pile of the Persian carpet, pushing her long skirt high. He tore open his pants. Buttons flew, skittering. The insides of her thighs were burning hot. He thrust himself against her, and she arched her back, shuddering.

'In, in!' she hissed. 'Put it into me!'

She bit his shoulder. She grabbed his buttocks, nails digging into him as if she was trying to pull all of him inside her, and she said 'Oh,' and then she said 'Oh, hold me tight. Oh, Jesus, hold me, I'm going,' and he felt the long lovely inner clenching of her. He closed his eyes and went with her, all the strength of his body merging with all the strength of hers, holding her tight, tighter, until he could not any more, until there was nothing left, until he slowly and gently and gently and slowly let her go.

After a while she sighed and sat up. Her hair was in disarray across her bared shoulders. The torn blouse hung from her waistband. She kissed him.

'What are we going to do now?' he said, thinking of all the things that could never again be as they had been before.

She smiled again, like a cat this time.

'We're going to take all our clothes off,' she said, tossing back her hair. 'And then we're going to do it properly!'

And that was how it began.

Catherine. As he watched her cross the room, he was consumed by waves of lust. He wanted to boast how good they were together. She had no shame. He had never known a woman like that. She would do anything he wanted her to do. When they made love, he felt hollow afterwards, so intense were his feelings.

'Let me,' she said in the bath.

She took the soap. When there was plenty of lather on her hands she soaped his body, working downwards. When she took hold of him she giggled.

She kneaded and stroked him; the reaction was instant.

'Oooh,' she said. 'I never!'

'Yes, you did,' he grinned. 'About an hour ago.'

'Might do it again,' she said. 'If you asked me nicely.'

He was afraid to keep looking at her, so sure was he that everyone would be able to see what was in his eyes. His whole body ached with the need to touch her. He sometimes wondered whether her husband had any inkling that they were lovers. No, he decided. Billy thought only of cards, whisky, business. Love played no part in his daily life. Catherine was just another ornament in his house, like the Tompion clocks and the

Canalettos and the Chinese carpets.

'You don't love him,' he said to Catherine.

'I love you, James,' she said.

'Then come away with me.'

'No, my darling. That could never be.'

'To hell with them all! To hell with everything except you and me!'

'It's a lovely dream, James,' she said softly. 'But that's all it will ever be.'

The Priestman house was a huge folly of a place, half house and half castle, standing just below the Stanford house on Nob Hill. There were often a dozen house guests. They might stay a week, a fortnight, a month, and never see their host more than a couple of times. Each evening, in the great salon with its ormolu-framed mirrors and priceless furniture, beautifully gowned women and men in evening suits greeted each other gravely. Perfume wafted on the soft summer air. Lights twinkled in San Francisco bay, far below. Liveried servants passed through the room with silver trays of champagne in crystal glasses.

'Well, James, how the hell are you?' Billy Priestman said, moving towards him as James came down the stairs. His broad-planed face was set, purposeful. Over Billy's shoulder he saw Catherine. She smiled and touched her lips with two fingers. Their secret passed between them like electricity.

'Want to talk to you, James,' Billy said.

'Fire away.'

'Not here,' Billy growled impatiently. 'This is business. Bring your drink into the library.'

James followed his host into the library. It was a huge room, impeccably furnished. How stupid it was that metal dug out of the hostile earth could buy things as beautiful as this, James thought. The polished rosewood shelves were packed with valuable books in fine bindings, their gilded titles gleaming in the flickering firelight. The fireplace was of the baronial variety.

13

Above it were two cavalry sabres crossed over a shield, on which there was a crest with a Latin motto: *Deus nobis haec otia fecit.* A suit of armour stood in one corner. Warlike emblems for a doctor turned mining millionaire, James thought.

'Want another?' Billy said, using his chin to point at James's glass. He bit off the end of a cigar and spat it into the fireplace.

'No, thanks,' James said. 'What's this all about, Billy?'

James cradled the heavy crystal glass in his hand and leaned back in the leather wing-chair. Whatever Billy was leading up to, he was not going to allow himself to be hurried.

'My ma died of cholera in '37,' Billy said, pouring himself half a tumblerful of bourbon from the crystal decanter. 'The kids, too. Left my poor old Pa with nothing, except me. Just what he probably didn't need. Anyway, when Jim Marshall found gold on the American, we were right here in California. My pa went prospecting, just like every other damned fool in the world. And I went with him. I was just twelve years old. I worked like a nigger for two years, and we never found shit.'

James had heard it all before. He guessed Billy liked to tell it. Maybe it made him feel good, to be so rich now and to think of that skinny twelve-year-old kid up to his waist in the icy water of the American river, panning for gold they never found.

'What my pa did,' Billy said, 'was he took up selling patent medicines. The miners would buy any kind of medicine if they thought it might do them any good. Pa could lance boils, stitch up knife wounds, things like that. Learned as he went along, he said. Pretty soon they were treating him like a real doctor. By the time the gold fever gave out, he had a practice. Everyone knew him.'

The butler soundlessly opened the door and coughed discreetly.

14

'What?' Billy snapped.

'Madam asked me to tell you that dinner is ready, sir,' the butler said.

'Tell them to wait,' Billy said. He turned to James as though the butler did not exist. 'That's how old 'Doc' Priestman got respectable. And rich in the process.'

'Plenty did,' James observed.

'Right,' Billy said. 'Thing was, pa was about as well organised as a kitten with a ball of wool. Papers everywhere, in boxes in the attic, in safety deposit boxes. He had bank accounts all over town. I never had the time to sort it all out. But young Willie did.'

He would, James thought. William was Billy's son. He was about the same age as James's son, Lee, but there the resemblance ended. Willie Priestman was worth walking a long way to avoid.

'He found something?'

'Pa had about as much money sense as a chicken,' Billy replied. 'I guess my ma knew it, too. Seems like, whenever she could, she took some of his money and bought land with it.'

'Land?'

'Surprised me, too,' Billy said. 'Parcels of prime land up in the Oregon Territory. Carolina, too. And in Virginia.'

'Virginia?' James said. For the first time what Billy was saying interested him.

'Not your neck of the woods.' Billy said, with a small smile that showed he had noted James's quickened interest. 'Further north, around Fairfax Court House.'

Belmont, the family home of the Starr family, was near Fredericksburg, Virginia. Fairfax Court House was about forty miles northeast, just a few miles outside the capital. James hadn't lived in the East since the end of the War, but his brother Andrew, who had rebuilt Belmont and restored its reputation as one of the great stud farms of America, might well be interested.

'How much land?' James asked.

'Five hundred acres.'

'That would be worth quite a few dollars now.'

'Just so,' Billy said, puffing on his cigar and squinting through the smoke. 'You interested?'

'I'm just a New Mexico lawyer, Billy,' James said. 'But my brother might be. How much are you asking?'

'A song, as they say. If you'll both do me a favour.'

'What kind of favour?'

'You know anything about mining, James?'

'Not enough to write a book about it,' James said. He was not surprised by Billy's change of tack. Billy never approached anything head-on. His tactics were always oblique. He started to take a cigar out of his pocket, but before he could do so, Billy jumped up and came across with a humidor.

'Try one of these,' he urged. 'Corona Coronas. From Cuba. Rolled between the thighs of dusky Cuban virgins.'

He waited until James's cigar was properly lit before returning to his own chair. Then he leaned forward, as though to impart something of great importance.

'Mines need two things most,' he said.

'Water and timber,' James supplied.

'Right!' Billy said, slapping his knee. 'You know we spent more'n two million bringing water into Virginia City? It's a fact! The mines alone use nearly three million gallons a day. And we need trees more'n we need water. Hundreds of millions of feet of timber below-ground, for shafts and props and galleries and floors. Millions more feet for fuel.'

'And?'

'Let me put it to you straight,' Billy said. 'We need timber, bad. Make no bones about it. But we can't get ahold of any. Bill Clark has got all sorts of timber-land up around Missoula in Montana. Marcus Daly like to bought up half the damned Territory. Now he's negotiating with the Northern Pacific for more. If me and my partners don't get ourselves more timber-land . . .' He left it hanging.

'What's all this got to do with me?' James said.

'I'm coming to it, I'm coming to it!' Billy said. 'See, the only land with the quantity of timber on it we need is public-domain land, James.'

'You can't get title to public-domain land,' James said.

'Shit, I know that!' Billy said, scornfully. 'Damned stupid laws. Hear me, James, if we don't get timber, we'll have to stop mining. It'd set the business back ten years. That's why I'm talking to you. I want you to get your brother to talk to his father-in-law, that Senator – what's his name?'

'McCabe,' James said, 'Angus McCabe.'

'That's the fellow!' Billy said. 'He's got the pull out there in Montana, and in Washington. Get him to see how important this timber business is to us, James. And to him.'

'Senator McCabe wouldn't listen, Billy,' James said. 'He's a conservationist. He's already had suits brought against Daly. And some others. He wouldn't sit still while public-domain land was deeded to a wealthy corporation like yours.'

'Andrew could persuade him.'

'I don't think so.'

'There are a hundred thousand reasons why he ought to think about it.'

'What?' James said, not believing what he had just heard.

'A hundred thousand dollars,' Billy said, evenly. 'Paid into any bank McCabe cares to name, the day we get title to that timber-land in Montana.'

'I see,' James said. 'And we get the Fairfax land, is that it?'

'Knew you'd catch my drift,' Billy said through a wreath of tobacco smoke.

'You must be crazy,' James said.

'What's the matter?' Billy said, genuinely surprised.

17

'Isn't it enough?'

Shaking his head angrily, as James got up out of his chair and strode across to the library door, yanking it open. Billy watched him without speaking, as James turned and faced him.

'Damn you, Billy!' he said.

Billy Priestman shook his head sadly, a philosopher watching folly he cannot prevent.

'I'll get the land,' he said. 'Some other way.'

'You're crooked enough,' James said, and slammed the door.

Billy got the land. Nothing that Senator Angus McCabe or Andrew Starr could do made any difference. When a man with Billy Priestman's millions decided to use them as a club, he usually got his way. James often wondered in later years whether the bitterness of the fight for the Montana land had contributed to old Angus's final illness. As for Billy, he never again alluded to their conversation. Neither of them forgot it; neither really forgave. In Billy's world only fools turned up their noses at doing a friend a favour. The time always came when you would need a similar favour in return. There was no point in principles. The man who had the gold made the rules, not the man with principles.

'He wasn't always like that, you know,' Catherine said, when James told her about Billy's attempt to bribe him. 'He used to be so . . . gallant.' She pronounced it in the French style, *galant*. It sounded courtly.

'He isn't any more,' James growled. 'I don't recall when he ever was.'

'Oh, James, it's a long story,' Catherine said, laying a hand on his forearm. 'A long, boring story.' How could she tell him? It would seem like begging for understanding, and she could never allow herself that, not even with James. All the things Billy was now – a cynical, heavy-drinking power-broker who would

18

trample on anyone who got in his way – had come about because of what he had once been: an idealistic young man who wanted to be a doctor more than anything else in the world. When he had come back to San Francisco after the war, with his diploma from the medical school in Baltimore, it had been the most natural thing in the world for him to become his father's assistant and locum. In those days, the average doctor got no more than a year's formal training, followed, if he was lucky, by a practical apprenticeship, so Billy was better qualified that most to practise. Then in 1874, the first state legislation governing the licensing of doctors had been passed, followed two years later by the Medical Practitioners' Act, which made licensing obligatory. Embittered by what he saw as a law which took no account of a decade of successful practice, Billy refused to sit the qualifying examination. Instead, he sold the practice; it was the first time she ever saw him rotten, stinking drunk. He told everyone he was rich from his mining investments – he had bought $2 shares in the Consolidated Virginia mine in Nevada in 1871; by 1875 each share was worth $700 – and that henceforth he planned to devote himself to having a good time.

'I'm forty years old, dammit!' he said to his cronies. 'Man can't do same damned thing all his life!'

He soon attracted hangers-on. A whole hard-drinking, tobacco-chewing, poker-playing crew of them. They knew every girl in every French restaurant in the city, not to mention the other kind who worked in the parlour houses up on the Barbary Coast. Once Billy started going there, the little that remained of his marriage to Catherine was finished: she would have nothing to do with him. He could get as drunk as a fiddler's bitch, sit up all night playing poker at ten thousand dollars a hand, and she would bear his morning grouchiness with equanimity. He could stake his entire personal fortune on a hunch, and she would support him, even encourage him. But she could not

19

bear him to touch her any more. The thought of what he might bring back from one of those parlour houses terrified her. Sometimes refusing him made her feel selfish and cruel, but she did not dare to take the chance of forgiving him. So all the love Billy might have had was lavished instead on Willie and Marie. She was a rich woman in her own right: there was nothing that they could not have.

It took her a long time to realise that they blamed her for the way Billy was. When she finally understood this, Catherine resigned herself to being lonely for the rest of her life. Infidelity never occurred to her. She knew that some men thought her beautiful, but she turned a deaf ear to their compliments.

Until James.

Just thinking about him made her feel as if her entire body was blushing. She was gluttonous for his love. It was as if she wanted to explore every sensation known to the human body with him. She thought deliciously shameless thoughts about him as she lay in bed.

'Cock' she would say, thinking of it sliding inside her, the solid presence of it, while Billy snored in the other bed.

She loved him. No doubt of that, she thought. They had talked about the future. What they could do, what they could not. James's life centred on his law practice in New Mexico, his ranch at Cloudcroft, his wife, Linda, and his son and daughters. Catherine's revolved just as irrevocably around Billy's, in San Francisco, her son and daughter.

'You ought to get a divorce,' James told her.

'Nice people don't divorce, James,' she said. 'You ought to know that. They . . . separate. They arrange little evasions. To outsiders, their life appears normal. They share a bedroom, even though there isn't any love between them any more. But they do not divorce.'

'You don't love him,' he said angrily.

'No. And yet, yes,' she said. 'And even if I divorced

20

him, James, would you leave Linda? Would you walk away from everything you've achieved in New Mexico?'

'Yes!' he said.

'No, my darling,' Catherine said, softly. 'No, you would not. And even if you would, I would not let you.'

James shook his head in that angry way he had. It all seemed like such a damned waste. The constant having to find excuses for yet another trip to San Francisco, that uneasy feeling that Linda knew his real reason for coming out here so often. It nagged at him because he loved her, too, in another way, a way that had become like second nature over the years. Yet he loved Catherine, and he was fond of her daughter, Marie. Her son Willie he emphatically did not like. It was James's considered opinion that nobody could love Willie Priestman.

'How long will you be here this time?' Catherine asked him.

'A week, ten days,' he said. 'I want Lee to see something of the city, it's his first visit. The usual things. Seal Rocks, the boat trip round the bay. Maybe we'll go up to Sacramento for a few days.'

'He's a fine-looking boy.'

'Don't let him hear you calling him a boy. He's twenty one.'

'Same as William.' She was the only person who called her son that. Everyone else called him Willie, although not out of affection.

'He's here?'

'Yes. Spring vacation.'

'How does he like Harvard?'

'He professes not to. But he's been elected to Hasty Pudding.'

'That's good.'

'How are the girls?'

James's daughter Portland was nineteen now, her

sister Rachel fifteen.

'They're at school, back East. They spend the short vacations at Belmont with Andrew and Diana. Aunt Louisa sees to it they don't get into any trouble.'

Although she was in fact younger than both James and his brother, Andrew, Louisa Starr, widow of James's cousin Jesse, was the undisputed mistress of Belmont. Aunt Louisa believed in piety, chastity and honour, and woe betide anyone who transgressed. She permitted no smoking, and the mildest swear-word would attract a withering response from her. Dressed always in black, she was a formidable old tyrant whom everyone in the family delighted in conspiring to thwart. It was well known that she had a 'past'. No one had ever dared to ask her about it.

'From what you've told me about Aunt Louisa, I'm sure they won't!' Catherine smiled. 'Now, about Friday. You will come, won't you?'

'Dinner, you said. For how many?'

'About forty.'

'Oh, God,' James groaned.

'Bring Lee,' she said. 'Please, darling?'

'Maybe you could bribe me,' he said, sliding his hand down her naked belly.

'Next time,' she said, throwing back the bedclothes. 'I must go.' He had rented an apartment in a square overlooking Russian Hill. They called it their den of iniquity.

'I bet you say that to all the boys,' he said. He watched her walk across the room, marvelling that this lovely woman loved him.

'Fool,' she said, making as if to throw her shoe at him.

'You're serious? About me bringing Lee?'

'Of course. There'll be some young people there. He'll enjoy it.'

Everyone called James's son Lee, although his first name was David. James had added the second name,

22

Lee, when his brother Andrew told him that he would call his first child Grant, after his old wartime commander. As it turned out, Diana had a daughter, not a son. By then Lee was christened, and the name stuck. Now James was rather glad to have somehow saluted that great soldier under whom he had once served.

'Quite a place,' Lee Starr observed, as the coach pulled up outside the Priestman house that evening. Because it was Lee's first visit to San Francisco, they were staying at the Palace Hotel. When he visited the city alone, James stayed at the Priestman home.

'You know what Ezra Carver said when he first saw it?' he said to his son. 'This is the kind of place God would have built if He had had the money.'

Ezra had made a fortune during the Civil War, not all of it legitimately. Now he was a railroad tycoon. His Ohio, Kansas and California railroad was almost completed, inching up the Sacramento valley towards San Francisco. For him to know the Priestmans was as natural in the California order of things as the rising of the sun. They were all one breed: robber barons, Andrew called them. You might be astonished, or even disgusted by their single-minded pursuit of the dollar, but you could not deny that they were good at it. James found them all hard to admire, particularly Billy. Maybe I hate him all the more to justify the way I feel about Catherine, he thought, nearer to the truth than he realised.

'What's he like?' Lee asked, as they alighted from the coach.

'Billy? Let's see. Not big. Your height, maybe. Heavy-built, though; two hundred pounds and more. Mouth like a steel trap. Deep-set eyes. Full whiskers.'

'No, Dad,' Lee said, gently, 'I mean, what is he *like*?'

'My opinion? I think he's a miserly, self-centred, self-

23

righteous, egotistical bastard!'

'But apart from that?' Lee grinned. 'Do you like him?' They walked up the marble steps towards the brightly lit doorway. 'Or are you just jealous because he's got so much money?'

'He can buy everything except taste,' James said.

'Miaow!' Lee said, grinning even more widely.

The ballroom in which the guests were being received was crowded and warm. Servants poured champagne at a long table covered with a white damask cloth. Down the opposite side of the room was another table groaning beneath the weight of canapés and other delicacies of every conceivable kind.

'*Sacré*-pink!' Lee murmered. 'Caviar in buckets?'

'That's Billy,' James said. 'Mister Subtle.'

'Who's that trying to catch your eye?' Lee said. 'Over to your right. Inspector General's Department.'

James glanced right. An officer wearing the insignia of a lieutenant-colonel in the Inspector General's Department raised his hand, beckoning. Well over six feet tall, he had hard, but pleasant features beneath a crop of iron-grey hair.

'Henry Lawton, by God!' James said. 'Lee, come and meet one of the best soldiers in the business!'

They crossed the room and James extended his hand. Lawton shook it, smiling. 'Well, James,' he said. 'How the hell are you, anyway? You look just as ugly as I remember.'

'I'm fine as snake hair, Henry,' James said. 'I see they gave you some more gold braid. Expect they got nobody old enough to wear that much but you.'

'They can't give it all to old Nelson Miles,' Lawton grinned, referring to the Commanding General of the United States Army. 'And who's this young man?'

'My son, Lee. Lee, shake hands with Colonel Henry Lawton, the man who captured Geronimo.'

'Hell, James, I never caught that old bastard, that was Charlie Gatewood,' Lawton said. He turned to Lee.

'Well, Lee. Are you in college?'

'The Academy, sir,' Lee said, awed to be talking to such a famous soldier. Lawton had fought in twenty-eight major battles during the Civil War, and won the Medal of Honour, America's highest military award, at the battle of Atlanta.

'West Point, eh? Wish I'd had the chance,' Lawton said. 'You're set on being a soldier, like all the Starrs? What branch of the service do you have in mind?'

'Cavalry, sir,' Lee said.

'Good choice. You get your pa to write me if there's anything I can do for you. I want to talk to you, James. I need your advice.'

'Professional or personal?'

'Is there a difference?'

'One costs more than the other.'

James's eyes told Lee to leave them alone, and so he made his excuses and went across the room towards the buffet, more to have a destination than because he wanted anything to eat. He was halfway across the room when a drawling voice stopped him.

'Well, well, if it isn't cousin Lee! Fresh from the frontier, are we?'

Lee turned to see Willie Priestman smiling at him. There was no friendliness in Willie's eyes, however. He was tall, a spindly, gangling fellow with a long, oval face cut in half by a thin nose that plunged from his high forehead into his silky moustache, beneath which was an uncompromising slit of a mouth which hinted at the iron will hiding behind the bland exterior. The dark-haired girl at his side watched Lee with frank interest. She's waiting to see Willie cut strips off my hide, Lee thought.

'Willie,' he said. 'How are you?'

'Mother said you were here,' Willie said. 'I imagine you find it all a little different to New Mexico.'

'Everywhere is different to New Mexico,' Lee said, determined not to let Willie's jibes annoy him. 'Won't

25

you introduce me to your lady friend?'

'You'd best beware, Marietta,' Willie said. 'Lee's the hot-blooded type. His Spanish heritage, you know. Lee, this is Marietta Powell. Marietta, my cousin Lee Starr.'

'What's all this about a Spanish heritage?' Marietta Powell said, wrinkling her nose in what Lee was sure she thought was an irresistible manner.

'That's Willie's subtle way of telling you that I am half-Mexican,' Lee said. 'Are you a San Franciscan?'

She giggled, as if he was silly for not knowing, and looked at Willie.

'Marietta's father is one of the wealthiest men in California,' Willie said, speaking slowly and distinctly, as if for a backward student. 'You've heard of Powell Street? It was named for him.'

Lee smiled, but didn't rise to Willie's bait. Instead he asked a question. 'Tell me, Willie, how are you enjoying Harvard?'

'Not a lot,' Willie said. 'Classes on the hour, regulations, roll-calls, assignments. Damned fools ragging you in the Yard. One simply has to endure it.'

He pretended a fashionable world-weariness, but Lee was not fooled by it. Willie Priestman was a very sharp fellow. He had done the Grand Tour when he was ten. He came back with enough French and German to hold an intelligent conversation with the graduate who had been his tutor on the trip. He had a talent for getting what he wanted.

'Any idea what you're going to do when you leave?'

'I've been working on the *Lampoon*,' Willie said. 'When I graduate, I'll take over one of my father's papers here in San Francisco. The *Inquirer*.'

'I'm impressed,' Lee said. He was not impressed by Willie. He was impressed by the fact that Willie had a father who could give him a newspaper to play with, the way other fathers might buy their sons a .22 hunting rifle.

'What about you, my dear fellow?' Willie said. 'Still at West Point?'

'Third year.'

'And then the Army?'

'Eldest sons always go into the Army in our family,' Lee said, more for Marietta Powell's benefit than Willie's. 'It's something of a tradition.'

'Oh, tradition!' Willie said, with a grimace. 'Not much damned money in that, is there?'

Anger flashed in Lee's eyes, and Willie saw it. At that precise moment the dinner gong resounded from the hall. Lee stifled his reply and Willie smirked.

'Let's go in, shall we?' he said to Marietta Powell. The girl simpered and tilted her nose just enough for Lee to see that he was being high-hatted. Somehow the silliness of it dissipated his anger like blown smoke. He grinned and went into the ornate dining-room. He found that he had been seated next to Willie's sister, Marie. She was petite, dark-haired, and very beautiful. By the end of the evening he had decided that he liked her very much indeed.

2

Willie Priestman always knew he was different to other boys. He did not know how he knew; he just *knew*. It wasn't anything to do with his father's wealth, although that was part of it. It wasn't that he was more privileged than ninety-nine per cent of the world's population. Willie felt *apart* from other people of his age. He would do so all his life.

At the age of twelve, he was trying to write stories. He liked using words. Words had power. Words could move people, inspire them, anger them, shame them. Words *were* power.

For his English homework, he wrote an essay called 'The Dark Street'. He stayed up late to finish it, poring over the battered copy of Roget's *Thesaurus* he had bought at John Rivett's bookshop in Market Street. His teacher, a tyrannical spinster called Miss Hill, accused him of having copied it from somewhere. First angrily, then impatiently, Willie refuted the accusation.

'William Priestman, you're a liar!' she snapped.

'I'm not a liar!' he shouted. 'Don't call me one!'

'Insolent boy!' she brayed. 'Report yourself to the Principal right this minute. This minute, do you hear me?'

The Principal was a horse-faced, middle-aged man with a heart condition. His name was Shadrack. There were a lot of jokes about that. Shadrack told Willie he must apologise to Miss Hill. Willie refused. The Principal threatened to cane him if he did not do as he was told. Willie told him he could cane him till his arm dropped off, but he would not admit to being a liar when he was not.

'Very well,' said the Principal. He opened a glass-fronted cupboard behind his desk. 'Touch your toes.'

He whacked Willie six times with the cane. When Willie straightened up, Shadrack looked uncomfortable, as though his heart hadn't been in it.

'Now, sir,' he said. 'Will you apologise to Miss Hill?'

'I've done nothing to apologise for,' Willie said.

Shadrack looked exasperated. He ran his hand through his thinning, grey hair and walked across to the window.

'You are a stupid boy, Priestman,' he said, looking out across the quadrangle. 'A very stubborn, stupid boy.'

Willie didn't answer. He knew who was stupid, and it wasn't him. Shadrack told Willie to go home. Next day, it was as if nothing had happened. Nothing was said, not by Shadrack, not by Miss Hill. Willie had won.

Everyone in the school seemed to know exactly what had happened. At recess, a boy named George Johnson-Jones, who was in Willie's class, found him in the quadrangle.

'Go on, Priestman, you can tell us,' he grinned. 'You did copy it, didn't you?'

Willie hit him in the mouth. He fell back, blood welling from his split lip.

'You bugger!' he shouted, and leaped at Willie. They were at once surrounded by a circle of shouting boys. The whole school was in the quad, and all of them came running as 'Judder' Jones and Willie scrapped like alley-cats. Willie was consumed by anger: the fact that his opponent was bigger and heavier than him meant nothing. He would have fought a sabre-toothed tiger at that moment. By the time the recess bell brought the fight to an end, both Willie and Judder Jones were a sorry sight. Willie had a welt under his right eye that had almost closed it. Judder Jones had a bloodied nose to go with his pulped lip, which was now swollen to the size of a half plum. Their knuckles were skinned; their shirts spotted with blood.

The chemistry teacher, Howard Roscoe, regarded them soberly as they entered the room. 'Well, Priestman,' he said to Willie. 'Have you been fighting, by any chance?' He seemed to be working at not smiling. Willie looked at Judder Jones.

'Fighting, sir?' he said, virtuously. 'Good Lord, no! I bumped into a door.'

'I see,' Roscoe said. 'And you, Johnson-Jones?'

'Same here, sir,' Judder said. 'Bumped into a door.'

'A door, is it?' Roscoe said drily. 'A revolving door, no doubt?'

It got a giggle, but more than that, it got Willie a reputation. Which was precisely to his liking. Cameraderie meant nothing to him. He did not need the boisterous approval of his peers. All he wanted was to be left alone.

'That all you want to do, read?' Billy would say to him. 'Don't you want to ride, or play football, or swim?'

'Not really,' Willie would reply, infuriating his father even more.

'Ought to go out and get some fresh air,' he shouted. 'Boy his age!'

Willie learned to ignore his father's remarks. They were all sound and fury, anyway, like Shakespeare's tale told by an idiot. Football, swimming, riding, those things were not important. Books were important.

Books showed Willie how little he knew – how little anyone knew. While they did not give him a contempt for education as such, they made him merciless with tutors who did not know their subjects, or adults whose opinions were not anchored on facts. If you knew the facts, you had power. You could do anything you wanted. Because people then began to assume you had the facts, even when you didn't.

If he became interested in something or someone, Willie would not rest until he had found out all there was to find out on the subject. Everything interested him.

At the age of nineteen, he entered Matthews Hall at Harvard University. He did so unwillingly: he had no desire to attend college.

'You'll go and you'll damned well like it!' Billy told his son.

I'll go, and damned if I'll like it, Willie thought rebelliously. And that was the way it was. In his brief stay at Harvard, Willie got himself a reputation for bizarre practical jokes and incredible largesse. As a scholar he was less successful. He didn't care about that. He had a job on the *Lampoon*. He was consumed with the job of learning all there was to know about newspapers. He sensed, rather than knew, that this was the direction he wanted to take. It was all there. Words. Knowledge. Power.

In 1886, Billy Priestman purchased the San Francisco *Inquirer*. In fact, he took it over as payment of a bad debt, and had no more interest in it than any of his other possessions. Willie, however, studied every issue of the paper avidly, comparing it with the other San Francisco papers, and later, to those from New York and Chicago to which he subscribed. He spent so much time studying the newspaper business that his college work fell off to nothing. The tutors warned him that he would never get through if he did not study seriously. Willie was not interested. He did not care whether they understood this, or whether they understood him. Willie knew he was not a popular man, and he suspected that he did not have the gift ever to be one. Well, he thought, to hell with that. He would get the power and the knowledge, and with them would come success. With success came popularity. Everybody loved a winner.

31

In his junior year he was asked to leave college. It was put to him that he was not benefiting from the opportunities that were available at Harvard. He left without a backward glance; at least he wouldn't have to pretend to talk through his nose any more. His father would kick up hell, of course: Billy was nothing if not predictable.

'What in the name of the Almighty do you plan to do with your life, lad?' Billy demanded. 'We've given you all the chances. You've taken none of them.'

'I know, Pa,' Willie said. 'But believe me, Harvard wouldn't have helped me to get where I want to go.'

'And where, pray, is that?' Billy asked.

Willie tried to ignore the sneer. You wouldn't sneer at Marie, he thought, no matter what crazy thing she said she wanted to do. It's always me. Well, I'll show you. One of these days, I'll show you.

'I want to run a newspaper,' Willie said. 'The *Inquirer*.'

'Is that all?' Billy said, heavily.

There it is again, Willie thought. Why do you always do it? If Marie said she wanted a newspaper, you'd have one delivered to her room tied with pink satin ribbons.

'I'm serious, Pa,' Willie said. 'It's what I want to do.'

'Great jumping Jesus!' Billy swore, biting off the end of one of his over-large cigars and spitting it in the general direction of the fireplace. 'Haven't I wasted enough damned money on that paper? I took it for a bad debt, and so far, all it's done is cost me more. I been waiting to give it to someone I hate!'

Then I'll be perfect, Willie thought. 'Give it to me,' he said. 'I'll make it pay.'

'You're serious?'

'Very.'

'How much a year you think you could make outa that damned rag anyway?' Billy said. 'Even if it was a success, I mean.'

'At a guess?' Willie said. 'A hundred thousand a year.'

32

'Shit, boy!' Billy said. 'That ain't money!'

That was the end of it for a while. Willie didn't mind; he had not expected to win the war in the first skirmish. He knew how to handle his father, and how to get what he wanted. All he had to do was wait for the right moment.

Billy told his son they would be going down to Santa Barbara, where they would spend two weeks on the vast sheep ranch Billy had bought. Willie knew what was going on in his father's mind. Billy was going to try the man-to-man, let's talk things out together, approach. Billy was sometimes full of shit. Willie hated Santa Barbara, but he went anyway.

San Julian ranch was a sprawling place located on four high plateaux and covering more than 250,000 acres. The place was managed by a shrewd old Yankee named Tom Long. Old Tom, as everyone called him, was a tall, coarse-looking man of about fifty-five, who dressed as roughly as any cowherd. Born in Bangor, Maine, he had kept a general store there before coming out to California. He ran a saloon in one of the mining towns for a couple of years, sold it at a profit, and took to cattle-dealing. He had been running his own ranch, a small place with about six thousand head of stock, when Billy bought San Julian, and persuaded Old Tom to join him as a quarter-share partner.

Willie resigned himself to a week of listless evenings playing draughts – neither his father nor Old Tom played chess – and listening to Old Tom's hoary anecdotes about life out here during the Civil War, or the pair of them discussing the price of land, mutton or wool. Or Old Tom's recipe for sheep-dip: tobacco water, sulphur and carbolic acid heated to 120° Fahrenheit. Willie was sure there was some of it in the whisky bottle from which the foreman ceremoniously poured their drinks each night.

At the end of the week, Billy took his son on to the porch and stood looking out across the rolling brown hills.

'Well, old lad,' Billy said expansively. 'What do you think?'

'What do I think about what?'

'The ranch,' Billy said. 'I'm offering you the chance to run it. Say the word, and it's yours. I'll sign the papers to – '

'Not a chance,' Willie said flatly. 'I wouldn't live down here for all the gold in California.'

'Too much like hard work, that it?' Billy said. He meant to sound cutting; it came out querulous.

'Pa, it's not that,' Willie said. 'It's just that . . . ranching isn't for me. I'd do all right at it. But I'd never be the best in the business. If I go into the newspaper business, I will be.'

'Newspapers!' Billy said, exasperatedly. 'Can't you think of anything else? How about one of the mines? I'll give you a share in the Consolidated Virginia. Or the Homestake.'

'I want the *Inquirer*,' Willie said.

'What about the people I've got running it now?' Billy asked his son. 'Could you deal with that?'

'Are you going to give me the chance?'

'They're tough nuts, Willie. They're liable not to like a snot-nosed kid coming in. Especially the owner's snot-nosed kid.'

'I want the paper, Pa,' Willie said, sensing that his father was weakening, that this was the moment. 'Nothing else. I'll never ask you for anything else.'

'Tell you what I'll do,' Billy said, savouring the moment. 'You take care of Roper and Williams, and the paper is yours. Fail, and *I* decide what you're going to do. Agreed?'

'Agreed,' Willie said. His father beamed with pleasure, confident he would win his bet. He did not know Willie.

Two weeks later, Willie Priestman walked up Montgomery Street and turned into Market. The huge frontage of the Palace Hotel loomed across the street. It was a bright, crisp morning with a fresh breeze coming in off the bay that snapped the flags on the buildings. The street was aclatter with people and trolleys and drays and hansoms. Willie hummed a little tune and smiled at passers-by, who frowned, as people often do if smiled at by someone unknown to them. Willie did not mind their frowns. Today was a very special day. Today, everything else being equal, he was going to begin his own life, on his own terms, as publisher and editor-in-chief of the San Francisco *Inquirer*. It was not much of a paper, not yet, but he would fix that. Meanwhile, he had a suite of offices at the corner of Market and Grant Streets, with reporters and copy editors and messengers and adding machines and presses and files and accountants and lawyers. He stopped for a moment and looked back along Market Street, savouring the way he felt. He remembered an old cowboy saying: got the world by the tail with a downhill pull. That was the way he felt. He was looking forward to the next few hours. I can do it, he told himself, and found the confidence thrilling. I can do this, and more than this, and perhaps more than anybody.

He stopped outside the *Inquirer* office. A man was gold-leafing the words 'William Lawrence Priestman, Propr' on the arched window above the main entrance. That's me, world, Willie thought. William Lawrence Priestman, at nobody's service.

The office was divided into two equal parts. On the right of the main doors was the city room. The chief editor was an ex-US cavalry major named Fred Mitchell. He was a bluff, tall man with a dour disposition. He seemed to do his job well enough, although from what Willie had been told, the man had as much charm as a dead horse. His assistant, Bill Schofield, sat opposite him, a red-haired, sharp-featured and ambitious young man with a flair for 'hot' copy which the dour Mitchell continually edited out of the paper. Well, time enough to change that later, Willie told himself, nodding in reply to the greetings of the staff. He did not thank Mitchell when the editor hurried over to open the lift-up counter to let him through.

'Tell Mr Roper and Mr Williams that I would like to see them in my office at exactly ten o'clock,' he said.

'Yes, sir,' Mitchell said, and hurried away, his face alight with suppressed curiosity. Willie glanced at the clock. It was a few minutes after nine. Let them squirm for an hour; good psychology.

They knocked on his door at precisely ten, and came in. Roper was a big man, fat around the middle, bald. He had apelike arms and hands, matted with coarse black hair. Lester Williams, coming in behind him, looked monkeylike in comparison.

'Gentlemen,' Willie said. 'Take a seat.'

'Thankee,' Roper said, sinking into a chair with an audible groan of relief. He had bad feet. Ten minutes' walk was purgatory to him. The boys in the city room said Old Ropey never hung up his stocking at Christmas, but stood it beside the bed. They said his wife had to sleep with all the windows open so she didn't suffocate from the smell. They said . . . well, they said a lot of things about Roper, and Mitchell, and Williams. Willie knew most of them. He paid one of the copy boys five dollars a week extra to come and tell him. He detested the man, an obsequious toady named Gryce, but he had no compunction about using him. You used any kind of weapon in a war.

'Profits, gentlemen,' he said to his visitors.

'Eh?' Roper said, sitting up. 'Beg pardon?'

'Profits,' Willie repeated. 'Why aren't there any?'

'Ah,' Roper said, and looked at Williams.

'Ah,' echoed Williams. 'Yes. That.'

'That,' Willie said. 'Precisely. My father acquired this newspaper five years ago, gentlemen. He has poured a lot of money into it. He has, in fact, kept it going in the

36

face of losses which would have persuaded any sane man to consign it to the Devil, along with everyone who works here!'

'Here, now, just a – ' Roper began. His mouth closed like a trap when Willie held up a peremptory hand.

'Despite those losses, however,' Willie said, 'and despite its falling circulation, you, gentlemen, live like pashas.'

'True, up to a point,' Roper started.

'True that it makes no profit, or true that you live like pashas?' Willie asked smoothly. 'Or both?'

'Well,' Williams said. 'The thing is, you're probably not –'

'*Au fait*,' Roper said, sliding in. 'Being new. Fresh to the game, as it were.'

'Nobody's ever asked – ' Williams said, with the same glance at Roper that seemed to follow his every sentence.

'About profits before,' Roper finished. 'Left it to us, see? To the experts.'

'Always,' Williams said. 'Everything.'

'Trust, you see,' Roper said heavily. There was a faint sheen of perspiration on his upper lip, but he was still confident. 'Difficult to describe. Know it when you see it, though. You'll see, young feller-me-lad. A year or two here, you'll see how it all works. Complicated business, if you don't understand it.'

'Immensely complicated,' Williams confirmed. 'You need years.'

'You couldn't explain it to me?' Willie asked. 'In layman's terms?'

Roper sucked in his breath as though shocked by the request.

'Difficult, difficult,' he said. 'It's so complex. Still, you're young, as I said. Plenty of time for us to show you the tricks of the trade.'

'Get to know the ropes,' Williams said. 'We'll take you through it. Step by step.'

'You're fired,' Willie said.

'What?' Roper barked, half-rising from the chair.

'Eh?' Williams squawked.

'You heard me,' Willie said, marvelling at his own calm. 'Get out. Don't come back. Your directorships are terminated. You no longer work for this newspaper.'

'Now just a damned minute!' Roper said, lurching to his feet. 'You can't get away with this!'

'Damned right he can't!' Williams said. 'We'll sue. You hear what I say? We'll sue!'

'Nothing would please me better than to get both of you into a court of law,' Willie said. 'And question you under oath. Let me tell you something, gentlemen. If you give me any trouble, I may just do it anyway!'

'You dare to threaten me?' Roper said, banging his hand flat on the desk. 'Me?' The meaty hand left a damp imprint on the leather top. Willie eyed it with distaste.

'It's not a threat,' he said. 'I mean every word of it.'

'Well, you've got goddamned gall, boy, I'll say that for you!' Roper burst out. 'Why, you snot-nose, I was putting newspapers together when you were still in didies. If it hadn't been for me – me and Les, here – this damned rag would have folded years ago!'

'That's right,' Williams said. 'We made it what it is today.'

'That, at least, is the truth,' Willie said.

'You throw us out now, and I'll make it my business to break you, sonny!' Roper said, venomously. 'I'll see to it you can't get permission to interview a dogcatcher. I've got the contacts in this town. I'll put you in the poorhouse and piss on your gruel!'

'There's the door,' Willie said. 'Fly at it.'

3

'Will I see you in New York?' Marie asked.

'Not much chance of that,' Lee said ruefully. 'They don't give us too many furloughs at the Academy. When do you plan to be there?'

'As soon as poss,' Marie said. 'I'm not as taken with San Francisco as its inhabitants.'

'You prefer New York?'

'Goodness, yes!' she said. 'I couldn't bear to stay in a city that was a thousand miles away from the next civilised place. One needs travel, excitement – don't you agree?'

'Absolutely,' Lee said. 'How long will you stay here?'

'Till I tire of it,' Marie said. 'Which on present indications will not be long.'

'I've enjoyed being with you, Marie,' Lee said.

'And I with you.'

'Funny . . .' he began, then stopped, flushing.

'What?'

'Nothing.'

'You were going to say *something*,' she said.

'It would have been out of line,' he said.

'Lee,' Marie smiled, putting her hand on his forearm in a movement so like her mother's that it startled him. He had not thought of her as being like Catherine, but in that moment she was her mother twenty years before. And for the first time he understood why his father called Catherine Priestman one of the most interesting damned women he knew. From a man not noted for his admiration of the opposite sex, that was praise indeed. He had a sneaking suspicion his father liked Catherine a lot more than he let on.

'I was going to say it was funny, to have been so close to you . . . and yet, not to . . . ' He gave it up, with a shrug.

'Did you think we might fall in love?' Marie said, in her characteristically forthright way.

'Well . . . no. I mean, yes. I mean, I thought we might, and it's funny, I haven't thought of you that way at all.'

'The compliments you pay a girl,' she smiled.

'Oh, damn it, Marie!' he said. 'It was *meant* right, but it came out wrong.'

'Dear Lee,' she said, snuggling against his arm, 'I know what you meant to say. And I'm glad. It's nice to be close to someone without all *that*.'

'You don't have a beau?'

'Good Lord, no!' she said. 'I value my freedom far too much to get involved with one man to the exclusion of all others.'

'You're very beautiful, Marie,' he said.

'Ah, the lad does know how, after all!'

'Maybe . . . if I kissed you?'

She smiled. 'Lovers is nice, but friends is better,' she said, softly. The carriage came over the crest of the hill and they could see the town below them, the forest of masts at the wharves. Beyond them lay the wide sweep of the bay, and the brown hills of Oakland on the other side.

'Pretty,' Lee said. 'Shame to leave.'

'Back to your Military Academy. Where exactly is West Point, anyway?'

'It's on the Hudson, about sixty miles north of New York City. Pretty forbidding location.'

'You don't like it much, do you?'

'I've never thought about like or dislike,' he said. 'But now you mention it, no, I'm not crazy about the place.'

'Why?'

'I don't know if I could put it into words.'

'Try,' she said. 'Maybe it will help.'

He made a gesture with his right hand. How could you tell someone who had never seen it what West Point was like? How could you explain the real traditions it embodied and the mock traditions it permitted, the first entirely admirable and the second utterly contemptible? He remembered how he had been when he first arrived there, excited and awed. He asked directions of a passing cadet, who treated him as if he were a leper and told him that until he had passed his entrance exam, until he was issued with a uniform and given the lowly rank of plebe, he was not a cadet, he was a *thing*.

'Understand me, sir?' the boy – for he was little more than a year senior to Lee – screamed. 'You are a thing, sir. A thing, sir, and do not forget it, sir!'

Lee was no scholar, but he got through the initial examination and became the proud possessor of a grey swallowtail uniform jacket with black frogging and gold buttons. He was allocated a cot in the South Barracks and issued with new blankets that stank of sheep oil. Another tradition, of the second kind: that freshmen, or plebes, always smelled of sheep oil.

'The first two years I was there I was more miserable than I have ever been anywhere in my whole life,' he said to Marie. 'Maths every morning, French every afternoon. I was luckier than some. Like I said, I'm no scholar, but I was usually somewhere in the middle of the class rankings. And I didn't get as many skins as some of the others.'

'Skins?'

'If you do something wrong, you get demerits,' he explained. 'Cadets call them skins. If you're at the bottom of the class, they say you're "among the immortals".'

'You weren't, though?'

41

In June the first classmen threw their hats into the air after their last parade, and then harried them around the Plain, stabbing them with bayonets or kicking them. After giving away or selling their blankets, uniforms, books and other truck, they left the academy forever. Each lower class then moved up, whereupon the Board of Visitors turned to the new boys.

On July 1, the entire faculty moved out of barracks and into camp, a tent city set up on the treeless Plain. Only the second classmen were exempted from this annual event, being permitted to leave on furlough until the summer encampment terminated at the end of August. More tradition.

There was no point telling her about the other traditions, the ones that required plebes to become beasts of burden for the upperclassmen, carting all their belongings back into the barracks for them. Nor the good old tradition of sadism, such as making burdened kids run to and from the barracks at the double in broiling August sunshine until they collapsed, and then awarding them demerits for damaging an upper-classman's property.

Instead he told Marie about the curriculum, which became progressively more interesting as it became more difficult. A third-year man like himself studied philosophy, which included mechanics, optics, astronomy and electricity, and advanced drawing. Those who needed to do so also began to learn riding. Those who already knew unlearned what they knew and learned it again the Army way.

'Cadets are not allowed to smoke,' he said, 'but, of course, plenty do. They have to run it to Benny's for cigars or liquor if they want it.'

'Benny's?'

'It's a tavern. Benny Havens' tavern. It's on the bank of the Hudson, just below a village called Buttermilk Falls.'

He told her how they saved meat and potatoes and

42

bread and butter for three days, filched from the dining-hall and smuggled out in forage caps from which the rattan hoops had been removed, and how all the cadets who had done this then congregated in someone's room for what they called a 'hash'. He told her about Flirtation Walk, where cadets strolled with young ladies after the weekly hop, and exchanged that most romantic of souvenirs, a tunic button, for a coy squeeze or a stolen kiss. But there was no point in telling her about the vicious boredom, or the ladies at Roe's Hotel who had what was known as 'cadet fever', or the endless hours spent walking extra rounds on guard duty to work off demerits, or watching someone you had grown to like going 'down the Canterberry road' to the station, dismissed from the Academy for poor marks or too many demerits, or both.

'Maybe I'll come up to see you,' Marie said. 'You can take me to the hop.'

'I'd be the envy of every man there if I did,' he said. 'As long as you wouldn't mind being the absolute centre of attraction, and as long as you wouldn't mind every other girl in the place being jealous and hating you.'

'Heavens!' Marie said. 'It sounds irresistible!'

'Then come,' he told her. But she never did, because when she went to New York she met an up-and-coming young Broadway songwriter named Irving Strasberg, and everything she had ever said or thought on the subject of lovers and friends went entirely out of her head.

4

'You're to stop seeing that damned songwriter,' Billy said. 'I won't have any arguments about it!'

'Oh, Daddy!' Marie said. 'Don't be such a bear!'

'No, Missie, I mean it!' Billy said. 'I won't have it, and there's an end to the whole thing!'

'Why?' Marie said. 'Give me one good reason.'

'Only one?'

'One will do.'

'All right,' Billy said heavily. 'He's a Jew.'

'What difference does that make?' Marie said. 'I'm not going to marry him.' *Am I?* she wondered. Irving had asked her. So far she had not answered. But she was not sure, not yet. It was all so unexpected, so sudden. She couldn't tell her father any of that. She knew what would happen if she did.

'I don't want you seeing him, that's all!' Billy said, louder this time. 'Goddamn it, Marie, he hasn't been off the boat ten minutes!'

'You're being silly, Daddy,' Marie said, adroitly moving the conversation into an area where she could control it. She knew how to handle her father. 'Irving Strasberg is one of the leading men in New York. Maybe the world. He is a millionaire several times over from his songs.'

'Songs!' Billy scoffed. 'Romantic tripe!'

'People like them,' Marie said spiritedly. 'Anyway, what's the difference between getting your money out of a hole in the ground and getting your money from

44

writing songs for people to sing? I would have thought you'd admire a man who came up from nowhere, the same way you did.'

'It's not the same,' Billy said. 'A Jew. A Jew is different.'

'You'd rather I married someone like Pomeroy, I suppose?' Marie said, scornfully. '"Oh, yes, sir, Mr Priestman, sir, I kiss your boots, Mr Priestman, sir, anything you say is just dandy with me, Mr Priestman, sir. Like to stand on my neck, Mr Priestman, sir? Be my guest, Mr Priestman, sir".'

'Pomeroy's a fine young man,' Billy huffed. 'Fine family. We've known them years, ever since they came out here in '69.'

'He's an HA,' Marie said.

'What?'

'A horse's – '

'Marie! I'll have none of that gutter talk in this house!'

Unless you talk it, she thought. 'I wish you'd get to know Irving, Daddy,' she said. 'He's really nice. And I think you'd have a lot in common.'

'I've got nothing in common with his type,' Billy grumbled. 'Damned mountebanks. *Song*writers! Hah!'

There was no point in going on with this, Marie decided. It was easier to let him have his way. And carry on doing just what she had always done: please herself. After all, what was he going to do? Cut her off without a cent? If he did that she would *have* to marry Irving. Maybe that was what she wanted anyway. She didn't know. When she was with him she knew. He was dark and intense, and his eyes were like black liquid. He had long eyelashes, and wavy hair. He was not tall, but that bothered him more than it bothered Marie.

'Is it very different?' she asked him. 'Being Jewish?'

'Only at Christmas,' he grinned.

'Don't make fun, Irving,' she said. 'I want to know.'

'Nobody's *different* because of their religion, Marie,' he said, 'or because they come from another country or

45

because their skin isn't white. People are people.'

'But you don't believe in Jesus Christ, do you?'

'Do you think that makes any difference to the way I feel about you?'

'I don't know,' she said. 'Does it?'

He thought of his mother, Leah. He thought of what she would say if he married Marie Priestman. A *shikse*. Marrying outside the religion would be liking slapping Mamma in the face. *Why couldn't you find a nice* Jewish *girl*?

I didn't fall in love with a Jewish girl, Mamma. I fell in love with this one. She is the one I was writing love songs to before I even knew she existed on the face of the earth.

'Marry me, Marie,' he said.

She did not answer. She never did when he said those words. It was as if in answering she would commit herself irrevocably, and knew it.

'Marry me,' he said again. 'We'll elope. We'll rent a yacht and cruise all through the Caribbean. Puerto Rico. The Virgin Islands. Cuba.'

'Elope?'

'I'll buy you the biggest diamond in Tiffany's,' he said. 'It'll be so vulgar the Four Hundred won't ever speak to you again as long as you live.'

What a scandal the whole thing would be! she thought. Headlines in the papers. What would her father say? What would Mama say? Wouldn't they all just be in the most awful tizz!

'Say you will,' Irving said. He took her hand, held it tight, kissed the fingers. 'You know I'm mad about you.'

'Oh, Irving,' she said, and let him kiss her. It was just like a dream. Wait till she told Louisa and Sally and the others. They'd just die with envy!

'Say "yes",' Irving said. 'Say you will.'

'I'll think about it,' she said.

'You're driving me crazy, you know that?' Irving said.

'Oh, Irving, be quiet and kiss me again,' she said.

46

Billy knew his daughter a lot better than she knew herself. He had spoiled her, he knew that. Maybe he'd done it on purpose. She'd always been his pet. It never occurred to him that the sheer weight of his love oppressed his daughter, sometimes even frightened her. Even if she had been able to tell him so, Billy would not have understood. How could love frighten you?

'Well, Missie,' he said. 'I've decided what I've decided. No more of Strasberg.'

'But Daddy, it's impossible!' Marie said. 'I'm bound to run into him, either here or in New York, or some-place.'

'No, you won't,' he said. 'Not for six months, anyway.'

Marie frowned. 'What does that mean?'

Billy reached into the inside pocket of his Prince Albert coat and pulled out a wad of papers. He slapped them on the occasional table. Marie looked at her father and then at the papers. Tickets, she thought. The legend *Trans-Pacific Steamship Company* in red across the top of them.

'You're going away?' she said, not comprehending at first.

'We are,' Billy said. 'You and I, Missie. Around the world.'

'Around the – ?'

'Hawaii first,' he said. 'Then Yokohama. Always wanted to go to Japan. Then Shanghai. Great Wall of China. Then Bangkok. Angkor Wat . . .'

His voice droned on. Marie didn't hear it. *No*, she was thinking. *He can't do this*. Another voice, a cynical one, answering in her mind. *Oh, yes he can.*

'I won't go!' she said.

Billy just smiled. 'We leave the day after tomorrow,' he said.

'I mean it, Daddy!' she said, her voice rising. 'I will not go!'

Billy kept on smiling.

'Yes, you will, Missie,' he said.

47

5

Although well over a quarter of a century had passed since Robert E. Lee surrendered at Appomattox Court House, Fredericksburg women still wore black on Confederate Memorial Day. Children in the local schools studied Washburn's incredibly biased *History of Virginia*, and stood every day at assembly while the principal led the whole school in singing 'The Sword of Lee'.

Forth from its scabbard, pure and *bright, flashed the sword of Lee.* Romantic words; Lee knew of no instance where Robert E. Lee had ever used his sword in battle, but that made no difference. This was the South. Down around Norfolk, Virginia, 'Jeb' Stuart's widow taught Sunday school. Once in a while James Starr went down there to see her. He said she didn't teach an awful lot of Scripture, but her wide-eyed charges got plenty of stories about how her dashing cavalryman husband had ridden right around the Union Army in '61.

What Lee liked most about Belmont was that things here stayed the same as they had been for as long as he could remember.

He walked up the hill towards the family burial plot. The afternoon was mild, almost balmy, the way it sometimes is in Virginia in the late fall. A Baltimore oriole threw a song at him out of a tall elm. Another picked it up effortlessly and improvised on it. Off to the west the mountains looked more purple than blue.

He looked back towards the house, feeling the warm

glow he always got when he looked at it. It looked permanent, as if it had earned its place in that long valley looking down towards the Rapidan. Well, it had, he thought. Sometimes when he stood in one of the airy, high-ceilinged rooms he felt that if he just closed his eyes and opened them again, the past would have come back, the way it had that time when he had stood in the garden of George Washington's mother's house in Fredericksburg and Uncle Andrew came out of the back door and told him he had once lain wounded beneath the same tree in whose shade Lee was standing.

'The whole garden was full of wounded and dying,' he said. 'The whole town.' That was after the battle of Spotsylvania Court House. Lee knew about that battle, and every other battle from that legendary war. His whole family history was inextricably linked with its events. His father had been with Jackson until Chancellorsville, and had lost an arm at Gettysburg. His uncle had been an officer on Grant's staff. Strangely enough, it was the half-mad Jesse, Aunt Louisa's husband, for whom he felt the most affinity. According to Aunt Louisa, he had been a sort of cross between Sir Lancelot and Robin Hood. Uncle Andrew said he was a hellion.

Aunt Louisa was a bit of a hellion herself, Lee thought. She was just about the most knot-headed old lady he had ever encountered. She gave the whole family a hard time: no smoking, no drinking, no cussing, mind your manners, wipe your feet, say 'Yes ma'am!' when I talk to you.

He sat on the low wall under the huge oak on the crest of the hill and lit a cigarette. You had to be this far from the house if you wanted to fool Aunt Louisa. Any nearer and that sharp beak of hers would go up in the air, and she would sniff, sniff, and say 'I *sincerely* trust no one has been smokin' in here?'

He looked around.

The little family cemetery held the last remains of

four generations of Starrs. On the far side lay David Starr, who had been exiled to the Colonies from England in 1775. His portrait hung in the library at Belmont. Everyone said Lee looked very like him.

'Skulking, Lee?'

It was his sister, Rachel. His parents always said that Lee had the luck, Porty had the brains, and Rachel had the looks. At twenty-two, she was beautiful in a dark-eyed, Spanish way. At least, that's what the fellows in Fredericksburg told Lee. She was just his sister. Beautiful or not beautiful. Just a sister. Lee laid down the book of poetry he had brought with him to read. Rachel picked it up and glanced at the cover.

'Verlaine?' she said. 'You in love, Bro?'

'Oh, shut up, Ray,' he said.

She just grinned. 'The lovely Constance,' she said. 'She walks in beauty . . .'

'Shut *up*, Ray!' Lee said, getting up. 'I'm going for a ride!'

'Can I come too?' she said, catching up with him. Her raven-black hair swung in the soft breeze. 'Oh, come on, Bro! Don't be mean!'

'All right,' Lee said, his anger dissipating. 'But no more about Constance Edmondson, hear?'

He had been in Fredericksburg a few days earlier. It made a change, but not much of one. The only time anything happened in Fredericksburg was during the street fair that took place on the first day of the spring term of court. There were side-shows and horse-trading, and a fair amount of drinking was done. It usually led to a few fist fights.

Lee was walking past the Rising Sun when someone spoke to him.

'Why, Lee Starr!' the breathy voice said. 'When did you get into town?'

He turned to face the most beautiful girl he had ever seen in his life. Heart-shaped face, blue eyes framed by golden curls, a smile to melt your heart, and dimples.

She was wearing a pale blue dress with a dark stripe, and a cloak around her shoulders. Lee heard himself gulp.

'Why, don't pretend you don't reckanahze me, you ol' heartbreaker, you!' the girl said.

'Constance?' he managed. 'Constance Edmondson?'

She was a tiny thing, just up to his shoulder. She cocked her head to one side when she smiled, wrinkling her nose. Her laugh was a silvery trill.

He walked through the town with her, in a trance. She was attending the Corcoran School of Art in Washington, she told him. He told her about Fort Omaha, about his friends Gates and Vaughan. He made what he did sound a lot more important than it was. He wanted to impress her.

The Edmondsons lived in a big house on Princess Anne Street. To get there they had to pass McCoy's Drug Store.

'I'd admire to buy you a glass of lemonade, Constance,' Lee said, more boldly than he felt. 'If you'd permit me.'

'Well,' she said. 'Ah don't want to staht no talk.'

They were there for more than an hour, talking; talking as if there were never to be a tomorrow and it must all be done now. He begged her to meet him again the following day. She agreed. And the next day, and the next. He called for her at her home, and her parents greeted him gravely, as if he were a stranger and not the same Lee Starr who had so often come to this house as a boy with dust-scuffed knees and tousled hair.

Yesterday they had ridden all the way down to Lake Anna and back, then walked across the fields from Belmont to Fredericksburg, leading the horses.

'You know Ah'll be leavin' tomorrow,' she said. 'Ah have to go back to school.'

'I know,' he said miserably. They walked in silence for a while. 'Maybe I could write to you.'

'No,' she said dolefully. 'It's not allowed.'

'But when will I see you again?'

51

'Ah don't know, Lee,' Constance said, not looking at him. 'Next summer, maybe? Unless you could come to Washington?'

He shook his head: impossible. Unless he could get a transfer. Maybe Uncle Andrew could arrange something. He knew everybody in Washington.

'I could talk to my uncle,' he said. 'Maybe he could fix something.'

'You think he might?' she said tremulously. She looked right into his eyes, her own bright blue eyes wide. 'Ah'd surely like that.'

'Oh, Constance!' he said. He took her in his arms and kissed her. She did not resist, but neither did she respond. It was like kissing a doll. Her reaction, however, was ecstatic.

'Why, Lee Starr!' she said. 'You . . . kissed me!'

'I'd like to do it again,' he said boldly.

'Don't you dare, now!' she scolded, but did not resist when he kissed her again. It was exactly the same as the first time. Her lack of response seemed strange. He put it down to shyness. Girls like Constance didn't allow just any man to kiss them whenever the mood took them, after all.

He was sure that his heart would break as he watched her train pull out of the depot heading north. They had vowed vows before she left. He would come to the capital and they would meet secretly. They would be true to each other while they were apart. His heart was swollen with love. He wanted to be whatever she wanted him to be; it swept over him like a tidal wave.

He walked back to Belmont in a dream, scuffing through the new-fallen leaves. When he got up to his room he did something he had never done before: he wrote a poem.

It's autumn.
Summer is ended
Leaves make a carpet

In the lane where we met
Summer is ended
Winter draws nearer
My love has left me
But I can't forget
Winter draws nearer
Spring is a dream
Here am I, waiting,
Loving you yet
Spring is a dream
Far in the future
But until then
It's autumn.

He never showed it to anyone, of course, but he kept it, to hold the magic of having Constance in his arms fixed in his mind. That was why he had shut Rachel up when she started to talk about Constance. It was too special for that.

They rode west towards Orange, and stopped to water the horses at Cedar Run. Rachel watched him with an impish smile lurking about her lips. Finally, she burst out laughing.

'What's so funny?' Lee said.

'You, Bro!' she giggled. 'Mooning about over Constance Edmondson! Your face looks like a wet weekend!'

'I don't want to talk about it,' he said.

'Oh, Lee, don't be pompous!' she said. 'Somebody's got to tell you, and I reckon it's just got to be me.'

'Tell me what?' he said.

'About Connie Edmondson,' Rachel said impatiently. 'Don't you know she's . . . fast?'

'How can you say a thing like that, Ray?' Lee snapped angrily. 'You don't know her at all!'

He was sickened, stunned. Shame and rage flooded his mind. He wanted to go somewhere and hide.

'I'm sorry, Bro,' Rachel said softly. 'Someone had to tell you.'

53

'Why?' he shouted. 'Why?'

He swung up on to the sorrel and kicked it into a run. Rachel followed him, more slowly. Poor old Lee, she thought. Never mind. He'll get over it.

And what about you? she asked herself. *You're pretty good at telling big brother the facts of life. Who's going to tell them to you?*

'Giddap!' she shouted, startling her horse. She lifted the animal into a gallop. The wind sang past her head and she wished it would whip away all the thoughts inside it.

The voice in her head would not go away. *Adulteress, adulteress,* it jeered. She was in love with her sister's husband. She thought of Huntington's hands on her body, and her breath caught in her throat.

How could it be so wrong when it was so good?

6

There was nowhere that you could go and not hear one of Irving Strasberg's songs. It was as if the whole world was singing them. Errand boys whistled them as they delivered groceries. The postman hummed 'The girl I love is like a melody' as he put their mail through the slot in the door of the house Billy had rented in York Terrace in London. As they walked in the Bois de Boulogne they could hear a band playing it through the trees.

They never spoke about Irving, but he was always there, always between them. Billy felt it; Marie knew it. She had not thought of being in love with Irving until now. Away from him, she could think of nothing else.

She was disappointed that he did not write to her. No, not disappointed, piqued. Annoyed. She determined to put him out of her mind and succeeded only in the opposite.

Marie loved travelling.

New cities excited her. The very act of going to the railroad station, boarding a train, hearing porters shouting in foreign languages, was exciting. She drank in the sights, the sounds, the smells of every place they visited. The smell of the upholstery, the clink of the cutlery in the dining car on the Orient Express. The noisy gabble of the *scugnazzi* crowding around them in Naples, the awe she felt descending into the tiny little room that housed the birthplace of Christ, the childlike, elegant, bizarre movements of the dancers in Bali. She loved every moment of the trip.

But if he loves me so much, why are there no letters from Irving?

When their boat sailed into New York harbour a tender came out to meet them. Between its masts hung a banner which said WELCOME HOME DARLING MARIE LOVE IRVING.

He met her at the gangplank. A coachman stepped forward carrying a huge basket of flowers. It made Marie perversely angry. Why was he bringing her flowers now?

'It's so wonderful to see you,' he said. 'Good to see you, too, sir. My man will get your bags.'

'No need for that,' Billy said.

'I'll take you to your hotel,' Irving continued. 'Where are you staying?'

'Let me say this so that you'll understand it, young man,' Billy fumed. 'I do not want you to get my bags, or take me to my hotel, or any other damned thing. And most importantly of all I want you to stay away from my daughter. If you do not, I will take a horse-whip to you. Am I making myself quite clear?'

'I'd have to hear that from Marie, sir,' Irving said. 'With all due respect.'

'Why didn't you write?' Marie said.

Irving frowned. 'But I did. Special delivery. To Rome. To Cairo. Everywhere.'

'But I never –' Marie looked at her father. Billy stared back at her and she saw the truth in his eyes.

'Daddy?' she said.

'Not here!' Billy said hoarsely. 'Not in front of this . . . riff–raff!'

'Yes, here!' Marie shouted, stamping her foot. A man coming down the gangplank hesitated, as though she had called his name. Head turned. Marie did not care. She could not believe what she had just learned.

'How many letters?' she asked. 'How *many*?'

'Missie, you are making a spectacle of yourself,' Billy

56

said, drawing himself up. 'Get into the coach and I'll take you to the hotel. Perhaps you'll get hold of yourself by the time we get there.'

'I'll do no such –'

'Do what I damned well tell you!' Billy Priestman shouted, and there was an agony in his voice that Marie had never heard there before. She moved involuntarily to obey, or perhaps to alleviate the hurt she sensed in him.

'Marie?' Irving said, reaching out a hand to touch her forearm.

'Don't touch her, you goddamned kike!' Billy Priestman shouted, and hit him clumsily. Irving fell backwards, careening into a knot of bystanders. A man grabbed him, and prevented him from falling. A bright red blotch marked Irving's cheekbone. He made no attempt to retaliate. Inside his head he heard the mob screaming *Bei Zhidov*! and he was a child again, in Russia.

One night, two dragoons had got into a fight at the Yama, shouting that one of the girls had picked their pockets. They reeled noisily off into the night, throwing drunken curses over their epauletted shoulders.

'We'll be back, you whore bitches!' they yelled. The usual thing. Frightened the girls to death. If I had a rouble for every time one of those loud-mouths has said that, one of the girls said, I'd have a palace on the Taganka. Everyone laughed, even the *kotzki*, the pimps.

The Yama, the Pit, was the red-light district, a few blocks of shabby two-storeyed houses with gingerbread fretwork and dingy lace curtains. The best houses were on Bolshaya Yamskaya; three roubles a visit, ten roubles the night. Huddled against and behind it was the Malaya Yamskaya, where the going rate was fifty kopecks and two roubles would buy you any aberration you could conceive. Robbery was a way of life; episodes such as the fight between the dragoons were common-place.

But this time was different.

This time the dragoons came back.

They came back accompanied by a hundred or so of their fellow soldiers from the barracks. They swarmed into the Yama like a pestilence, kicking down doors, beating up the girls and the pimps. A man was killed; two girls, another man. A fire started somewhere. The police stayed well clear. Not worth getting your head broken to save anyone in the Yama.

The disorder spread like a stain, out of the Yama and into the nearby Jewish quarter, taking on a different form as it did.

Bei Zhidov! screamed the mob. Kill the Jews!

Terrified men and women scattered like sparrows before the mindless mob. Shop windows were smashed in, doors torn off their hinges, shelves ransacked by the thieves who came in the wake of the rampaging mob. There was a Russian word for all this: *pogrom*, devastation. Screaming women ran towards the lighted streets, seeking help that would never come. Nobody cared what happened to Jews. The raging mob filled the streets like a river. They burst into houses and flung furniture and clothing into the streets to be trampled and smashed. When they tired of that, they dragged many of the helpless inmates to the stinking Yauza River nearby, shoving them down the slimy banks into the putrid slop, commanding horrified spectators to spit upon them and defile them with mud.

Moses Strasbregyanov and his family were spared this humiliation, although that was of little consolation to them. The fire which swept out of the Yama destroyed their home and everything in it. They had nothing except the clothes in which they stood shivering in the wake of the mob. Moses' oldest son, Isidore, fourteen years old and small for his age, stared at the wreckage of the only home that he had ever known. His dark eyes were filled with hatred. He clutched the thin body of his little sister, Sarah, and listened to the sound of his mother crying.

'*Dushka*, *Dushka*, it could be worse,' his father was saying. 'At least we're still alive, thank God. We have the children, we have each other. We can start again.'

Isidore looked at the burning house, at his baby brother Aaron huddled in a quilt that Leah had hastily wrapped around him.

'Why didn't you kill them?' Isidore shouted at his father. 'Why didn't you kill the men who did this?'

He would always remember the houses burning, the stink of fear. He never forgave his father for not fighting, for being that kind of Jew.

He thought of Moses now as he watched Billy Priestman shoulder his way roughly through the crowd on the pier.

Marie looked back over her shoulder, mute appeal in her eyes. Forgive me, try to understand, what can I do? The look could have meant any, or all, or none of those things.

'You all right, Mr Strasberg?' his coachman said.

'I'm fine, Henry,' Irving said. 'Let's get into the carriage. I want to see where they're going.'

'Anything you say, Mr Strasberg.'

Anything you say, Mr Strasberg. It wasn't like that for a very long time. They had had nothing when they came to America, less than nothing. They had received letters from his father's brother, Jacob, who was a *cantor* in a synagogue in New York. He said there was a better life to be had in America. And, Isidore thought, anywhere is better than here.

That is where we will go, Moses said.

But we don't know how to get there, Papa, Leah said. Where is it, this America? And where will we get the money to go there?

'We'll get the money, *Dushka*,' Moses said softly.

59

'You'll see. We'll get the money and everything will be different.'

They travelled through the Jewish Pale to Latvia. It took them almost a year. Sarah died on the way. They buried her beside the road near a small town whose name Irving could no longer remember. From Riga they got a boat to Hamburg. Moses worked for a shoemaker until he had enough money to buy tickets for New York.

They disembarked at Castle Garden. The circular building was jammed with people. There was nobody to meet them and they did not know where to go. There were no seats in the courtyard. You either stood or sat on the cold pavement. Night fell. The men talked together in low tones. They all wanted to know the same things: what was happening, what was going to happen next, when would it happen. The ones who had been waiting longest told them: you have to pass through here, to be cleansed. To get to New York, you must pass through this Gehenna that stinks of human waste and despair.

After two days Jacob found them. He had changed his name to Strasberg.

'More American,' he said, banging himself on the chest. 'Strasberg.'

'Sdrazbyerg,' Moses said.

After a week or two, he found work as a *shomer*, the supervisor in a kosher slaughterhouse. It was lowly work but it put bread on the table. Izzy and Aaron learned American on the street, and hard-pressed teachers at the public school taught them numbers, simple spelling, how to write.

The older people wanted the youngsters to retain their religion. No matter how little they earned, they put aside a few cents for a *malamud*. So Moses became a *malamud*, working the early shift at the abbatoir so as to keep evenings free for teaching Hebrew. He was old-fashioned. He would not work on the *shabat* or even

60

touch money. He became deputy *cantor* at his brother's synagogue. Izzy loved *shul*. *Kol Nidre* on the Day of Atonement made his heart ache, it was so beautiful. During the week he had a job, selling the *Evening Journal*. It wasn't much, just a few cents a day. Every night he put what he had earned into his mother's apron.

And now he had millions.

Broadway was crowded, as always. Horse-drawn trolleys clanked their bells. Fashionably dressed men and women walked arm in arm, stopping to look in store windows. The coach ahead of them turned on to Fifth Avenue as they trotted past Madison Square. Stern's department store, the Eden Musee, old Mrs William Colford Schermerhorn's mansion slid by. North of the square, the old brownstones were all being converted into business premises or torn down, to be replaced by fashionable milliners, dressmakers, jewellers. At Thirtieth Street, the ornate frontage of the ten-storey whitestone Holland House, its main door flanked by pillars and gryphon-like creatures mounted on stone balls, came into view. The coach ahead went on past it.

'The Waldorf,' Irving said. 'It has to be.'

'You want me to stop, sir?' Henry asked.

'Around the corner,' Irving said. 'Let me out and then go home, Henry.'

He went into the Waldorf through the doorway on the Thirty-third Street side. The great marble lobby was abuzz with sound. Many of the banquettes were full. From time to time the *ting!* of the desk clerk's bell and his shout 'Front, please!' cut through the soft thunder of voices. Everyone came here; mainly to see, sometimes to be seen. *Le tout* New York knew that in their Fifth Avenue chateaux, the incredibly rich members of the upper classes could entertain a hundred guests for dinner at an hour's notice. At such hotels as the Waldorf, anyone who had the money could do the same.

61

Irving went into the bar and sat at one of the tables. When the waiter came, he ordered a glass of champagne.

'Will that be all, sir?'

'I'd like to find out what suite Mr Priestman is in,' Irving told him. 'He just checked in.'

'I'll make inquiries, sir,' the waiter said. Irving looked around. There was no one here that he knew. He wasn't much for sitting alone in bars, but right now he didn't want company. The waiter came back with his glass of champagne.

'Mr Priestman and his daughter are in Suite Four-fourteen, sir,' he said.

Irving thanked him and handed him a silver dollar.

'Thank you, sir,' the waiter said, and went away. It was all so hushed, so polite, so . . . ordered, Irving thought. A long way from the saloons and beer halls of the lower East Side where he used to sell the *Journal*. He wasn't allowed inside. He could see through the swing doors, though, and watch the waiters passing foaming glasses of beer over the heads of the patrons. Sometimes he could hear music, a rackety old piano being pounded. The air was always blue with smoke, and there was sawdust on the bare planked floors.

Sometimes, when there was a lull, the waiters would drape their damp towels over their arms, form a quartet or a sextet, and sing in harmony.

> *There's an old mill by a tavern,*
> *Where the gentle breezes play*
> *And the night birds sing the sweetest song of love . . .*

Izzy would listen to the songs, entranced. The harmonies, the strange, affecting lilt of the melodies, left him spellbound. This was not the dark, passionate music of Russia, or the elegaic, sad hymns of the *shul*. This was American music, and he loved it. He had a natural ear. He only had to hear a song twice and he could sing it perfectly. He had a sweet, clear young voice. One day he stood on a street corner and sang one of the songs that he had heard. Passers-by stopped to listen for a moment, smiling. One or two of them threw pennies into the cloth cap he had put at his feet. Izzy was dazzled: he had doubled his income just by singing a song!

When he got home that night he told his parents he wanted to be a singing waiter. Moses was stunned, horrified.

'Better you should want to be a *faygeleh*!' he shouted. 'A *shagetz*!'

'Moses!' Leah said, shocked beyond belief.

'But Pa, I can make good money!' Izzy said. 'And it's what I want to do!'

'Want, want? Who's care what you want? You'll do what I'm say!' Moses shouted.

'I won't!' Izzy shouted back at his father. 'You can't make me!'

'Silence!' Moses roared, and hit him across the face. Leah stood like a statue, her mouth open. Aaron's eyes flicked from his father to Izzy and back again. Moses glared at his son, anger holding back the regret in his eyes.

'You hit me,' Izzy said, wonderingly.

'A *paatch*,' Moses muttered. 'Nothing.'

'You think that will stop me?'

'You hear me now, Izzy. You hear me,' Moses said. 'No son of mine sings in saloons! No son of mine!'

And Izzy heard the mob screaming *Bei Zhidov!* and remembered how he had felt that night, and his heart filled with contempt.

'What will you do?' he said scornfully. 'Hit me again?'

He ran away from home.

Occasionally he got a one-night job in a tavern. The crowds liked him, a dark-eyed boy who sang songs about home and mother that brought maudlin tears to their eyes. The Bowery grapevine started working for

Izzy. In those days, song publishers paid entertainers to sing their songs onstage or in saloons. One of the biggest was Gus van Bleecker. He was a giant of a man in a loud checked suit. He smelled of cigars, whisky and bay rum. He was a 'name' in variety, or vaudeville, as they were beginning to call it.

'Heard about you, son,' he said to Izzy. 'Heard you sing real nice. Come and sit down with me. Have a drink.'

'Thanks,' Izzy said, dazzled. 'I'll have a beer.'

He didn't usually drink in the daytime. The beer made him light-headed, but he would have been light-headed anyway. He, Izzy Strasberg, was sitting with Gus van Bleecker drinking beer!

'Know Tony Pastor's?' Gus asked him.

'Sure,' Izzy said. Everyone knew Tony Pastor's Music Hall. It was at Fourteenth Street on Union Square. All the headliners wanted to play there. Vaudeville was becoming smart.

'I've got a week's spot there,' Gus said. 'Two weeks if they like me.'

'I'm sure they will, Mr van Bleecker,' Izzy said.

'Call me Gus,' Gus said expansively. 'I hope you're right, son. Thing is, I need something new. Something different. Can't play Tony Pastor's with the same old act. But I got me a doody of an idea.'

'You do?' Izzy said, trying to concentrate and wishing he hadn't drunk the beer so quickly.

'Sure do,' Gus said, breezily. 'Want another?'

Before Izzy could refuse, Gus had signalled the waiter and two more foaming mugs were plonked on to the table in front of them. Gus quaffed his with apparent relish. Izzy followed suit; no use letting Gus think he was a pantywaist.

'Here's my idea, son,' Gus said. 'I want you to be in the act with me.'

'Me?' Izzy said, astonished.

'Not on the stage, you understand,' Gus said. 'In the

64

audience, but working for me.'

'I see,' Izzy said. He drank some more beer.

'Now here's the how of it, son. I think it will work a treat. You sit down in the audience. I come on. I sing my songs – I've got a lot of new ones, good stuff, ten dollars some of them cost. Now when I get through singing, you'll get up and encore the number. Spontaneous, like. You get the idea?'

'I think so,' Izzy said, frowning. 'The audience thinks I'm one of them. Then – '

'Then I say "There's a boy down there with a wonderful voice, folks! What say we get him to stand up and sing that song again? Only this time, you all join in!"'

'And I stand up – '

'And I say "Give that boy a spotlight!"'

And it was a hell of a success. It sold sheet music, which was the aim of all the parties. Izzy loved every single moment of it. Especially the singing.

'Give that boy a spotlight!' Gus van Bleecker would shout, and Izzy would sing and sing and sing. He could not believe anyone in the world could be more fortunate than he. He was singing and getting paid for it. The pennies had turned into dollars. He was in the show business.

The vaudeville world became his world, its people his people. He was surprised at how many of them were Jewish. Many of them were on the look-out for 'speciality' material, especially the comedians. They soon discovered that Izzy, with his infallible ear for dialects and street talk, could provide it. At first he sold them jokes. Two dollars a joke, then five, then ten. Later he started to work with fellows who could write tunes. It was so easy; he could never figure out why anyone would find it difficult to put words to a tune. They just rolled right out of his head. 'Sadie's Perfume' was one success. 'My Beautiful Marie From Sunny Napoli' and 'Wait Till You Meet Her Mamma'

65

followed. It was when these songs were published that Izzy's name was changed yet again. When he typed up the lyrics to send to the printers, he submitted them with the byline 'I. Strasberg'. The printer, wanting to use his full name but not knowing what it was, took a chance and printed it as 'Irving' instead of 'Isidore'. When he saw what had happened Izzy was not altogether displeased. It had a nice ring to it.

Irving Strasberg.

He went into the lobby of the Waldorf and sat there until he saw Billy Priestman by the front desk. Irving went immediately to the house telephones and called Suite 414. Marie answered.

'It's me, Irving,' he said.

'Oh,' she said doubtfully. 'Where are you?'

'Downstairs,' he said. 'Can you get out?'

'Well . . . ' she said.

'Meet me at the Thirty-third Street entrance in ten minutes,' he said, and hung up.

They were married in upstate New York two nights later, and two days after that, set sail for the Caribbean in a chartered yacht, the *Melanie*.

7

They stood naked in the middle of the room. He lifted her and she put her legs around his middle, laying her head on his shoulder. Her long, golden-brown hair swung. Slowly, slowly, he lowered her, and slowly, slowly felt her enclose him. She murmured wordlessly and moved against him.

'Katey,' he whispered. 'Come on, Katey.'

'Ah, darling,' she whispered back. 'Darling.'

Their movements were languid, liquid.

'Now?' she said.

'Yes,' he said. 'Yes, yes, yes, yes, yes, yes.'

They slid apart. He knelt on the carpeted floor, and she faced him, smiling. She kissed him on the mouth. Her lips were slack and hot.

'You'll kill me,' he said. 'You know that?'

'What a way to die!' she giggled.

'What would you do with the body?'

'Toss it out of the window,' she said. 'Happens all the time in San Francisco. Nobody would even notice.'

'Just another stiff,' he said.

'Not any more,' she said, giggling again.

He padded across the room, putting on a robe, and poured two more glasses of champagne from the bottle in the silver cooler. He took them across to the bed on a tray. Catherine sprawled on the coverlet, arms wide. She sat up to take the glass of wine from his hand.

'I can't stay long, darling,' she said.

'Marie?'

'I promised I'd go and see her.'

'How is she?'

'She's terribly weak. But her temperature is nearly normal now. Unless there's a relapse, the worst is over.'

'She's got the best doctors in San Francisco,' James said. 'There'll be no relapse.'

'Do you know anything about typhoid?'

'I know it's a fever, and I know it can kill you.'

'If only they hadn't gone to Cuba.'

'Is that where they think she caught it?'

'Likeliest place, according to Dr Cosgrove.'

'She'll be fine, Katey. Don't worry.'

'I hope you're right.'

Actually he knew a lot about typhoid, but he wasn't going to tell any of it to Catherine. From what she'd told him, Marie had picked up a classic case. She could have caught it off a carrier, or from milk – which she'd drunk with rum, like a lot of tourists – or half a hundred other ways. Three weeks after they got back from their trip she was complaining of headaches and suffering nosebleeds. Her temperature went up jerkily until it was a hundred and one. That was when Irving called in the doctors. At the end of the first week the small pink spots of typhoid appeared on her chest and abdomen and she was rushed into hospital. She lapsed into a muttering delirium. Irving was at her bedside day and night, haggard and drawn.

'He blamed himself,' Catherine said.

'I'll bet Billy gave him hell,' James remarked.

'Billy won't even speak to him,' Catherine said. 'He's been beside himself ever since they ran off together.'

'I'd have paid money to be there when he found out,' James grinned.

'No, you wouldn't,' she said.

She thought at first that Billy might go mad, so intense was his reaction to the news that Marie had eloped with Irving Strasberg. He raged and swore, sweeping furniture out of his way as he strode through the house like an enraged bull. He got roaring, fighting drunk and had to be brought home from the Merchants' Exchange after knocking down someone who had unwittingly asked him how his daughter was. He acted, Catherine thought, exactly like a jilted lover, and she was at a loss to understand why.

She finished the wine and got dressed. It was getting late. The sun was dipping behind the crest of Angel Island. In the slanting rays coming in through the tall windows overlooking Russian Square, dust motes danced like tiny planets in a strange galaxy. She wanted to stay with James, draw on his strength. She did not want to go back to the hospital, to the smell of formaldehyde, starched linen, sickliness. Seeing her daughter's wan, thinned face, and the great dark shadows beneath her eyes had frightened Catherine. Death was something you expected to come for you long before it came for your children.

'Will you walk down the hill with me?' she said.

'I'll come to the hospital, if you like.'

'No,' she said. 'Better not.'

'Maybe you're right.'

She clung to him. 'James, James, tell me she's going to be all right.'

He said the reassuring things she needed to hear, holding her close, kissing her eyes and her hair, and trying to give her courage the only way he knew how. She was afraid, and her fear touched his own heart. There were so many things that could still go wrong. Marie could be left with deafness, or impaired memory, or suffer an internal haemorrhage. She could . . . He closed his mind to such thoughts. She would be fine. There was going to be no relapse. Why should there be? She was a healthy girl; the best doctors in town were treating her. He said all these things again to Catherine, and perhaps, for a while, she believed them.

'Hold me close, James,' she said, her voice muffled against his chest. 'I'm so afraid.'

He got her coat and they went down to the street. There were only a few people about. A mild breeze came in off the bay, bringing the smell of sea and salt. She heard a newsboy shouting on the corner. A trolley clanged and drowned some of the words but she stopped, frozen.

'James?' she said, choking with dread.

'Katey? What is it?' James said, turning to her. Her face was as white as a sheet. She pointed at the newsboy's placard. It lifted in the wind and then settled. The headline screamed at them.

PRIESTMAN HEIRESS DIES OF TYPHOID!!!

'Read all about it!' the newsboy shouted. 'Extra! Extra!'

'She's – it can't be!' he said. But they both knew it was true, and they both knew what it meant. Marie had died while they had been making love. And where, Billy Priestman would want to know, had she been? Catherine stood on the street corner and looked at James with horrified eyes.

'What are we going to do?' she whispered. 'For God's sake, James, tell me! What are we going to do?'

8

Dead.

How could she be dead? he thought. It had all happened so fast, so cruelly fast. Only minutes ago her lovely eyes had lost their light and he had thought: she's just gone to sleep, that's all it is.

The doctor put his hand on Irving's shoulder.

'I'm sorry,' he said.

Irving frowned. Sorry for what?

'Mr Strasberg,' the doctor said. 'Your wife is dead.'

Dead.

Who invented that awful word?

Dead meant never any more. Dead meant gone. Dead meant no more anything. A locked door outside a closed room that would never be opened again.

'Can I stay here?' Irving whispered. 'Just for a while?'

'Of course,' the doctor said.

He went out silently. Irving did not even know he was gone. He stared at Marie's silent form. We were happy, he thought. Why did it have to be us? He was numb in mind and body. I ought to be crying, he thought. But there were no tears in him. How long he sat there he did not know. In the end he got stiffly up from the hard hospital chair and went outside. A nurse came over to him and said something. Forms to be signed.

'Not now,' he said. He went out into the street. There were people everywhere. He hated them. Nobody cared about Marie. Nobody cared about him. Bastards! he wanted to shout at them. Don't you know my wife is dead?

People hurried by. One or two of them looked at him curiously. Nobody stopped. Tears of anger filled Irving's eyes. Bastards, bastards, he thought. Nobody cares about anybody in this fucking world.

He walked down the hill. The sea glittered between the buildings. The world was just the same. Marie was dead, but nothing else was changed. It seemed utterly, cruelly unfair. The tears filled his eyes again and he dashed them away. None of that, he told himself. They won't get any of that from me.

He found himself walking towards the Priestman house. Someone would have to tell them. He would rather it was him than anyone else. He hoped Catherine would be there. At least Catherine didn't hate him. The old man did. Irving saw it in Billy's eyes, a black, killing hate. And Willie, too. Only with Willie it was not hate, it was contempt.

He knocked on the door. Jameson, the butler, answered it.

'Mr Strasberg, sir,' he said. 'How – ?' He stopped when he saw Irving's face. 'Oh, sir,' he said.

'Is Mrs Priestman here?'

'Madam is in Santa Barbara, sir,' Jameson said. 'She is not expected back until this evening.'

'Mr Priestman?'

'He is in the study, sir. I'll tell him you are here.'

'No!' Irving said, more sharply than he had intended. 'No, Jameson. I'd better just go in.'

'Yes, sir,' the butler said.

Irving went up the stairs to Billy's panelled study and opened the door. Billy was sitting in his wing-chair by the fire, his feet propped up on a footstool. He was reading some papers and did not look up as Irving entered the room.

'What is it?' he said.

Irving said nothing. He thought the silence would go

72

on for ever, but he did not know how to start, how to break the news. Billy looked up. Irving did not need to speak. Billy Priestman took one look at his face, and knew.

'She's gone?' he said hoarsely. His eyes were empty, unfocused, as if he were sleep-walking. Irving nodded, struggling to keep back his tears. He did not trust himself to speak as well.

'Gone,' Billy whispered. 'So fast. So very fast.'

'I'm sorry,' Irving whispered. 'I'm so sorry, sir.'

It was all Irving had to offer, some sort of sympathy. Everything else inside him felt dead. Yet somehow the words seemed to anger Billy Priestman. Irving saw anger flood his red-rimmed eyes.

'You're sorry, are you?' Billy sneered, a vein throbbing in his temple. 'Sorry! You steal my little girl, you take her to some pest hole, you kill her – and then, you kike bastard, you come here and tell me that you're *sorry*?'

Inside his head Irving heard only the one word. It reverberated in his head like the screams of the men in the hot, dark streets of the ghetto. *Bei Zhidov!* they had shouted. Kill the Jews, the sheenies, the kikes!

Irving took a step forward, fury flashing in his eyes, the shouts of *Bei Zhidov* echoing in his head, the smell of burning, the memory of old men with broken faces sobbing in the putrid slime of the Yauza. The anger on Billy Priestman's face turned to alarm and he backed away, holding up his hands.

'No, don't . . . ' he said.

The anger went out of Irving like exhaled smoke. He felt exhausted. The two men stood looking at each other for long, long moments. Then Billy Priestman drowned his own fear with assumed rage.

'Get out!' he screeched. 'Get out of my house, you – '

He did not have the courage to say it. Irving shook his head.

'You contemptible bastard!' he said.

He walked out of the house and down the hill towards the Embarcadero. His heart was a stone on which the words Billy Priestman had spoken were engraved forever. He would never forget or forgive them.

9

'Come away, Pa', Willie said. 'Come away, now.'

Billy Priestman shook his head, his face twisted as though with pain. Rain drove at them from a leaden sky as if they were its enemy, misting in a fine spray on the dripping umbrella, sluicing down the yellow slickers they were wearing. Everyone else had gone.

'She never understood,' Billy mumbled. 'Never understood.'

'What didn't she understand?'

Billy shook his head again. The smell of liquor came off him like heat off a stove. His face was wet with tears or rain, or both.

'Pa, let's go now,' Willie said. Standing around in this murderous downpour was a shortcut to pneumonia, he thought. He hated illness of any kind. He was bone-tired. That's when it gets you, he thought, when your resistance is low. His mother's death, so quickly on the heels of Marie's, had knocked him sideways. Billy, too. His father had simply quit functioning, sitting hour after long hour in his big leather chair in the library, staring at nothing. Willie had perforce taken up the slack, running his own business and looking after his father's extensive affairs at the same time.

'My fault,' Billy said. 'My stupid fault.'

'No, Pa,' Willie said gently. 'You mustn't blame yourself.'

'Made her do it,' Billy said.

'No,' Willie said, putting a clumsy hand on his

75

father's shoulder. 'It was . . because of Marie.'

Yet again, Billy shook his head hopelessly.

'Bastard,' he muttered.

Willie frowned. He had the eeriest feeling he and his father were talking about different things. Water trickled down his neck and he shivered. Got to get the hell out of this rain before I catch my death of cold, he thought. That would be marvellous, wouldn't it? Another Priestman death, like some bizarre epidemic.

'Let's go home, Pa,' he said, more forcefully this time. He pointed with his chin at the two gravediggers huddled beneath a yew tree fifty yards away and looking as miserable as half-drowned cats. 'They're . . . waiting.'

Rain bounced off the tombstones and made misty haloes around the upturned faces of the stone angels. Willie took his father's arm and, reluctantly, Billy turned away from the grave.

'Tomorrow,' he said.

'All right, Pa, tomorrow,' Willie said gently. 'We'll come back tomorrow.'

They got into the coach, stripping off their rain-drenched slickers. The driver clucked the horses into movement and they clattered out of the cemetery. It was cheerless and damp inside the swaying carriage. Rivulets of water ran down the windows. Neither man spoke until they turned into Sacramento Street.

'I loved her, you know,' Billy said abruptly.

'I know, Pa,' Willie said soothingly.

'Marie,' Billy said testily. 'I loved her. That's why she was . . . taken. A punishment.'

'Why would it be a punishment?'

Billy did not answer, and Willie did not pursue the subject. His father wasn't making much sense, but grief did that sometimes. As for himself, he felt nothing yet. Maybe he would later. They said that happened sometimes. As a child he had adored his mother, but when he was fourteen, that changed. He was old enough to see the chasm that separated his parents, and in the way of unforgiving adolescence, blamed her for it. As for Marie, they had never been close. She laughed at him too much, and he had never liked that. She laughed when he told her he disapproved of the fast Society set she ran around with, laughed and became even more provocative. Let Willie tell her he disliked a person, and Marie would do her utmost to befriend and charm them. She cultivated the Starrs, whom Willie found snobbish and boring, and as for Irving Strasberg . . . The man had been a guttersnipe whom no amount of money or fame could redeem. Marie had taken him to her heart. Well, much good it had done her.

He got out of the carriage beneath the *porte-cochère* and smiled automatically at the servant who came running with an umbrella he did not need. He went into the house, his face impassive, noting that his father headed straight for the whisky decanter. For the next four hours he listened, saying little, as bishops and soldiers and civic leaders and local politicians recited their encomiums. He had to stifle a sardonic grin. What would that perspiring, fat-faced fool of a cleric say if he *knew*? Probably faint dead away, the dumb old fart, Willie thought.

He had managed it all rather well, he thought. It had been a stroke of good fortune that the owner of the Pacific Coast Hotel recognised the name Priestman, and had the good sense to send for Willie before he called the police. Willie instructed him to do absolutely nothing until he arrived. No doctor, no police, nothing. The man, whose name was Thaddeus Taylor, was happy to oblige. Satisfied, Willie got in a carriage and went to see a doctor he knew, Carleton Dawson. Dawson had a smart practice on Polk Street.

'My dear Mr Priestman!' he said, when the maid showed Willie in. 'This is a pleasant surprise. What can I do for you?'

Willie told him.

'You can't be serious, sir!' Dawson said, aghast. 'What you're suggestin' is quite out of the question! Why, I would be struck off –'

'Spare me the histrionics,' Willie said. 'I want you to do what I say.'

'But, Mr Priestman, I –'

'Do you remember Julie Donaldson?' Willie said. There was a long silence before Dawson spoke.

'Yes,' he said, so quietly as to be almost inaudible.

'Then you will not have forgotten that I was of some service to you in that matter?'

'No,' Dawson said. Willie could hear the hate in his voice. He smiled. He liked a good hater, and Dawson had plenty to hate him for. The doctor had made improper advances towards a woman patient. She mentioned it to a friend, who told one of Willie's reporters. Smelling a good story, Willie sent a pretty girl reporter named Julie Donaldson to visit Dawson as a new patient. He told her to take off her clothes behind a screen. When she was undressed, he came up behind her, grasping both her breasts. Julie Donaldson drove her elbow backwards into his abdomen and stamped on his instep at the same time. Dawson reeled back, eyes popping with shock. When Julie Donaldson revealed that she was a reporter with the *Inquirer*, she thought he might die on the spot, so suffused with horror was his face. He begged her not to file the story, promised her a thousand dollars to forget what he called the 'unfortunate incident'.

Willie gave the girl a thousand-dollar bonus and told her he would handle the story himself. Dawson was a bigwig in the local Democratic Party, and might prove useful at some later date. Willie was already thinking about politics: governor, senator, president, the route was not difficult for a man with the right connections and the right money. What was it they said? It takes three things to become president. The first is money, the second is money, and the third is money. He called on Dawson and told him what he had done.

'I'm forever in your debt, Mr Priestman,' Dawson told him fulsomely. 'I'll never forget what you've done, sir, never. And I'll pay you back, I promise.'

'You most certainly will,' said Willie.

Willie took Dawson with him down the coast to San Luis Obispo in his private train. While Dawson examined Catherine's body, Willie took Thaddeus Taylor to one side. Taylor was a squat, swarthy man with a heavy moustache, and a pendulous belly, across which was draped a heavy gold watch-chain with a gold nugget pendant.

'Mr Taylor,' he said. 'A private word.'

'Yes, sir, Mr Priestman, sir,' Taylor said, rubbing his flabby paws together. 'Anthing you say, Mr Priestman.'

'Yes, yes,' Willie said. 'Now, sir. How many people other than yourself know about my mother's . . . death?'

'Just three, Mr Priestman,' Taylor said. 'The maid who found her. My under-manager, Mr Lane. And myself, of course.'

'Did she . . . was there a note? Anything at all?'

'No, sir, nothing.'

'You're absolutely sure, Mr Taylor?'

'When I realised who it . . . that it was your mother, Mr Priestman, I was especially diligent, especially. I can assure you there was no note of any kind.'

'Good,' Willie said. He looked around as someone knocked at the door. Taylor opened it to admit Carleton Dawson. The doctor set his Gladstone bag on Taylor's desk and turned to face Willie.

'Well?' Willie said. 'Have you been able to ascertain the cause of death, doctor?'

'Heart failure,' Dawson said.

'Heart f——?' Taylor started up out of his chair. Willie fixed him with a stare, and Taylor slowly sank back into a sitting position, his thick-lipped mouth slightly open.

'It is my opinion that Mrs Priestman suffered a cardio-vascular arrest,' Dawson said smoothly. 'Whilst that in itself might not necessarily have proven fatal, she had taken a small amount of laudanum – ' He looked up as Taylor made a small sound, then continued urbanely, 'which was sufficient to depress the motor functions and so cause death. I have the laudanum bottle here. As you see, it is practically full. Perhaps one dose has been taken, no more.'

'It was empty,' Taylor said wonderingly, as if to himself.

Dawson smiled forgivingly. 'You are mistaken, sir. I shall certify death from natural causes.'

He looked at Willie. Willie looked at Taylor. The silence lengthened until, at last, the hotelier pasted on a smile that did not reach his eyes.

'Well, gentlemen,' he said, his voice shaky. 'I would. Ah, I'm not sure . . . that I . . . my reputation here . . .'

'My dear Taylor!' Willie said, getting to his feet. 'How crass of me! You must have been worried sick about all this, and here am I thinking only of myself. It's – ' He put a little break into his voice; rather well, he thought. 'With it being my . . . mother, you know. I . . .' He waved a hand, vaguely. It worked like a charm.

'Oh, Mr Priestman, forgive me!' Taylor said. 'It's just that . . . in the hotel business . . . people talk, you know. The staff. Other guests. One's reputation, such a fragile thing . . .'

'Of course, of course!' Willie said, putting on a brave smile. 'I had given some thought to it on my way down here, Mr Taylor. Thaddeus, is it not?'

'Yes, sir,' Taylor beamed. 'Thaddeus.' The unease in his eyes was giving way to cupidity. Stupid prick, Willie thought.

'If it would not offend,' he said. 'I would like to express my gratitude to you in some, ah, tangible way, Thaddeus. As my poor way of thanking you. A bonus, one might call it. A thousand dollars, say? And perhaps something for your manager, and the maid?'

'That's very generous, Wil – Mr Priestman,' Taylor breathed. 'I said to myself as you came through the door, there's a generous man if I ever – '

The maid, a Mexican woman of about fifty, and the under-manager, Percival Lane, were summoned. The latter was a limp-wristed fellow in a dove-grey suit. Willie told them what he proposed.

'You're really awf'ly kind,' Lane said, gushing. 'It's not necessary, you know.'

'I know,' Willie said, chilling Lane into silence. 'Dawson, show them the death certificate.'

Dawson handed the document to the maid, who read it and shrugged. Lane's eyes widened as he read it, and he looked at Thaddeus Taylor for guidance. It was not forthcoming.

'Now sign this piece of paper,' Willie said.

'What is it?' Taylor asked.

'It says that you have read the death certificate issued by Dr Carleton Dawson of San Francisco, which states that Catherine Priestman died of natural causes, while a guest at this hotel,' Willie said. 'It further states that you have no reason to question that finding.'

'But . . . ?' Lane said, very tentatively, still looking at Taylor. The swarthy fat man shook his head. Willie took a bundle of bills out of his pocket and put them on the desk. Greedy eyes followed his every movement.

'Sign,' Willie said.

Much later, on their way back up the coast to San Francisco in Willie's train, Dawson finally summoned the courage to say what he had been wanting to say.

'You really are a ruthless bastard, Priestman,' he said.

'Yes,' Willie agreed. 'I am.'

All the way back to town, one question nagged away at his mind. Why? Why had Catherine killed herself? Why had she chosen to go so far from home to do it? Perhaps he would never know. The only person who could answer his questions was his father, and he loved him too much to subject him to more hurt now. Billy was hurting badly enough over Marie.

He always loved her more than me, Willie thought. He had never minded, knowing that one day his achievements would make his father proud, and Billy would see who the *real* love had always come from.

So Catherine was buried in hallowed ground alongside her daughter, and the bishop droned his homilies about the great ship of life dropping off passengers, and may there be no moaning of the bar, while the rain thrashed the trees and drenched the large crowd of friends who had come to the funeral.

At last the house was empty. Jameson came to inquire whether there was anything Willie wanted before he retired.

'Nothing, thank you, Jameson,' Willie said. Jameson turned to go, and turned back as Willie asked a final question.

'You father is in the library, Mr William,' Jameson said. 'I fear he has drunk rather a lot this evening.'

'Don't worry,' Willie said. 'I'll put him to bed. Thank you, Jameson. Good night.'

'Good night, sir,' Jameson said, and withdrew. Willie poured himself a whisky and went along the darkened corridor towards the library. One of the twin doors was ajar, and he could see his father, chin on chest, in front of the dying fire.

'Zat?' Billy said.

'Me, Pa,' Willie said, wondering at the hostility in his father's voice.

'C'min,' Billy said. 'S'down. Va drink.'

'I've got one.'

Billy picked up the bottle on the occasional table beside his chair, and sloshed whisky into his glass. Some of it spilled on to the table and the carpet.

'Pa,' Willie said gently. 'Haven't you had enough?'

'Haven't had tha' mush,' Billy said, and Willie could see the foolish grin twist on his father's face. Grief, he thought, wondering why it was hitting his father so hard and not touching him at all.

'It'll be all right, Pa,' he said softly touching Billy's forearm. Billy jerked it away as if Willie's fingers were red-hot.

'Tush me!' he said, angrily. 'Don' tush me. Bassud, I am. Dirty shitty bassud.'

'No, Pa,' Willie said. 'No you're not.'

'Killed her, di'n' I?' Billy said.

'What are you talking about?' Willie said, ice touching his heart. Did he know? How could he know?

'You do' know,' Billy said. 'You weren't there. You don't remember. I remember. I remember . . . '

'Tell me what you're talking about, Pa,' Willie said.

'Y'mother,' Billy said, staring at the red embers in the hearth as if to read words written in them. 'Marie. She was dying. Y'mother wasn't there. Sent people all over sh . . . all over, looking for her. Dis'peared. Said she's vis'tin someone. She's visitin' someone, all right. That bassud. Thass who.'

'Who?'

'Comin' to that, comin' to that,' Billy said, waving a hand. 'Fine mother, eh? My baby dying, 'n she's in bed with that bassud.'

'What?' Willie shouted, rage coursing through him. 'Who?'

'Starr!' Billy croaked. 'James Starr, that one-armed bassud. Him and your mother – '

'You knew that?' Willie hissed, getting up to stand in front of his father. 'You knew, and you said nothing?'

Billy shook his head wearily. 'More to it than that, boy,' he said. 'Siddown. Listen. Listen.'

'I'll kill him!' Willie said.

'Thass what I said,' Billy nodded. 'Kill the bassud. But *her*! What about *her*? She was just as bad. Worse. She di'n' even deny it. Said she was sorry. 'magine that – sorry! I said she's cheap'st bitch inna world. Said she was a dirty, no-good tramp. Hit her. You know that?

Hit her with my fist.' He held up a trembling hand, as if he could not believe it had ever been used for such a thing. 'Begged me to forgive her, Willie. On her knees, sobbing, begging. All I wanted was . . . nothing. Marie was dead, see? Didn't matter any more. Told her to get out. Your mother. Get out, I said. Get your filthy body out of my sight and out of my house, and – ' He stopped, shaking, tears coursing down his cheeks.

'She never spoke,' he said. 'Just went out, silent, like a ghost. Know what I did? I got drunk. Thass a good one, isn' it?'

'You couldn't have known,' Willie said gently. 'You were hurt, angry. It's understandable.'

Billy looked at his son. The firelight was almost gone now, but Willie could see what was in his father's eyes.

Willie said nothing. He didn't know how to say what needed to be said.

Billy sighed. He got up very slowly and put his hand on his son's shoulder.

'I think I'll go on up now,' he said.

Willie helped him to his room, and got him into his nightshirt. Billy rolled on to the bed, and then, to Willie's dismay, he started crying.

'O God!' he sobbed. 'O God, why did you take her?'

'It's all right, Pa,' Willie said. 'I've taken care of everything. There's no need to cry.'

'O God,' Billy mumbled. Willie stayed for a while, stroking his father's hand until the sobbing turned to a whimper, and then stopped altogether. When he judged that his father's regular breathing meant that Billy was asleep, he stole out of the room.

'Marie,' Billy said into the silence.

10

Pacific Coast Hotel
San Luis Obispo

My dearest,

I hardly know how to write this letter to you. I had the most awful scene with Billy. He made me confess 'my sin'. He called me things that lacerated my soul, awful, filthy words.

I am glad now that I made you leave San Francisco and not attend Marie's funeral. There would probably have been an ugly scene. Billy has not drawn a sober breath since our darling died. I begged him to forgive me, promised never to see you again. He told me that he would ruin us both. Me first, then you, he said.

As soon as the funeral was over, I left the house. I could not bear to be under the same roof as Billy, to suffer his accusing glare, his foul language. I have come here to try to find some surcease from the awful guilt that haunts me. I cannot help but feel that my daughter's death is in some way a punishment for loving you. I need you so desperately now, but that cannot ever be again. And so I write to say goodbye to you, my dearest. I weep to know that I shall never see your dear sweet face again, or kiss you, or hold you against my breast.

I love you, I love you.

    Goodbye, my darling. Forgive me.

                    Your
                    Catherine

James learned the rest later. There could have been no pain, they said, as if physical pain was the only kind there was.

He did not, could not attend her funeral. He knew that if he were to see Billy Priestman he would kill him. He was beyond grief, in some limbo of feelinglessness. Only a little while ago he had held her in his arms, felt the soft, singing strengths of her body moving in rhythm with his own.

His wife, Linda, was a wise woman. She saw, and she understood what had happened to her man. She had realised what was happening right from the beginning. For a while, she wanted to die. Then she wanted to strike back, to hurt both of them for what they had done to her. She gave no sign of it to James, although it seared her heart every time she helped him pack to leave New Mexico for another trip to San Francisco, to *her*. Linda was a wise woman, but she was a woman first and wise second. She hated Catherine Priestman as she had never hated anyone in all her life. The hate lay like black vomit in the pit of her stomach.

Why? Why, why, why?

Over and over, the same question. What did this woman have that she, Linda, could not offer her man? What was it that she, Linda, no longer had that this woman had?

Why? Why, why, why?

Later, she began to try to understand, and that was the hardest thing she had ever done in her life. She knew now that he would never leave her. Time was on her side. She could wait, even if she hated while she was waiting. It would come. There was pain in it for them, too. She saw that sometimes in her husband's eyes, and knew that he loved her, too, but not the same way, not the way it had once been. She hated Catherine for that more than anything, but still she gave no sign. When he came home, she was there, the same.

Now Catherine was dead and Linda could feel no pity

for her. No sorrow. Sadness for her man, because he was sad. But that was all. Another part of her was fiercely glad because it was over at last.

Now the wounds were made, and they were deep. Some of them might heal. Most of them would not. She saw the hatred in her husband's eyes whenever he spoke of the Priestmans.

And knew that in the Priestmans the same hatred must also be burning.

That was how it ended.

That was how it began.

BOOK TWO

HATE

11

'That bastard,' James said, shaking his head. 'That demented bastard!'

'What's happened, James?' Linda said.

'He's done it again!' James said. 'Look at this!' He angrily tossed his copy of the Roswell *Pioneer* across the table. Linda picked it up and read the story. It had to do with James's standing for commissioner for the newly formed Gonzalez County, and his involvement in setting up the finance for the drilling of the first artesian well on Will Prager's property at Roswell. 'The irrepressible greed of lawyer Starr, with his unsavoury methods and unprincipled cohorts, is again in evidence . . . only one arm, but the hand at the end of it is capacious and canny . . . a record that would stink a Ute out of his tepee . . . unworthy to serve in any public office, and certainly not one involving the handling of developmental finances . . .'

It was a thorough hatchet job of the sort that Willie Priestman knew only too well how to engineer. The *Pioneer* was a Priestman paper: indeed, Willie had bought it as one of the many weapons he and his father were using to bar whatever progress James tried to make. When he stood for the Territorial Legislature in 1894, they pulled out all the stops. Large donations to the campaigns of the opposing candidates arrived anonymously. Editorials appeared in the Priestman papers in Santa Fé, Albuquerque and Roswell casting calumny after outright lie on his record. Throughout the campaign the Priestmans mailed flyers to every member of the Territorial Legislature, on whose faces red-lettered slogans were printed: VOTE FOR STARR, A MAN WHO WOULDN'T STEAL A RED-HOT STOVE! IF YOU THINK YOUR CONGRESSMAN NEEDS BRIBING, VOTE STARR AND WATCH IT HAPPEN! VOTE, STARR, A MAN WHO WILL STOOP TO ANY CHALLENGE! Inside the envelopes were transcripts of newspaper items that had appeared over the years, all carefully chosen to show James in the worst possible light. They were smear tactics, but they worked. James was not elected.

'I'm not going to sit still for this!' he said now. 'Damned if I am. I'll go out to San Francisco. Maybe there's some way to talk sense into the man.'

'I'll come with you,' Linda said.

'No, *corazón*,' he said gently. 'You stay home. Rest. That will do you more good than all those hours in a train. It'll only be for a few days.'

Linda nodded, her sigh a mixture of relief and exasperation. She did not know what was the matter with her these days. She had always been as healthy as a horse, but for the past few months, it seemed that the mildest physical work exhausted her. Her appetite had fallen off to nothing. She was thirsty all the time.

James took the next train to San Francisco.

Billy Priestman received him in the study of the big house, his face like stone. The years had not been kind to him. He was unhealthy-looking, overweight. The breath wheezed in his chest when he spoke.

'You've got a damned nerve, coming here,' he said. 'Speak your piece and get out!'

'Billy, we've got to talk,' James said. 'This stupid feud between us has got to stop. It's pointless, it's – '

'Getting to you, is it?' Billy sneered. 'Must be, to bring you crawling all the way out here. Well, I'll tell you this, Starr. I haven't even begun on you yet!'

'Billy, what happened, happened,' James said. 'No–

body regrets it more than I. But it's over, Billy, it's in the past.'

'You came here to tell me that?' Billy said. 'Well, I'll give you full marks for gall, you bastard!'

'Everybody got hurt, you know,' James said softly. 'Not just you.'

'Hurt?' Billy blazed. 'You talk to me about hurt, damn you! I was in a hospital, watching my daughter die, while you . . . were – '

He shook his head, the hate a live coal in the black ash of his eyes. The house was still and cold. There were no more memories in it any more. They had all been replaced by hatred.

'She admitted everything, you know,' Billy said. 'I made her tell me. She begged me, on her knees, said she'd never see you again, she'd do anything. I told her then, as I'm telling you now, Starr – that I'd ruin you!'

'You're crazy,' James said. 'You're a crazy man.'

'You'll find out how crazy I am!' Billy Priestman said. 'When I'm finished with you, you'll have nothing, Starr. *Nothing!*'

'What I've got I got the hard way, Billy,' James said. 'You'll find taking it off me a bigger job than you're cut out for.'

'We'll see about that!' Billy hissed. 'I'm going to make you pay for what you did. You and all your damned tribe! Now – get out of my house! If you ever try to come here again, I'll kill you!'

'Look at me shaking,' James said contemptuously. There was nothing you could do with a man that full of hate. 'Go ahead, Billy. Do your damnedest!'

Billy Priestman did just that. He spent thousands of dollars trying to stall James's political career. He made donations to any candidate who would run against him. He shamelessly bribed political writers, editors, journalists. Billy didn't care what he spent, and that kind of money has a way of getting results. His bagman in Santa Fé was a vain and venal creature named

93

Mortimer Ashby, son of a family which owned vast tracts of land on the Cieneguilla Grant. He was personal assistant to William Romero, a member of the Territorial Legislature, and as such, he knew everyone. That made him dangerous. The movers and shakers of New Mexico Territory were ruthless men. They took their whisky straight and played their poker seriously. They were a clan, and James was a member; but business, after all, was business. Clients began to drift away from the law firm of Elkham & Starr. Loans were called prior to their due date. Something had to give, and James was damned if it was going to be him.

'Sam,' he said to his partner, Sam Elkham. 'I'm going to stop that sonofabitch Ashby cold!'

'Tell me how,' Sam said.

'What do we know about him?'

'He's a pimp,' Sam said. 'We've used him once or twice.'

Ashby could arrange for a batch of young, clean and willing girls from south of the line to be present at Santa Fé or Albuquerque political gatherings. His own predilections were in another direction.

'Could we nail him on that?' Sam wondered.

'No,' James said flatly.

'Got to be something nice and tight,' Sam said. 'But what?'

'I'll work on it,' James told him.

It took him a while, but he came up with just what was needed. Ashby was one of a group who were trying to push a spurious bill through the Territorial Legislature which would validate around two hundred thousand dollars worth of warrants for pay and maintenance of the New Mexico militia during the Apache campaigns. Governor Thornton had stated categorically that he would veto the bill if it reached him, since he believed that most of the warrants were fictitious. Manuel Torres, the shrewd and unprincipled Santa Fé merchant who was the largest holder of these warrants, came to see James.

'I don't know whether the damned warrants I've got are real or fake, James,' he said, angrily grinding out his cigar in the ashtray on James's desk. 'But if Thornton vetoes that bill, I'm out one hell of a lot of money.'

'By the same token, Manuel, if you push them through and they're fake, you'll go to jail,' James reminded him.

'What about unloading them on someone?' Sam Elkham said. He was standing with his shoulder against the door jamb, wearing that cynical smile James knew so well.

'Who the hell would be dumb enough to buy them?' Torres said, looking from James to his partner in surprise.

'You mean who I think you mean, Sam?'

'Damned right,' Elkham said.

The one thing they knew for sure about Mortimer Ashby was that he was greedy and gullible. If he could be made to believe that the legislature was going to honour the warrants, he would buy them. James went to see the governor. Thornton was adamant: he would not allow crooks to bilk the Territorial treasury, even if it meant that honest men remained unpaid.

'You're absolutely right, governor,' James said. 'It's a problem. Mind if I make a suggestion?'

'Go right ahead.'

'Why not let whoever owns the paper present it? But ask the Department of Justice to send someone out here to examine every warrant, and decide which is genuine and which is forged. That way, you don't lose votes and anyone trying to defraud the government gets jumped on by the Justice people.'

Thornton steepled his fingers and touched them to his lips, a frown on his handsome forehead. Then he looked up and smiled.

'James,' he said, 'you're a genius.'

'Ain't that the truth?' James grinned.

It was easy after that. Elkham & Starr saw to it that the first person to be informed that the governor was no longer intending to veto the bill was William Romero. No mention, however, was made of the Department of Justice. Next day, Mortimer Ashby called in to James's office on the Plaza.

'Starr,' he said casually. 'I was passing the door. Thought I'd say hello.'

James had never made any attempt to conceal his dislike of Mortimer Ashby, and he did not do so now.

'I'm busy,' he snapped.

'Just wanted a quick word,' Ashby said.

James looked up, fixing Ashby with a hostile stare. 'Ashby,' he said levelly. 'Billy Priestman is trying to put me out of business. You're his man. I've got nothing to say to you. Besides which, I'm up to my ass in work on these militia warrants. Manuel Torres has got a bundle of them, and the damned things aren't worth a shit!'

'How many have you got?'

'About eighty-five thousand dollars worth, at face value.'

'Interested in selling?'

James allowed himself to look astonished. 'They're not worth a damn, Ashby. What's the catch?'

'No catch,' Ashby said.

'Thornton will veto that bill of yours for sure,' James said. 'You know something nobody else knows?'

'I'll give you forty-two and a half thousand for the paper,' Ashby said.

'You got a damned nerve!' James said, disgustedly.

'You said yourself Thornton will veto that bill,' Ashby said, affecting impatience. 'Then they won't be worth sticking on a nail in the outhouse.'

'Ashby,' James said. 'What the hell you up to?'

'Do you want to sell or don't you, Starr?' Ashby said, as if it didn't matter one way or the other to him. He could not conceal the flicker of greed in his eyes, and James felt almost sorry for him. Here was the son of one of the richest men in New Mexico Territory, who did not need money, but who could not resist sticking it to Elkham & Starr. It was when times got tough that you really found out who your friends were, James thought. And your enemies.

'Let me think about it,' he said.

'I'll be back at noon,' Ashby told him.

'You're not giving me much time, Ashby.'

'Take it or leave it,' Ashby said, flicking imaginary dust off the lapels of his dove-grey Prince Albert.

James watched him leave. There was no pity in his eyes. When a man was fighting for his life, he had to use any weapon he could lay his hand on. Ashby would probably go to prison for grand larceny. What would he get? A year, two? What would two years in a penitentiary do to a man like Ashby? Convicts showed the third sex little mercy. Well, if Ashby didn't like being shot at with real bullets, he shouldn't have joined the Army, James thought, dismissing the man from his mind.

Winning a battle, however, did not win the war. Billy Priestman had more than one string to his bow. Now he went after Huntington Carver, the husband of James's daughter Portland. Huntington was already in trouble, and Billy Priestman saw to it that his troubles multiplied. Huntington, not yet thirty-five, had taken over his father Ezra's railroad, the Ohio, Kansas & California, after Ezra — a man they'd nicknamed 'the Back Bay Bastard' in New York financial circles – died of a heart attack. To put the debt-ridden railroad back on its feet and get the rails to San Francisco, Huntington had cut a lot of corners and trodden on plenty of toes. He was no better, and certainly no worse, than a lot of other railroad boomers of his day. Then the depression of 1893 shot his plans to pieces, wiping out projected profits and reducing investment to a trickle. Like a vulture scenting carrion, Matthias Bryant, a former government auditor of railroads, approached Huntington with a 'report' which 'examined, in detail', the origins of the financing, the operational characteristics, and the political manipulation which had been employed, both by Huntington and his father, to effect the completion of the OKC. Bryant offered to sell the only copy of his report to Huntington for fifty thousand dollars. Huntington kicked the man into the street, whereupon Bryant went straight to Willie Priestman, who knew exactly how to use Bryant's information. The 1894 Pullman strike, although it had failed, had left memories of wretched suffering and deep bitterness towards the railroads. Polemics against them began to appear in the *Inquirer* chain, and were quickly picked up by the others. The Priestman papers, busy as they were with their crusade against Spanish atrocities in Cuba, were always willing to find space in which to excoriate anyone connected with the Starr family. Even when Huntington published Bryant's letters, proving that the man had been trying to blackmail him, some of the mud still stuck.

'They're trying to crucify a dead man,' Huntington bitterly told his friends. His second-mortgage bonds, representing the OKC's debt to the government and amounting to about thirteen million dollars, would fall due in a year. The annual simple interest on this sum, paid by the government, was more than three quarters of a million dollars. By the time the bonds began maturing, the government would have paid out nearly forty million dollars on behalf of the OKC.

'What have you got in the way of credits?' Andrew Starr asked Huntington, when they met in Washington.

'At the very best, around eight million,' Huntington said. 'If I don't find a loophole someplace, the OKC is a write-off.'

'Not to mention you,' Andrew reminded him.

'I've got a year,' Huntington said. 'They've put over the refunding measure because of the election. Can you do anything? Talk to McKinley, maybe?'

'I can try,' Andrew said. 'He'll be favourably inclined, but I don't know what he'd be able to do. Can I give you some advice, Huntington?'

'Certainly, sir.'

'Put your private affairs in order,' Andrew said forthrightly. 'You know what I'm referring to.'

Huntington flushed. 'This is a damnable intrusion,' he said. 'I don't think you – '

'If Willie Priestman's jackals fasten on to the details of your personal life, young man, you'll be finished on Capitol Hill,' Andrew said. 'Don't bother to protest. I'm a shade too old for hypocrisy. We both know what I'm talking about. Attend to it.'

'Yes, sir,' Huntington said. You arrogant old piss-artist, he thought. He was careful, however, not to let his feelings show. Huntington was every inch his father's son, and he knew better than to alienate so potent an ally as Andrew.

He had no intention of doing what Andrew was suggesting. Andrew Starr didn't know a whisper from a big wind. Most of all, Andrew Starr did not have to live with his vain, self-centred niece, who thought of nothing but her overblown, overpriced, overstuffed mansion on Fifth Avenue, and her standing with Ward McAllister's glitteringly boring Four Hundred.

Just the same, Huntington thought, it would pay to be circumspect. The way things were poised now, a scandal would do him no good at all. He decided to go and see Rachel the minute he got back to New York.

Portland was waiting for him at the station. He made no attempt to hide his surprise.

'What on earth brings you down here?' he said.

'I want you to go somewhere with me, Huntington,' she said.

'Can't it wait?' he asked querulously. 'I've just had a long, dusty train ride, and . . .'

He stopped when he saw her face. Portland had never

looked at him as she was looking at him now. There was a contempt, an anger in her eyes that he had never seen before.

'I have a carriage waiting,' she said, signalling for a porter. She did not speak until they were rattling out of the station, and then only when he asked her a question.

'I said, "where are we going?"' he repeated.

'226 West Forty-eighth Street,' Portland replied, her face impassive. *Jesus!* Huntington thought. *Oh, Jesus Christ in the morning!*

'What's this all about, Porty?' he said, fighting the apprehension that was trying to close his throat.

'Perhaps nothing,' she said, not looking at him. 'We will see when we get there.'

The coach pulled to a stop outside an elegant town house. Without waiting for her husband to help her down, Portland alighted from the coach and told the driver to wait. Then she crossed the sidewalk and rang the bell.

'I never realised you enjoyed melodrama so much, my dear,' Huntington said. Portland tossed her head and said nothing. A maid opened the door. She looked blankly at Portland, and then smiled when she saw Huntington.

'Good evening, Mr Carver, sir,' she said.

She stood to one side. No use pretending any more, Huntington thought. I'll just have to brazen it out. How the hell did she find out? He followed Portland into the room. Rachel got up from her chair. She made a helpless gesture towards the man sitting next to her. It was Willie Priestman.

'Well, well,' Huntington said. 'I might have known.'

'He made me send for her, Huntington!' Rachel said. 'I didn't know what to do. He said – '

'It's all right, Ray,' Huntington said gently.

Willie Priestman got up out of his chair and came across towards Portland.

'You'll be wondering what all this is about, Mrs

100

Carver,' he said. 'My name is William Lawrence Priestman. You may have heard of me.'

'Yes,' Portland said. 'I've heard of you.' She was uneasy, off balance. I wonder what she expected, Huntington thought. Something like this? Nothing at all like this?

'I . . . suggested that your sister send you that note,' Willie said. 'She took a little persuading.' He allowed himself a small, self-satisfied smile that blew the cork of Huntington's bottled anger.

'I ought to break your damned neck!' he shouted at Willie. 'You goddamned hyena!'

Willie looked at him speculatively. 'You could give it a try, Carver,' he said. 'There's nothing in it for age or weight.'

Huntington took a step forward, but before he could take another, his wife stopped him with a word.

'Don't!' she hissed. He half turned to face her and saw what was in her eyes. He could have taken anger or hatred; but her disgust stunned him. She pushed past him and confronted Rachel, who flinched, even though Portland had made no overt move.

'Is it what I think it is?' Portland hissed. 'Is it, Rachel? Is that what this gentleman has brought me here to hear?'

Willie Priestman gave a barking laugh. 'I'm called a lot of things, Mrs Carver. "Gentleman" isn't a word they use much.'

'You're a — ' Huntington began, but Willie silenced him with a lifted hand.

'I've heard all I want to from you, Carver,' he said. 'It's your wife I wish to talk to. Mrs Carver?'

'What do you want?' Rachel asked, tonelessly, sitting down in the chair, her shoulders slumped.

Willie smiled. 'I want Huntington Carver to resign the presidency of the Ohio, Kansas & California railroad. In my favour.'

'You must be insane!' Huntington snapped. 'I'd never — '

'And if he does not?' Portland said quietly.

'Then on Monday morning, madam, every news-paper in the Priestman chain will carry the story of your husband and your sister.'

'There is no story!' Rachel said. 'Porty, listen to me!'

'Mrs Carver?' Priestman said.

'You shall have my husband's resignation,' Portland told him. 'Have the papers drawn up.'

'Are you crazy, too?' Huntington shouted. 'You don't think I'm going to let this gutter-animal blackmail *me*, do you?'

'You have no choice but to do as he says, Huntington,' Portland said, as if she was reading the words from a printed page. 'If this story were to become public – '

'Let him publish, and be damned!' Huntington said hotly. 'That wouldn't be the end of the world!'

'It would be the end of *my* world, Huntington,' Portland said, with quiet dignity. 'And the end of your son's.'

'You can't get away with this!' Huntington shouted. 'I won't let you!'

Willie ignored him, his eyes on Portland Carver. She took a deep breath, squaring her shoulders, then looked at her husband.

'I am leaving,' she said. 'Perhaps you will accompany me to the carriage, Mr Priestman?'

'Of course,' Willie replied.

'I shall wait exactly one minute, Huntington,' Portland said. 'Then I shall go. With you, or without you.'

'You expect me to decide in one minute?'

'Huntington, I don't care,' Portland said, utter weariness swamping her voice. She turned and went out of the room, and Willie Priestman followed her. The door closed quietly behind him.

'Ray?' Huntington said.

'You're going, aren't you?' she said, not looking up.

'I can't – I've got,' he said, agonised. 'Or I'll lose everything!'

'You already have,' she said.

In the street, Portland was waiting in the carriage, looking straight ahead. She did not acknowledge his arrival. Willie Priestman nodded gravely, as though he had predicted things would come out this way, and he was moderately pleased that they had.

'Be at my office in the morning,' he said. 'Ten-thirty, sharp!'

The coach pulled away without another word being spoken. Willie paid it no heed. He had known that battle was won from the moment Huntington Carver walked into the room and saw him there. Willie's mind was already busy on another problem: the matter of James Starr's son, Lee. The last he'd heard of him, Lee was in the cavalry at Fort Omaha, Nebraska. It would be not quite so easy to bring him down. But there would be a way. Willie was sure there would be a way. And he would find it.

ALASKA HO!

Who has not heard of Captain Jack Crawford! Poet, Author, Scout, loved and honoured by Army Men for his uprightness and integrity, high in the regard and trust of the newspaper profession! Captain Jack counts among his friends most of the prominent men in the country, beginning with President McKinley! Experienced, vigorous and shrewd, he will lead and direct under this Corporation an expedition of practical and expert miners in the new Alaska Gold Fields. Mother Lode Claims will be taken up for this Company to be sold at enormous profits, often without expending much capital in their development. There are no promoters' shares and no concealed profits. Every share guaranteed. Write for prospectus.

Klondike broadsheet, summer, 1897

12

'Maybe that's what we ought to do,' Gates said. 'Quit the damned Army an' go huntin' gold in the Klondike.'

'You, quit the Army?' Chris Vaughan said. 'That'll be the day. You never had it so good!'

'You could put in for a transfer,' Lee said, looking up from his novel. 'I hear the Eighth and Ninth are up there already. Freezing to death.'

'All the same,' Gates said lugubriously. 'Says here they're bringing nuggets the size of baseballs out of that country.' He turned the page of the month-old newspaper he had been reading.

'Sure,' Lee said. 'All you have to do is kick the moss out of the way, and there's the gold, lying on the ground.'

'Sounds tempting,' Gates grinned.

'I had a sort of great-uncle who was a 'forty-niner, Chuck,' Lee said. 'My pa told me him and his son spent two years looking for gold up around Mokelumne Hill. Never found shit, my pa said.'

'Plenty did,' Gates said, reluctant to give up the dream.

'And a damned sight more didn't,' Vaughan said flatly, ending the discussion. 'You got a soft berth, Charlie m'boy. Be thankful for it.'

'How did you get into the service anyway, Chuck?' Lee asked, laying his book aside. It was called *Quo Vadis*, and it was pretty turgid reading. Aunt Louisa had sent it to him. She sent him lots of books, always the same kind. She probably thought he was in need of moral uplift.

'You recall what happened in '93?' Gates said.

'Everybody knows that,' Vaughan grinned. 'Boston won the pennant.'

'No, you damfool!' Gates said. 'I'm talkin' about the Panic.'

Hard times had struck the country like an avalanche that year. The value of the silver dollar fell seven cents in gold. There was an enormous run on the banks. Labour uprisings took place which the militia either would not or could not suppress. Mobs burned and looted railway cars belonging to the Pullman company in Chicago. Federal troops were ordered in by the President to protect the mails and restore order. The hard times persisted into the following year, in which there was a national railway strike. Thousands upon thousands of men were thrown out of work. Many of them elected to enlist.

'You joined up then?' Lee said.

'In Lubbock, Texas,' Gates nodded. 'First thing I knowed I was on my way to fight Injuns in Wyoming with Adna Chaffee.'

'You see any action?'

'Sure he did,' Vaughan drawled. 'He went out single-handed and arrested six reservation Injuns for peeing against the wall of the guardhouse.'

'Take no notice o' him,' Gates grinned. 'He's only jealous 'cause he ain't never rolled up with no Injun girl in his blankets.'

'Never had the clap,' Vaughan said. 'I'm not jealous about that, either.'

'Come on, you two!' Lee said. Vaughan and Gates spent most of their free time needling each other. It was hard to get either of them to remain serious for any length of time. It was as if, somehow, they shied away from serious talk.

Bit by bit, Lee had pieced their stories together.

Vaughan was English by birth and by tradition, although he had lived in America since he was nineteen and considered himself as good an American as the next man. His accent, however, remained more English than anything else, his mental processes crisp and logical, and he was outspoken to a degree which frequently flustered some of the other company commanders. Vaughan and Gates had served together at Fort Larned in Kansas prior to their posting to Omaha. Gates was a 'ranker' – an enlisted man who had earned promotion to officerhood. Vaughan had entered the service with a commission in New Hampshire. He never spoke of his family, and Lee often wondered if the name he used was not his own. Many a man had joined the Army to get away from his past. Chris reacted to questions the way a tortoise reacts to touch: by retreating into his shell.

The year moved slowly on.

Willie Priestman's chain of newspapers continued to fulminate against the Spanish oppression of the plucky rebels in Cuba. It was cheap and nasty stuff, done with a bludgeon rather than a scalpel. Most of the story was told in headlines which gradually decreased in type size down the page. The prose was of a kind: oratorical, hortatory. People bought the yellow press for sensation, not news, and they bought by the million. Willie's enterprises must be doing very well, Lee thought. A letter from his sister Portland, announcing the birth of a son, called Huntington after his father, also brought the news that Willie and Marietta had a third child, this time a daughter. She was to be called Catherine, and the choice surprised Lee. It was a name with a sad legacy.

Fall drew in. The colours of the land changed subtly. The leaves sifted reluctantly to earth from the cotton-woods. The garrison at Fort Omaha readied itself for the onslaught of winter. The regiment was at peacetime strength, around sixty men to a company. There were twelve companies in all, but with a number of officers on detached service – a euphemism for recruiting – and

107

leave, it devolved upon seven or eight junior officers to keep things ticking over: drills, shooting practice, lectures, civic duties such as providing honour guards for parades in the town. Because of the hard times of previous years, the quality of the troopers was higher than usual. The Army could not always be so choosy. There would be precious little room for the 'snowbirds' this year, Lee thought. The homeless wanderers who enlisted in the fall every year to escape the rigours of winter were known as snowbirds, perhaps also because, with monotonous regularity, they flew away every spring, deserting in droves.

Fort Omaha lay about two miles from the Missouri and maybe four from the town itself. The land between Omaha and the fort was level. South and west were gently rolling hillocks of dark and fertile soil and lush buffalo grass. Cottonwoods grew along the creeks. The climate was ideal, rarely more than ninety in summer or below zero in winter. Game was still easy to find, and there were plenty of catfish in the river. It had been home to David Lee Starr ever since 1891, when he had thrown his cap into the air with the rest of his class at West Point, and come out to Omaha as a second lieutenant of cavalry, just too late to see any fighting in the last Indian battles up in the Dakotas, and unsuccessful in his application for a posting to Texas, where there were border troubles.

It was almost dark now. He sat on the veranda and watched the hills on the horizon merging with the purpling sky. Inside, he could hear Chris Vaughan singing. '*Oh, the moonlight's fair tonight along the Wabash,*' his friend sang, '*from the fields there comes the scent of new-mown hay. Through the sycamores the candlelight* – Hey, Lee! Shall I light the lamp?'

'What?' Lee said, shaking himself out of his reverie. 'Oh, yes, sure. I've got a report to write, anyway.'

He went inside and closed the screen door. The rooms he shared with his fellow lieutenant were simply furnished but comfortable. A pot-bellied stove in the corner, a sofa, a roll-top desk, a couple of battered armchairs, their tin trunks with Indian blankets thrown over them: that was about the sum of their joint possessions.

'Is Chuck coming around?' Lee asked. 'He said something about calling in after retreat.'

'He'll be along,' Chris said. He was a tall, slender, good-looking man, with almost white blond hair and shrewd grey eyes. Even with his uniform tunic and boots off he looked elegant. Chris was one of those men who look good in whatever they wear. He always made Lee feel like an unmade bed.

'You heard any more about this new CO?' Chris said.

'Not a word,' Lee said. 'The Old Man isn't giving anything away.'

'The Old Man' was Brigadier-General Walter Clancy, Sixth United States Cavalry, and he would not have been amused to hear his younger officers refer to him in such disrespectful manner. He was a martinet of the old school who believed that the best possible thing for young officers was drill, drill and then more drill again. His coming retirement was viewed by everyone on the post with mixed feelings. You knew where you were with General Clancy. You knew what you could get away with, and what to expect if you didn't get away with it.

The door opened and Gates came in. He was a big man, wide-shouldered and heavily-built. He looked as if he might go to fat when he got older. He had an earnest face that concealed a dry, lazily humorous outlook on life.

'All right,' he said. 'Where's the booze?'

'Usual place,' Vaughan said. 'Leave a little in the bottle, if you can hold yourself in check.'

'I'll pay you back the end of the month,' Gates said, uncorking the whisky bottle and pouring himself a drink. 'Anyone else?'

'After tattoo,' Lee said. 'I'm calling the roll.'

'I'll join you,' Chris said, coming out of the alcove which was their kitchen. He had been washing some

109

socks. The steamy smell of wet wool came into the room with him. 'I was just asking Lee if he'd heard anything more about General Moffatt,' he said. 'He hasn't. You?'

'I heard he's a sumbitch,' Gates said. 'From a long way back.'

'Who told you that?'

'I just heard it around the post.'

General Moffatt's record was not one to be compared with any of the great soldiers. He had spent the War between the States comfortably ensconced in the Gulf States with the rank of colonel, and most of his serving life in the South-west, latterly as Commanding Officer at Fort Riley, Kansas.

'Working his way·back East,' Gates remarked, as Chris Vaughan recited the known facts again.

'They say he's got a daughter,' Lee offered. 'Name of Jennifer.'

'Beautiful?' Vaughan said hopefully.

'Spit an' image of her daddy,' Gates grinned.

'Holy shit!' Vaughan said. 'Really?'

'Should make post dances real lively,' Gates said. 'Time comes, likely I'll introduce you, Chris. Wouldn't be surprised if Miss Moffatt isn't just the right type for you. Little homemaker, you know? Darn your socks, wash your shirts, feed you right, keep you off the liquor.'

'Don't do me any favours.'

'Be a pleasure,' Gates said. 'You want another drink?'

'You're too kind,' Vaughan said. 'That's *our* booze you're being so free with, you know.'

'Told you I'd pay you back come pay day,' Gates said. 'How can you live with a guy this stingy, Lee?'

'It's not easy,' Lee smiled.

Their easy camaraderie came from many long hours spent in such banter. Lee valued their friendship greatly, for the daily routine of army life, while often strangely comforting, was also crashingly monotonous.

Reveille was at sunrise. Inspection came twenty-five minutes later. After breakfast, the troopers cleaned their rifles, polished breastplates and cartridge boxes and buttons ready for the full-dress parade at nine. After the raising of the flag and the playing of the national anthem by the post band, the officers would move to the front and doff their hats to the commanding officer. Then the troops were marched past in review, company by company.

Immediately after parade, the guard was mounted. Soldiers not on guard duty were drilled for an hour prior to being assigned to work details: shoeing horses, policing the reservation, repairing boots, carpentry, cleaning. Dinner was at one. Roll-call of retreat, when the flag was lowered and the soft, sad sounds of the bugle lay on the silent evening, was at sunset. Tattoo, another roll-call, was at nine. At nine-thirty taps was sounded on the drums for lights out.

In their spare time the men played cards or shot craps, wrote letters, squabbled good-naturedly over whether or not Bob Fitzsimmons would ever have beaten Jim Corbett if 'Gentleman Jim' had still been in his prime. The officers played bridge or held whist drives, played chess or draughts, read; once a month they dined with the commanding officer at his quarters. There were few excitements. Days went by, more days, and more. The golden haze of summer sharpened into the etched hardness of fall and winter, and the great plains closed in on themselves as the snow whistled down from the north and clad the world in an icy blanket. Then would come the greening, and the cycle would begin anew.

From his father, Lee heard the family news as it happened. Lee's sister Portland had bought a fine house on Fifth Avenue, James wrote. Porty has always wanted to live in the East, Lee remembered. Of Uncle Andrew's three daughters, Mary was married and settled down in Chicago, where her husband, Daniel Hampson, was in the mail-order business and doing very well. Joanna, the second eldest, was engaged to the son of James's law partner, Stephen Elkham. Lee remembered

111

Steve, a freckled, red-haired kid who liked to tie tin cans to cats' tails and always lied to get out of trouble. Steve had landed Lee more tannings than anyone else he ever knew. He did not like Steve Elkham and he did not envy his cousin one little bit. Sarah, Andrew's youngest daughter, was teaching at a girls' school in Boston. She was a bit of a 'Bohemian'. Lee had always liked Sarah best of all the Starr girls.

General Moffatt arrived three days later.

He invited them to an informal meeting in the Officers' Mess the night after his arrival, and was introduced to each officer by the outgoing commander, General Clancy. Lee studied the new man as the introductions were made. Moffatt was red-faced and overweight, with the broken veins of a heavy drinker. He wore his hair too long for a man of his age, and his watery eyes were shifty. Hair, beard and moustache were liberally sprinkled with grey. His voice was measured, ponderous. He spoke like a man who has grown pleased with the sound of what he says.

'Well, gentlemen,' he told them. 'I am honoured to be your new commanding officer, and I am confident that we're all going to get along just fine. However, to ensure that none of you will be under the slightest misapprehension, I intend to make my position clear from the outset. First and foremost, I demand and expect to receive one hundred per cent loyalty from each and every man on this post – no exceptions! Secondly, I will not tolerate sloppy conduct of any kind. Off the post or on it, I expect every man to comport himself correctly. Any soldier, and especially any officer brought before me for infractions of acceptable behaviour or dress may expect to be dealt with severely. Severely,' he said again. as if savouring the word. He glared at them from beneath heavy brows as if daring anyone to speak. No one did. 'Thirdly, you will find that I am what they call a "book" man. I believe that the book is there for good reasons. Go by the book and you will have no arguments from me.

112

Deviate from it at your peril, gentlemen. At your peril. And finally, this: in my command, I permit only one standard – excellence. Standard performance will be treated as sub-standard, and sub-standard performance will in no wise be tolerated. Do I make myself perfectly clear, gentlemen?'

'Yes, sir!' the assembled officers chorused.

'Good. One more thing. You will find me a hard taskmaster, gentlemen, but you will discover that I am fair. I expect nothing of any man that I do not expect of myself.' He waited a few pregnant moments, as if again expecting someone to speak. Then he nodded. 'Very well. That is all. Dismissed, gentlemen!'

'Well, boys,' Chris said, as he, Gates and Lee walked back across the parade ground towards their quarters. 'What do you think of our new commanding officer?'

'You liked him,' Gates said.

'Love at first sight,' Chris replied.

'Me, too,' Gates added.

'I could tell,' Chris said. 'I saw it in your eyes.'

'How about you, Lee?' Gates said.

'He seemed all right,' Lee argued. 'You're just not giving him a chance. He's new. Maybe he was nervous.'

'Sure,' Gates said.

'Come on!' Lee said. 'I've seen a lot worse than him. So have you!'

'He's right, you know,' Gates told Vaughan.

'Maybe,' Vaughan said darkly. 'But I never came across one that started off with so many *threats*. He doesn't know anything about us. Why does he think he has to start off by threatening us?'

'He was just stating his case,' Lee said. 'Letting us know where he stands. Maybe he overdid it a bit. I don't think we ought to take it to heart. This is a good outfit. Once he sees that, he'll relax.'

'Okay, okay.' Gates spread his hands in surrender. 'Anythin' you say, babe. But you watch out. That old boy is trouble.'

113

13

The public wanted scandal.

Willie Priestman gave it to them.

They wanted sensation. He gave them that, too. They didn't want to know what had been said at some committee down at City Hall. They wanted to know the juicy story of the love-nest the councillor chairing the committee had set up on Kearney Street for his mistress, paid for out of city funds.

Willie learned one thing very quickly. Big-headline news does not happen obligingly every day. Sometimes you have to make it happen yourself. When Roper and Williams sued the *Inquirer*, he crucified them in his pages. Long before the case was due to come to court, the two men withdrew it. They were whipped and they knew it. The way Willie had manipulated public opinion, they would have been lucky not to end up paying him damages. As one of his minions said at the time, not admiringly, 'If you were to put Willie Priestman into a pit full of snakes, he'd either end up king snake or dead!'

Only winning counted to him. The best revenge was to succeed.

He fired Mitchell and put Schofield into the editor's chair. He got on well with the red-haired, sharp-tongued Ohioan. Bill Schofield had come out to California six years earlier and started as a copy boy, working his way up by sheer energy and talent. As soon as Mitchell was gone, he blossomed. With Willie urging him on, Schofield harried and bullied the reporters into bringing in the kind of stories that sold papers. He worked fourteen, sixteen hours a day. He was a single man, alone in San Francisco. The paper was his bride, his work, his life.

'Where's the picture to go with this story about the lost kid?' he would bawl at some luckless reporter. Pictures, drawings, sketches, maps all played an important part in the layout of the *Inquirer's* front page.

'Couldn't get one, Bill,' the reporter said.

'You mean the mother didn't have a picture of her kid?' Schofield shouted. 'What kind of shit are you trying to give me, Lafferty?'

'Well, I couldn't very well ask her – '

'Get out of here!' Schofield yelled. 'And don't come back without a picture of that kid. Even if you have to steal it!'

The size of the headlines increased. Forty-two point, sixty-four point, eighty-six point. Schofield and Willie agonised for hours over exactly the right words to use.

'I want *stories*!' Willie would shout at the daily conferences. 'Stories, not goddamned *news*!'

Scandals all contained the same ingredients: bribery, lies, sex, power, fame. Its rules were simple, Willie told them. If some clerk in an obscure city office accepted a bribe for altering a zoning ordinance, or a beat policeman took a side of ham for not noticing the cockroaches in some greasy spoon, that was not scandal. But if a civic dignitary was accused of accepting one hundred thousand dollars in bribes, or keeping a showgirl in a fancy apartment, *that* was scandal and *that* was a story.

No sacrifice was too great for Willie. He did without a private life, without proper food. The paper was everything. He needed nothing else. His excitement fed upon itself and created more. He knew he was on the verge of something big, a breakthrough. How it would come, what it would be, he could not foretell. He wanted to do things in a way that had not been done before. He wanted people to stop in the street and say *look!*

'What about this actress?' he said to Schofield. 'She really do that?'

'She did, Chief,' Schofield grinned.

'Ten whiskies?'

'That's what she claims.'

'How you planning to run it?'

Schofield pushed a piece of paper across the desk. Willie looked at it and made a face.

'Slow,' he said.

'"Mayor's daughter tells all" is slow?'

'Slow,' Willie said. 'What does the man do?'

'Lawyer.'

'Big time?'

'Nah.'

'Anything on him?'

'Clean as a whistle.'

'All right,' Willie said. 'Try this.' He pushed the paper back at Schofield, who pursed his lips.

'Nearly, Chief,' Schofield said. 'Not bad.'

'You got a nerve, you bastard,' Willie said. 'You're going to improve it?'

'One hundred per cent,' Schofield said, scribbling. He pushed the paper back across the desk. Willie read it and grinned. 'Copy!' he yelled.

ORGY SCANDAL IN FRISCO LOVE-NEST
MAYOR'S DAUGHTER TELLS ALL
ADMITS DRINKING TEN WHISKIES AND
DANCING NUDE
CITY LAWYER'S SHOCKING SECRET LIFE

The headlines screamed off the page. Willie had no illusions about their worth as literature or, for that matter, fact. They sold papers. That was all he was interested in. Anybody who bought such crap was a sucker, anyway, a moron who neither knew nor cared what was happening in the real world. Let the *Times* and

116

the *Tribune* provide the in-depth reporting. It would never make anyone rich. The public wanted vice, sin, sex, scandal. Somebody had to give it to them. Willie put up a hundred-dollar prize for the best headline of the week by a staffer. He cut the prizewinners out of the paper and stuck them on a wall in his office.

ACTRESS REPORTED POISON VICTIM IN VENGEANCE PLOT

THE FRENCH AMBASSADOR AND THE ICE CUBES

MY HUSBAND, OUR PUPILS AND ME: HEADMISTRESS SPEAKS

SOLD INTO BONDAGE: JAPANESE GIRL'S STORY

and Willie's favourite:

BRIDE-TO-BE DANCED IN MEN'S PYJAMAS ON WEDDING EVE

'Everybody get excited!' he would yell at his reporters as they left the editorial room after the morning conference. 'Then you'll get me excited!'

'My God, Charlie,' a newcomer once asked one of the older reporters, 'don't he ever relax?'

The older man made a wry face. 'Sure he does,' he said. 'When the Late Night Final comes off the presses, he sits down and looks through it for, oh, anything up to two or three minutes.'

'You got to slow down, boy,' Billy Priestman told his son. 'Have some fun. There's more to life than work, work, work, you know.'

'Work's fun to me, Pa.'

'You really love that damned business, don't you?' Billy said, wonderingly.

'You thought I was going to make a hash of it, didn't you?' Willie said.

'You've done well,' Billy admitted grudgingly. 'Although there's plenty round town with nothing good to say about the way you do it.'

'You know what I tell them Pa? I tell them the *Inquirer* is like a generator. It isn't beautiful, but by God! it gives off sparks!'

'You don't want to go making your name mud around town, boy,' Billy glowered. 'You may find yourself on everybody's blacklist.'

Willie smiled. 'I'm going to be rich, Pa,' he said. 'This is only the beginning. I'm going to take over some other papers. One day there'll be a chain of them, all over the country. I won't just be rich, I'll be powerful. There won't be any doors I can't open.'

'Don't suppose there's any damned room in the newspaper business for modesty,' Billy said. 'Which is just as well for you.'

He got up from the table and told Jameson to bring coffee in the library. 'Join me?' he said.

Willie shook his head. 'Got to get back to the paper,' he said. 'Maybe tomorrow.'

'Like to talk to you,' Billy said. 'Won't take a minute.'

Surprised, Willie followed his father into the library. It was his favourite room in the house. Gradually, he was throwing out all the junk his father had bought to fill the shelves, and replacing it with genuine collector's items. Willie would not have gone so far as to say that he was a bibliomane, but something in him wanted to collect things, and anything printed interested him. Only a few days ago, he had bought a copy of Shelley's *Queen Mab*, with manuscript revisions by the poet himself, a first edition of 1813 in the original boards. He had not read it yet, nor many of the other rarities he had bought. There would be time for that one day, but not yet.

'You know Cosmo Powell's girl,' Billy said. 'Marietta.'

'Of course I do,' Willie said, impatiently looking at his watch. 'What about her?'

'She's joining us on the yacht for the weekend,' Billy said. 'We'll sail down to Santa Barbara.'

'Us?'

Billy nodded. 'I want you to be there.'

'What is this, Pa?' Willie said.

'Just do like I say,' Billy said, ignoring the question. 'You'll enjoy it.'

'Another time, Pa,' Willie said. 'There's a big story breaking. Some immigrants were lynched in New Or – '

'Let Schofield handle it,' Billy said. 'Cosmo Powell owns three newspapers.'

Cosmo Powell's father had been a forty-niner who struck it rich at Mokelumne Hill and had the good sense to put the money into land. Cosmo had struck it nearly as rich as a stockbroker. When he wasn't making money he was chasing skirts, a handsome, vain man who wore custom-tailored suits from Savile Row in London, and who fancied himself a connoisseur of food and wine. And Marietta was his only daughter.

Willie thought.

'I'll be there,' he said.

'Thought you might,' his father replied.

They were married with due splendour the following June. An archbishop attended the ceremony, and there was a reception for a thousand people in the evening. Willie and Marietta spent their honeymoon aboard Billy's yacht. Every detail of the 'love match of the decade' was chronicled in the pages of the *Inquirer*. The bride's gown, the guest list, the menus, the furnishings on board the Priestman yacht were all described in ornate prose.

The marriage was many things, but it was no love match. The way Willie looked at it, if he had to marry anyone it might as well be someone with money. As a wedding present, her father gave Willie his faltering New York newspaper, the *Clarion*. Willie reciprocated by buying Marietta a Los Angeles newspaper, the *Mirror*. He changed the names of both to *Inquirer*. Reporters were instructed to always refer to the Priestman 'chain'. Willie was on his way to realising his ambition. Three newspapers to make over, instead of one, speeded him up rather than slowing him down. He had to do it, to work, work, work. He needed the action, the drama, the planning, the urgency. He could not abide idleness, in himself or anyone else. He hired the best writers, he paid the best money, he commissioned the best artists. There was no job on the paper that he could not do as well as any of the men doing them. Willie was a good writer, a good editor, a good publisher. He knew that the stuff he published was trash, but that didn't matter a tuppenny damn. It was the *best*.

Above all, Willie was an innovator.

He knew what his competitors, the staider and more conservative publishers, thought of his style. He didn't give a fart in a windstorm about that. He knew, without knowing how he knew, that he was right; and when they began to copy him, Willie did not see that as victory but as confirmation of his judgement. He knew that success would bring them all flocking to court him, and that was the only victory worth having. All the rest wasn't worth what a dog does to a lamp-post.

Be independent, run your own show. That was the way to do it. And kick ass. Always, no matter how well things are going. There was no substitute for sheer hard work, and the only way to get that was to kick ass.

In 1892, Marietta gave him a son, whom they christened William Priestman III. Two years later another son was born and named Isaiah after Willie's grandfather. Willie bought a new house, big even by Californian standards, and installed his family in it. There were butlers and maids and nannies and nurses. Willie was hardly aware of their existence. He was on the move: to Los Angeles, to New York, to Chicago

120

and back to California. His detractors sneered; 'a vacuum with a typewriter', they called him. Circulation kept on rising. He bought another newspaper, and another: Atlanta, Cincinnatti, St. Louis. A new word entered his daily life: syndication. New circulation-boosters included an agony column devoted entirely to etiquette, presided over by Emily Brocklehurst of the Naragansett Brocklehursts; and a tittle-tattle column entitled 'Talk of the Town' which chronicled the doings of the wealthy and fashionable.

In 1896, Marietta's third child, a daughter, was born. Willie left the choice of names to his wife. Marietta, thinking to please her ailing father-in-law, chose the name Catherine. All it did was to set Billy off on a ten-day drinking jag, although if it hadn't been that, likely something else would have done just as well.

Billy drank a lot these days. Willie was aware of it, and knew that he ought to do something about it, but he was at a loss to know what the something was. Billy never got so drunk that he didn't know what he was doing, although he was taking aboard a lot more liquor than was healthy. According to the quacks, heavy drinking was often caused by deep, burning, inex-pressible anger. Could that be true? What could be causing it? Somehow Willie was unable to bring himself to ask his father direct, personal questions, no matter how much Marietta told him he should.

'He's got it under control,' he told her.

'No, Willie,' she said. 'It's got *him* under control, and one of these days it will take over completely.'

'My little expert,' he said, indulgently kissing the top of her head. 'Don't worry your pretty head about it. He's a tough old turkey.'

He decided to have a real talk with his father. As soon as there was time. It was just that he was always so damned busy. And never more than now, with the revolt in Cuba. Willie had always known that one day a crusade would come along, something he could use to

121

propel the *Inquirer* chain into the multi-million-copy sales he had always envisioned. Cuba was it.

The story broke early in February, 1895, with a brief despatch to the effect that an insurrection had broken out in Cuba. The Spanish Minister in Washington, the government in Havana, were prompt in reporting that there was no revolt, just a show of force by some bandits. Willie sent one of his reporters to the offices of the Spanish-language paper *El Porvenir* in New York. He came back with information that made Willie stop the presses, remake the front page, and inform America, in ringing headlines, that there was indeed a

REVOLT IN CUBA

OFFICIAL DENIALS DISCOUNTED

TWO PROVINCES UNDER MARTIAL LAW

HEAVY FIGHTING IN MATANZAS AND SANTIAGO DE CUBA

Willie's instinct was right. Cuba swiftly became the dominant topic, and the *Inquirer* chain fanned the flames. In March, a cargo ship was fired on and chased twenty-five miles by a Spanish gunboat. Willie beautifully gauged the outburst of martial ardour that this 'outrage to the flag' – the phrase he insisted be used in every one of his ten newspapers – created.

'This country is spoiling for war!' he told his editors. 'Our stance is and will be that it is the duty and destiny of the United States to take possession of Cuba, if necessary over the dead body of Spain!'

Teams of *Inquirer* reporters went down to New Orleans and Tampa, to get the latest atrocity stories from the refugees who were arriving from Cuba. The continuous fighting had ruined the sugar crop. There was no money, no food. Famine brought disease, which threatened to spread to the United States. As the year went on, Willie sent men to Havana itself, with instructions to attach themselves to the staff of the rebel leader, General Gomez.

'Don't think you're going to sit in the bar of the Hotel Havana and drink rum punch all day, either,' he told them. 'I want hot copy from you, and I want lots of it!'

He got his hot copy. The Cubans knew exactly what the *Americanos* wanted, and made sure they got it. Stories of battles, rapes and other atrocities were splashed day after day across the pages of the Priestman papers. Willie wrote the editorials, fulminating against the Spanish oppression, demanding to know when the United States was planning to intervene. Someone asked him whether he knew for a fact that the stories he printed were true.

'They're true after I print them,' Willie retorted, and in a way he was right. Nobody really cared about truth any more. Cuba was a tortured land, where a decadent tyranny, unable to suppress the heroic aspirations of its people, was systematically and bloodily exterminating them. As the new year opened, General Don Valeriano Weyler y Nicolau was appointed to succeed the military commander in Cuba, Martinez Campos. Willie went after Weyler – whom he referred to always as 'Butcher' – without mercy.

'BUTCHER' WEYLER'S BLOODY METHODS
WAR AGAINST UNARMED CIVILIANS
MURDER AND BRUTALITY

A few days later he stepped up the voltage.

NEWEST INSTANCES OF 'BUTCHER' WEYLER'S TERROR
AS MANY AS 100,000 CUBANS IN RECONCENTRATION CAMPS
DISEASE RAMPANT
HUNDREDS DYING OF STARVATION

Circulation was going up and up. He was fighting in the big time now, his competitors were Pulitzer and Hearst. They all sensationalised; but none of them had the inventiveness of Billy Schofield.

ATROCITIES COMMITTED BY 'BUTCHER' WEYLER'S TROOPS

'DISGUSTING' ACTIONS OF OFFICERS

TESTIMONY OF AMERICAN WOMAN

Willie's finger was on the pulse of national sentiment. A nice little war with Spain, some politicians were saying, could be a mighty fine thing. Willie saw to it that their views received an airing in the *Inquirers*.

'Do you want to lead the country to war, man?' one appalled congressman asked him.

'If it'll sell papers, sure,' Willie said.

That was all he was interested in, and he constantly invented new ways of boosting circulation. He ran contests in the paper, offering cash prizes or food hampers. There were balloon races, firework displays that drew huge crowds. Willie appeared at them all, shaking hands and kissing babies as shamelessly as any politician. 'Mingling with the unwashed,' he called it. But it sold papers.

He invited his readers to write to the editors of his papers, expressing their views. It was cheap copy and, again, it sold papers. He created a special section in the papers which he called 'Your Problem Page'. At first it dealt with mundane things: how to fix household appliances, and so on. The whole section was tossed out *en bloc* when one day, sifting through the piles of mail that came into the office every day now, Willie came across a letter from a young woman in Queens who wanted to know whether it was proper to allow a young man, whom she had gone out with only twice, to kiss her. She signed herself 'Worried', and in a flash, Willie knew he had a bonanza.

124

'Schófield!' he yelled, and fifteen minutes later the 'Women's Problem Page' was born. It was an immediate, roaring success. The letters came in thousands, from 'Pining' of North Beach, or 'Young Mother' of Brooklyn, who poured out their hearts for other 'worrieds' and 'pinings' and 'young mothers' to read on the way home from the factory, or the store, or the office. He installed a man full-time on each paper to handle this mail. Before long, everyone called the incumbent 'the sob-sister'. The sob-sister on the New York paper was Max Hardy, a squat, fat and ugly man who looked like a cigar-smoking toad, and who was reputed to have the foulest vocabulary of any Priestman staffer. He came to Willie one day with a problem.

'W.L.,' he said – everyone was required, nowadays, to address Willie by his initials; a favoured few were permitted the familiarity of 'Chief' – 'I want off of this asshole job.'

'Why?' Willie said.

'Because it's fucking boring me fucking mindless,' Hardy said. He held up a sheaf of letters clutched in his fat fist. 'There isn't one fucking letter in this whole shitbag of a post that's worth wiping your fucking ass on.'

'So?' Willie said.

'So?' Hardy shouted. 'So? So what the fuck am I expected to put in the fucking column if there aren't any fucking letters, for Christ's sake?'

'See this?' Willie said, holding up a pencil.

Hardy frowned, not getting it. 'Yes?' he said, dubiously.

'See this?' Willie said, picking up a ruled pad.

Hardy's toad face split into a grin around the stump of the cigar. 'You mean I can write the fucking things myself?'

'I mean you'd better,' Willie said. 'Or I'll kick your ass off this paper!'

William Lawrence Priestman, if you please. He

125

insisted on the use of his full name now. He was already a celebrity, and on his way to being a legend. He loved it.

He was a rich man who did not need money.

He was a powerful man who did not need friends.

He did favours for people who did not forget them.

He endowed scholarships, schools, colleges, and in doing so, learned the inside moves of city politicking.

He had everything he wanted – except one thing.

He wanted a war.

War with Spain was his wish, his dream, his ambition. He knew it would be the making of the newspaper chain, he knew it as certainly as he knew his own name. What dispatches he could send back from Cuba! What stories, what scoops!

'A million copies a day!' he told his editors. 'That's what I want. A million a day!'

'Maybe we'll do it, Chief,' Schofield said. 'If there's a war.'

'You run the paper,' Willie told him. 'I'll see to the war!'

New York *Inquirer*,
September 28, 1897

EDITORIAL
HOW LONG, O LORD?

How long before the oppressed Cuban people, crushed beneath the heel of the Spanish tyrant, tortured and starved and beaten by the bloodthirsty troops commanded by 'Butcher' Weyler, can hope for deliverance? Is it not time for us to say, as civilised human beings, as a Nation, that CUBA HAS BLED ENOUGH?

14

There was a street in Georgetown that Washington insiders knew. It was quite narrow, and there were only a few street lights, whose fitful light ensured the anonymity of the men who went there. It was called Cable Street on maps. Less charitable men referred to it scathingly as Faggot Alley.

Henry Starr stood on the corner opposite the street and wished to God he could stop himself from coming here. It was too risky. He had too much to lose. If it ever got out that Andrew Starr, the confidant of Presidents, had a cousin who frequented places like this . . . And yet he could not stay away, even though he hated it now. He was old, and they were always particularly cruel to older men.

Yet . . . he could not just turn and walk away. This was the only place where he could find what he needed. Just thinking about it excited him. He looked at his watch. Nine o'clock. He nodded, as though making a decision, and then strode across the street, head down.

As he walked down Cable Street, darker shadows moved in the darkness. Whispers pursued him. He did not stop. He wasn't looking for one of the kind that plied their trade from a doorway. You never knew what they might have.

At the lower end of the street there were lights, and he heard the sound of a zither being played in the Cafe Vienna. Lanterns suspended above the tables shed pools of light on the chequered tablecloths. A slim figure rose from one of the nearer tables, and Henry's heart went *bump* the way it always did.

'Hello,' he said, breathlessly.

'He*llo*.'

'Warm night.'

'Yes, it is. But pleasant.' Inane. Stupid. Henry clenched his sweating palms, praying silently.

'Would you by any chance have a light?'

'Certainly.'

Let it be different tonight, Henry prayed. Make him really what he looks as if he is. Don't let him be one of the other sort. I want to love him. I want him to love me.

'The trouble with weather like this,' the young man said, 'is that you're so *hot* all the time.'

He arched his eyebrows, and Henry felt a thrill course through his body at the *double-entendre*.

'Saturdays are always so lonesome in a strange town,' he said. He saw the disbelief in the young man's eyes, and chose to ignore it. 'Don't you think?'

'You're from out of town, then?' the young man said.

'Yes,' Henry lied. 'I wish I knew someplace to go where people are laughing and . . . having fun. You know.'

'There are a couple of places not far from here,' the young man said. '*Très gai.*'

'Mmmm,' Henry said, touching his lips with his tongue. 'Sounds wonderful. Perhaps you'd let me buy you a drink?'

'Or something,' the boy said. 'Anything you fancy, especially?'

'Let me think about that,' Henry said, as he fell into step. The boy was slim, athletically built. His skin was marbled white, his hair blue–black. His eyes were dark shadowed pools. As they left the circle of light his hand brushed Henry's erection. Please, Henry prayed. This time, let it be different. Please.

When he came to, one side of his head felt completely numb. Disoriented, he tried to stand and could not. He seemed unable to open his right eye. For a terrifying moment he thought he had had a stroke, and then he remembered, drowning in shame.

It had been a set-up, a variation on the ages-old badger game. The boy had taken him into an alley where two men were waiting. Henry had begged them not to hurt him, but that was all part of the fun to them. He remembered the names they had called him, and shuddered. Yes, that was what he was. And this was his punishment.

He raised his head and saw that he was in an alley off a main street. The same alley? If so, he was not far from help. He tried to get up again, and found that he could not. His right leg, from the hip to the foot, was totally numb. He felt the lumps on his face with a shaking hand. His tongue felt swollen and raw inside his mouth. It rasped on a broken tooth.

Bastards, he thought, without anger. There was no point in anger. What had happened to him happened to lots of men like him, and there was nothing you could do about it.

He managed to struggle into a sitting position, and propped his back against the wall. He could see street lights at the end of the alley, about twenty yards away. Once in a while, figures hurried by.

'Help!' he called weakly. 'Somebody help me!'

He wondered what time it was. He did not bother trying to take out his watch, because it would not be there, any more than his money, or his tie-pin or his silver cuff-links. Vultures never left meat on the bones.

A man appeared at the end of the alley. 'Help!' Henry called. 'Help me!'

The man disappeared from sight, then reappeared. Henry saw him peer into the alley, and called out again.

'Is anyone there?' the man called.

'Here!' Henry shouted as loudly as he could. 'I've been robbed. Help me!'

The man came edgily into the alley, as though expecting at any moment to be robbed himself. He was dressed in evening clothes, with a white silk scarf looped carelessly around his neck, and a silver-topped cane held ready in his right hand.

'My God!' he said, when he saw Henry's face. 'What the devil happened to you?'

'I was attacked by three men and robbed,' Henry said. 'They beat me up and left me here. Can you help me to stand up?'

'Here,' the man said. 'Get your arm around my shoulder and we'll see what we can do.' He knelt down beside Henry, and, with a surge of strength Henry had not expected in so slightly built a man, got Henry to his feet.

'Put your weight on your foot,' he said. Henry did as he was bid. There was no pain. Nothing broken then, he thought. Thank God for small mercies.

'I'm very grateful to you, Mr – ?'

'Ashby,' the man said. 'Mortimer Ashby.'

'I'm Henry St–anley,' Henry said, catching himself just in time. 'Lucky for me you were passing. What time is it?'

'After two,' Ashby said. 'Do you live near by?'

'No,' Henry said. 'I'm from out of town. Cincinnati.'

'Look, you're in a mess,' Ashby said. 'I've an apartment near here. Why don't you come back there and clean up?'

'You're very kind,' Henry said.

'My dear fellow, I'm glad to help. Only hope someone will do the same for me if I ever find myself in the same fix.'

'Pray God you never do,' Henry said piously. He stamped his foot on the ground, and felt the first faint signals of the oncoming pins and needles. His clothes were dusty and torn, and he knew he was going to get a shock when he looked in the mirror, but that was all right. Worse things than this had happened to him. Much worse.

As he hobbled along, Henry parried all Ashby's questions with well-rehearsed lies. Henry was a consummate liar: he had decades of practice behind him. He knew the best lies were the general ones: you could support them with true facts. So he told Ashby that he lived in Cincinnati, Ohio, a city he knew well, and that there, as opposed to Fredericksburg, Virginia, he and his wife Ann ran a small horse farm. Safe ground; he could answer questions on Cincinnati and horses all night if need be. Yes, he had a daughter, Ruth, who was grown up and married to a fine man. They lived in the South, near Richmond. Yes, he was in town on business, just for a few days. Due to leave tomorrow, as a matter of fact. He was so busy keeping up this pose that he failed to note exactly which way they got to Ashby's apartment, and found he no longer had any idea where the alley was.

'Here we are,' Ashby said, as they stopped outside a big brownstone house. 'I've an apartment on the ground floor. Can you manage the stoop?'

'I'm fine,' Henry said. His whole body was a mass of throbbing aches now. The side of his head was still numb. His ear had no feeling in it whatsoever: it felt like a piece of pastry stuck on the side of his head.

'In here,' Ashby said, opening doors. Henry heard a match being struck, smelled gas. Then the mantle flared into yellow light and he saw he was in a large drawing-room with half-closed sliding mahogany doors. Through the gap he saw the adjoining room was a bedroom. There were bookshelves on one wall, an ornate marble fireplace flanked by stone jars stuffed with dried reeds and bulrushes, with a huge turtle shell covering the actual fireplace itself. In the bay window stood a walnut Challen baby grand piano, on which was a collection of photographs in silver frames. A leather chesterfield faced the fireplace, with two matching armchairs at either side.

'I like your apartment,' Henry said.

'Thank you,' Ashby replied. 'Here, let me take your coat. I'll show you where the bathroom is. You can clean yourself up a bit while I make some coffee. Or would you prefer something stronger?'

'If I may,' Henry said, 'I'd like both.'

'And both you shall have!' Ashby smiled.

When Henry came back into the drawing-room, Ashby was pouring the coffee from a silver pot into fine bone china cups. A bottle of Courvoisier and two crystal balloon glasses stood on a silver tray nearby.

'Very handsome,' Henry said.

'I believe in buying good things,' Ashby said. 'Only fools believe you can get anything worth having without paying for it.'

'I couldn't agree more,' Henry said. Ashby picked up the bottle of cognac and raised his eyebrows. Henry nodded. Ashby poured a generous measure into one of the glasses and handed it to him.

'Now,' Ashby said. 'Tell me the truth, Henry.'

'The tr – what do you mean?' Henry stuttered.

'My dear fellow, spare me!' Ashby said, holding up an elegantly manicured hand. 'I'm not altogether a fool, you know. And you're by no means the first man to have been beaten up by those treacherous little *tarts*!'

There was enough feeling in his voice for Henry to realise that Ashby was speaking from experience. And so, without words, their relationship abruptly changed. Each now recognised the other for what he was.

'Yes, yes, I'm "on the inside", too,' Ashby said. 'I do not, however, soil my hands on the cheap queans of Cable Street.'

Henry was silent. He wanted desperately to ask Ashby a thousand questions; knew he would utter none of them.

'It was just . . . being from out of town,' he said.

Ashby just looked at him, the patrician face set in an

expression of suppressed impatience. A good-looking man, Henry thought. Ashby was of medium height, slim, elegant even when sitting. His clothes fitted him as only hand-made clothing can. A wealthy man, certainly. Ashby ran a thin hand through his silvering hair. For the first time Henry noticed the effeminate movement of the head as he did so. I ought to have known, he thought.

'Henry,' Ashby said, lighting a cigarette that he took from a thin gold case, 'you and I are going to get nowhere unless we're frank with each other.'

'How do you mean?' Henry fenced.

'I mean it's time you stopped answering my questions with questions,' Ashby said, 'and told me the truth about yourself. Perhaps I may be able to help you. To . . . ah, prevent your making another mistake like the one you made tonight.'

'How could you do that?' Henry said, then cursed himself as he realised he had asked another question. Ashby saw his awareness, and raised a hand.

'It's all right, my dear fellow,' he said. 'I understand perfectly, I assure you. After all, why should you trust me? We've only just met. And I wouldn't mind wagering you've found, as I have, that those, ah, how shall I put it? Those similarly afflicted to ourselves are usually no more trustworthy than that boy you picked up tonight.'

'Yes,' Henry said. 'That's true.'

'Then I shall give you my bona-fides first,' Ashby said. 'And you can decide whether you can trust me when I have done so.'

'Why?' Henry asked. 'Why would you want to do anything for me?'

'Let's just say it pleases my vanity,' Ashby said. 'Now: you'll stay here the rest of the night. I've a spare room, it's no problem. Tomorrow we'll pick up your things from your hotel and bring them here. And tomorrow evening . . . ' He stopped, seeing Henry's hand pushed palm out towards him. 'Something wrong?'

'I lied to you,' Henry said. 'I'm not staying at an hotel. I'm not from out of town. My name isn't – '

'Enough, my dear fellow!' Ashby said, expansively. 'Quite enough for now! We can go into the gory details tomorrow.'

Henry nodded dumbly. 'I just . . . wanted you to know.'

'It's a good start, Henry,' Ashby smiled. 'A very good start.'

The following evening they travelled by coach to a house on the far side of Georgetown, near Dumbarton Oaks. It was a solid, respectable-looking mansion with a semicircular gravel drive and an imposing portico. Ashby, dressed in evening clothes as he had been the night before, waited till the coach had clattered away before he pressed the bell. Henry noticed that he pressed it in a certain way, like a signal.

The door silently opened.

They went into a hall lit only by a dim red light. The smell of incense threaded through the warm air. The woman who had opened the door was small, slight, red-headed and very pretty.

'How lovely to see you again, Merlin,' she said to Ashby. 'And you have brought a friend! How are we to call you, sir?'

'No names are used here,' Ashby said softly to Henry. 'You'll see why shortly.'

'Call me . . . Ishmael,' Henry said, on the spur of the moment.

Ashby smiled. 'Very *good*,' he murmered. 'Melville, no less!'

'Won't you follow me, please?' the woman said. As they walked down the long, shadowed hall, Ashby whispered to Henry that the woman's name was Lacy

135

May. They went through a screen of hanging bead curtains into a softly lit room in which the scent of the incense was very strong. When his eyes became accustomed to the gloom, Henry saw that all around the D-shaped room, reclining on velvet cushions embroidered with golden thread, were naked young men of every size and colour. All of them smiled lazily at the new arrivals. One or two moved across the room slowly, like prowling panthers, their oiled bodies sleek and proud.

'Gentlemen,' Lacy May said, and with a rush of shock that he had not expected, Henry saw for the first time that Lacy May, too, was male.

'Well . . . Ishmael,' Ashby smiled. 'What do you think?'

'It's . . . incredible,' Henry said, swallowing. His throat was tight, and he could feel the long, slow throb of desire in his loins.

'Something to drink, gentlemen?' Lacy May asked.

'Champagne, I think,' Ashby said. 'While we study the menu.'

Lacy May gave a little trilling laugh and went out of the room. The boys – some of them very young indeed, Henry realised – returned their gaze with indolent, knowing looks.

'Do they . . . will they . . . ?' Henry tried to get a question past the thickness in his throat.

'Anything,' Ashby said.

Henry thought briefly about money, and realised that he did not care what it cost. He had never realised there were such places. All these years, and he had never known! What follies he could have spared himself, what humiliations he could have avoided! Here was what he had always dreamed of finding, a safe and private place where all his dreams and all his fantasies could be made to come true.

Lacy May came back with the champagne, and they sat at one of the tables facing into the semicircle of the room. From time to time one of the boys would come by their table, arrogant and yet – to Henry – vulnerable, and perhaps touch one of them on the face, or run fingers through their hair. Their eyes were all the same, knowing, full of promises.

'May,' Ashby said. 'Won't you ask Young Adonis to join us for a glass of wine?'

Lacy May smiled and nodded to one of the young men, who got up and walked across the room, smiling a small triumphant smile. He was as handsome as the god from whom he had taken his name, with the well-defined musculature of an athlete. His hair was ash-white, his eyes a startling blue. He sat next to Ashby and put his hand on Ashby's thigh while Ashby poured him a glass of champagne.

'I'm glad you chose me again,' Adonis said.

'I chose you because I like you, Adonis,' Ashby said. 'Very much.' He kissed Adonis on the mouth. Beneath the table Adonis's fingers were busy.

'Now, now,' Ashby said, lifting Adonis's hand and putting it on the table. 'Not so fast, my dear.'

'Oh,' Adonis said, pouting prettily.

'Ishmael,' Ashby said softly. 'Have you . . . decided?'

Henry nodded, and Ashby signalled Lacy May to come to the table. Henry pointed to the youth who had caught his eye, dark-haired and marble-skinned like the boy from Cable Street.

'You've impeccable taste, Ishmael,' Lacy May said. 'Impeccable.' She beckoned to the boy, who uncoiled himself languidly, his every movement firing Henry's desire, and came across the room. His lips were very red. He drew attention to them by touching them with the tip of his tongue as he sat down. On his naked right shoulder was a tattoo.

'This is Butterfly,' Lacy May said.

'The tattoo,' Henry croaked.

'Do you like it?' Butterfly smiled.

'It's lovely,' Henry managed. 'And so are you.'

137

'Ooh,' Butterfly said. 'How sweet. What's your name, you nice man?'

'H – Ishmael,' Henry said.

'And what is your pleasure?'

Henry smiled dreamily. He was floating in a sea of sweet sexual anticipation, a paradise where nobody reviled him, or called him a dirty old man, a heaven where there was incense and comfort, a glass of wine and a private room instead of some squalid deadfall or even more squalid alley. Sexual fantasies followed each other through his head like nymphs gambolling in some mythological meadow.

'Could we . . . go, now?' he said to Butterfly.

'Well,' Butterfly said, drawing the word out. 'What about my wine?'

'I'll have a bottle sent up,' Henry said.

'That's different,' Butterfly said, managing to touch Henry as he stood up. Trembling with desire, Henry followed him across the room towards the stairs. Mortimer Ashby watched him go. A smile touched his lips.

15

The trouble with her parents, Sarah thought angrily, was they were so damned perfect. Consequently they couldn't take imperfection in anyone else, least of all in their youngest daughter.

Look at them, for God's sake! she thought, in their sixties and still acting as if they were in the first year of their marriage! They weren't really perfect, of course. In fact, they fought like cat and dog, fiercely and often. When the immovable force of Andrew's conservative approach to problems came up against the irresistible object of Diana's determination to change things, the noise could be heard all over Fredericksburg. Their fights were furious and frequent, but never at any time were they remotely personal. When whatever needed to be decided had been decided, the argument was forgotten as if it had never occurred. Andrew and Diana Starr knew each other very, very well. They were among the blessed few who actually liked each other after more than a quarter of a century together.

And not only were they well-nigh perfect, Sarah thought, they expected everyone else to live up to their high standards. Expected, note, not hoped. Well, if there was one thing that Sarah was sure of, it was that she was a long, long way from perfect.

'How many times are we going to go through this with you, Sarah?' Andrew asked, keeping the anger out of his voice. Anger never worked with his children. He sometimes wondered whether there was any damned thing that did.

'I don't know,' Sarah said sullenly.

'"I don't know" isn't an answer, Sarah,' Diana said.

Sarah said nothing. Well, there was nothing to say. They were right when they told her that they had talked like this before. They were right when they said she had made the same mistake before. They were right, they were right, they were always so damned right. She wondered whether they knew how much their always being right made her hate them.

'This man, David Liddell,' Diana said. 'Tell us about him.'

'I've told you,' Sarah said. 'Over and over again. He's a writer. From Boston. I met him in New York.'

'At a party, you said?'

On the Staten Island ferryboat, actually, Sarah thought, imagining the look on her parents' faces if she were to tell them the truth. 'Yes,' she said. 'Some friends in the Village.'

'The Village,' Diana said, managing to make the two words express everything she felt about Sarah's life, David Liddell, and the kind of people one was bound to meet in Greenwich Village.

'And now you want to go to Boston.'

'Yes.'

'To be with this Liddell person.'

'That's right.'

'Sarah, you're being very foolish,' Andrew said. 'And very irresponsible. I might even use stronger words. Not decent.'

'Oh, Father, don't be so old-fashioned,' Sarah said. 'Young people these days don't live by such outdated notions!'

'Since when was decency an outdated notion?' Andrew said, unable this time to keep the anger out of his voice. Diana heard it and intervened.

'What your father means is that we cannot approve your relationship with this man, Sarah. He is . . . we

140

want something better for you. Someone with a good background, an income – '

'Oh, money!' Sarah said, scornfully. 'I was wondering how long it would be before we got to that!'

'Well,' Diana said, 'has he any money?'

'Whether he has or he hasn't makes no difference to me!'

'Ah,' Diana said. 'Then he hasn't.'

'David's not having any money doesn't make him worthless!' Sarah protested. 'You don't love someone because they have money or haven't!'

'There are those who do, Sarah,' Andrew said gently.

'David's not like that!' she flared. 'He loves me!'

'Love doesn't buy the groceries!' Diana snapped back. 'What is your precious David going to support you on, pray? He has no profession, no income.'

'He's a writer,' Sarah said. 'An artist. It takes time – '

'Meanwhile, how will you live?'

'I can work,' Sarah said. 'We'll manage until David gets his start. We'll get by.'

'You'll get by,' Andrew repeated, 'and that's about the sum of it.' He made a theatrical production out of a sigh. 'You're a grown woman, Sarah, and we can't stop you from doing anything you have a mind to do. But we will not help you realise this folly, do you understand?'

'Is that supposed to frighten me?' Sarah sneered.

'Darling, we want you to be happy,' Diana said, seeing the storm clouds gathering again. 'It's simply that we think this . . . liaison is unwise. You're thinking with your heart and not your head.' She paused, pleased that she had managed not to say 'again':

'We know nothing about him,' Andrew said. 'His background, his family – '

'Family, family, family, that's all you ever hear around here!' Sarah shouted. 'I'm *buried* in family, don't you understand? Buried in cousins and uncles and grandfathers and ancestors and all their important

141

friends and all their impeccable connections! I don't want any of it! I don't need it! I want something better!'

'There may well come a time when you will find there is nothing so good,' Andrew reminded her quietly.

'I doubt it,' Sarah retorted.

'So might I have done, at your age,' Andrew said. 'That doesn't make it any the less true.'

'Father, I've made up my mind,' Sarah said. 'This is what I want. And you're not going to stop me.'

'We've told you how we feel, Sarah,' Andrew said. 'What I want you to understand quite clearly is that we will not help you. Not now, and not in the future.'

'I don't care!' Sarah said spiritedly.

'I think that's what makes us so sad,' Andrew said. 'We can see so clearly how you feel, while you cannot understand how we feel.'

You always feel the same way, Sarah thought. You want things under your control. You want to call the tune and watch everybody dancing to see if they make a mistake. Like Mary, mousy and docile, or Joanna, who hated horses but became a champion rider because *you* wished it. Well, you're not going to make me knuckle under to rules in which I don't believe.

'I understand,' she said. 'But you don't.'

She got up and marched out of the room, slamming the door. Andrew looked at his wife and grimaced. Diana shook her head.

'Oh, Andrew,' she sighed. 'I could weep.'

'I know, love,' he said, going across to her and putting his arm around her shoulder. Through the tall window he watched his daughter striding down the path towards the stables. How many times had he watched her do that, her head up, her back straight, that ain't-afraid-o'-nothin' expression on her face?

She always was the spunky one, he thought. Mary was sweet and gentle-natured, Joanna self-centred, vain. It was Sarah, the one he'd always called the runt of the litter, who'd surprised him with her determination to cut her own path, live her life her own way. She was seven kinds of damned fool, but there were times when Andrew found himself close to admiring her, and perhaps even envying her. Mostly, he worried about her.

But then, everybody worried about Sarah.

Everybody, that was, except Sarah herself. She was a small girl, with dark, naturally curly hair and grey eyes that shone with intelligence. Folks said she looked a lot like Mary Starr, the sister of her grandfather. She had the same rebellious streak, Andrew thought, that was for sure.

She had an attractive smile and a good figure, and she was a natural flirt. There were always boys around, carrying her books home from school, coming down from college to visit. Any man with three daughters, Andrew used to say, got a degree in romance before his oldest girl was eighteen. He could tell the degree of smittenness just by the expression on a pimpled face. Sarah was always in and out of love, succumbing – and suffering – the way other young people caught hay fever or summer colds, and as frequently. That was fine when she was a youngster, but as she grew older, he began to realise that Sarah was too good-natured ever to question a man's motives. And as if they knew it, too, all the bad hats, the no-gooders and the no-hopers homed in on her. She was young, she was pretty and she was gullible. She was also, one day, going to be quite wealthy. That was more than enough to attract adventurers, and there had been stormy scenes featuring more than a few.

But Sarah went on falling in love. And as regularly, out of love. Her reactions were always much the same. First, distressed and chastened; then, after a while, angry, determined never again to let herself be fooled. Three, four, six months later she would be in love again, and this time it was always going to be different.

143

Then home she would come to Belmont, to be consoled by her Aunt Louisa. Sarah was Louisa's favourite of all the Starr girls. She supported Sarah's every barmy notion, as if, Andrew grumbled, letting her make the same mistake over and over would teach her not to make it. He knew better than to argue with Louisa, however. She had a whim of steel. Her word had been law at Belmont for a long time. She was a big woman for someone so small, Andrew always said.

'You think she'll ever learn, Andrew?' Diana sighed.

'Maybe,' he said, not really believing it.

16

Jennifer Moffatt was not beautiful. She knew that. But she was attractive to men. She knew that, too. She stood about five feet eight, tall for a girl, but not too tall. She was not fashionably full-breasted, but she had a good figure, and a slender waist that looked as though it could be easily spanned by two male hands. She had fine dark eyes, and high cheekbones that gave her face, with its slightly swarthy skin, a faintly Spanish look. She was warm, intelligent, and humorous, yet she managed to keep at bay the many bachelor officers she had met in a lifetime of living on Army camps. It was not long before every young officer at Omaha Barracks had introduced himself, and pressed her to accompany him to the monthly post dance, or for a carriage ride, or even – as one or two of the bolder souls tried – a promenade along the river. All had been firmly turned down. It was something Jenny had had plenty of practice at.

After a couple of months, all but the most smitten had given up on her. 'Hard-hearted,' they said. 'Chilly Lily' they called her. There was even a rumour that she was secretly in love with a young officer serving out West.

In fact, Jenny's reserve was due not to any undying love, nor to coldness of nature, but to her mother's almost-hostile protectiveness. Laura Moffatt knew all about being madly in love with some penniless young man. No daughter of hers was going to make the same error, suffer the same heartbreak.

When Laura's own parents had discovered that their daughter was madly in love with a penniless medical student, they whisked her out of Baltimore and off on the Grand Tour, war or no war. When she came back, they had everything arranged, and Laura was married grandly to Whittier Moffatt, scion of a very old Massachusetts family. Whittier's mother's people had come over on the *Mayflower*.

Whittier's military career had been less than glorious, and his postings distinctly unglamorous. It had taken Laura only a very short time to realise that he was spineless, and that unless she pushed him and pushed him, he would never amount to anything. It had taken her only a little longer to come to terms with being married to a man she had never loved and would never love. She thought of herself as *accustomed* to Whittier, and over the years had rationalised her youthful romance into a folly from which she had been delivered. She had no intention of allowing Jennifer, her only child, to become embroiled in a similar situation. Love, Laura had decided, was a risk to any woman. The world was not well lost for it.

So the young officers were charmingly turned away, not because Jenny did not like them, or was not attracted by them, but because of Laura. Let Jenny spend too long with any one of them, or allow her manner to become a trifle too warm, and one of her mother's 'talks' would inevitably follow. They were always the same: extended and tedious. It was simpler to avoid them by doing as Laura bade.

Even so, Jenny Moffatt knew what she wanted, and felt that when it came along she would know instinctively. Quite how, or where, or when, did not matter. She would know. No romantic mush, no sweet talk, no moonlight and roses would be necessary. And he would be a soldier. Of that Jenny was even more certain, although she did not know why. Except, perhaps, that she rarely met any young man who

146

was not a soldier.

Her life at Omaha Barracks was much the same as it had been at other military posts where her father had served. She read, she sewed, she studied the piano, she rode every day. There were shopping expeditions into town, and once in a while a longer trip, to St. Louis or New York. Around her smaller world the larger world of the Army moved, its activities punctuated by the unchanging cadences of bugle and drum. Reveille and roll-call, mess-call and retreat, day after eventless day. The newspapers were full of talk of war with Spain, but it was hard to make a connection between the headlines and the young men in their freshly pressed uniforms who came dutifully to the Moffatt house to pay their respects, or crowded around begging for a dance at the monthly 'hop'.

The post dance was held in the echoing gymnasium on the southern perimeter of the parade ground. It was more eagerly looked forward to than any other social event on the calendar. Young ladies from Omaha drove up with their parents, eyes ashine with anticipation. Refreshments were provided from mess funds, and the post band supplied the music. There was intense competition for the privilege of dancing with the commanding officer's daughter, and many a young hopeful privately promised himself on the eve of the dance that *this* would be the occasion when Jenny Moffatt would bestow upon him that special smile that would tell him she was his.

The band swung into a schottische, and the gentlemen led their ladies out on to the floor. It had been liberally sprinkled with French chalk before the dance, and now, after an hour, it was splendidly treacherous. Because it was a fine night, all the windows of the gymnasium were open, and through them peeked children in their nightdresses, rosy-cheeked, wide-eyed, giggling. Every once in a while one of the wives would go over and tell them to *scat*! and they would flee, only to shyly reappear minutes later.

'My dance, I believe, ma'am?'

Jennifer looked up to see Lieutenant Starr smiling down at her. He was very dark, very handsome, she thought. Someone had told her his mother was Spanish. Maybe that was where he got that black hair and those long, dark eyelashes. She moved into his arms and they swung out on the floor. Laura Moffatt watched them, her face expressionless.

'I really like dancing with you, Miss Moffatt,' Lee said. 'You're one of the few girls I know who can really dance.'

'Why thank you, Lieutenant,' Jenny smiled. 'You're not so bad yourself.'

'Not usually,' he grinned. 'It must be you.'

'I've been flattered before, Lieutenant,' she said. 'It doesn't work on me.'

'It wasn't flattery,' he said. 'That's not my style.'

'What is your style?'

'I'm the dead-serious type,' he said.

'I've met a few of those, too,' Jenny replied.

'I'm sure you have, ma'am,' he said. 'There isn't a bachelor officer on the post wouldn't cheerfully throttle me if it meant he could have this dance with you. You've got us all at your feet.'

'You, too, Lieutenant?'

'Me, too, ma'am. No question about it, I'm sunk.'

'But you're not the flattering type.'

'No,' he said, looking directly into her eyes. She felt that first tug of engaged emotion and in the same instant became aware of his body, muscular and pliant. She imagined him making love to her, and the thought made her heart bump. *Jennifer*! she scolded herself. She could not look at him for a moment.

'Where are you from, Lieutenant Starr?' she said.

'New Mexico,' he said. 'We've had this conversation before, you know.'

'What do you mean?'

'At the dance last month. Same questions. Same answers. That's how you keep us all at arm's length, isn't it?'

'I'd . . . forgotten, that's all,' Jenny said, with just the hint of a toss of the head. Impudent fellow!

'Couldn't we get past the primary conversations?' he asked her. 'I'd like to know what you think, what you feel, what you believe. Where you come from, what your parents do, that stuff doesn't matter.'

'I was merely making –'

'Polite conversation, I know,' he said. 'But we're wasting time, you see. If we only talk about the weather and what the papers say, the dance will be over. And we still won't know the first thing about each other.'

'You're crazy,' she said, smiling in spite of herself.

'It's not crazy, Jenny Moffatt,' he said. 'It's the only sensible thing. What kind of little girl were you? Shy, I'll bet.'

'No, I wasn't!' she said. 'I was . . . quiet. That's not the same thing.'

'Only child.'

'That's right.'

'I've got two sisters. And hundreds of cousins. One big unhappy family.'

'Unhappy?'

'It's a joke,' he said. 'What about you?'

'Lots of cousins,' she said. 'Down Richmond way. One big unhappy family.' She smiled to show him that it, too, was a joke, but it was not. The Hibberts were a mightily unhappy lot, and she did her best to stay well away from all of them.

'Where would you go,' he asked abruptly, 'if you could pick anywhere in the world?'

'Anywhere?' Jenny tilted her head to one side. 'Paris, I think. Or maybe Florence.'

'Good choice,' he said. 'I'll come with you.'

'When shall we leave?' Jenny said, entering into the game.

'We could sneak out now,' he stage whispered. 'Nobody would notice.'

'Down the river to New Orleans,' she said.

'Pick up a ship for New York.'

'See the sights for a couple of days.'

'Then sail for Europe,' he said.

Jenny gave a huge mock-sigh. 'Just one thing,' she said. 'We hardly know each other, Lieutenant.'

'True,' Lee said. 'Maybe we should take care of that first. Go to Europe a little later.'

Once again she felt that engaging of her emotions. Their eyes met. No shy glance this time: something passed between them.

'Yes,' Jenny said softly, the words coming almost unwilled. 'I think that would be better.'

The dance ended. Lieutenant Starr led her back to where her mother and father were sitting. Laura Moffatt watched them cross the room, her lips pursed.

'Thank you, Lieutenant,' Jenny said, in her soft, clear voice. 'It was most enjoyable.'

'It certainly was, ma'am.' Lee bowed to Laura, who had not missed the look that passed between him and her daughter, something invisible that Laura saw as clearly as if it had been made of mahogany, and knew it for what it was.

'Lieutenant Starr certainly seems to have made quite an impression on you, Jennifer,' she said stiffly. 'What did he have to say that was so all-fired fascinating?'

'We were talking about travel,' Jenny said.

'That all?' Whittier asked. He sounded disappointed, Jenny thought, as though he had hoped for more. Laura Moffatt said nothing. She sat very still, a faraway look in her eyes that did not go away when the next dance began and the next young officer came to waltz with her daughter.

Across the room, Chris Vaughan and Chuck Gates had watched the entire scene with undisguised interest.

'Ahah,' Gates said.

'Ahah, indeed,' Vaughan echoed.

Lee joined them on the stag line, his face stuck in a foolish smile.

'Havin' a nice time, Lieutenant?' Gates asked.

'Splendid,' Lee said, turning to look towards the Moffatts. Gates and Vaughan snickered, and he swung around to hush them, thus missing the stony glare that Laura Moffatt directed his way.

'What's so funny?' Lee frowned.

'Sssssssssplennnnnnnndid!' Gates mocked.

'Shows, does it?' Lee grinned.

'Just a tad,' Gates said.

'Boy, you in a heap o' trouble,' Vaughan warned, in a white-trash accent. 'A *heap* o' trouble!'

'Ah, go suck a duck!' Lee retorted inelegantly.

'You just keep that old saying in mind, boy,' Vaughan said. '"You got to watch out when you start in chasin' a girl you don't end up catchin' her mother".'

'Who said that?' Lee challenged.

'I did,' Vaughan said.

'And he *knows*,' Gates grinned.

Across the room, Jennifer Moffatt was leaving the dance floor with the young officer she had waltzed with. Andy Grover, Lee thought, and he's got the same foolish grin on his face that I had after I danced with her. At that moment, Jenny turned towards Lee and their eyes met. He smiled. She smiled back, and the way she smiled made his world tilt sideways.

151

The Washington *Inquirer*
February 16, 1898

THE MAINE BLOWN UP!

Awful Disaster to United States Battle Ship
in Harbor of Havana

Number of Killed or Missing, 253.

Lieutenant Jenkins and Engineer Merritt
Among the Number

Cause of the Disaster Unknown

Question of Whether It Was Accident Aboard
Or Blow Without

Comment of Various Officials

17

'I must say, Jennifer, that I think you are seeing far too much of this young man,' Laura Moffatt said, without looking up from the embroidery she was working on. She nodded once, as if to emphasise her words, and shifted the embroidery nearer to the light. Laura always had something 'creative' in hand. People admired her for her industry. I don't like to waste precious time just *sitting*, she told them, as if inactivity were a pernicious disease.

Jenny looked up from her book, surprised by the abruptness of her mother's remark. They had been alone all evening, and spoken little. It was cosy and quiet in the house, a cheery fire crackling in the stone fireplace. General Moffatt was dining out with some visiting 'brass' at Delmonico's in Omaha. He would not be back until late. I might have known what she was up to, Jenny thought. She's been waiting for her chance.

'You mean Lee?' she said.

'You know very well whom I mean, miss!' Laura said tartly, her eyes on the embroidery.

'But, Mama, we see each other only two or three times a week,' Jenny protested. 'Other girls –'

'I'm not concerned with what other girls do!' Laura said firmly. She laid the sewing down and turned to face her daughter. 'It's you that I am concerned with, my dear.'

'I understand that, Mama,' Jenny said. 'But Lee is such a dear friend. Life here would be very dull if I did not have his company.'

'There are plenty of other young officers on the post,' Laura said. 'I am sure that any of them would be honoured to be your escort. Yet you see only this Lieutenant Starr.'

'I – I don't care for the others, Mama,' Jenny said. 'I have to say I find most them very . . . limited. In their conversation, in every way.'

'I find it hard to believe that Lieutenant Starr is so accomplished,' Laura said. 'He evinces little sign of it when he comes here.'

'Oh, Mama, you don't know him as I do!' Jenny said. 'Naturally, he's quiet when he visits the house. Papa is his commanding officer. But he's not like that really. He's such . . . *fun*!' The warmth of her voice was a signal to her mother. Laura watched her daughter closely.

'Fun in what way?' she asked, artlessly.

'Oh, fun to be with,' Jenny said. 'To talk to. You know, Mama, we talk all the time.' A dreamy note had come into her voice that Laura did not fail to notice. 'About anything! Everything! About life, and all the places we want to go, and books, and poetry, and music. He talks a lot about his family. Did you know that his great-grandfather went with the Lewis and Clark expedition? Lee says they must have camped quite close to here in 1804.'

'Yes, yes,' Laura said. 'The Starrs are well known in Army circles. But that's not what I want to talk to you about, Jennifer.'

'What *did* you want to talk to me about, Mama?' Jenny said, knowing the answer. All her life her mother had been telling her the same things: and they all began with *don't*. Don't tell anyone your secrets. Don't rely on anyone. Don't give your affection to any one person to the exclusion of all others. Don't commit yourself in any way. It was simply unwise, Laura said.

If only she knew.

Jenny let her mind fill with the memory of being in Lee's arms, the feeling of his mouth on hers, the sturdy thunder of his heart against her own. He loved her. Hidden in a chocolate box at the back of the wardrobe in her bedroom were the letters and poems that he had written to her. He had loaned her the book she was reading, poems by W. B. Yeats. He had underlined one called 'To An Isle In the Water':

> *Shy one, shy one,*
> *Shy one of my heart*
> *She moves in the firelight*
> *Pensively apart*

She loved him to read poetry to her. He said that, if war had not been coming, he would have asked her to marry him.

And what do you think I would reply if he did, Mama? Jenny wondered. Did her mother know anything at all about what went on inside her daughter's head? Did any mother, ever?

'I want you to stop seeing Lieutenant Starr, Jennifer,' she heard her mother saying. 'I thing your friendship with him is . . . ill–advised. I have already spoken to your father, and he agrees with me.'

'But, Mama, that's utterly unfair! There's no reason for it!'

'If your father and I say it, that is enough reason, young lady!' Laura said, her voice hardening. She would have to be firm. If that was not enough . . .

'I think the very least you could do is tell me why,' Jenny said, her head coming up. 'I'm not a child any more, Mama. I have a mind of my own.'

'I know that,' Laura answered. 'And I respect your feelings. More than you know. But you must realise our position in this, Jennifer. How it looks. To the wives of the other officers, to everyone.'

'It's none of their business!' Jenny said.

'But it is, my dear,' Laura said sweetly. 'An Army

155

post is like one great big family. Very little remains secret for long. And one or two people have mentioned to me that . . . well, that you and Lieutenant Starr are rather . . . how shall I put it?' She made a gesture, as much as to say: no word exists to express the meaning I want. 'Too . . . *involved.*' That was it, she thought, that was exactly the word. She watched Jennifer's face carefully, and noted her reaction. Ah, she thought angrily. Then it's gone as far as that.

'Oh, I think it's hateful that people should spy upon one and then tattle!' Jenny said, getting up from the chair and crossing the room towards the window. The constant wind moaned softly. Eddies of drifting snow danced pirouettes across the snow-covered parade ground. The lighted windows of the adjutant's office shone bravely in the blackness.

'Darling, listen to me,' Laura said. 'Come, sit here beside me.'

Jenny came away from the window and sat down on a stool in front of the fire beside her mother's armchair. I don't want to listen to this, she thought, knowing she had no choice. That was the trouble with parents. You *had* to listen. You couldn't say that they had no wisdom to impart that you would want to learn. How could two people like her parents, who never exchanged any of those tender, loving gestures that people who loved each other could not help but exchange, think they were qualified to talk to her about *love*? They didn't know what love was. Maybe they had, once, a long time ago. But they had let it die, and forgotten it.

They were old. What could two old people know about how young people felt today? It was all different now, all changed.

But still she knew she would have to listen to it.

I will not get angry, she told herself.

But she knew she would.

18

'Sit down, Lieutenant,' General Moffatt said.

Lee sat down uneasily. The General's summons had been abrupt, although not entirely unexpected. The atmosphere in the house was strained and tense. Mrs Moffatt sat to one side, sewing. She did not greet Lee. There was so sign of Jenny.

'I imagine you know why I have asked you to come to see me,' the General said, clearing his throat with a sound not unlike a bark. 'What?'

The watery eyes were even shiftier than usual, and Lee's heart sank. Whatever was going to happen, it was not going to be good.

'Yes, sir, I believe I do,' he said. 'It's Jenny, isn't it?'

'Jennifer,' Moffatt corrected him. 'Yes. Hm. Been seeing a lot of each other, haven't you?'

'Yes, sir. In fact, I – ' As he spoke Lee saw Laura Moffatt's head come sharply up, and saw in her eyes a dislike so intense that it was like a blow. In mid-word he changed 'love' to 'like' and the sentence came out, 'I like her very much indeed.'

He wondered whether Mrs Moffatt had noticed the split-second hesitation.

She had.

'Jennifer is very young,' Moffatt said. 'Too young to be . . . tied down in any way.'

'Is that how she feels, sir?' Lee said. He tried to say it artlessly, but Moffatt caught the slight nuance of malice and flushed angrily.

'Jennifer is my daughter!' he snapped. 'What she feels or does not feel does not enter into this discussion. Do you understand me, Lieutenant?'

'Yes, sir.' There was no profit in allowing his anger to show. If he got into contention with Old Fuss and Feathers, as Moffatt was disrespectfully known around the post, he could only lose.

'I expect that any day now the regiment will be put on war footing,' Moffatt said. 'It seems likely there will be war with Spain, and should that prove to be the case, I shall immediately apply for combatant duties.'

'Yes, sir, of course,' Lee said.

'That being so, Lieutenant, you can see why I would prefer that your relationship with my daughter ceases forthwith.'

'Sir?' He had expected to be told to surrender his monopoly. But not this.

'I believe you heard me correctly, Lieutenant.'

'But . . . why, sir? We like each other very much. I –'

Moffatt's face went a shade purpler, and he put one hand flat on the small table at his side. It made a small but definite sound, and its meaning was very clear: *enough*, the gesture said.

'I have no intention of discussing this further with you, sir!' Moffatt said, his voice going up. He glanced at his wife. Laura Moffatt was watching Lee's face very closely, as if trying to read his mind.

'Then may I respectfully request your permission to see Jenny one last time, sir, to explain – ?'

'Lieutenant, I will not tell you a –'

'Whittier, let me talk to the young man,' Laura Moffatt said, coming across the room and laying her hand on her husband's arm. 'There is no need for raised voices.' She turned to Lee and smiled sweetly.

'Jennifer is a little . . . headstrong,' she said. 'Girls of her age often are. I remember when I was younger . . . ah! but that's another story.' She smiled her Southern-belle smile. She was being so gracious, Lee thought, it

158

almost perfumed the air. 'It has nothing at all to do with you, you see. Nothing whatever. But my husband and I feel – no, we *know* – that Jennifer is too young for any permanent attachment. As my husband just said, things look very uncertain at the moment. We are only thinking of her welfare. Trying to spare her any unnecessary unhappiness. I'm sure you understand how a mother would feel in such a situation?'

'Yes, ma'am,' Lee said. 'I understand perfectly.' He saw the brief flash of response in her eyes and cursed himself for again letting his tongue get the better of his judgment. But it was damnably hard not to.

'Good, good,' Mrs Moffatt cooed. 'I was sure you would. Perhaps you will call by tomorrow at two to say goodbye to her.'

'Goodbye, ma'am?'

'Yes,' Mrs Moffatt said, the venom showing in her eyes as she slid the knife in. 'She's going to stay with my family in Charleston for the summer. If there is a war, she'll stay there until it is over.'

'In that case, ma'am, may I again respectfully request that you allow me to see Jenny alone just once before she goes?'

'I am afraid,' Laura Moffatt said, far too sweetly, 'that that would be out of the question.'

'May I ask why?' Lee said.

Something in the words set off the explosion: he was never quite sure why afterwards. Whittier Moffatt lurched to his feet and confronted Lee, his face mottled with rage. His wife started to say something, but he shook his head like an enraged bull.

'Why?' he roared, spittle flecking his lips. 'You damn impertinent puppy, you ask *why*? Then I will tell you!'

'Whittier,' Mrs Moffatt said, touching his arm. He ignored her, his eyes fixed on Lee's face.

'I'll give it to you straight!' Moffatt shouted. 'No daughter of mine is going to marry a goddamned half-breed! Do I make myself clear?'

159

Lee felt the blood drain from his face. His anger froze in him. He could not believe what he had just heard.

'Sir?' he croaked.

'You heard me!' Moffatt raged, his voice even louder than before. 'You asked for the truth, and now you know it. I don't want you or anyone of your kind near my girl, and if I find out that you've tried to see her, I will have you broken, do you hear me? I'll have you kicked out of this man's army so fast your head will spin. That is all, Lieutenant!'

Lee stood staring at both of them for a long, long moment. He had never wanted to kill a man before, but the urge to grab General Moffatt's wattled throat between strong hands and throttle him surged through Lee like a tide.

'General,' he said, mastering his emotions with an enormous effort. 'What you just said makes me ashamed to serve in the same regiment as you.'

'I think you had better leave, Lieutenant,' Mrs Moffatt said coldly.

'Thank you,' Lee replied. 'I could use some clean air.' He turned on his heel without saluting and went out of the house. It was a beautiful spring afternoon. A catbird flicked its long tail and gave its mewing call in a nearby tree. He went around the rear of the enlisted men's barracks and vomited into the dust. Eyes watering, panting, he leaned against the cool stone of the building, shaking his head.

Half-breed.

It was the ugliest thing he had ever heard.

Slowly, he made his way back to his quarters. Vaughan was not there, and Lee was grateful: he did not want to talk to anyone for a while. The evening shadows drew in as he sat on the edge of his bed, staring at the wall.

I'll have to quit, he thought.

And do what?

I don't know. But I can't stay here. Under *his* command.

160

He hated the thought of leaving Vaughan and Gates.

But he would have to. Have to.

Half-breed.

The words shimmered inside his head like a cluster of fireflies. Hatred of Whittier Moffatt and his affectatious wife coursed through him.

And Jenny?

He ached with the need to see her, talk to her. Had she known what they were going to say to him? He could not bring himself to believe that. Then where was she while it was going on? Why had she not been there to defend him? What kind of love was that?

O Jenny, he thought.

He heard footsteps on the wooden porch, and looked up. Chris Vaughan came in, smiling.

'You dog!' he said to Lee.

'What?' Lee said dully. Vaughan did not notice his mood, or perhaps merely chose to ignore it.

'I have tidings to impart,' Vaughan said. 'From a certain lady.'

'Jenny?'

'Very hush-hush, she was, about the whole thing,' Vaughan said. 'You'd have thought the Pinkertons were after her, the way she kept looking over her shoulder.'

'Chris!' Lee said warningly. Vaughan grinned.

'Sorry,' he said. 'Rear of the stables, immediately after retreat. She said she'll only be able to stay a moment.'

Lee's heart soared. The dreadful gloom that had descended on him after his interview with General and Mrs Moffatt lifted and he smiled for the first time in hours.

'Chris,' he said, the smile growing wider, 'I love you. You know that?'

'I say, careful!' Vaughan said, with an exaggerated look of caution to right and to left. 'You'll have everyone talking!'

'Don't care!' Lee said. 'I love you!'

161

'Aw, go soak your head,' Vaughan retorted. 'Before that damned grin splits your face in half!'

The following day a straight-faced Lieutenant Lee Starr bade farewell to Jennifer Moffatt in the presence of her watchful parents. He wished her a safe journey and a wonderful vacation in Charleston. She thanked him kindly, and they shook hands.

A week later, Lee tendered his resignation, and it was accepted without regret by his commanding officer. He did not tell Gates and Vaughan his reasons for resigning; nor did he allow anything they said to sway him. He had made his decision and it was final.

One month later, Lee and Jennifer were married by a justice of the peace, then headed west, to spend their honeymoon on James Starr's ranch in New Mexico.

New York *Inquirer*
March 3, 1898

THE
WAR
SHIP
MAINE
WAS
SPLIT
IN
TWO
BY
AN
ENEMY'S
SECRET
INFERNAL
MACHINE!!!

19

The telegram from Secretary Cortelyou wasted no words. THE PRESIDENT WANTS TO SEE YOU, it said. Andrew Starr took the next train to Washington. He had a pretty shrewd idea what it was McKinley wanted to see him about, and all the way up to the capital, he pondered deeply on the question of war with Spain.

He was an old man now, and he had heard the phrase 'manifest destiny' used many times to justify action by the United States outside its own borders. But never the way it was being used over the Cuban question since the revolution against Spanish rule which had broken out in '95. American capital was deeply involved in Cuban sugar-raising and refining, not to mention mining and shipping, all of which had suffered heavily in the insurrection. Another matter of pressing concern was the excesses of the Spanish general sent to quell the rising. The belief had now become widespread that America must intervene if she was not to be false to her destiny.

Cleveland had resisted the pressure, but Cleveland had been a president who cared more for principle than for the adulation of the mob. Andrew did not think McKinley was that kind of tough.

The train rattled on through the night. Andrew was glad to be away from the heavy burden of family problems which had beset him for the part year. First, the trouble with Sarah. Then Henry. Poor Henry, he thought. I hope he's found some kind of peace at last. At least they had managed to bury the scandal with him.

It had begun about a year ago.

He was in his study at Belmont when Louisa came in. She was dressed in black, as always. Her hair was quite white. She was a big woman for someone so small, he thought.

'I've got to talk to you, Andrew,' she said, peremptory to the point of rudeness. 'You been smokin' in here?'

'No,' Andrew lied. No use getting into an argument.

'You know my feelings,' Louisa said, turning her head this way and that, as if to catch an errant wisp of smoke which would give Andrew away. 'Tobacco's an instrument of Satan!'

'What do you want to talk to me about, Louisa?' Andrew said. Louisa's little tyrannies did not bother him. He had decided long ago that, if anything, they were a kind of cement which held everyone else in the family together. Family unity came in all shapes and sizes: outwitting Aunt Louisa was one of them.

'About Henry,' Louisa said.

Henry was Andrew's cousin; he had resigned his army commission at the end of the War between the States and taken on the management of the Boston factory where Sam had manufactured repeating rifles since 1863. There wasn't much of a market for them any more, and Henry, who was not cut out to be the manager of a factory at best, soon got his walking papers. Andrew had brought Henry down to Fredericksburg and given him the job of assistant manager at one of the stud farms he had bought along the Rapidan, about twelve miles from Belmont. Henry soon demonstrated a flair for horse-breeding which no one – least of all Henry himself – had dreamed he might possess. The stud became highly profitable, and Henry started making real money for the first time in his life. The house on the Rapidan had been enlarged into a pleasant, rambling mansion in the Colonial style. Henry and his wife Ann had just become grandparents for the second time.

'What's the matter with Henry?' Andrew said.

'Trouble,' Louisa said flatly. Andrew made a grimace. He had never envisaged himself as a man to whom the world would bring its troubles, as a child might bring a dead bird to its mother. Yet somehow, that seemed to be the rôle life had handed him, both at home and in business. Every Republican president since Sam Grant had availed himself of Andrew's judgment. And the family. Well, it got to be that you eventually realised there never was going to be any end to it. You were in the same fix as a doctor: no matter how many people you cured, there were always going to be more sick people waiting outside to see you.

'What kind of trouble?' he asked Louisa, wondering why Henry had not come to see him personally. Too frightened, probably, he decided. Andrew and his brother James had always called Henry 'Mary Ann', because he was such an old woman.

'It's nasty, Andrew,' Louisa sighed, sitting down. She let out a long, tired sigh. 'Dirty-nasty.'

'A woman?'

'Worse,' she said. 'Boys.'

'You're sure about this?'

Louisa said nothing. She looked at Andrew, her eyes holding his.

'All right,' Andrew said. 'Let's hear it.'

'Ann came to see me,' Louisa said.

Ann believed Henry had put his aberration behind him, Louisa said. He had promised his wife that he would never again slide back into that half-world, and he had kept his promise for a long, long time. But then success came, and with success, money. More money than Henry had ever had in his whole life. Money for good clothes, for hotel suites, for fine food, for champagne. He got in with a fast crowd at Saratoga.

There were always people who pandered to the tastes of the wealthy, as long as there was money in it for them. The temptation was put in Henry's way, and it was all downhill from there.

'Henry says there are . . . letters. A man has them. He wants one hundred thousand dollars for them.'

'Or?'

'He'll take them to Willie Priestman.'

'His name?'

'Mortimer Ashby.'

'Do we know him?'

'He was a small-time politician out in New Mexico. Working for Billy Priestman. Your brother and Sam Elkham put him out of business. I gather he went to prison.'

'Ah,' Andrew said.

Ashby's tastes were the same as Henry's, Louisa went on. When he found Henry, beaten up by street louts and lying in an alley, he had taken him to his apartment. Whatever transpired there – Louisa's patricianly elevated nose emphasised her lack of desire to know any of the details – it was clear that Ashby had learned Henry's real identity, and deliberately set out to entrap him.

'There's a house in Georgetown,' Louisa said. 'A male . . . house of assignment. They do anything for money. Ashby took Henry there. Henry seems to have developed an attachment for one of the . . . boys.'

'And Ashby used the boy, is that it?'

'The two of them were in it together. Ashby paid the boy. He encouraged Henry to write him letters. Love letters. The boy was called Butterfly.'

'What?'

'They all have names like that,' Louisa said, impatiently. 'My Lord, Andrew Starr, you're old-fashioned!'

'It's nothing to be ashamed of,' Andrew retorted.

Anyway, Louisa went on, once they had the letters,

all they had to do was hire a Pinkerton agent to make an affidavit of Henry's visits to the house, and they had a package.

'I've no doubt it gave that slimy creature a real thrill to tell Henry what he planned to do.'

'I'm surprised he didn't go straight to Priestman,' Andrew said.

'Probably reckons he can get more out of us.'

'He's wrong,' Andrew said grimly. 'How is Henry?'

'About how you'd imagine,' Louisa replied. 'He's a weak reed, Andrew. Always was. He can't help the way he is. What I'm afraid of is that even if we get him out of this, he'll slide back. You mark my words.'

'You may be right,' Andrew said. 'Doesn't alter the fact we've got to do something about this Ashby fellow. Got any ideas?'

'You could pay up,' Louisa said, with a sly grin.

'Don't hang upside down from the chandelier waiting till I do,' Andrew said. 'We've got to move fast, Louisa. Fight fire with fire. Hit Ashby so hard he won't ever know what happened. That will take some planning.'

Louisa got up out of her chair and stood with her arms akimbo. There was a light in her eyes that he hadn't seen for a long time. He was glad she was on his side.

'You going to fight clean, Andrew Starr? Or dirty?'

Andrew grinned, although there was no mirth in the smile. 'Clean if I can,' he said. 'Dirty if I have to.'

He arranged to meet Mortimer Ashby. It was all done very politely, one gentleman discussing a business proposition with another.

'We only have your word that you have these letters,' Andrew said.

'That's right,' Ashby said equably. 'But I'm sure Henry will have admitted he wrote them by now.'

'A hundred thousand dollars is a great deal of money.'

Ashby shrugged. 'How much is your reputation worth?'

'You won't listen to reason? Turn the letters over to me and forget the whole thing?'

'Are you mad, sir?' Mortimer Ashby said. 'Or do you think perhaps that I am?'

'I can't budge you on the price?'

'A hundred thousand,' Ashby said. 'Not a cent less.'

'I'll need a little time to get that much cash together,' Andrew said.

'You can have forty-eight hours.'

Andrew sighed. 'I'll . . . I'll do my best,' he said, managing to look defeated.

'I'm sure you will,' Ashby said smoothly. 'You really haven't any alternative, have you?'

Not damned much, Andrew thought, as he left the hotel. He had a lot to do, and all of it depended upon Ashby's going to Lacy May's house. Louisa was taking care of that end of things. He had no doubt whatsoever that she would persuade Butterfly to call Ashby and tell him there was trouble, that he should come over.

Not far from the house, Andrew had rented a disused warehouse. Even now, some of the most skilled scenery construction experts in Washington were working there. The actors and actresses were all briefed; the costumes and props had all been obtained. They had been told that it was an elaborate practical joke, and in a way, Andrew thought grimly, it was.

They let Ashby have enough time to start talking to Butterfly. Then Andrew gave the signal, and the 'police' wagon pounded up to the door of the house. Three hefty 'policemen' and a 'detective' hammered on the doors. Others went around the back to make sure nobody escaped that way. The door was opened, and they pushed their way in. Within five minutes they were out again, with the boy manacled to Mortimer Ashby. Piling them into the wagon, the 'police' rushed them to the 'station house'. It looked exactly like the real thing. Ashby was taken inside, formally charged, and thrown into a cell. Nothing he said seemed to have any effect on his captors. He was refused permission to contact anyone.

'I demand to see an attorney!' he shouted. 'It is my constitutional right to see an attorney!'

'Tomorrow,' said the unfeeling patrolman, who seemed to be the only one on duty. 'When you appear before the magistrates.'

And with that he had to be content.

Two hours passed, three. The place was eerily silent. Then a man came down the corridor to Ashby's cell. He was dressed in civilian clothes, and he looked very grave. Ashby rushed to the door of the cell, but the man waved him back.

'Open up,' he told the patrolman.

He came into the cell, told Ashby to sit down, and took a seat in the other chair, facing Ashby across the stark wooden table.

'Do you know a Maurice Templeton?' he said.

'No,' Ashby said. 'Who are you?'

'My name is Naisby. Chief Inspector Naisby, Vice Squad,' the man said. He was thickset, powerfully built, with world-weary eyes and slicked-down brown hair.

'I refuse to answer any more questions until I have seen my attorney,' Ashby said.

'You sure you don't know this man?' Naisby persisted. He put a photograph on the table. It was the boy, Butterfly.

'Is that his name?' Ashby said.

'You know him, then?'

'The police – your men arrested him at the same time as they arrested me.'

'He is a known homosexual, Mr Ashby,' Naisby said. 'Do you want to tell me what your business was at that house?'

Ashby swallowed and shook his head. 'No.'

'Then I must conclude that you were at that house for an immoral and obscene purpose.'

'That is not true,' Ashby snapped.

'He's confessed, Mr Ashby,' Naisby said. 'He's told us everything.'

'Confessed?'

'The boy you know as Butterfly. He's told us all about you.'

'You're lying.'

'If you say so, Mr Ashby.'

'What . . . what has he said?'

'Do you know the owner of the house you were arrested in?'

'No.'

'You're quite sure?'

'Of course I'm sure!' Ashby snapped.

'That's funny, sir,' Naisby said. 'According to the deeds, the owner of that house is you.'

'What?' Ashby shouted. 'What did you say?'

'The deeds name you as owner of the house, Mr Ashby. Do you realise what the penalty is for running a house of male prostitution?'

'This is insanity!' Ashby protested. 'I no more own that house than you do, Inspector!'

Naisby opened his briefcase and brought out a document. He laid it on the table, turning it so that Ashby could see it.

'Good God!' Ashby said. 'Where did you get this?'

'Is that your name?'

'Yes.'

'Your signature?'

'I never signed these papers!' Ashby cried. 'That signature is forged!'

'Why would anyone forge your signature on the deeds to a house, Mr Ashby?' Naisby said.

'To . . . so that something like this . . . yes, that's it, someone wants to get me put away. I know who, yes, I know who! It's that damned Andrew Starr, isn't it?'

'I beg your pardon?'

'It's all a big frame-up!' Ashby shrieked. 'Can't you see it, man? Can't you see it?'

171

'Mr Ashby, you're obviously upset,' Naisby said. 'I'll come back and see you later . . . '

'No, no, no, don't go, you've got to listen to me!' Ashby said, almost hysterically. 'Don't leave me here! I've got to get help. Get in touch with Willie Priestman! Tell him what has happened to me!'

'Would that be the Mr Priestman that runs the newspapers, sir?' Naisby said.

'That's him!' Ashby said. 'Get hold of him. He'll tell you what's behind all this!'

'If I was you, Mr Ashby, I'd be careful of telling the newspapers to come down here,' Naisby said. 'You're going before the magistrate in the morning, charged with keeping a homosexual brothel. We've got all your boys under arrest, you know. Every one of them has offered to give evidence to save his own skin. I'd be less than fair if I didn't tell you I think you'll go down for twenty years' hard labour.'

'Tw . . . ' Ashby couldn't finish the word, let alone the phrase. All at once his skin turned a dirty grey, and he slumped in the chair as if all the wind had been sucked out of his body.

'Why don't you make it easy on yourself?' Naisby said. 'Tell us exactly what you were doing at that house. It'll go easier on you if you co-operate with us.'

Ashby shook his head, his eyes unfocused.

'Leave me alone,' he whispered. 'Got to think.'

Naisby nodded and got up, rapping on the cell bars. The policeman came along the corridor and opened the cell, and Naisby walked briskly away as the policeman locked it again. Silence descended on the building. In the windowless cell, Mortimer Ashby paced to and fro, his mind seething with fear and anger.

No damned way were they going to pin something like this on him! No damned way! But they had the evidence – the deeds with his name on them, the confessions of the boys! God, what had they said? There must be some way to prove that he was not the owner of the house! But he had no idea who the real owner was. It was his word against the deeds. There was no question who a court would believe. What *else* had the boys told them? Suppose word of all this got back to New Mexico? My God, the old man would cut him off without a penny!

Back and forth he paced, back and forth. He had no idea what time it was, how long he had been in this place. They would take him in front of a magistrate in the morning. There were bound to be reporters there. They always hung around the magistrate courts, waiting, like hyenas, for tasty scraps they could turn into spicy headlines.

'Officer!' he screeched. 'Officer!'

In ten minutes, Naisby was back.

'You have something to tell me, Mr Ashby?'

'Sit down,' Ashby said. 'I'll tell you everything.'

When the confession was written out and signed, Ashby was taken to his apartment, and there he handed over the letters written by Henry which proved his story. He was then taken back to the police station, to await his appearance before the magistrate the following morning.

As soon as he was in the cell, the actors left the building. The one who had played the part of Chief Inspector Naisby, real name Nicholas Austin, hurried to Andrew's house on Thirty-fourth Street.

'He's still in the cell?' Andrew asked.

'Still there,' Austin grinned. 'He'll find it's open. Sooner or later. Then he'll catch on.'

'I'd love to see his face when he does,' Louisa said. 'You've done well, Nicholas. Thank you. Thank your people for us.'

'It was more than a pleasure, ma'am,' Austin said. 'It was fun. One of my best performances. Damned shame I didn't have but an audience of one!'

After he was gone, Andrew carefully burned all the letters in the fireplace. Then he poured himself a stiff whisky. He looked at Louisa, eyebrows raised. She was smiling.

'Pour one for me,' she said.

It was all over.

Except for one thing.

When he heard what they had done, Henry Starr went into the far stable at the Rapidan stud and blew out his brains with an old .44 Army model Colt. He left a note.

'I know you all acted for the best,' it said, 'but I cannot go on, knowing I might again succumb to the temptations that brought all this about. I beg you to forgive me, especially my dearest wife, Ann.'

They buried him on the knoll above the house, in the family graveyard. Poor Henry, Andrew thought, as the train pulled into Alexandria station. Poor everybody. He wondered what had happened to Mortimer Ashby. Nothing good, he hoped.

When he got to the White House, he learned that the President and Mrs McKinley were listening to a piano recital in the Blue Room. Mrs McKinley was sitting close to the pianist. She looked frail and unwell. The President, a burly, imposing man, sat on a sofa in the middle of the room. There were about two dozen people present. McKinley looked up and saw Andrew. He made a gesture: come and sit here.

'As soon as this piece is finished, go and speak to Mrs McKinley,' he said. 'Then go through to the Red Room. I'll join you in a moment.'

Andrew did as he was told, and said hello to one or two people he recognised. Then he went into the Red Room. McKinley came in with Mark Hanna. The Ohio business tycoon was a strange sort, Andrew thought, not for the first time. When he was with McKinley he resembled nothing so much as a farm boy a-courting. What the attraction was, Andrew had no idea, but there was no arguing that Hanna was devoted to the

174

President. He had been the driving force that pushed McKinley into the White House – 'advertised him like a damned patent medicine,' as Teddy Roosevelt said.

'Sorry to drag you up here, Andrew,' he said. He sat down. McKinley sat next to him, resting his head on his hands. His whole demeanour was that of a man in great distress.

'I had to see you,' the President said, hoarsely. 'I'm . . . my wife is in poorer health than usual. Seems like I haven't slept more than three hours a night for weeks.'

'Damned newspapers!' Hanna growled. 'Baying for war. They'll have it whether we want it or not!'

'No, sir!' McKinley said, speaking more forcefully. 'There'll be no war. No war!'

'This Cuban business is very . . . volatile, Mr President,' Andrew said. 'Hanna is right. The newspapers –'

'And the people,' Hanna interjected.

'The mood is for war,' Andrew said. 'You must not ignore it, sir. And don't forget, the Spanish fleet has taken up position in the harbour of Santiago de Cuba. They're playing confrontation, sir, whether we want it or not.'

'I know it, I know, I know!' McKinley said, and broke down, crying like a child. Hanna looked at Andrew. Andrew put his hand on the President's heaving shoulder and remained silent. After a while, the big man sniffled and looked up.

'I'd better go back in,' he said. 'Are my eyes red?'

'Blow your nose hard as you go in,' Andrew suggested. 'Then they'll all think that's what caused it.'

'Yes, yes, good idea,' McKinley said, getting up. He looked at Andrew. 'Do you really think I'll have to go to war?'

Andrew spread his hand. 'You're damned if you don't, Mr President. And you're damned if you do!'

'Damned,' McKinley said softly. 'Aye, you're right, Andrew. He's right, isn't he, Mark?'

175

'As usual, Mr President,' Hanna said.

McKinley went across to the door and then stopped with his hand on the doorknob. 'Can you both stay?' he said.

Both men nodded, and McKinley managed a smile of sorts. 'We'll talk later,' he said, and went back into the piano recital. They heard him blow his nose like a trumpet as the door closed.

20

'Someone coming,' Jenny said.

Lee looked up from his newspaper. You saw the dust long before you saw the rider, in this country. Although it was still April, the ground was already baked. He stood up and unhooked the field glasses hanging on the porch rail. The red shirt, the way the approaching rider sat his horse, meant only one person.

'Bill Brainerd,' he said.

The ranch was set amid sheltering blackjack oaks on the lower springs of the Rio Feliz. It was a beautiful, lonely place. James Starr had bought the land in 1866 from a man named Casey, and it had been his home ever since. He had never regretted leaving Belmont in his brother Andrew's hands and coming west after the Civil War. There was nothing in Virginia for any man who'd fought for the South. In the Territories, you could begin again. He had found his lovely Mexican wife, Linda, in Texas, and brought her north to New Mexico. Over the years, he enlarged the original two-room building to a sprawling, comfortable, ten-room adobe house, snug and warm in the fierce mountain winters, cool and welcoming during the lambent summers. When his law practice began to flourish, James bought a house in Santa Fé. But the Flying J was his first love. Overseeing the management of the eighty-thousand-acre spread was the solid, capable man who now rode into the front yard of the ranchhouse and swung down from the saddle.

'Evenin', Lee,' he said, coming up the steps. He took

off his hat and wiped his forehead with a forearm. 'Ma'am.'

'Will you have some coffee, Bill?' Jenny said.

'Or something stronger?' Lee added. Brainerd gave a grin and an aw-shucks shrug. Lee nodded and sloshed a generous measure of bourbon into a tumbler. He raised it to eye level and squinted through the glass at the sinking sun. 'Way below the yardarm,' he announced. '*Salud*!'

Bill clinked his glass against Lee's and took a sip of the whisky. He hitched his rump on to the porch rail and tossed his battered Stetson on to one of the cane chairs.

'Been over to Tularosa,' he said.

Lee nodded. Jenny picked up her sewing again. They had learned early on that Bill Brainerd moved at his own speed.

'Big excitement over there,' Bill went on.

'That so?' Lee said, taking a sip of whisky.

'You know Georgie Curry?'

'Know of him,' Lee said. 'Pa knows him better.'

'He's busier'n a hen drinkin' a can o' paint,' Bill said. 'Seems like the Governor called for volunteers for a cavalry regiment, an' George has already set up a recruitin' office.'

'He's got a commission?'

'Reckons it's a foregone conclusion,' Bill said. 'You know George, you know he's pretty damn' pleased with hisself, most o' the time.'

Lee looked at his wife, and she smiled, laying aside the sewing.

'You want to go,' she said.

'Jen – ' he began. He wanted to tell her what he felt, what it was like to be Army born, Army bred, that it was the family tradition always to answer the call to arms.

'You don't have to say it,' she said, laying her hand on his arm. 'You forget, my darling, I'm an Army brat myself.'

178

'You're the most beautiful damned Army brat I ever saw,' Lee said. He got up out of his chair and took her in his arms and kissed her.

'Lee!' she protested.

'Hell, Bill's seen a pretty girl get kissed before, haven't you, Bill?'

'Kissed a couple m'self,' Bill grinned.

'When will you go?' Jenny said, looking into her husband's eyes and hoping that none of the fear was showing. She knew there would be many times in her life when she would have to watch him go off to some unnamed battlefield in some unknown place, to watch him go and know he might come back sick, or maimed, or never come back at all. Their moments in the sun had been lovely, and all too brief. But never for one moment had Jenny deceived herself into believing that her man's rift with the Army was anything other than temporary.

He was Army.

And that was that.

'I'll wire Gilly Otero,' Lee said. 'Offer to serve in any capacity he likes. I ought to get a captaincy with any luck.' His thoughts were already running ahead, making the first decisions, forming the outlines of plans. 'I'll go on up to Roswell. See if I can persuade some of the boys to join up with me.'

'I'll come with you,' Jenny said.

'Just to Roswell, Jen,' Lee warned.

'We can talk about that later,' she said. Lee looked at Bill Brainerd. Bill smiled and gave an almost infinitesimal shrug. It was a man-signal: *what can you do with them?*

'Another drink, Bill,' Lee offered.

'Don't b'lieve I will,' Bill said, unhitching his buttock from the porch rail. 'Got to go talk to Connie about goin' up to Roswell. If it's all the same to you.'

'Oh, Bill!' Jenny said. 'You, too?'

'Ma'am,' Bill Brainerd said gravely, 'I been listenin'

179

to my daddy talk about *his* war since I was four years old. Seems to me I'd kinda like to have one of my own to talk about to my kids one day.'

'But who'll run the ranch?' Jenny wanted to know.

'Shucks, Connie can,' the foreman said. 'She mostly does, anyway. Besides, it ain't gonna take long to pacify them dagoes. I reckon we'll be back in time to pick the apples.' He straightened up and gave Lee his best shot at a military salute.

'Permission to leave, Captain?' he said.

'Carry on,' Lee grinned. He turned to see Jenny watching him. Her hands were on her hips, her arms akimbo, and there was a not altogether assumed touch of exasperation in her eyes.

'Come inside, you,' she said. 'I want to talk to you.'

'We can talk out here,' he protested.

'What I want to say can't be said standing up,' she said. The exasperation was gone; a bold challenge had replaced it.

'That's different,' he said, and followed her in.

21

It was cold now, as dawn broke.

In the first grey-green moments of the day, the waters of the bay were almost still. Off to the left, floating in mists the colour of smoke, a jungled peninsula rose sharply to two thousand feet, the broken summits betraying their volcanic origin.

Bataan.

George Dewey felt the cold tea he had drunk earlier lying like mud in his belly. Don't let me be sick, he prayed, to no one in particular. Everything had been perfect thus far. They had left Mirs Bay on April 27, two days after the formal announcement of war with Spain, and arrived off Manila at midnight on the thirtieth.

'Keep her at eight knots!' he said.

'Eight knots, aye!' came the reply.

The fleet moved forward, *Olympia* in the van. From the peak of every vessel floated the largest regulation ensigns being displayed. After *Olympia* came *Baltimore*, *Raleigh*, *Petrel*, *Concord* and *Boston*.

The sky lightened shortly before five, and the fleet was sighted by the shore batteries, which opened up with a thundering rumble. Shells trundled overhead like passing freight trains, and huge towers of water erupted behind and between the moving ships. *Concord* replied, but Dewey stopped her after two shots. They had not come to make war on civilians.

At 5.06, *Olympia* shook from stem to stern as the first

of the submarine mines exploded. The helmsman, a tall young fellow with straight black hair and boyish features, looked nervously at the Commodore.

'Steady as she goes!' Dewey said. 'Steady, now!'

'There they are, Commodore!' Stickney shouted. 'There's the Spanish fleet!'

They were moored just outside a point of low land, which reached out like a lobster's claw to protect the inner anchorage of Cavite Bay. Most prominently in view was a cream-coloured vessel moored head and stern, with her port battery to seaward.

'Can you make her out, Mr Stickney?' Dewey asked his aide.

'She's the *Castilla*, sir,' Stickney called. 'She's got steam up. They all have!'

They could see them all clearly now: behind the *Castilla*, moving to and fro within the confines of the bay, were the Spanish flagship, *Reina Cristina*, the *Isla de Luzon*, the *Isla de Cuba*, the *Don Juan de Austria*, the *Don Antonio de Ullua*, the *Marques del Duero*, the *General Lezo*, the *Argos*, several torpedo boats and the transport ship *Isla de Mindanao*, which was steaming away at full speed from the scene of the imminent encounter.

'Kindly ask Captain Gridley what the range is,' Dewey said, leaning forward, knuckles white as he held the brass rail of the flying bridge.

'Range six thousand yards, sir, and closing!'

Dewey nodded. Almost as if his nod had been a signal, a puff of pure white smoke burst from the bushes lining the red clay shore ahead, contrasting starkly with the bright green foliage. The shell screamed over the advancing American fleet to splash ineffectually half a mile behind them.

Now the gunners on the *Reina Cristina* opened up. They overcorrected their elevation, and the shells fell well ahead of the *Olympia*, although one or two of them passed between her masts on the rebound from the water. One by one all the other Spanish ships began to fire, and the sound of the cannonade became one long rolling thunder of sound.

Still Dewey gave no sign. He watched the roiling smoke of the shore batteries and the battleships ahead of him as if they were a firework display, and no more dangerous. The shells whistled and roared overhead, turning the water of the bay into a maelstrom. Dewey took the grey travelling-cap from his head and ran his hand through his hair, and as he did, a shell burst directly above him. He flinched automatically, as fragments of shrapnel clattered on to the decks below.

Down there a boatswain's mate, hand on the lockstring of the after five-inch gun, sprang up and shouted 'Remember the *Maine*, boys! Remember the *Maine*!'

There were two hundred men tensely standing by their guns. Every one of them took off his hat and cheered. The hoarse shouting was repeated in the turrets and fire rooms and throughout the battle-ready decks of the ship.

Dewey took out his watch and looked at it. The time was 5.41 a.m.

'You may fire when you are ready, Captain Gridley!' he said.

'Fire when ready, aye!'

The first gun to fire was the starboard eight-incher, and within moments the entire fleet was engaged, the huge guns hurling shell after 250-pound shell towards the smoke-wreathed Spanish ships two and a half miles away. Shells screamed towards the American vessels in an awful iron shower; above them, time-shells burst, scattering red hot fragments of metal, which hissed in the churning sea, or rattled on the decks, cutting rigging, holing lifeboats. Near the wardroom of the *Olympia*, a shell fragment cut the signal halyards from the hands of Lieutenant Brumby as he stood on the after bridge. Another gouged a hole the size of a football in the deck; still another rattled against the bridge railing.

On *Baltimore*, eight men were wounded when a shell ripped up the main deck, disabled a six-inch gun, and exploded some three-pounder shells. *Boston* was hit and set afire, and a shell passed directly through her foremast. The fire was quickly extinguished, while *Boston* continued to hurl shells towards the Spaniards.

'When the devil is he going to give it to them properly?' a smoke-stained ensign muttered on the deck of *Baltimore*. 'How long's he going to wait?'

'What's your range, Captain Gridley?' Dewey shouted.

'Four thousand yards, sir!'

'Very good,' Dewey said. 'Helmsman, bring her to starboard. We'll go broadside!'

'Starboard, aye!'

'That's it, that's it, a touch more, hold her on two twenty!'

'Two twenty it is, sir!'

'Right,' Dewey said. He rubbed his hands together briskly. 'Open up with all guns!'

After two and a half hours, the two fleets disengaged, great giants exhausted by hurling thunderbolts. Dewey's gunnery officers reported to him that *Olympia* had insufficient ammunition for another two hours' fighting. *Baltimore* was much better fixed: he gave the order for her to take the lead.

At 10.50 the signal for close action was hoisted again. At 11.16 *Baltimore* began firing at the Spanish ships, making a series of hits as if at target practice. *Olympia* followed, the other battleships behind her as before. The *Castilla* was burning fiercely, and the *Reina Cristina*, whose magazines had exploded, was sinking. Dewey now signalled the smaller ships, *Raleigh*, *Petrel* and *Concord* to go into the harbour and destroy the rest of the Spanish fleet at close range.

He had long since thrown up the cold tea that had been his breakfast. He surveyed the blazing ships in Cavite harbour with red-rimmed eyes. Seamen were leaping into the water from the blazing ships. Even as he watched, the *Don Antonio de Ulloa* lurched over and began to sink.

'Signal to disengage!' he shouted to the flag officer.

'Disengage, aye!'

He saw the white flag being run up the flagpole over the Spanish arsenal ashore, and heard the ragged cheers of his men. Sirens and foghorns sounded across the bay from the American ships. It was all over. They had won.

He felt damnably tired. I wonder what happened to my uniform cap? he thought.

22

Laura Moffatt wished she could stay in San Francisco
for ever, to shop for her clothes at the City of Paris, to
browse over the books and magazines in Zellerbachs, to
wander through Gump's on Market Street looking at
French figurines and other imported antiques, or
meander through the markets, to buy fish or vegetables,
or pumpernickel bread at the New Era German Bakery.
After the drab sameness of life at Omaha Barracks, San
Francisco was like a paradise, and she blessed each day
the chance that had put her husband and Elwell Otis in
the same law school in Harvard.

After fifteen years of unsung and unspectacular
service in a succession of equally unsung and
unspectacular Army posts, Laura had begged her
husband's old college chum to get him a decent
appointment. Ellie had got Whittier into the then brand-
new School of Application for Infantry and Cavalry –
the officers' training school – at Fort Leavenworth. For
the first time in years, Laura found herself near a decent-
sized town where you could buy civilised food and
halfway fashionable clothes. Such things were important to her. For a while, Kansas City satisfied the
craving inside her for new places, for an excitement she
only vaguely recognised she needed. There was an
unrealised yearning in her to become celebrated, as, for
instance, Libby Custer had always been. But Laura
knew perfectly well that her husband was not and never
would be 'Army', the way the dashing, glamourous

Custer had been. Whittier was a desk soldier. He lacked imagination. Most importantly, he had never gone to the Academy, and Laura was sure, although she did not pretend to understand how it worked, that having gone to West Point was the way to the top in the Army. The Academy officers got the best postings; men like Whittier got whatever was left. Worst of all was that her husband had no 'push'. He was punctilious and severe, he was fastidious and vain, but he had no gumption. After Leavenworth, determined never again to spend years drying out like a prune in some God-forsaken frontier sink-hole, Laura Moffatt took her husband's career in hand. In future his postings would be a matter for mutual discussion and decision she told him. In other words, she would decide, for Whittier Moffatt was as indecisive as hiccups.

On Monday, April 25, 1898, President McKinley sent his message requesting Congress to pass a resolution declaring that a state of war existed between the United States and Spain. Congress immediately acquiesced. Doubt no longer remained. America was at war.

Volunteers flocked to the recruiting booths in thousands to answer the President's call. The Navy was blockading Cuba. Commodore Dewey and the Pacific Squadron were en route for Manila, to crush any portion of the Spanish fleet which might be there. The nation was aflame with the martial spirit. On May 4, McKinley authorised the Commanding General of the Army, Nelson A. Miles, to assemble troops for the invasion of the Philippine Islands. Miles organised the Philippine Expedition Force from three infantry and three artillery battalions, a total of five thousand men. Command of this force, Eight Corps, was given to a sixty-two-year-old veteran of the Civil War, Major-General Wesley Merritt. He had been one of the famous 'boy generals' like Custer, breveted six times for gallantry in the field.

'West Point, of course,' Laura Moffatt observed acidly.

'He's said to be a fine soldier, my dear,' Whittier said, looking up from his newspaper. 'Anyway, he won't have the command for long. Ellie Otis is going to take over, so I'm told.'

'In the Philippines?'

'It's only a rumour.'

Laura went to the bookshelf and got down the atlas. She knew nothing about the Philippines – who did, for Heaven's sake? The map had dotted lines connecting the great Pacific ports with each other, the distances in tiny numerals. San Francisco to Honolulu was 2,090 miles. Honolulu to Manila was another 4,760. Seven thousand miles! The names stirred her imagination: Mindanao, Luzon. She turned to the back pages, where the vital statistics of each country were shown. 7,083 islands, she read, 4,000 of which have no name. Area about the same as the British Isles, 1,152 miles from north to south. 87 dialects, the major ones being Tagalog, Visayan, Bicol, Pampango and Pangasinan. Most educated people and many natives speak Spanish. Hot season March to June. Rainy season July to October. November to March cool and fairly dry. Industries sugar cane, pineapples, tobacco, rice. There were volcanoes, jungle! It sounded exotic, sensuous, exciting.

Laura wrote to Elwell Otis that very night.

The transfer to California was the best thing that had happened to Laura in a decade. She did not care that her husband was working eighteen hours a day to effect the expedition which Congress had decreed. She had San Francisco all to herself. If that meant she had to put up with Whittier's grumbles, it was well worth it. What did she care that there was no plan of mobilisation, no higher organisation, no provision for the assembling or transportation of an overseas expedition? The longer it took Merritt and his staff to draw up the plan, create the organisation, assemble and transport the Corps to Manila, the longer Laura Moffatt would have. To be in San Francisco. And to be with the man she had been in

188

love with, all those years ago in Baltimore.

Billy Priestman.

They met at a glittering gala, held in the world-famous Grand Court of the Palace Hotel to welcome General Merritt to the city. There was a sumptuous dinner – a banquet was the only word to describe it – with cuisine by Raphael Weill. After the banquet there were the usual speeches. She sat through them, as she had sat through less grand functions, half listening to the words being spoken, most of her attention on the clothes and jewellery of the women sitting around her. Layers of cigar smoke eddied upwards and swirled around the three hundred gas lights which illuminated the scene. Later, the band of the 14th Infantry would play and there would be dancing. Laura was not looking forward to the dancing. Most of Whittier's friends were as old and as clumsy as he was, and all of them were elephantinely gallant. Not a few of them breathed stertorously in her ear and pressed their lower parts against her body while dancing. She permitted herself a slight shudder of disgust. There had been none of that nonsense with Whittier from the day she brought Jennifer home from the Army hospital. They slept in separate beds. He had never questioned her decision, which Laura knew was the right one. Men were animals if you allowed them to be.

The tall, dignified Merritt was speaking now. He was telling his glittering audience that the war would change many things, that old men like himself would at last be kicked aside to make way for good, new, young officers who would get the kind of experience only to be found on the battlefield. Laura let her attention and her eyes wander, lingering briefly on the hulking form of Elwell Otis. Why doesn't he have those awful side-whiskers trimmed? she wondered. Next to Otis sat an elderly woman wearing an outrageous crimson dress, cut sufficiently low at the neck to display a positively vulgar diamond necklace that had probably cost thousands at

189

Shreve & Co. Diamond earrings, too, Laura noted, and a bracelet as showy as the necklace. I wonder who she is? Laura thought. Someone pretty high up the social ladder, if she can get away with a dress like that at a party like this. Her glance touched the face of the man sitting next to the lady in red, moved on, returned.

Is it? she thought. She felt a flush touch her cheeks, and for a moment the room swam before her eyes. Could it be?

It was him.

Billy.

She had been in Baltimore, at Miss Rathbone's Academy on Mulberry Street, and he had been a student at the University hospital. She remembered him as he had been then, a good-looking boy with brown hair and shy brown eyes. The man he had become looked unhappy and unwell, with deep frown lines between his eyes. How old would he be now? Over sixty, she remembered. She joined in the applause as General Merritt finished speaking, and turned to the man sitting on her right, a San Franciscan named Livingston who had bored her all evening talking about his clothing store on Polk Street, and his success in persuading people to wear the new-fangled ready-to-wear clothes that were all the rage.

'Who is that man?' she asked. 'The one sitting next to the lady in the red dress?'

'That's Billy Priestman,' he said.

'And the lady. Is that his wife?'

'Bless my soul, ma'am, no it's not!' Livingston smiled. 'That's Agnes Fothergill. Related to the Coits.'

I was right, then, Laura thought. Anyone related to the Coits was high in the San Francisco pecking order.

'Which one is Mrs Priestman?' she asked.

'Ain't one,' Livingston told her. 'Mrs P. died, oh, ten years ago. Billy lives alone. Got a great big place up on Nob Hill. Well, he can afford it!'

'He's rich?'

'As Croesus,' Livingston said, a note of envy in his voice. 'Made millions from the Nevada mines. Millions!'

'Perhaps you'd introduce me,' she said. 'Later?'

'Be glad to, ma'am,' Livingston said. 'Glad to.'

Billy did not recognise her at first, and treated her with puzzled courtesy, his demeanour that of a man waiting for the earliest opportunity to get away. Laura managed to keep his attention until Livingston saw someone he wanted to speak to, and moved away.

'You don't remember me, do you?' she said, almost shyly. Billy's eyes sharpened for a moment, and he frowned. There was no reason on earth for him to recognise her, she thought. She must have altered over the years. She could see the changes in him.

'I'm Laura Hibbert,' she said softly.

'Laura Hib –?' The frown remained, and then all at once it cleared, like dark clouds blowing away to let through sunshine. He looked much more like the boy she remembered when he smiled. 'Laura Hibbert!' he said. 'I can't believe it!' He shook his head in disbelief.

'How are you, Billy?'

'What happened to you?' he said. 'Where have you been all these years? Why didn't you –?'

He stopped, and they both laughed self-consciously.

'Thirty years,' she said.

'Thirty-five,' he corrected her.

'What happened to us, Billy?' she said, her voice gentled by long-ago memories. 'We were so much in love.'

'We were just kids,' he said. 'It was wartime. Things happen, Laura. Can I call you Laura? I don't know what your name is now. You're married, of course?'

'My name is Moffatt. My husband is a soldier. He's on General Merritt's staff. I'll introduce you –'

'No,' Billy said. 'I'd rather not meet him.'

They were silent for a moment as a waiter brought cognac on a silver tray. Billy took a glass, and they waited until the man was out of earshot.

'You just – disappeared,' Laura said. 'I looked for you at the hospital. Everywhere. Nobody knew where you'd gone.'

'I was sent to Gettysburg. After the battle. There weren't enough doctors. They needed anyone they could get. Even students. When I got back to Baltimore, you'd gone.'

'My parents found out about . . . about us,' Laura said, plunging. 'They came and took me away. We went on the Grand Tour. Me and my broken heart.'

And I made a vow never to let anyone ever again hurt me the way you did, she thought.

'Was that when you met your . . . husband?'

'When I came back. His name is Whittier Moffatt. Brevet Brigadier–General.'

'I'm impressed,' Billy said.

'Tell me about you.'

'It's a long story.'

'I want to hear it.'

'Have lunch with me tomorrow,' he said.

'Oh, I – I couldn't do that,' she replied, flustered by his directness.

'Supper, then?' he said. 'Or lunch the next day. Dammit, Laura, I'm not trying to seduce you!'

She laughed, realising that it was a long time since she had so spontaneously done so. Billy was right. What possible harm could there be in two old, old friends, who had not seen each other for more than thirty years, having lunch together?

'I'd love to have lunch with you,' she smiled.

'Capital!' Billy said. 'I'll take you to Marchand's.'

They had their lunch, and then another, and then another. They had lobster at Delmonico's, pheasant in the splendid dining-room of the Palace Hotel. They ate at Maison Riche and the Maison d'Orée and the Sutro Castle Cliff House. They walked for hours afterwards in Golden Gate Park among the cyclists and the dog-carts and the stylish gentry in their fashionable carriages, and they had tea in the beautiful Japanese Tea Garden with its kimono-clad waitresses and tinkling miniature waterfall.

They talked and talked and talked.

Billy told Laura about his daughter's death, and Catherine's soon after. He told her about his son, William, the newspaper tycoon, who was even now making plans to go to Cuba and publish a newspaper right where the war was happening. She told him of her life in the Army, the places she had seen, the birth of her daughter.

'Only one child?' Billy asked.

'Only one,' Laura nodded. She had never wanted another after that ordeal. 'Her name is Jennifer.'

'Is she with you in San Francisco?'

'No, she lives in New Mexico with her husband.'

'A rancher?'

'His name is Starr.'

'Any relation to a man named James Starr?'

'His son,' Laura said. 'Do you know him?'

'I know James Starr,' Billy said, and she saw hatred glowing in his eyes. Without knowing why she told Billy the story of her husband's confrontation with Lee, and their daughter's subsequent elopement.

'One day I intend to make that young man bitterly regret turning my daughter against me,' Laura finished. 'If I could find some way to – ' She stopped, aware that Billy was watching her closely. Her emotions warred within her. All her life Laura had kept her passions to herself, never showing dislike, never permitting herself any kind of outburst. She always found a way to repay slights, to obtain redress. She plotted revenge the way chess-players plan their games. Revenge, said the Spanish proverb, was a dish best eaten cold. Laura never forgot that. Yet now, every instinct cried out in her to confide in Billy Priestman. It was astonishing: she had not really known him for more than three weeks, yet already she felt closer to him than to any other man she had ever met. Like a flood sweeping over her came the realisation that she wanted, she *needed* someone to be close to. Who better than the man she had once loved, the man who she could . . . She closed off the thought. She would not permit herself such folly. Billy was still watching her.

'You're a good hater, Laura,' he observed. 'Like me.'

'Yes,' she said slowly. 'I am a good hater.'

'We're like each other,' he said. 'Maybe that's why we get along so well.'

She smiled and laid a hand on his arm. 'Dear Billy,' she said softly. 'You have made San Francisco such a wonderful experience for me. I'll never forget it, never.'

'You could . . . stay,' he said, looking away as though what he had just said was entirely inconsequential. Laura felt as though someone had taken all the breath out of her body.

'You must not say such things,' she whispered.

'I'm rich,' he said. 'And I'm lonely. I haven't enjoyed myself like this for years. Seems a damned shame to end it, that's all.'

'Too late,' Laura said, very softly. She felt girlish, loved, almost disappointed that he had not pressed her harder, while simultaneously glad that he had not. 'Let's just be friends. Could we? Very close, intimate friends?'

Billy found her hand and squeezed it gently, then kissed her forehead. 'Dear Laura,' he said. 'If that is your wish . . . so be it.'

She sighed, and he thought, *stupid bitch, she's swallowed it.* In Laura Moffatt God had put a weapon into his hands with which to smite the Starrs yet again. It was well worth playing up to the woman to get that. He'd have played stage door Johnnie to a Barbary Coast drab, let alone this posturing simpleton. He half listened as she talked about her daughter's letters, and how Lee Starr was planning to go to Cuba with Roosevelt's volunteers.

'If there was some way of breaking up that marriage,' Laura said, 'I'd do it tomorrow!'

'Perhaps we can find a way,' he said.

'Do you think so, Billy?' she said, looking into his eyes.

'You just leave it all to me,' he said.

She sighed and leaned her head against his shoulder. *Stupid bitch*, he thought again.

BOOK THREE

WAR

23

'I been in some fuck–ups,' Bill Brainerd said, as the *Yucatan* finally weighed anchor and began to move across Tampa Bay. 'But this is the fucked–uppest fuck–up I ever saw. Beggin' the Captain's pardon.'

He had a point, Lee thought. Getting the Army out of the makeshift barracks at Tampa and on to the flotilla of thirty-two ships had been an exercise in chaos. Come to think of it, the raising of the expeditionary force to go to Cuba had been an exercise in chaos right from the start.

He and Brainerd recruited forty men in Roswell, and took them to Santa Fé, where they were mustered–in. New Mexico raised five troops of volunteer cavalry, which would form one of eight squadrons making up the 1st Volunteer US Cavalry regiment. Some of the men's wives came to see them off. It was a sparkling May morning. Crowds surged around them as they marched to the depôt. Bands played. There were brave smiles, a few tears.

'Wish me luck,' the men said.
'Look after yourself,' the women said.
'We'll be back before you know it.'
'I'll miss you.'

Then the goodbyes and the kisses and the cheers and the shouts and the band playing were drowned by the shrill blast of the engine whistle, signalling departure. The women clung to the men for one last embrace, one final kiss. The train began to move. Watching the faces of the women, Lee was glad that he had persuaded

Jenny to stay at the ranch with Connie Brainerd.

They travelled up over Raton and across to Dodge City, Kansas. There was little to eat: hard tack, some canned beef, coffee. The quartermaster had no funds yet. It did not bother the men. They were in good spirits. They played a lot of poker, drank, told stories, slept fitfully as the train trundled southwards towards San Antonio. There was a festive mood aboard, as if they were going to a party.

Some party, Lee thought.

When they got to San Antonio they unloaded the horses and saddled up. On Commerce Street they saw a man tacking a sign to a streetcar. TAKE THIS CAR FOR THE EXPOSITION GROUNDS WHERE ROOSEVELT'S ROUGH RIDERS ARE CAMPED.

'That us?' Brainerd asked. '"Rough Riders"?'

'I guess it must be,' Lee said.

'Rough Riders,' Brainerd repeated, disgust in his voice. They rode across town to the encampment. They found the Arizona Squadron had preceded them by a day. Their railroad cars already sported signs proclaiming them 'Wood's Woolies'. Colonel Leonard Wood was the commander of the regiment. Some of the troops from Indian Territory had signs that read 'Roosevelt's Cowboys'. Lieutenant-Colonel Theodore Roosevelt, the former Assistant Secretary of the Navy, was Wood's deputy. Since Wood was in Washington, making sure that his regiment got the best possible equipment, Roosevelt was in command.

They slept on benches or on the ground for two nights until their equipment arrived. Lee spent the waiting-time looking around the town. He was especially interested in the ruined Alamo, scene of a battle about which he had heard stories all his life. His Spanish grandfather had actually fought in it.

A few days later they were issued with uniforms, tents and other accoutrements. Colonel Wood had obviously been successful in Washington: they were

200

among the élite few equipped with the new Krag-Jørgensen carbine.

Next day horses arrived for the enlisted men.

Drilling commenced. Chaos ensued.

It was immediately clear that Colonel Roosevelt knew a lot of things about a lot of things, but he didn't know shit about drilling. In short order, he retired, leaving the duty to Major Alex Brodie. Roosevelt's ignorance of basic drill formations perturbed Lee, who had always made a point of studying his commanding officers. Both his father and Uncle Andrew, when speaking of their own field experiences, had always insisted upon the importance of having confidence in your superiors.

'Man who's going to die carrying out someone's orders,' James said, 'has to be sure the fellow who gave them isn't a jackass.' They told stories of volunteer regiments in the War – there had only ever been the one, as far as they were concerned – whose colonels, elected by the men they were to lead, 'had no more conception of battle conditions than a chipmunk. The price of their learning was the slaughter of the men who had elected them.

Of Colonel Leonard Wood, Lee had few doubts, even though Wood had come into the Army by the back door, as it were. He was a graduate of Harvard Medical School who had become a civilian contract surgeon with the Army, distinguishing himself in the Geronimo campaign, in which he won a Medal of Honour. Lee's one reservation was that Wood had received the colonelcy of the regiment through his friendship with Roosevelt and some other prominent Republican politicians.

Roosevelt was another matter. He was a politician, turned soldier for reasons yet to be discovered. Fame, glory, prestige? The son of a well-to-do New York merchant, Roosevelt had been a weak and sickly child plagued by asthma and poor sight. He had toughened

201

himself up with strenuous exercise, ranching in the Dakotas, hunting in the wilderness. It was as if he was always looking for a chance to show off.

'He would have been in a dozen duels if this had been a time for fighting them,' Uncle Andrew said of him. 'It's as if he's addicted to adrenaline.'

Maybe he was, Lee thought, but he wondered whether inside the boom-bang balloon front Roosevelt presented to the world there might not be a scared little boy hiding. If there was, he concluded, Roosevelt was doing a hell of a job hiding him.

On May 29 the regiment left San Antonio by train for Tampa, Florida. It was a long, hot, unpleasant journey of some eleven hundred miles, every one of them sweaty, humid and uncomfortable. Squalls of rain lashed the slow-moving train.

Eighteen miles from Tampa the train was sidetracked by the railroad engineers. They said there was no way of getting the train into Tampa. Everything was jammed solid.

'Usual Army fuck-up,' someone said. 'Hurry up and wait.'

There was no shade worth the name; the horses in the slatted cattle-cars were suffering badly in the heat. Lee gave orders for the doors to be opened on both sides to let in what faint breeze there was.

'How long do you suppose we'll be held up here?' he asked the engineer. The man looked down from his platform and, while he did not exactly sneer, made it abundantly clear that he had no time for stupid questions.

'You just go back inside an' set, sonny,' he said, spitting close to Lee's feet. 'We'll let you know when it's time to move out.'

'We've been here six hours,' Lee protested. 'Our animals are suffering.'

'You got a chaplain aboard?' the engineer said.

'I'm not sure,' Lee said. 'Why?'

'You could get him to pray,' the engineer replied. The conductor snickered.

'I'll ask you one more time,' Lee said, in his most reasonable tone of voice. 'There's a stockyard a couple of miles up the track. There'll be water there. Can't you just move us that far, so we can water the horses?'

'I told you already, soldier boy!' the engineer said. 'We can't move till we gets *orders* to move. How long's it take for somethin' as simple as that to get into your skull, anyways?'

He looked at his conductor as though expecting applause for slapping down this shave-tail. Lee looked at his first lieutenant and sighed.

'Engineer?' he said.

'What the hell you wuh – wuh-wuh –'

'You know what this is in my hand?'

'It – it's – it's –'

'It's a Colt .45 Army model,' Lee said pleasantly. 'And it's aimed right at your belly.'

'See here –' the conductor began. His mouth kept moving, but no noise emerged when Bill Brainerd turned to face him. Brainerd had no weapon in his hand, nor did he make any threatening movement. But the narrow-faced conductor saw what was in the big man's eyes, and it froze his marrow.

'Get down from there!' Lee snapped. The engineer climbed down warily. His eyes never left the gun in Lee's hand.

'What's your name, mister?' Lee said.

'Patterson,' the engineer answered. 'Harry Patterson. And I'd like to know just what the hell you think you're –'

'Mr Patterson, I'm taking your train,' Lee said. 'Lieutenant Brainerd, get a detail and place these men under arrest. Lock them in the caboose. If they give you any trouble, tie them up!'

'You can't take my train!' Patterson said angrily. He was a beefy, red-faced man of about forty, with heavily freckled skin and gingery hair already thinning at the front.

203

'You just watch me,' Lee said, grinning. 'All right, Lieutenant.'

'Big man,' Patterson sneered. 'Hiding behind a gun.'

Lee looked at him, and then at Brainerd. He shook his head, as if mystified, and without a word, stuck the pistol back into the holster at his belt.

'I'm still taking your train, Patterson,' he said softly. 'Want to try and stop me?'

Patterson glared at him for several long moments, his fingers curling and uncurling. Lee eased his weight on to the balls of his feet and waited.

'Ah,' Patterson said, half turning away. 'To hell.'

'Carry on, Lieutenant,' Lee said, relaxing. Brainerd saluted, grinning, and marched the two men off to the rear. Within another ten minutes Lee had two of his men, Morgan Nelson and Tom Hall of Roswell, moving the train out of the siding.

They watered the horses at the stockyard, saddled up, and rode the rest of the way into Tampa, leaving two men behind to guard the train. News of Lee's encounter with the engineer had obviously spread. The men were cheerful again, telling jokes as they rode along. By the time they reached town, word had already been telegraphed to the Adjutant-General's office by the railroad company. Lee was ordered to report immediately to Colonel Roosevelt.

At close quarters, the man seemed more forbidding, dourer than the genial, hail-fellow-well-met of the parade ground. He was a big man with wide shoulders and a thick throat. The silver oak leaves and the golden initials USV shone on his undress uniform jacket. The usually beaming smile was conspicuously absent. The steel-rimmed glasses glinted as he looked up at Lee.

'Well, Captain,' he said brusquely. 'What the deuce is this all about?'

'Sir?'

'Adjutant-General's made a report on your conduct, sir. I'll read it to you. "Captain Starr's action in commandeering the train blah blah blah an arbitrary and unjustified action calculated to blah blah blah and therefore recommend to Colonel Wood that Captain Starr be severely reprimanded blah blah blah." ' He looked up. 'Anything to say?'

'No, sir,' Lee said.

'Nothing in mitigation?'

'No, sir.'

'Hmm,' Roosevelt said. 'Colonel Wood is presently away from camp. That makes it my responsibility to reprimand you.'

'Yes, sir.' Lee wished he would get on with it.

'Let me say, Captain, that I am surprised,' Roosevelt said, getting up from his camp chair and coming around the table. 'Surprised, and worse, annoyed. Now, why the hell did you wait seven hours before you kicked that damned engineer off the train?'

On June 7, General Shafter abruptly announced that he would sail the following morning at daybreak with such troops as were already on board the transports. All hell immediately broke loose. The eager volunteers literally fought each other to get to the port and on to one of the ships. Embarkation degenerated into a milling shambles. The railroad which connected Port Tampa with the camp was a single track, while at the port itself there was only one ramshackle pier from which men and supplies could board ship. The ships had to enter a canal to get to the pier.

The 9th Infantry stole a wagon from the 6th, leaving them to get to the port the best way they could. The 71st New York stopped a train allocated to the 13th Infantry and commandeered it at bayonet point. The 13th in turn commandeered another empty train and some cattle-cars, rousting an engineer from his bed to drive the wood-burning locomotive they 'liberated'. At 10.30 a.m. on the morning of departure they steamed triumphantly up to the pier, cheering.

In the welter of confusion surrounding embarkation, vital equipment that should have been loaded was left behind, including irreplaceable medical supplies. Batteries were loaded on one vessel, their ammunition on another. Regiments were broken up and scattered on different transports. When Roosevelt tried to get aboard the *Yucatan* he discovered that it had also been allocated to the 71st New York and the 2nd Infantry. When the fur stopped flying, Teddy had his ship, albeit with four companies of the 2nd aboard as well. It was at this juncture that Brainerd made his comment about Army foul-ups, and it was hard to argue with his judgment.

Lee found accommodation for his troop on the upper deck. Those who had blankets or overcoats laid them down wherever they could find space.

'Why couldn't we have bunks, Captain?' one of the men asked. 'There was plenty down below.'

'Go down there four days from now, and ask me again,' Lee said. He had inspected the cramped, foetid, below-decks accommodation, with its slatted pine cots and tiny portholes, and opted for the open air.

It was a good decision.

They had hardly cleared Tampa Bay when word was received aboard Shafter's HQ ship, the *Segurança*, that the Navy had sighted Spanish warships. The transports were diverted to Key West, where they wallowed and sweltered for a week in the muddy, humid June heat. Conditions aboard grew steadily worse. For reasons nobody understood, the Commissary Department had bought little of the canned corned beef which was staple Army fare in the absence of fresh meat, and substituted something they called 'canned roast beef'. It was, in fact, boiled beef, but it looked and tasted like stringy slime. The men hated it worse than any other single thing they had to endure during the voyage and the later campaign.

The boats rolled out of Key West, heading across the

Straits of Florida. Their best speed was around seven knots, often slower. On June 18 they saw the green slopes of Cuba rising out of the horizon. Spirits rose. Men crowded to the rails to get their first look at the enemy coast. The ocean was green-blue. Once in a while they saw dolphins. They were eager to get ashore, see some action.

'First time I was ever on a ship,' they said. 'And I hope to God it's the last.'

In the course of the next day they rounded the harsh, grey terraced flanks of Cape Maysi, with its long finger running into the sea. They found a breeze there, and the ships began to lurch and wallow. Before long the men were crowding to the rails for another reason, and, as is often the case, the seasickness proved infectious. Brainerd and Lee spent a lot of hours holding the bucking bodies of retching troopers as they groaned their hard tack and coffee into the faceless sea.

'Oh, Jesus, Jesus,' one of the lads sobbed. 'How long is this going to last?'

'Just keep on pukin' till you feel somethin' round an' hairy comin' up, son,' Brainerd advised. 'Then hold on to that: it's your asshole.'

Two days later the fleet hove-to off Daiquiri, with the serene and lofty peaks of the Sierra Maestra looming to the north. The landing force was to be two infantry divisions and one dismounted cavalry division, plus two and a half thousand volunteers, including the Rough Riders. Disembarkation was almost as much of a disaster as the loading had been. Some of the ships' captains balked at coming close to shore and the possible fire of Spanish guns. Horses were dropped overboard, whinnying in frantic panic, to swim ashore as best they could. Many swam out to sea and perished. The landing became a brutal tale of lost equipment and drowned animals and injured men. It took five days to get them all ashore. Finally, it was done. Six thousand men were on the beach at Daiquiri with General Lawton, the remainder further along the coast at Siboney with Wheeler.

General Shafter, grossly corpulent, sweating profusely in his woollen uniform and immense white sun helmet, was still aboard the *Segurança*, suffering from fever and recurring gout. He sent orders that the expedition take up strong defensive positions along the coast. 'Fighting Joe' Wheeler, predictably insubordinate, decided to give his cavalrymen something to do, and sent them into the jungle to locate the Spanish defences under the command of Brigadier-General Samuel Young.

'Bring me back a few Spanish onions, Sam!' he bade the Pennsylvanian, and Young promised to try. He advanced from Siboney in two columns, the 1st and 10th Cavalry on the left, Roosevelt's Rough Riders taking the right.

They plunged into the jungle, and into Hell. Between close-growing eucalyptus, bamboo and banyan, matted vines made impenetrable walls. Underfoot lay sharp outcroppings of rock, fibrous undergrowth, flowers and plants of exotic shapes and hues. Animals and insects none of them had ever seen scuttled about. The endless screech of brilliantly plumaged birds echoed around them. Spanish bayonet plants jagged and pulled at them as they passed. To go forward at all was to fight, and to fight was to be exhausted and drenched with sweat, while the inside of the mouth became parched, the tongue swollen with thirst.

All at once, they stumbled on the rearguard of the retreating Spanish army. Lee saw the flashes of rifle-fire amidst the trees and yelled at his men to hit the ground.

Up ahead, Colonel Roosevelt and the skirmishers were caught in column, and Lee saw three or four of the troopers fold silently to the ground. Bullets whacked into tree trunks over their heads or *zapp-zipped* through the close-growing leaves. The damp earth smelled of the grave. Lee got to his knees, pistol in hand.

'D Troop!' he yelled. 'Forward! Fire at will!'

'Come on, boys!' he heard Brainerd yell. 'This way to Santiago!'

The troopers began shouting hoarsely and Lee started forward ahead of them, not looking back. He fired his revolver at the yellow gunflashes up ahead. Whether or not he hit anything or anybody he could not tell. All around he heard the sound of shouting. Branches whipped across his face as he blundered forward, half-blind.

'Keep in line, now, boys, keep in line!' he heard Sergeant Alley shouting. 'Aim low, now! Kneel and fire! That's it, kneel and fire!'

Inch by inch, foot by foot, they advanced through the resisting jungle, firing at phantoms. Once in a while, Lee saw the sprawled body of a Spanish soldier. Some of them lay wounded and bleeding against the boles of great trees. One extended a hand towards Lee as he advanced.

'*Socorro, por favor,*' he said. '*Agua. Agua.*'

'Disarm that man!' Lee shouted to a nearby trooper. 'Then give him some water!'

'Sir!' the trooper shouted, and ran to obey. Lee watched as he kicked the soldier's Mauser rifle to one side, and knelt down to give the man a drink from his canteen. Then the scene was swallowed up in the jungle behind him as he moved forward. All around now he could hear the sound of the other troops advancing. Somewhere up ahead he thought he heard the familiar shout of Colonel Roosevelt. He dashed the sweat from his eyes and grinned. You had to say that for the old turkey-buzzard: at least he led from the front.

All at once the intensity of the Spanish fire ahead increased, and a hail of lead stormed through the trees, tearing down branches, thwacking into the trunks of the big trees, sometimes gouging out great chunks of bark, which went whickering into the gloomy shadows. Still the Americans moved forward. Lee pushed through a stand of close-growing bushes and stopped. To his right he heard a low keening sound, somewhere between a sob and a scream. He pulled the screen of leaves back and saw a young trooper lying face down on the ground.

The boy looked up in panic when he heard Lee's approach. Shame flooded his eyes when he saw the officer's insignia, but he did not move. His eyes were red with weeping. A string of mucus hung from his nose.

'I can't!' he sobbed. 'I can't, I can't!'

Lee squatted on his haunches beside the boy. F Troop, he noted automatically. One of Max Luna's boys.

'Come on, son,' he said. 'You've got to do it.'

The boy shook his head, his face still averted. As he did, another Spanish fusillade rattled through the trees above their heads. The boy gave a little scream and buried his face in the dirt. His toes kicked into the loam and his body squirmed with fear.

'O God, O God, O God, O God,' he mumbled. 'O God, O God, O God.'

'What's your name, soldier?'

The boy sat up. His uniform was covered with leaves and stained with mud, his face swollen with crying. He flinched visibly each time a bullet hummed through the air above them.

'W-W-Woodward, sir,' he gulped. 'Trooper John Woodward, F Troop, 1st Vol – uh!' He flinched again as a bullet slammed into a nearby tree.

'Where you from, Johnny?' Lee asked, acting as if nothing had happened.

'Tularosa, sir,' Woodward said.

'Your family there?'

'Yes, sir,' Woodward said. A faint flush stained his puffy face. He was thinking about his folks back home, of his own shame.

'You think you're the only one that's scared,

trooper?' Lee said, making a gesture that encompassed the jungle, the Spanish forces up ahead, the whole war.

'I can't do it, Captain!' the boy burst out. 'I can't go into that an' get kilt! I just can't do it?'

'Why not?'

'I – just can't, that's all.'

'You just going to wait here?'

'I don't know,' Woodward said. His face grew sullen. 'But I sure as hell ain't goin' anyplace else!'

'Is it because you wet your pants?' Lee said. Woodward flushed beet-red and averted his eyes. There was a long silence, and then he nodded.

'The boys will all laugh at me,' he muttered.

'The hell they will,' Lee said. 'Every man in the regiment will have wet pants by now. There's a creek up ahead, Johnny.'

Johnny Woodward looked at him with shining eyes, hope returning. Maybe nobody would ever know. If *everyone* had wet pants . . .?

'Come on, son,' he said, getting up. 'We got a war to fight.'

Woodward scrambled to his feet, brushing the detritus from his tunic and wiping his nose with the sleeve. He picked up the Krag and checked the breech was clean.

Lee could see him still thinking, maybe it will be all right, maybe no one will ever know.

'Get moving, soldier!' he said brusquely. Woodward snapped him a salute, and Lee returned it. Then Woodward ran off into the trees, rifle ported across his chest. Lee hurried after his own men. A small smile touched his sweaty face. Sure as hell hope there really is a creek somewhere up ahead, he thought.

Within another ten minutes he caught up with Brainerd and the rest of the troop. They plunged down a sharp incline and into a brackish line of almost motionless water. Good luck, Woodward, Lee thought. The sound of Spanish rifle-fire seemed less fierce, and he

211

surmised that they must be pulling back. Then all at once, as they came up the rise on the far side of the creek, the trees thinned out, and they advanced into a huge clearing.

'Pull the line together!' he shouted to the sergeants. 'Move ahead in skirmish order!'

They advanced at a fast walk across the clearing towards the Spanish entrenchments. Perhaps halfway between them and the jungle on the far side, they could see enemy soldiers fleeing into the trees. Standing beneath the American flag planted on the edge of the entrenchments, Lee saw Colonel Roosevelt shouting orders for the advance to halt. Bugles sang recall; the men fell panting to the damp and spongy earth, lungs labouring, exhausted by heat and fatigue and fear. Lee felt the strength drain out of his body like water out of a bath, to be replaced by an enormous inertia.

After a while he limped over to where Bill Brainerd lay sprawled on the ground, his head pillowed on his hat, which he had folded up on a log. The rest of the troop lay scattered all around.

'Captain,' Brainerd said. 'You mind if I don't get up?'

'At ease,' Lee said. 'I'll join you.'

He sank to the ground and sighed. Just walking across the clearing seemed to have taken more out of him than all his exertions during the running fight through the jungle.

'How you feeling?' Brainerd asked, without looking at him.

'All right,' Lee said. 'I thought I'd be scared, but I wasn't.'

'Me either,' Brainerd said. 'Too damned busy, I guess.'

'Uh-huh,' Lee said. Then after a moment: 'Feels good, though.'

'You're damned right.'

'I sure could use a drink.'

'Me, too.'

He wanted to talk about it some more, but an instinct told him not to. All that needed saying had been said.

He had learned how not to be afraid.

The next thing he would have to learn was how to kill. He wondered how he would feel about that.

The rest of the force moved up from Daiquiri, and bivouacs were established on either side of the Aguadores at El Pozo and Los Mangos. Mosquitoes whined over the encampments in clouds, and such food as there was, was dire: sowbelly, and coffee so bad that the men spat it out and said: if this was the best coffee they could get, damned if they wouldn't drink the cook's dishwater, and if this was the cook's dishwater, damned if they wouldn't try the coffee. Even so, El Pozo was infinitely preferable to the beach at Siboney, where land crabs and tarantulas had crawled over them while they slept, and most of the food was spoiled.

Roll-call revealed that they had lost two men, both wounded in the jungle fighting and taken to the divisional hospital. A further eighteen were down with either malaria or dysentery, or both. Word filtered up from Siboney that there were no doctors down at Division, just corps sergeants who had only one kind of pill to give the sick, whatever their illness. Wounded men lay on cots in open tents, their mouths, eyes and nostrils full of flies they were too weak to swat.

Shortly after retreat a young lieutenant brought Lee an invitation to call on General Lawton at Division. Lee found his way to headquarters and presented himself to Lawson's adjutant. He found the stern-looking Ohioan poring over a makeshift map, which had been drawn for him by his scouts. The hissing spirit-lamp cast a yellow glow through the canvas. Lawton smiled as Lee came in and saluted.

'Well, young man, it's good to see you,' he said. 'I heard you were in that little skirmish at Guasimas.'

'Yes, sir.'

'You're with the Rough Riders, I see. Didn't make regular cavalry, then?'

'I did, sir,' Lee said. 'But I resigned my commission.'

'Where was this?'

'Fort Omaha, sir. Sixth Cavalry.'

'Sixth Cavalry,' Lawton mused. 'That would be Whittier Moffatt's regiment, wouldn't it?'

'Yes, sir.'

'Whittier Moffatt, eh?' Lawton said, as if to himself. 'Care to tell me what happened, young man?'

'Perhaps some other time, General,' Lee said. 'With respect. General Moffatt is my father-in-law, you see.'

'I didn't know that,' Lawson said, the curiosity very apparent in his eyes. He was silent for a moment, then shook his shoulders side to side, a most unusual movement. 'Your Colonel,' he said. 'Roosevelt.'

'Yes, sir?'

'What does he think this is, a damned political campaign?' Lawton said. 'I never saw such a headline hogger!'

'Begging the General's pardon,' Lee said. 'I don't think it's Colonel Roosevelt's fault. The newspaper reporters are down on General Shafter. They're going out of their way to give any glory there is to someone else. Colonel Roosevelt . . .'

'Never mind, never mind,' Lawton said testily. 'Called you here to say something. Apologise. Promised your father years ago I'd try and do something for you. Clean went out of my mind. Things might have been different if I'd remembered. So, that's my way of apologising. Except to say that if the day should come when I can do something for you, I want you to get in touch with me. Will you do that?'

'There is something you can do for me right now, sir,' Lee said. 'If you would be so kind.'

'What's that?' Lawton frowned.

'My father always said the worst thing about being in

214

battle is that you never understand what the strategy is, the tactics, the intention of your commanding officers. I wondered if you would tell me, sir.'

Lawton pursed his lips. 'Suppose I were to tell you, and tomorrow you were captured by the Spaniards? They'd know our plan.'

'Would that alter it at all, General?'

'I doubt it,' Lawton smiled. 'General Shafter is not renowned for his flexib – ahem! You will, of course, forget I said that.'

'Of course, General,' Lee grinned.

'Now,' Lawton said. 'The plan. Come around the table and take a look at this map. I'll try to explain it. Over here on the left, is Santiago. Between us and it rise the Spanish defences. The first on Kettle Hill, then behind that on San Juan Hill, and behind that again, Fort Canosa. Their other principal strong point is at El Caney, about three miles north of here. Shafter's plan is for my division to march there and clear the right flank while Kent and Sumner take their divisions along the Santiago road, deploy below San Juan Hill, and wait for me to join them. Then we shall attack the heights in concert.'

'I see,' Lee said. 'How long do you think it will take you to capture El Caney, General?'

'Two hours, three at the most,' Lawton said. 'Then we'll march south to flank Don Diego, and thrash him. Any questions?'

'No General,' Lee said. 'It sounds pretty simple.'

'Let's hope it is, my boy,' Lawton said. He stuck out his hand, and Lee shook it. 'Good luck tomorrow.'

'Thank you, General,' Lee said. 'Good hunting.'

Lawton smiled. 'Look me up in Santiago,' he said. 'I'll buy you a drink.'

Lee saluted, turned on his heel and left. He walked slowly back to the Rough Rider encampment, engrossed in thought. In his mind's eye, he saw the battlefields of morning, thousands of men moving across the ground like deadly ants, killing and being killed, all part of a vast plan of which not more than a couple of hundred of them were aware. And each man was a walking bundle of fears and hopes and dreams, be he American or Spaniard, and any one of them might be the one who made the plan succeed or made it fail, some hero or some coward as yet unknown, burrowed now in blankets to keep the insistent mosquitoes at bay. He looked up at the sullen tropic sky. To his surprise, he realised he was looking forward to the morning.

Lawton's division was in position around El Caney by daybreak, after an all-night march. Sumner and Kent formed their divisions to pass through the dense country along the Aguadores River, and thence through cultivated fields and over high ridges to their goal of San Juan.

That was the plan.

But the plan didn't work.

Lawton could not budge the Spaniards at El Caney. They were well dug in, their resistance more fierce and heroic than any encountered thus far in the fighting. The American artillery was ineffective, and the black powder rifles of the Massachusetts volunteers made them such easy targets for the Spanish Mausers that their line was held only by the arrival of Bates's cavalry brigade. Not until around four in the afternoon, when the Spanish began to run out of ammunition, was any progress made.

Meanwhile, Jacob Kent and Samuel Sumner's divisions took more than six hours to hack their way through the close-growing forests to Las Guamas Creek. In reaching it, they were sitting ducks for the entrenched Spanish soldiers, who laid a murderous fire into the close-packed phalanxes of advancing Americans. An observation balloon, towed along, provided a perfect aiming-in point for the Krupp quick-firing guns on the heights. Discovering a poor road south of the main one, Kent moved troops on to it to speed up the advance and deployment. But the leading regiment, the 71st New York Volunteers, panicked and broke under the savage enfilade coming at them. They threw themselves into the bushes screaming with fear, or simply lay down on the trail and refused to budge. Because of the press of Regulars following them, they could not retreat. No inducement on the face of God's earth could persuade them to go forward into that hailstorm of death. Faces set with contempt, the Regulars of the 9th and 13th Infantry stepped over and past and around the terrified volunteers and kept steadily on, exposed to the same vicious fire from the same, as yet unseen foe. Eventually, the line was established, straggling along the San Juan River, some on the eastern bank, others on the west.

On the far right of this straggling line, the 1st Volunteers lay in skirmish order, with Kettle Hill beyond. They had no idea what was happening elsewhere. The heat was almost tangible. Artillery no longer rumbled behind them. Ammunition was low. No orders came.

Bill Brainerd eased over to where Lee was lying, his field-glasses trained on the crest of the hill. As far as he could make out, the Spanish troops had dug in on the actual crest, not the tactical crest a little below. It was damned poor judgment on some Spanish officer's part, he thought. Troops rising to fire would skyline themselves, giving the Americans silhouetted targets to aim at. Always supposing they got a chance to raise their heads: the stuttering, ceaseless waves of Mauser fire rolled down on them without respite. Any trooper unwise enough to cut loose with his Springfield immediately gave away his position with a balloon of powdersmoke, which drew a vicious enfilading fire.

'How's it look up there?' Brainerd said. His voice was croaky, as if he had a sore throat.

'It's not going to be a day at the beach,' Lee said grimly. Between the fortified Spanish positions on the

217

crest of San Juan Hill and where he lay, rose a smaller hillock, crowned by what, as far as he could see, were small ranch buildings and outhouses. Near them was a huge copper kettle. Probably used for sugar refining, he decided.

'When the hell they going to let us take a crack at it?' Brainerd grumbled. 'Why do we have to squat here doing nothing while them garlics pour it on to us?'

'We'll be moving out soon,' Lee said. 'What time is it?'

'Coming up to one,' Brainerd said, 'and three degrees hotter than Hell.'

A bullet whipped above their heads, and they flinched. The flesh crawled constantly with apprehension – the possibility that somewhere an unseen finger was pulling an unseen trigger, to send a bullet smashing into your body.

'We're gettin' low on ammunition, Captain,' Brainerd said. 'Somebody better say piss or get off of this pot.'

They heard cheering and looked around. Colonel Roosevelt was coming out of the woods on his horse, Little Texas. He wore a campaign hat with a blue polka-dot kerchief tied to it. He looked as if he was going for a canter in Rock Creek Park.

'All right, boys!' he was shouting. 'Let's walk up to the top of this hill!'

He rode off fast. Lee saw Roosevelt's orderly, Henry Bardshar, go running after him. The rest of the men moved more slowly. Coloured troopers from the 9th Infantry, and a sprinkling of 1st Infantry joined them, going up the slight incline towards Kettle Hill. The Spanish fire seemed to redouble in intensity. The men were moving out of cover, cheering. Lee stifled the impulse to call them back: they looked pathetic, doomed. Up on the hill, Roosevelt came up against a wire fence. He leaped off Little Texas and turned him loose, shouting and waving his hat. A trooper on Lee's right knelt and fired up into a tree. A Spanish sniper screamed in agony as the heavy bullet tore upwards through his body. He fell out of the tree like a sack of earth and crashed to the ground.

Now Lee could see the Spanish troops running out of the buildings at the top of Kettle Hill, and the cheering Americans blazing away at them as they ran. Smoke drifted across the slope like October ground mist. Someone planted a guidon on the hill next to the copper kettle. Lee reached the shelter of the bullet-pocked ranch buildings just as the Spanish troops unleashed a murderous mixture of rifle and artillery fire on their position from San Juan Hill.

'Bastards got the range of every damned rock on this fuckin' island!' a panting trooper said, sliding for shelter behind the great kettle. Bullets spanged off it. Shrapnel from the shells exploding overhead whistled and twittered around them.

Off to the left, they could see troops going forward up San Juan Hill. They were moving in bunches, ten here, twenty there, creeping up the sunswept hill. A flaming hail of bullets roared at them from the crest, but still they moved doggedly through the long grass. No drums sounded, no bugles; just the ragged blue line moving slowly up the steep hill, like a ribbon unfolding. The men walked with their rifles ported across their chests, as if they were fording a thigh-deep stream.

'Look at those bastards!' somebody shouted. 'Will you look at those sonsofbitches!'

The men around Lee started cheering as they saw the tall, commanding figure of General Hawkins, readily recognisable because of his white hair and goatee beard, rallying his men. A few moments later they heard the unmistakable sound of the three Gatling guns coming into action. Up on the crest, great chunks of earth flew into the air around the Spanish entrenchments. He saw men clambering out, running in panic.

'Look at them coffee-grinders givin' it to the dagoes!' someone yelled. The troops were approaching the crest of the hill. Lee glanced around, looking for the familiar figure of Teddy Roosevelt. He saw the Colonel waving his hat and shouting hoarsely, his words lost in the rippling thunder of the rifle volleys. Roosevelt started forward at a run, stopped, came back. No one was following him. He shouted again. Lee heard some of the words this time, snatches between the thunderous roar of the Mauser fire now enveloping the crest of San Juan Hill.

'. . . up the hill . . . next line of trenches . . . on the command . . .'

'All right, men!' Lee shouted, scrambling to his feet. 'Let's move on up the hill!'

He heard the warm whip of bullets as he moved forward, slipping and scrambling on the greasy grass. Up ahead was a line of palm trees. The skirmishers raked their foliage with bullets, but there were no guerillas up there. Rough Riders, white regulars and coloured, they all went forward together, shouting, firing as they ran. They saw Spanish soldiers jumping up out of the trenches and running to the rear, and they cheered as they pursued them.

'Kneel and fire!' Lee shouted to the men nearest him. 'Pick your targets!'

The Krags snapped spitefully all along the line. He saw Spanish soldiers throw up their arms and tumble back off the skyline. He risked a look around. His men and the regulars were scattered all along the right flank of San Juan Hill. Up ahead, he could see Roosevelt, waving his campaign hat. He was shouting something, but again it was lost in the rattle of small-arms fire. Crazy man, Lee thought, it's a wonder he hasn't been shot twenty times. If the Spaniards knew who he was . . .

'How you doin', Captain?' he heard someone shout. He looked around and saw Brainerd grinning at him, ten yards away on the right, slightly downhill. Brainerd looked stiff and uneasy, like a man who knows there is quicksand nearby. To Lee's left, Billy Landrie advanced with the squadron's standard. He lifted his Krag in greeting. The guidon with its crossed sabres and red 'D' flapped in a momentary breath of wind.

The line was coming to the crest now. It was amazing how many American soldiers there seemed to be, all at once. They laid a heavy fire into the packed Spanish trenches ahead. Screaming men tried to climb out, but were shot off their feet and slid back into the culverts. Now the Americans could see that the trenches were filled with dead soldiers in the light blue and white uniform of the Spanish army. An officer stood on the last crest above Lee, shouting at his retreating men, waving a sword. Lee ran at him, his Colt .45 cocked in his hand. The Spanish officer turned, and Lee saw the surprise and fear on his swarthy face. The man lifted a pistol, and the bullet whapped past Lee. He heard someone grunt behind him, and in the same moment he fired his own pistol. The Spanish officer was smashed off his feet by the heavy slug, and fell, dead or dying, half in and half out of the trench. Lee turned to help the man who had been hit by the Spaniard's bullet. There were two or three dead Americans lying nearby, nobody wounded. Young Billy Landrie ran up, his face shining with sweat and pride. All around Lee, cheering American soldiers drove the Spaniards down the steep declivity on the far side of San Juan Hill. Below them, in serried jumble, they could see the red roofs of Santiago, and the dark blue gleam of the harbour beyond.

'Plant that flag where our boys can see it, Billy!' Lee sang out. The boy drove the yellow silk guidon into the earth. Looking up, Lee saw the Stars and Stripes floating above the abandoned Spanish trenches. One by one, his men began straggling in, dusty, sweaty, exhausted, but smiling, all of them smiling.

'Well, Captain, looks like we done her,' said a

familiar voice. Lee felt a rush of relief as he turned to see Bill Brainerd limping down the slope towards him. There was blood on the leg of his pants.

'You hurt, Bill?' he said.

'Just a nick,' Brainerd said. 'I'll live.'

At that moment, they saw Colonel Roosevelt coming along the crest of the hill. They took off their hats and gave him a tired, broken cheer.

It wasn't much, but it was all they had left.

24

By the time Commodore Dewey's Asiatic Squadron had thrashed the Spanish Navy in Manila Bay, Willie Priestman's papers were thundering successes. Three of them were selling over a million copies a day. Willie himself was like a dynamo. The 'splendid little war' he had for so long advocated had come to pass. He had been right, just as he had always known he would be.

'Just takes the damned politicians longer to realise it than it took me,' he told his cronies. He had plenty of cronies now. Membership in all the right clubs, seats in the Diamond Horseshoe. Everyone wanted to be his friend. Just as he'd always said they would. Money and power was all it took. He accepted the fact as he accepted rain. He needed them no more and no less now than he had when they wouldn't speak to him. Willie Priestman didn't need anyone besides Willie Priestman.

He heard that Teddy Roosevelt had resigned as Assistant Secretary of the Navy in order to raise a regiment of volunteers. Willie decided to go him one better. He wrote to President McKinley offering to equip, arm and mount, at his personal expense, a regiment of cavalry to fight in Cuba. What he did not tell McKinley was that he proposed to lead the regiment himself. After all, he was an excellent horseman. What dispatches he could send back from the front line! What stories!

McKinley turned him down.

Willie wasn't particularly upset. Undaunted, he offered to arm his steam yacht *Sunday Girl* and take her down to the Caribbean – provided that he could command her. That offer, too, was graciously declined. Willie became irritated. The President was just being woodenheaded, letting politics get in the way of good sense. The *Inquirer* chain had been all out for Bryan in the election. Willie was a Democrat and McKinley was a Republican, but that shouldn't get in the way when there was a war on. Well, to hell with McKinley and to hell with the men who were advising him, Hanna and that damned soft-voiced Andrew Starr. This was Willie's war and nobody was going to keep him away from it.

'Schofield!' he bellowed.

His chief editor came in fast. He knew Willie's every intonation, and that bellow signalled one thing only: action, now.

'Yessir?'

'I want to charter a boat.'

Schofield didn't blink. He had heard much stranger demands than that from Willie Priestman. He had also learned a long time ago not to ask why.

'How big?' he said.

'Big?' Willie said. 'How the hell do I know how big? Big enough to take thirty or forty people. Machinery. Everything we'd need to print a paper on board.'

'The Navy's commandeering everything that will float,' Schofield said. 'It might take a while.'

'How long? A week, two – what?'

'Ten days,' Schofield said, plunging.

'Make it eight,' Willie said. 'Now get everyone in here. Reporters, rewrite men, artists. I want a conference in half an hour.'

'Right,' Schofield said. 'Anything else?'

'Who makes lightweight printing presses?'

Schofield was stumped. He stuck out his lip, spread his arms and raised his shoulders.

'Find out,' Willie said. 'Fast. I want two lightweight

presses, but big enough to turn out special editions. I want enough men to write the stories, and enough comps to set them. We'll have to take everything with us: type fonts, ink, formes, stackers. Act just as if we were starting a new paper, Schoey. Everything we'd need. Paper, cutters, everything. Then get it on a ship and we'll get going.'

'We going to Cuba, Chief?'

'Where else, you dumb turkey?' Willie snapped.

Willie got his war.

He got the story of how Hamilton Fish, scion of the upper crust New York family, was killed in the fight at Las Guasimas. He got the story of Kent's blundering before the battle for San Juan Hill, and printed it. He wrote eulogies on the death of Colonel Charles Wikoff, killed directing the 13th Infantry to their positions past the cowering soldiers of the 71st New York, who simply lay down and refused to advance into the Spanish fire. He wrote another for Lieutenant Jules Garesche Ord, killed at the very moment that his men carried the crest of San Juan Hill. He printed his newspaper with boiler plate and original copy, distributing it free to the men in the trenches. His easily recognisable figure was very soon familiar all around the front. The horse he rode was not big, but Willie was: his feet dangled down well below the animal's belly. He wore a black suit and a jaunty flat-brimmed skimmer with a scarlet band and a scarlet tie to match.

On July 3, the Spanish fleet, bottled up in Santiago harbour, steamed out in battle array to meet head-on the waiting American fleet. Nobody had expected it: certainly not the naval officer commanding, Admiral William T. Sampson, who had sent the battleships *Suwanee* and *Massachusetts* to Guantánamo to refuel, and was himself en route to Daiquiri aboard the *New York*, accompanied by *Hist* and *Ericsson*. At exactly thirty-one minutes past nine o'clock in the morning, the general alarm rang. Aboard the *Maria Teresa*, Captain Victor Concas y Palau asked permission of Admiral Pascual Cervera y Topere to open fire; receiving it, he ordered bugles blown to signal the beginning of the battle. Aboard *Brooklyn*, Commodore Winfield Scott Schley, commanding in Admiral Sampson's absence, rushed to the platform he had constructed around the conning tower, joined by Captain Francis A. Cook. As they reached it, the navigator, Lieutenant Hodgson, sang out a warning.

'Commodore, they're coming right for us!'

'Well,' Schley yelled back. 'Go right for them!'

The Spanish ships were all out of the harbour now: *Maria Teresa* in the lead, followed by *Vizcaya*, *Colon*, *Oquendo*, *Furor* and *Pluton*. They steamed west along the coast as the mighty guns on the American ships volleyed and thundered.

Behind the American squadron, already beginning to spread out as the Spaniards moved westwards at thirteen knots, forged a second fleet, that of the press boats, tearing along in a frenzy of excitement.

Willie Priestman was on the bridge of his own boat, rushing from side to side like a madman, trying to see through the roiling clouds of smoke that lay on the water like fog as the giant ships battered away at each other.

'What the hell is going on?' he kept shouting. 'Can anybody see what's going on?'

'There goes the *Gloucester*!' somebody yelled. Willie rushed to the starboard wing of the bridge as J.P. Morgan's yacht, in peacetime called *Corsair*, rushed off towards the mouth of the harbour, Old Glory snapping at the masthead. Plumes of water lifted from the sea as shells from enemy destroyers she was pursuing fell around her.

'Damn my eyes, she'll be sunk by our own ships!' Willie howled. 'She's going right under their fire!'

The rapid fire batteries of the *Indiana, Iowa* and *Oregon* were wreaking havoc on the small Spanish ships. All at once a great column of steam fringed with coal dust, spouted a hundred and fifty feet in the air as *Pluton's* boiler exploded. *Gloucester* swung her attention to the second destroyer, concentrating all her fire on *Furor*. They were no more than six hundred yards apart when *Pluton* careened against the rocky shore and blew up. As *Furor* turned to face *Gloucester*, she was smashed apart by shells from *New York*, which had come up at full speeed from the east. Willie saw the flags go up on *Gloucester*: 'enemy vessels destroyed'. He heard ragged cheering from the *New York* as she surged through the waves, a bone in her teeth. Admiral Sampson, still wearing the spurs and leggings he had put on to ride to his meeting with General Shafter, was hurrying to join the rest of his squadron. The decks of his flagship trembled with the screw's vibrations.

'Goddammit, the Spaniards are getting away!' Willie shouted. 'They're going to get clean away!'

Most of the American ships had been four or five miles to the south-east at the beginning of the action, and were being left behind. Even *Brooklyn* was well astern of the leading Spanish ship, and *Texas* was already out of it. Only *Oregon* had full steam up, with Admiral Sampson in *New York* far to the rear. It looked like the battle was going to fizzle out. In fact, the Spanish ships were in trouble, although the Americans did not yet know it. There was a fatal weakness in every ship in Cervera's fleet: their decks were made of wood, and all of them were on fire. The *Teresa* was the first to fall out of line, her whole centre a mass of flames, a towering pillar of smoke ascending from her stern. She was beached and abandoned about six miles west of the Morro. A few minutes later, *Oquendo* brought up just beyond her, rolling and staggering like a drunken thing as 'Fighting Bob' Evans of the *Iowa* pounded her to pieces. Her decks and cabins were blazing fore and aft;

there was fire down below. One of her guns burst, wiping out the crew and blinding the gunner. Her interior was a furnace. As she hit the beach, the flames burned away her halliards and the flags came fluttering down. *Gloucester* came up, with the fleet of press boats close astern.

'Don't cheer, boys!' Willie shouted. 'Those poor devils are dying!'

'Maybe we ought to stand in, Captain, and help them?' Schofield said to Captain Holmes, commander of Willie's 'flagship'. Holmes squinted at Willie and moved his sodden cigar from one side of his mouth to the other, saying nothing.

Willie stared into the distance, where the long plumes of smoke marked the location of the American battleships. The roar of guns was now like muted thunder.

'Take her in, Bob,' he said. 'Let's see what we can do for those poor unfortunate bastards.'

He felt daring, apprehensive. If the ammunition magazines blew up . . . There was a tenseness in his throat, a dryness which was not thirst, and little chilly surges in his body that no red flannel belly-warmer would have banished. They put out their boats to rescue the Spanish crews from the fire and from the Cuban insurgents who were waiting to butcher them on the beach when they landed. Doing the best they could for the wounded and the badly burned, the flotilla headed back towards Siboney, while *Gloucester* raced off in the wake of the fleet. By the time Willie got ashore, the great naval battle of Santiago was ended. *Vizcaya* had run for the shore at Aserraderos, where a month before the enormous General Shafter had climbed the hill on a stout-hearted mule. As she touched, the fire inside her rose in a great column above her smokestacks; her ammunition began exploding, and her side plating was literally red hot. Evans came alongside in *Gloucester* to help hoist Captain Eulate overside. He was bleeding

228

from three wounds, his head bound with a bloody kerchief. At about a quarter past one, the last Spanish ship, *Colón*, ran out of steam, and her speed fell off, putting her within range of *Oregon*'s thirteen-inch guns. Commodore Paredes put down his ship's helm, running her hard and fast aground. As a final shell from *Oregon* fell beneath her stern, *Colón* struck her colours. The bugle, all but drowned in the rolling waves of cheers coming from the American ship, sounded 'Cease firing', and the band struck up 'The Star Spangled Banner'.

Willie learned all this later, and it made headlines across the nation, the most joyous Fourth of July since 1863, when beleaguered Washington received the news that Vicksburg had fallen and Lee had been defeated at Gettysburg. When he got to Siboney he knew nothing of the great victory. He was filthy and bone-tired, his clothes torn and blood-spattered. He wanted nothing in the world so much as he wanted to fall on a cot and sleep. But he went instead to his cabin to write what he always thought was the greatest story he ever filed, the rescue of the Spanish sailors off the *Oquendo*.

'You who have never seen war in all its terrible glory [he wrote] cannot conceive what it was like to be there on that day. There, wrecked and burning, lies the great Spanish ship. *Oquendo*, she was called. Nothing now but a great hulk of wrecked iron, glowing with intense heat. Everywhere in the water there are boxes and uniforms, trunks, papers. And here and there, the poor, butchered bodies of the dead. Going alongside, all we could see through the choking smoke was twenty or thirty men crowded on the forecastle or hanging by ropes from her bows, screaming as their bare flesh touched the red-hot iron of the vessel. The burning ship, her plates burst outward the roar of the flames in her belly, the constant explosions of ammunition, the cries of the wretches we were pulling out of the water into our gallant little boats, all these you can only imagine. The water was not too deep, and some of the wounded had collapsed, exhausted or dying, on sandspits between the blazing hulk and the shore. From bushes on the beach, Cuban insurgents had opened fire on them. With a glass I could clearly see the bullets hitting the water near them. Sharks, made ravenous by the blood of the wounded, were attacking from the other side. Soon our boat was filled with crying, groaning, screaming men, terribly mangled, dying. The effect of our shell fire had been terrific. The *Oquendo* was not a ship; she was a slaughter pen.

'This is your war.'

Of course, he never printed it.

Siboney was a shambles. Companies had been brigaded or camped here and there in a helter-skelter pattern over the western section of the town, in rambling lanes, in a foundry, in a machine shop and in storehouses. At the front, on the hard-won crest of San Juan Hill, Fighting Joe Wheeler's division was entrenched. Word was that around four thousand 'garlics' – the American sobriquet for Spanish soldiers – had evaded Calixto Garcia's Cuban force and managed to get into Santiago. The battle itself had simmered down to a siege.

Willie went up to Shafter's headquarters, sited on a creek between La Redonda and Los Mangos. He presented his card to the adjutant. In due course, he was ushered into The Presence. Shafter sat in a wooden revolving chair, his great belly hanging between his thighs, islands of sweat on his pants and shirt. He looked ugly and unhealthy.

'How's the gout, General?' Willie asked.

'Same,' Shafter said abruptly. He had little time for

the press corps at best, and less for such as Willie Priestman. 'What can I do for you?'

'I heard you cabled Washington that you plan to hold your present position.'

'Correct.'

'For how long, General?'

'That I cannot say, Mr Priestman. Until General Toral surrenders.'

'You think that he will?'

'I hope that he will. I am no butcher, sir. The cost of storming the defences of Santiago will be high. Perhaps higher than all we have suffered here so far. I would rather avoid that if it is possible.'

'But General Toral has already rejected your demand for surrender. You must attack, surely?'

'Mr Priestman. You are not a military man. I am. Let me put this to you as simply as possible. The victory of our fleet has removed the only strategic reason for wishing to take Santiago. There is no point in throwing infantry against the city's considerable defences to secure an objective which has ceased to have any military value. It is therefore my intention to try to persuade General Toral to surrender, if I can find a way for him honourably to do so.'

'Should we not, for our own honour, go ahead and attack – and force him to surrender?' Willie said.

A touch of angry colour stained Shafter's cheeks: he knew the implied insult had been aimed at him.

'Bloodshed, Mr Priestman, is a necessary evil,' he said. 'Not a desired end. I'm not here to earn glory by fighting needless battles. I am here to secure the end of the war with the greatest economy of life.'

'The rainy season will be on us at any moment.' Willie observed. 'If you wait too long, you'll either be cut off by hurricanes or wiped out by yellow jack.'

'You cannot imagine that I am unaware of it, sir?' Shafter said.

'So you're going to sit tight and that's all?' Willie said.

'That isn't much to tell my readers, General.'

Shafter turned his head and looked at Willie as he might have looked at a lizard.

'I do not feel the need to justify either my thoughts or my strategy to you, Mr Priestman. Or any other damned newspaper reporter.'

'I'm not a newspaper reporter, General. I'm a newspaper publisher. You'd do well to remember the difference!'

'I don't give a damn what you are!' snapped the short-tempered Shafter. 'I treat all reptiles alike!'

'Shafter,' Willie said, getting up and lifting the tent flap. 'You just made one of the worst mistakes you ever made in your life.'

'Get the hell out of here!' Shafter threw after him. 'And don't be in any hurry to come back!'

After that Willie went for Shafter without mercy. The special pack-trains of three mules that went up to headquarters every day from Colonel Astor's yacht, two mules carrying ice and the other one champagne, were brought to the attention of a sensation-loving public. On July 6, Willie stage-managed the publication of all Shafter's telegrams, aggravating enormously the hostility that already existed between Army and Navy in Cuba, and doing the corpulent Shafter's reputation no good whatsoever. He even contrived, and it was not easy in the surge of celebration which followed it, to infer that most of the credit for the surrender of Santiago, which took place on July 17, belonged not to Shafter but to the newly arrived General Nelson Miles.

But by that time, General William Shafter had other problems on his mind. For with the fall of the city, and the relaxation of the battle tension, malaria and yellow fever swept through the Fifth Army Corps like a forest fire. Santiago de Cuba was a pesthole, full of refugees and half-starved natives who knew not a word of the English language, and had to be forcibly prevented from defecating in the streets. Within four days of the ceremonies of surrender outside the Governor's Palace, the Army's sanitation squads were burning more than five hundred cubic yards of refuse a day, and still not keeping up. In the trenches the men were dropping faster than the corpsmen could carry them down the hill and put them in the wagons bound for Siboney. Sanitation was impossible in the crude shelters and tents clinging to the slope of San Juan Hill. Flies and mosquitoes swarmed in clouds as each day the torrential rains washed half-buried corpses and decomposing mules from their shallow graves. There was hardly a soldier in the Army who wasn't filthy, lousy and sick.

THE TRUTH ABOUT THE CUBAN WAR!!!

AN EXPEDITION PREPARED IN IGNORANCE AND CONDUCTED IN A SERIES OF BLUNDERS

WRETCHED CONDITIONS IN CAMPS

TYPHOID AND MALARIA

HORROR OF THE HOSPITAL SHIPS

WE NAME THE GUILTY MEN!!!

'I want to make it so hot for that fat old fool that he sweats off thirty pounds, Schoey!' Willie told his editorial chief. 'Stick it to him, you hear me? Make the demand to send the soldiers home stronger. Never mind about investigations. Keep on after the pest camps and the horror ships. Keep on about how Shafter's vacillating has brought all this about. That's the way to really hurt the old bastard!'

To tell the truth, he was sick of Shafter, sick of Cuba, sick of the whole goddamned war. It wasn't selling papers any more. Even when Willie put considerable effort into trying to make a hero out of Nelson Miles, and Miles's Puerto Rico campaign as a model of military efficiency, the damned public simply turned their nose up at it. The cost of operating the boats, shipping supplies down from New York, and sending voluminous cables to keep the wheels turning back in the States, was gobbling up enormous chunks of Willie's profits. In addition, dealers were forgetting to cut their orders between battles, so that returns were swamping the warehouses. Yet Willie hated to leave unfinished his feud with Shafter. I'll get that fat bastard before I go, he vowed. But how?

He burned a lot of midnight oil before deciding that the answer was a petition, signed by as many officers and men as could be persuaded to put their names to it. The petition would, boldly and simply, demand that Shafter immediately arrange for replacements to be sent to Cuba, and that the brave men who had won the victory, and were now suffering agonies of privation and illness, be sent home. When it became apparent to the War Department that Shafter was not in command of his Army, but that the Army was giving Shafter orders, he would be finished. Willie went gleefully to work, printing up thousands of petition forms, placards and posters for distribution all over the island. The first parcels were sent out on a Thursday morning. Shortly after noon of that day, a squad of military police marched down to the quay where Willie's boat was moored. They were led by a squat, broken-nosed sergeant who looked as if he could bite pieces out of a cast-iron stove. He came aboard the *Marietta* and informed Willie that he had orders to conduct Willie to General Shafter's headquarters.

'You know who I am, sergeant?' Willie asked.

'Yes, sir,' the sergeant said.

'Then you'll know it's not smart to get on my wrong side. I'm a powerful man, sergeant.'

'Yes, sir,' the sergeant said.

'Very good,' Willie said. 'Now, here's what you do. You go back up to the palace, and tell that fat-arsed old goat that I don't take orders – from him or anyone else!'

'Sorry, sir,' the sergeant said. 'I can't do that. My

234

orders are to bring you up to Headquarters, Mr Priestman. And that's what I plan to do.'

'Then you'll have to drag me there!' Willie snapped.

'We can do that, too,' the sergeant said. 'If you prefer it that way.'

He shifted his feet slightly, and flexed his meaty hands. There was no hostility in his eyes, only a certain curiosity, as if he was wondering how many times he would have to hit Willie before Willie fell down.

'You can't,' Willie did not know whether to be angry or afraid, and came out somewhere between both. 'You wouldn't dare!'

'The General said "Right away" Mr Priestman,' the sergeant said. 'I don't want to keep him waiting.'

Humiliated and angry, Willie got his coat and let them march him to Shafter's headquarters in the Governor's Palace. Shafter, sweating like a bull, his great bulk encased only in shirt and trousers, was standing behind an ornate desk which had once been the property of General José Toral, talking in a torrent of words into a telephone. Couriers and aides constantly dashed up and away down the corridors outside. Shafter looked up as Willie was brought in.

'Mr Priestman,' he said. He looked at the sergeant. Something passed between them, and Shafter smiled. He looked at Willie in that detached, speculative way he had, and rubbed his ear.

'May I sit down?' Willie asked.

'You won't be here long enough,' Shafter said venomously. 'I'm kicking you out of Cuba, Priestman.'

'You can't do that!' Willie said, starting forward and then stopping as Shafter's glare met his own. 'You don't dare do anything so high-handed!'

Shafter contemptuously tossed a copy of Willie's petition on to the desk.

'If you were a soldier, I might have had you shot for that! As it is, you'll be off the island of Cuba within twenty-four hours, Priestman, or I'll put you in jail and

235

throw the key away!'

'I demand that you reconsider!' Willie said. 'I have a right to be here. The public has a right to know –'

Shafter made an impatient gesture. 'The Associated Press office will take care of that,' he said. 'Far better than jackals like you. Goodbye, sir!'

'I won't stand for this! I'll take this right to the top –' The words congealed in Willie's throat as Shafter got slowly to his feet. He was a very big man indeed, weighing around three hundred pounds. His voice was thick with the anger he was struggling to restrain.

'Sergeant!' he said loudly. As if he had been waiting for his cue, the tough-looking MP sergeant reappeared.

'Sah?'

'Escort this . . . gentleman back whence he came,' Shafter said. 'And make sure that he is off the island by noon tomorrow.'

'Very good, sir!'

Shafter looked at Willie, then shook his massive head, like a man convinced he is wasting his time whatever he says.

'Carry on, sergeant,' he said, wearily.

At sunset that evening, Willie Priestman stood on the deck of his ship and watched the squat silhouette of Morro Castle fall astern and gradually disappear below the horizon. He was glad to be leaving the damned place, even though his feud with Shafter had ended so unsatisfactorily. Well, he could take care of that in New York. Already it seemed unimportant. He itched to be back in the States again. He had big things to do.

The New York *Inquirer*
August 9, 1898

SPAIN SURRENDERS!!!!!!!

———

IMMEDIATE CESSATION OF HOSTILITIES AGREED

———

TERMS OF PROTOCOL PRESENTED

———

PUERTO RICO, GUAM TO BE CEDED TO U.S.

———

OUR ARMY WILL OCCUPY CUBA, PHILIPPINES

———

GENERAL WESLEY MERRITT TO SIGN TREATY IN PARIS

———

CUBAN EXPEDITIONARY FORCE ALREADY EMBARKED FOR HOMEWARD JOURNEY

———

CONCERN OVER YELLOW FEVER VICTIMS

25

'I have to go to Boston,' Lee said.

Jenny opened her mouth to protest: it was too soon, he looked so wasted, so weak. But she knew her man.

'When?' was all she said.

'I don't know. As soon as possible. I have to see Sarah.'

'About David Liddell?'

'That's right.'

David Liddell had died aboard the ship on his way home. Yellow fever. Most of the men on the trip either had it or had just recovered from it. When they arrived at Montauk Point from Santiago early in September, the survivors of the Cuban Expeditionary Force were a pitiful sight. Jenny would never forget as long as she lived how racked and ill her husband looked as he came down the gangplank and on to the pier, thin, underweight, yellow as a lemon. And he was one of the lucky ones. Many men came off the ships on stretchers, and even more had never made it to the ships.

Nothing was too good for the Rough Riders. Roosevelt opened his home at Oyster Bay to them, as did many other generous New Yorkers. Everyone treated them like royalty. They found it difficult to pay for a drink or a meal.

Lee wanted none of that.

He had lost too many good men. Losing them in battle might have been bearable. Losing them to disease and fever was not. He told her some of it. Heavy rains pouring down, no tents for shelter, every man for himself, standing in trenches a foot deep in water, day and night. When the sun came out the soldiers would wring out their wet clothes and blankets and hang them on branches, or on the roofs of their makeshift shelters, where they steamed and stiffened. There was never enough food, and what there was – sowbelly, hard tack, and coffee beans so hard the men had to crack them between rocks – was so poor they grew weak from malnutrition. Sanitation was at best rudimentary. Liquor sellers and whores were allowed to come and go as they pleased. The temperature climbed off the scale, sometimes over 130°. In such conditions it was hardly surprising that disease ensued; that it would spread widely was inevitable.

There was malaria.

The shivers came first. No matter what you did, you couldn't get warm. After maybe an hour or two, the shivering stopped. Then you grew hot, and hotter and hotter, until you felt as if your skin was going to burn right off your body. Your legs and arms and spine became an agonising mass of intense, throbbing, incessant pain which lasted eight or nine or ten endless, grinding hours. At last the fever broke, and you lay exhausted in filthy clothes soaked by your own sweat, too weak to sit up, unable to eat, barely managing to sip lukewarm water. You were over it. Until the next time.

Then there was yellow fever.

Nobody knew what to do about it. It came on much faster than malaria. Your skin turned banana yellow, and you started to vomit. You burned up with fever, one, two, three days of it. It might slacken off a bit on the second or third day; it might not. Either way, it would get worse. Your temperature went way up again, and the spasmodic vomiting recurred. This time it had blood in it. You might get a rash, or nosebleeds. Your urine turned black, what there was of it. Or you couldn't pass water at all, and died in that kind of agony.

239

Like David Liddell.

One of the medics came looking for Lee on the ship, a thin-faced, harassed-looking corps sergeant with a three-day stubble on his chin.

'We've got a guy in sick bay asking to see you, Captain,' he said. 'Name of Liddell.'

Lee frowned. 'Liddell? What outfit?'

'71st New York, I think. He said to tell you he knows your cousin Sarah.'

They went down a companionway to lower deck, and along a corridor whose cream-painted metal walls were slick with condensation. The hold had been converted into a sick-bay; alternate hatch slats had been removed to let in some ventilation. It was suffocatingly hot. Around the walls of the hold cheap pine cots stood in closely packed rows. The stink of disinfectant and sweat fought unsuccessfully with a sharper stench that Lee now knew all too well, the copper tang of death. The medic gestured towards a bed. In it lay a gaunt, dark-haired trooper. He looked as if he was in his late thirties; actually, he was twenty-four years old. His wide brown eyes took a moment to focus when Lee came to the bedside and spoke his name.

'You wanted to see me, soldier?'

'Wanted to ask you something, Captain,' Liddell said. 'A favour.'

'Go ahead.'

'I've got this . . . premonition. That I'm not . . . going to make it.' Sweat sheened his face, and his breathing was laboured, as if he had run hard in a hot sun.

'Yellow jack?' Lee said, knowing the answer.

'I . . . oh, shit, Captain, I wish they'd just kill me, get it over with,' Liddell gasped. 'Kill' – pant – 'Me.'

'What do you want me to do?'

'Go. See. Sarah. Your cousin.' Liddell's voice dropped to a whisper, and his chest heaved with effort. 'Tell her.'

'Tell her what?' Lee said, leaning forward. Liddell's hand clutched his wrist. There was no strength in it. He thrashed his head from side to side, trying to get enough breath into his body. Lee wiped the sweat out of his eyes.

'Jesus,' Liddell said. 'Jesus.'

'Take it easy. Take your time.'

'Running out' – pant – 'Time.'

'Let me do the talking,' Lee said. 'You just nod or shake your head, if you can. Okay?'

Liddell nodded. Lee could see him fighting the pain inside his body. The yellow cast of the skin was pale and sickly, and the bitten lips bloodless. Lee had seen too many men in Liddell's condition to harbour any doubts: this man was dying.

'You want me to go to Boston and see Sarah,' he said. 'You want me to tell her about – this?'

Liddell shook his head.

'You want me to tell her something else?'

Nod. Lee looked into the huge brown eyes, saw the agonised plea and understood it.

'You want me to tell her you were killed in action?'

Nod.

'How well did you know Sarah?'

'Love,' Liddell said.

'You were in love with her?'

Nod.

'And she with you?'

Nod.

'Were you planning to marry?'

Nod.

'But you volunteered for Cuba.'

Nod.

'I'll hold up my hand and show you a finger for each year you knew her,' Lee said. 'One. Two.'

Nod.

'You knew her for two years. In Boston.'

Nod.

'Is she still a teacher?'

Nod.

'Where can I find her?'

'Letter,' Liddell gasped. 'Locker.'

'All right,' Lee said. 'I'll get it later. Is that all you want me to do, find her and tell her you died in action?'

Shake.

'Something else?'

Nod. Lee frowned. Liddell seemed to understand the frown and lifted a sticklike arm from under the sodden sheet. He touched his fingers to his lips.

'You want me to tell her you love her.'

Nod. Liddell's eyes closed. His breathing was laboured and irregular. All at once he sat up, his eyes quite blank, and leaned over the side of the cot, vomiting bright red blood. Lee instinctively recoiled from the dreadful spatter, yelling for a corps man. An orderly came running, swabs and towels and sponge in hand. He lifted Liddell gently back into the bed, cleaning off his face and mouth.

'I'll have to ask you to leave, Captain,' he said. 'This man's dying.'

'I know,' Lee said.

He opened Liddell's locker and looked inside. The letter was easy to find. 'I'm taking this,' he told the orderly.

'Sure,' the man said. 'He won't need it any more.'

'He's dead?'

Nod.

Lee went back to the tiny cabin he was sharing with Brainerd, Landrie and Morgan Nelson. He sat for a long time on his narrow cot, thinking about Sarah Starr and David Liddell. Then he took the letter out of the envelope and read it.

My dearest,

I have just come home from St Mary's and I am sitting at the table looking out through the window at the garden. It has been very hot today and I am very tired. I miss you terribly. I thought it might get better after a while, but if anything it is worse. I manage all right during the daytime, with school work filling my hours. But sometimes the nights seem endless and I long to see you, touch you, kiss you. I wonder where you are, and pray that God will watch over you. I wonder where you will be when this letter finally reaches you, if it ever does.

Dearest, writing what comes next is very hard for me to do, but I know that you would want to know. I am going to have a baby. Our baby. I am awed and frightened by the thought, and I do not quite know what to do. I can only hope that you will be back home when he arrives. I am sure it will be a boy. I want him to have your eyes. And your name. Please do not be angry at me for telling you all this. You are the only one in all the world with whom I want to share this news. Don't worry about me. I am a healthy girl; as you always used to say, healthy as a farm horse.

There is nothing new to tell you. It will soon be time for the summer recess, and I will have plenty of leisure time to make clothes for the baby and write to you.

May God protect and keep you safe for me while we are far apart, my darling. Across the endless miles of ocean I send you all my deepest love. Until we meet again.

Your own, Sarah

When her husband showed her the letter, Jenny did some arithmetic in her head. Sarah had probably got pregnant just before David Liddell left with his regiment. Late May, then. She would be five months pregnant now.

'Don't you think she may have gone home?' she said. 'To Belmont?'

'Sarah hated Belmont,' Lee said. 'My guess is she'll be

243

toughing it out in Boston.'

That was all he could do, guess. Like all cousins, the Starrs knew each other intimately, but not well. They had all been close, like a litter of puppies, when they were kids. The years had scattered them.

The address on the letter was not far from South Station in Boston. Lee and Jenny went there in a hansom. It was a warm day, with a hint of fall in the air. Fallen leaves skittered across the common. A stone-faced woman wearing a pinafore and a mob cap answered their knock on the door of the house in Tuets Street.

'Gone, she is, long since,' the woman snapped when they asked for Sarah Starr. She had a marked Irish accent. 'And good riddance.' She eyed them up and down, priced Jenny's coat and shoes. Expensive, her little eyes said. Her manner softened slightly. 'Is it relations you are?'

'Cousins,' Lee said. 'We're just passing through town. Thought we'd look her up. When did she leave?'

'The end of July.'

'You said "good riddance" . . . ?' Jenny said.

'She was expecting,' the woman said, folding her arms across her scrawny chest. 'I'll have none of that in my house, I told her.'

'Do you know where she went?'

'Nor do I care,' the woman said, her glare daring them to take issue.

'Thank you for your help, Mrs . . . ?'

'Parker,' she said. 'And I can tell you this for nothing: you'll be wasting your time looking for her at that school. They gave her her walking papers, all right. As soon as they found out she was – about her condition.'

You told them, Jenny thought. It wasn't a guess. She *knew*. It was there in the woman's beady eyes for anyone to see. They were a type. In earlier times, they had stoned sinners and burned witches.

'How lucky she was,' Jenny said sweetly, 'to have a

friend like you.'

The Irishwoman's face went red with anger and she put her fists on her hips, arms akimbo, jaw sticking out.

'*What*?' she screeched in disbelief. 'What did you say?'

'You'll have to forgive my wife, Mrs Parker,' Lee said, as Jenny turned on her heel and climbed angrily into the hansom. 'She's upset about Sarah.'

'I see,' the woman said, still angry, but mollified by Lee's soft tones.

'What she meant was that one can see your character immediately, Mrs Parker. It shines from your eyes. It is in the way you speak, the way you stand. There can be no doubt whatsoever about it.' My God, he thought, she's *simpering*. He opened the door and got into the hansom. He beamed at her through the open window.

'Not the slightest doubt,' he said, smiling radiantly. 'You are, without question, a vicious, mindless bitch!'

The hansom set off down the street, pursued by her screams. Three days later, they returned to New York and from there went down to Belmont. Aunt Louisa might know where Sarah was. Nobody in Boston seemed to.

UNCLE TOM'S CABIN

A Great & Moral Play

BRING THE CHILDREN

Give Them An Ideal & Lasting Lesson
In American History

HIGH-CLASS SPECIALTIES BETWEEN
THE ACTS

SEE The Death of Little Eva!!!

SEE The Frolicsome Topsy!!

SEE The Kind & Affectionate Uncle Tom!!!

SEE The Hard-hearted Legree!!!

Theatre Playbill, 1899

26

The place was not quite squalid; neither was it clean. A woman of about fifty wearing a white apron let Sarah in and took her into a back room. The walls were covered with dark-green patterned wallpaper. On one side was an army cot, and in the centre of the room a table with a leather-covered top. Another table stood to one side. Sarah saw the glint of instruments and averted her eyes, unable to look at them. In one corner of the room was a cloth screen with a metal frame on wheels, the kind they used in hospitals.

'Shall we take care of the business first, dear?' the woman said. 'You've brought the money, I take it?'

Sarah opened her purse and counted out the hundred dollars. It was every penny she had saved over two long years, scrimping on everything, so that when David came back – well, there was no point thinking about that. David was not coming back.

'I'm Mrs Terson,' the woman said.

'Do you – are you the one . . .?'

'No, dear. That's Mrs Henry. She'll be here in a minute. You pop behind that screen and take off your clothes.'

Sarah nodded dumbly and went behind the screen. She heard someone come into the room as she undressed.

'All right,' she heard the woman's voice say. 'Where is she?'

Mrs Terson came up to the screen. 'Ready, dear?' she

said. *No!* Sarah wanted to scream at the top of her voice. She came out from behind the screen, naked and shivering. A sturdy, ample-bosomed woman with rosy cheeks stood by the table.

'Come along, lamb,' she said.

To the slaughter, Sarah thought. They laid her down on the table with her hips on the edge. The Terson woman pulled her legs apart and put them into two metal surgical stirrups. The rosy-cheeked woman turned the gas high. Yellow light flooded the room. Sarah concentrated on watching the mantle, white hot in the flame.

'I'm Sally Henry,' the stout woman said, smiling. She had bright blue eyes and corn yellow hair. Pretty, once, Sarah thought. Mrs Henry put on a dark-green smock and muttered something to Mrs Terson. Then she bent over Sarah. She put two fingers into Sarah's vaginal canal, holding the cervix with her fingers. With her other hand she felt Sarah's stomach, checking the size and position of the uterus.

'Steady now, lamb,' she said. Sarah felt something cold and metallic pushing apart the walls of her vagina. It didn't hurt, but the metal felt alien and hostile inside her. The woman did other things with instruments. They clicked, metal on metal. She worked slowly and methodically, as if she were milking a cow.

She picked up another instrument, hesitated. She looked at Sarah. 'This will hurt a bit, lamb,' she said.

OhpleaseGodno, ohpleaseGodno, ohpleaseGodno –

The pain was like white light, deep, deep inside. It was so intense that Sarah could not scream. Cold sweat drenched her from head to foot. The woman grunted as she scraped and scraped, pushing the curette higher. It was agony beyond anything Sarah had ever thought possible. Her body trembled uncontrollably and she pushed her knuckles into her mouth to stem the screams she wanted to utter. It took no more than a few minutes, but they felt like an eternity in which nothing existed except the searing, awful pain.

'There, lamb,' the woman said, straightening up. One by one she removed the bloody instruments, putting them into a tin bowl of hot water that Mrs Terson brought. Sarah watched her blood staining the water: pink, pinker, red. Waves of pain swept over her as the emptied uterus began to contract. She moaned like an animal, her body heaving on the sweat-slick leather.

Sally Henry went out of the room. Mrs Terson swabbed Sarah with antiseptic. The fumes made her want to vomit.

'Now, now,' Mrs Terson said. 'Now, now.'

'Oh God!' Sarah wailed. 'Oh God, Oh God!'

'Now, now,' the woman said. 'Don't fret, dear. You're going to be all right. You'll see.'

Sarah shook her head, sobbing with loss. The woman helped her off the table and put her on the army cot, covering her with a blanket.

'Half an hour and you'll be fine, dear,' she said. 'I'll get you a cup of tea.'

By the time she came back with the tea, Sarah had managed to partially control the shivering. The tea was hot, sweet, wonderful. She asked for more.

'You're lucky to have Mrs Henry,' the woman said when she brought it. 'Trained nurse, you know. Didn't mess you up like some would've.' She took the empty cup and stood up. 'You can go now,' she said. Sarah got up off the cot. Her legs felt like jelly. Mrs Terson helped her to put on her clothes, and gave her two sanitary pads to wear.

'Go home and stay in bed for twenty-four hours,' she said. 'You understand, dear?'

Sarah nodded dumbly.

'You should be all right,' Mrs Terson said. 'But if you start bleeding, you call a doctor straight away. Don't come back here. No matter what.'

'Call a doctor,' Sarah muttered. 'Don't come back.'

'That's a dear,' the old woman said. She patted Sarah's shoulder and led her along the hall into the vestibule. Sarah went down the steps and walked up the street, carefully, like an elderly woman. She managed to hold back the tears until she got to her rooms.

She stayed in bed for three days.

Until Solomon Bush came looking for her.

She did not recognise him at first. He was wearing a suit, a shirt and tie. His shoes were very shiny. He had a pearl grey Homburg hat in his hands.

'Yes?' Sarah said, frowning. 'What is it?'

'You don't know me?' he said.

'I – is it . . . Mr Bush?'

'That's me!' he said, leaning back a little and tapping his chest. 'Solomon Bush. Your student.'

'I'm afraid I can't ask you in,' Sarah said, making a gesture. 'I've been – unwell.'

'You don't look so good,' he said. 'Pale.'

'I'll be all right,' she said. She waited for him to say whatever it was he had come to say. He said nothing, just stood at the door with the anxious-to-please look on his face that she remembered from the school.

'Mr Bush,' she said gently. 'I can't stand at the door all day. Will you please tell me what you want?'

'I was worried about you,' he said.

Sarah frowned. 'Why should you worry about me?'

'I don't know,' he said. 'They told me at your lodgings that you had left.'

'Left!' she said with a mirthless smile. 'Oh, yes.'

'You look thin,' he said. 'Like you didn't eat.'

'I've eaten,' she lied. *Please go away*, she begged silently. Her legs were beginning to quiver. It was all she could do to hold back the tears of weakness.

'You won't come back? To the school?'

'There's no chance of that.'

'What will you do?'

250

Would the damned man never go? she thought. What the devil business of his was it what she did?

'I must go, Mr Bush,' she said. 'But thank you for calling.'

'I want to talk to you,' he said. The cowlike eyes were wide with the fear of rejection. He turned the brim of the grey hat nervously with strong, square-ended fingers.

'Another time, perhaps,' she said, feeling her head spin slightly. She grabbed the door jamb for support, and knew he had noticed.

'There's a café,' he said. 'Just along the street. A cup of tea, some soup. Would it hurt?'

Soup, she thought. Saliva flooded her mouth.

'I'm afraid –'

'Mrs Liddell,' he said quietly, 'you can die from such pride.'

Sarah stood for a moment, irresolute. Then she nodded. 'I'll get my coat,' she said.

He helped her on with it, and offered his arm. She took it without protest and he smiled, as if he had won a prize. A nice man, she thought, a simple man. She remembered thinking that before, when he had joined her class.

'You're from Germany, aren't you?' she said.

'Poland,' he said. 'A place you never heard of.'

'Tell me.'

'It is called Oświecim.'

'You're right,' she smiled. 'Is it a town?'

'Very small place,' Solomon said.

'How long have you been in America?'

'Since I was twelve. A long time.'

'And what do you do?'

He shrugged, as if apologising in advance for what he was going to say. 'I am a scrap dealer. Junk. I buy and sell.'

'Since you were twelve?' she said.

'I started when I was fourteen,' Sol said. 'As soon as I

251

had learned enough English.'

After the Tsar was killed in 1881, there were many *pogroms*. Poppa said it was a bad business and it would get worse. They would leave the Pale of Settlement and go to the new country, to America. They sold everything they owned, and there was just enough money to buy the boat tickets. The man who sold them the tickets said the boat was going to St. John's, in Nova Scotia. They asked if that was in America, and the man said it was. When they arrived they discovered that they were in Canada, but there was nothing they could do but make the best of it. Pyotr had no education and no money. He could not get work because he had no English. The only trade to which he could turn his hand was that of scavenger. He scoured the streets and docks, looking for scrap iron and hard metals which he could sell. His wife Manya raised chickens, and sold them and their eggs from door to door. After a few years, Pyotr changed his name to Peter, the family surname to Bush. By now he had built up a thriving little junk business, and in due course, he put Solomon to work in it as well. Sol was a good-looking, cheerful youngster. He often walked off with bargains someone less-liked might not have got.

He did not like being called a Polack, which was what the local people called anyone with an accent. But he had no time to go to school. At home they spoke Yiddish. Poppa learned only as much of the language of his new country as was necessary to conduct his business. In the evenings, he liked Manya and the boys to sing songs from the old country. What he wanted, he got. He was a domineering man. It was all he knew: women and children did what the man of the house told them to do. It was Manya's job to give the boys the love they needed. His was to earn the bread to feed them. No son of his would ever have to sleep with his grandmother, he said. Manya read the boys stories, and made their clothes, and learned their new language with them. She taught Sol to respect and look up to all women.

The men he talked to in St. John's all told Sol the same thing: you want to make your fortune, boy, you got to go down to Boston. Sol decided to take the plunge. Leo was old enough to take his place in the family business. Poppa could manage for a while. It never occurred to Sol that he might fail.

He had not been in Boston for a year when he got lucky, if you can call disaster lucky. On March 10, 1893, Boston was devastated by fire. Almost five million dollars' worth of property was destroyed. From the ruins, Solomon Bush made what was, to him, a fortune. He brought his family south, and allowed himself the satisfaction of making his father manager of the business. Things went well for them. They worked hard. Now they had a nice house, nice furniture. Momma was happy, Poppa was content. Such good sons, they had. All Sol needed now was a wife, Manya said. A nice girl. A nice Jewish girl, she meant. But Sol had no time for girls. He worked a fifteen-hour day, six days a week. He was big, healthy, strong, a bear of a man. He ate like a horse, slept like a log.

He knew that if he was going to get anywhere, he would have to learn proper English. That was when he enrolled at the Clifton Institute, one of the many 'colleges' which had sprung up to teach immigrants. The teacher in his class was an attractive brunette named Sarah Liddell. Sol found himself strongly attracted by her, but he did not have the remotest idea how to approach her. He followed her home, for no reason he understood. She called herself Mrs Liddell, but she had no husband. There was a mystery there. It fascinated him. In some strange way he wanted to take care of her. He had no idea why.

They went into the little café and sat at a table in a corner. They ordered soup, some bread.

'Maybe you'd like a proper meal? Some fish?'

'No,' Sarah said. 'Soup will be enough, thank you.'

'Maybe another time,' he said.

She avoided answering by asking a question. 'You knew no English when you came here?'

He shook his head. 'Nothing. Poppa still knows only a little. I never had any schooling worth the name. A man needs education. For business. To read, to write.'

He did not tell her that the reason he stayed in her class was not the English, not the reading and writing, but her. How could he tell her that?

'Enough about me,' he said. 'Tell me about you?'

'What do you want to know?' she fenced.

'There's something I don't understand,' he said. 'You are married. Yet you live alone. Is –'

'My husband was killed in the war,' she said. 'In Cuba.' She did not tell him the truth, that David had never been her husband. She had the feeling that to do so would shock Solomon, and she was right, it would have done.

'Then what will you do?' he said. 'If you have no work. Can you – I'm sorry, I shouldn't ask, maybe. But have you got any money?'

'Not a great deal,' Sarah confessed.

'No family?'

'My family live in . . . a long way away,' she said. 'I was too ill to go there. But when I'm stronger –'

'Let me help you,' he said.

'Why?' Sarah asked. There was no curiosity in her eyes. If anything, he thought, it was hostility. Why would she be angry because he wanted to help her?

'I want to know you better,' he said. 'I just don't know how to say it.'

She felt a surge of self-reproach. He was being kind in his clumsy way. It wasn't as if she couldn't use a friend. She would never go back to Belmont defeated: there was too much pride in her for that. Her parting from her parents had been a stormy one. Things had been said that wounded and hurt. She remembered the baffled

254

frustration in her father's eyes, the anger in her mother's.

But they had been right and she had been wrong.

How could she go back now and admit it? Liddell had been everything Andrew said he was. Her father said that by and large, you could divide humanity into two types: takers and givers. They were as necessary to each other as the frog and the scorpion in the fable. Takers always latched on to givers. Sarah, he said, was a giver; always had been open-hearted, romantic, generous, unaffected, impulsive. The greedy, the selfish, the envious – takers all – loved her type. David Liddell was a taker. He took her love, her devotion, with the same assured acceptance that he took her money. He volunteered for Cuba without consulting her, and told her it would be a wonderful experience for him. He gave no thought to what kind of an experience it would be for her.

When his ship sailed she felt more abandoned than she had ever felt in her life. Then angry, that he could so cavalierly walk out of her life. When he came back, she told herself, things would be different. She would be the taker and he would be the giver, for a change.

He would be a father. That would make all the difference, she knew.

But he never came back.

The letter from the War Department gave her the bare details of his death, nothing more. Its formal phrases were a sentence of death for the child inside her. She went ahead with the arrangements like a woman in a trance. It was as if it was all happening to someone else.

Until that night.

That awful night.

The rosy-cheeked woman grunting with effort, the relentless scrape, scrape, scrape inside her. That was how a woman paid for love. You gave yourself into the sweet abandon of it, the throbbing joining of it. You

255

laughed with the pleasure of it, wept with the joy of it. But the price you paid was cruel. She vowed she would never pay it again for any man.

Especially not this one, she thought.

She had heard from other teachers that it sometimes happened, one of the students would develop an amorous fixation, an attachment. The signs were easy to spot, they said. The student would be first in class, last to leave. He would bring flowers, or an apple, or candy for the teacher. He would always be the first to volunteer to clean the board, or run an errand. He would always try harder than everyone else, no matter what the standard of his work. There would be a yearning look in his eyes. She tried to remember whether she had noticed any of these signs in Solomon Bush, and had to confess to herself that she had not.

'I must go,' she said.

He opened his mouth as if to protest, then obviously thought better of it. He paid the bill and gave her his arm to walk back along the street. Leaves drifted down from the trees. The sky was a hard, fall blue. They reached the house without having spoken again.

'Thank you, Mr Bush,' Sarah said, extending her hand. 'It was very kind of you.'

He took her hand in his great paw. 'Can I come and see you again?' he said.

'I think not.'

'Tomorrow,' he persisted. 'The next day.'

'No,' Sarah said firmly.

'I'll come tomorrow,' he said. 'Same time. We'll have lunch.'

'I said *no*, Mr Bush!' Sarah said.

He shook his head. 'You don't mean it,' he said.

'I beg your pardon?'

'Mrs Liddell. Sarah. Forgive me. I can't say it clever. I want to see you again. You need someone now. You ain't got anyone. I'll be your friend. Just your friend. But I–I'm a good friend. I keep my word. You'll see.

256

Give me the chance and you'll see.'

'Mr Bush, I – '

'Sol,' he said. 'Call me Sol.'

'This is madness,' she said.

'Tomorrow!' he said. 'Lunch.' He shook her hand eagerly, like a farm boy, and hurried away quickly, as though to make sure she could not call after him that she had changed her mind. Sarah stood in front of the house, a bemused expression on her face, watching his broad back recede down the street. When he came tomorrow, she would simply tell him that she had no intention of going to lunch with him or anywhere else.

But she never did.

27

Las Vegas was normally a quiet little place, but not at the moment. To celebrate the first anniversary of their blooding at Las Guasimas, Roosevelt's Rough Riders had foregathered in the little New Mexican town, pitching their tents on the open prairie around it, swapping yarns all day and most of the June night, and putting a sizeable dent in the local beer and whisky supply. There wasn't a room to be had in the place. Even the old Montezuma, up at the Hot Springs, rebuilt and renamed The Phoenix, was jammed. Teddy Roosevelt, now governor of New York, came in a private railroad car loaned him by the owner of a Chicago newspaper. Alex Brodie brought in a large delegation from Arizona. Others streamed in from Texas and the Indian Territory. Everyone from New Mexico who had served in Cuba came up. The saloons echoed to the strains of 'There'll Be A Hot Time In The Old Town Tonight'. There were a few fights, nothing serious. During the day, the men ambled around the plaza with its gazebo and gardens, bought something to eat at the Mexican vegetable and poultry market, called in at the Old Adobe Hotel to hear about its one-time owner, Bob Ford, the man who shot Jesse James.

To Lee's surprise, Roosevelt sent for him. He told Brainerd, who made one of those what-the-hell-does-that-mean? kind of faces.

'Only one way to find out,' Lee said.

They were staying with the Manzanares family,

friends of his father's. They lived in a fine old house with an orchard, lawns and a fish pond, in Upper Vegas, one of the three villages between the town proper and the Hot Springs six miles above. Las Vegas was really two towns: the old Mexican adobe settlement on the west bank of the Gallinas River, and the rawer, newer American town on the east. Old Las Vegas was built around the plaza. From its four corners narrow streets of orange-coloured clay led out on to the surrounding plains. Skirting the plaza, Lee rode east on Bridge Street, crossing the dried-out river. East Las Vegas, with its saloons and hotels and the sprawling warehouses and stores of Otero Sellar, and Browne & Manzanares, was a crowded, bustling place. Lee tipped a salute to the loafers on the porch outside the Optic building. Behind the windows, shirt-sleeved men turned the pages of law books. Lee walked the horse down to the AT & SF depot, where Roosevelt's gilded Pullman sleeping coach stood on a nearby rail switch, guarded by two soldiers.

'Well!' Roosevelt said, when Lee was shown in. 'Good to see you again. Good to see you. How have you been?' He had put on some weight since Cuba, Lee thought, but he carried it well. He was wearing a dark blue serge suit, a white shirt with a soft collar, and a polka-dot four-in-hand. A heavy gold watch-chain was strung from one vest pocket to a buttonhole.

'I've been fine, sir,' Lee said. 'It's good to see you, too. And congratulations.'

'What? Oh, the governorship. Yes, yes. Pretty much of a walk-over, thanks to what you boys did down in Cuba. Now – can I offer you a drink?'

'A beer would be good.'

The white-jacketed steward nodded and looked at Roosevelt, who shook his head. They waited until the drink was brought on a silver tray and the coloured man withdrew, closing the door silently. Roosevelt sat down in an overstuffed chair, and waved Lee to another. He looked thoughtful and preoccupied.

'Have you been having fun with the boys?' he began.

'Some,' Lee said. 'And a lot of bushwah.'

'Yes,' Roosevelt grinned. 'You do get a lot of that, don't you? What have you been doing with yourself?'

'Getting to know my wife, mainly,' Lee said. 'We only got married a little while before the late unpleasantness.'

'Your father well?'

'You know him?'

'Slightly,' Roosevelt said. 'Know his brother better.'

'Uncle Andrew.'

'A good man,' Roosevelt said. 'I talked to him about you. Ever thought about coming East?'

'Permanently, you mean?'

'Plenty of opportunities for a young fellow like you,' Roosevelt said. 'War veteran, pretty wife, good family. You could do very nicely for yourself.'

Lee sipped the beer and said nothing.

'Keeping mum, eh?' Roosevelt said, allowing himself another brief grin, as if he rationed them carefully. 'Smart. I noticed it in Cuba. You think things out, go steadily. Your uncle says the same thing. He suggested I talk to you. Ask you whether you'd like to work for me.'

'We talked about it when I was in Virginia, Colonel,' Lee said. 'I told him then what I'm telling you now: I'm not interested in politics.'

'What *do* you want to do?'

'That's a good question, Colonel,' Lee said. 'And I'm not too sure I know the answer yet.'

Ever since he had come home from Cuba, he had been wondering what to do with his life. The main trouble was that he was qualified to do only one thing: to be a soldier. He said this to Roosevelt, who held up his hand.

'Everybody's got problems,' he said. 'You want to hear mine?'

'Thanks,' Lee grinned. 'But no, thanks.'

'You want another beer?'

'This is fine.'

Roosevelt leaned back in the chair, lips pursed. Then he nodded, as if making up his mind about something.

'They're after me to run for vice-president,' he said. 'Damned if I want to. But I can't see a way out.'

'You'll make a good vice-president, Colonel.'

'And they'll hang a "finished" label on my political chances!' Roosevelt said. 'Unless I have good men with me. Men like you.'

'I'm flattered, Colonel,' Lee said. 'But not tempted.'

'Pity,' Roosevelt said, his manner turning abrupt. 'Well, if that's your final word on it?' He got up out of the chair. Lee stood up and put down the empty glass.

'Suppose you could get back into the Army,' Roosevelt said. 'Is that what you want?'

'It's what I know.'

'They'd probably send you to the Philippines, you know. That's going to be a long, dirty war.'

'I didn't know there was any other kind.'

'I could probably pull a few strings,' Roosevelt said thoughtfully. 'I will, too, in return for a promise from you.'

'What's that, Colonel?'

'That you'll only sign on for a short hitch. And that when it's finished, you'll come work for me.'

'Doing what?' Lee asked. 'I don't know beans about politics.'

'Your uncle will teach you,' Roosevelt asserted confidently, 'or I will. Either way, I want your promise. If I can swing your reinstatement, will you come to work for me when you get out?'

'You're going to run for office?'

'Maybe in 1904.' Roosevelt said. 'Maybe.'

'The Presidency?'

'Maybe,' Roosevelt said. 'I don't know. It will depend on a lot of things. Well – what do you say?'

'One last question, Colonel. With all the people you've got to choose from – why do you want me?'

'That's easy,' Roosevelt said. 'You believe in the same things I do. Duty. Honour. Country. You're like Andrew Starr – you're honest. That's the kind of man I want at my side, whether it's on San Juan Hill or Capitol Hill.' He stuck out his hand and raised his eyebrows. 'Have we got a deal?'

Lee took his hand. 'Yes, sir,' he said. 'I believe we have.'

'Bully!' said Theodore Roosevelt, and this time the smile was wide and warm.

When Lee got back to the ranch, Jenny was not there. His father told him that she'd gone down to Las Cruces to visit her friend Laurey Clayton and was staying over a few days.

He told his father his decision, and James nodded gravely. He put a cigar into his mouth and got out his box of kitchen matches. Then he opened the box and took out a match. He pushed the matchbox hard against the cigar humidor and struck the match, puffing contentedly away at the cigar. He never allowed anyone to do things for him, never admitted to the fact that he had only one arm. The only concession Lee had ever seen his father make to his disability was to let Linda cut up his meat. You damned rock-headed old bastard, he thought fondly.

'Your mother's not well, boy,' James said to his son. 'You won't be leaving . . . right off?'

'No, Pa,' Lee said. 'It'll be a while till I hear from Colonel Roosevelt.'

'What made you decide to go back in?'

Lee shook his head, smiling. 'You know, Pa, it's funny. You've been asking me ever since I got back here what I was going to do with my life. Now, when I decide, you ask me why. Do you think I've done the

262

wrong thing?'

'Matter of fact,' James said, 'I do.'

'Tell me why.'

'It's not I don't understand how you feel about the Army, son,' James said. 'We all feel the same way.'

'What's your objection, then?'

'I think your timing's off,' James told his son. 'The man in the street thinks the war is over. Nobody wants to know any more.'

'It's not over in the Philippines,' Lee said. 'Not by a damned long chalk.'

'You think the Great American Public gives a damn about the Philippines?' James said, his voice rising. 'I misdoubt more than one man in a thousand knows where the goddamned place is!'

'That doesn't make it any less necessary to go.'

'No, it doesn't,' James sighed. 'But there'll be precious little glory in it, boy. It'll be a drawn-out, dirty guerilla war.'

'Like politics, you mean?' Lee asked, innocently. James guffawed. They shared a companionable silence.

'Suppose I can't complain if you want to do your duty,' he said, after a while. 'Was me taught you you had to.'

'You'd have preferred me to go East? Join up with Roosevelt?'

'Yes,' James said emphatically. 'I don't care for that make-believe cowboy one damned bit, but he's got to be a better bet than getting your head shot off in the Philippines.'

'They may not even send me out there,' Lee argued. 'We don't even know what regiment I'll be in.'

'You're half-Spanish, for Christ's sake!' James said impatiently. 'Where d'you think they'll send you? London?'

Another friendly silence ensued. Lee basked in it. He had not felt this close to his father for a long time. He wished there were some way he could let him know how much he loved him. Somehow men never got around to saying things like that.

'It's funny, you know, Pa,' he said, breaking the silence. 'I never wanted to be a soldier. I can remember when you told me I had a place at the Academy, all I could think was, no, I don't want to go.'

'You never said so,' James murmured.

'I didn't know how to tell you,' Lee said. 'How to say it.'

'Say it now,' James said softly.

'Well . . .' Lee shook his head. 'I remember I felt . . . resentful. And I thought: why does it have to be me? I – it was not having a choice that I hated.'

'What did you think you wanted to do?'

'I had no clear idea, Pa. Something artistic, maybe. Poetry. Music. Painting, maybe. But not the Army.'

'And then?'

'I stuck it out.' Lee said. 'I can remember thinking, I can do this. I'll get through to the other end and then I'll make my plans. If this is what they want me to do, then I'll do it.'

'You thought it was what we wanted?' James said. 'And all the time we thought it was what you wanted.'

'I know,' Lee said. 'That's what's funny about it. You see, somewhere in there, something happened. I got the bug. The Army bug.'

'Until you met up with Whittier Moffatt.'

'That old bastard.'

'Jenny hear from them?'

'She writes to her mother. She thinks I don't know.'

'Some things, it's better not to know,' James agreed. 'Women . . . ' He didn't develop the thought. 'One thing, though,' he said. 'I wish you'd let me break the news to your mother.'

Lee nodded. 'Whatever you say.'

'It won't be the best news she's ever had,' James said. 'Was she stronger, I wouldn't be so concerned. As it is . . .'

264

'That's what you meant about my timing?'

James nodded, lips pursed. 'Pretty much.'

'You think I ought to stay?'

'She wouldn't want that, son. She's a soldier's daughter, a soldier's wife. Now she's a soldier's mother. She knows about duty.'

Neither of them voiced the thought that was in both their minds. Linda's illness was of long standing, and nothing the doctors prescribed seemed to make much difference. She was listless and depressed, eating like a bird, her once softly rounded body skinny, her olive skin turned sallow.

'When do you expect to hear from the Adjutant-General's department?' James asked.

'Colonel Roosevelt said it would probably take a couple of months,' Lee told him.

James grinned mischievously. 'That ought to give you just about enough time to break the news to Jenny.'

'Wouldn't care to do it for me, would you?' Lee said.

'Not me, Mary Ann!' James said. 'That little gal of yours got a tongue that'd take the skin off a cigar-store Injun.'

'Don't I know it,' Lee said gloomily.

He had learned a lot of things about Jenny. Indeed, with the fond blindness of all new husbands, he believed he knew his wife very well. He knew she loved him fiercely, protectively, exclusively. He knew she was loyal, honest, frank. She had a brain and she was not afraid to use it: there was none of the dutiful wife in Jenny. Knowing all this, Lee had given considerable thought to how he was going to break the news to her. But he could not come up with a way of doing it which would avert the fireworks. Hell, he thought, hit her head-on and be done with it. Do it before she finds out some other way, from Ma or Connie or someone else.

'Colonel Roosevelt sent for me up at Las Vegas,' he said, as they washed the dishes on her first night back. 'Asked me if I wanted to go into politics with him.'

Jenny turned to face him, eyebrows raised, eyes wide with interest. 'And what did you tell him?'

'Told him I didn't think I was ready for politics. Not yet.'

'Darling, I think you're wrong!' Jenny said. 'I think you'd be very good at it.'

He laughed, a short, cynical sound. 'Sure! Making speeches to citizen groups and labour organisations, eating rubber chicken, shaking hands. Can't you just see me?'

'David Lee Starr, sometimes you amaze me!' Jenny said, putting her hands on her hips. She was surprised to realise how strongly she felt about this, but not so surprised as her husband was. 'Roosevelt is going to get to the top. You could go with him. What on earth would be wrong with that?'

Lee shook his head, doggedly polishing an already spotless plate. 'No, Jen. That's not for me, that palm-greasing, the smoke-filled rooms, the fixing. It repels me.'

'When we were in Virginia,' she said, 'I talked to your Aunt Diana. She told me about your Uncle Andrew. She said he could have run for President. He had every chance of being elected. But he would never do it.'

'I know,' Lee said, laying down the towel and the plate. 'I know why, too.'

'She said he was too honest, whatever that means.'

'It means he wanted to be able to tell the truth whenever *he* wanted to,' Lee said, quietly. 'And because he believed no job in the world was worth having that didn't allow you to do so.'

'Your father's not like that. He's a realist.'

'He prefers the word "pragmatist",' Lee smiled. 'Jen, come and sit down. I want to tell you something.'

A small frown touched her forehead. 'What's this?' she said.

'I'm going back into the Army, Jen.'

She just looked at him, her lips slightly parted. Then

he saw the anger flood into her eyes. She pulled her hands out of his grip and stalked across the the room, glaring out of the window into the black New Mexican night. He sat, saying nothing, watching her shoulders rise and fall.

'You bastard!' she said, so softly that he almost missed the words. 'You self-centred, arrogant bastard!'

'I thought – I thought you'd be glad,' he said lamely.

'Glad?' she hissed, whirling round to glare at him. 'Glad to be going back to being a widow in everything but fact? Glad to sit and wait, day after day, for someone to come to the door and tell me you're dead? Glad to manage on made-over clothes and live in some bug-hutch the Army hasn't gotten around to tearing down yet? Oh, damn you, Lee Starr, now I'm crying!'

'Jenny, darling –' Lee began. He went across to her and tried to put his arm around her shoulder. She spun angrily away from him.

'Don't you "there, there" me!' she blazed. 'I'm good and damned well mad at you, mister!'

'Then be good and damned well mad!' he yelled back. 'You know me. I'm Army. That's what I do!'

'You're not, you're not!' Jenny said, banging a balled fist on the table. 'You could be anything you want to be. Anything, anything!'

'Then let me be what I want to be,' Lee said quietly into the storm of her anger. 'A soldier.'

She stood silently with her head averted for what seemed a long time to both of them. Then, softly, Jenny spoke.

'How long have we got?' she said

'I don't know. A month, two.'

'That's not very long.' The anger burned inside her, but she controlled it. There was no point in being angry. He was Army. He had been Army when she fell in love with him. There was no difference between then and now. She loved him for what he was, not what she might make him become.

'Long enough,' he said. He came across the room and took her in his arms. He kissed her once, twice, sweetly, gently.

'I love you, Jen,' he said.

'And I love you, too,' she replied. 'You bastard.'

And if you think you are going off halfway around the world and leaving me behind, she thought, you have got one hell of a surprise coming your way, Lee Starr!

28

For a long, long time, Irving could not write. The very idea of writing songs seemed pointless. Who *cared*? Moon, June, blah. Songs were no vehicle for the intensity of his feelings. Nothing was. He was still a young man but he felt as if his life was finished. The society 'friends' he had known when Marie was alive very quickly disappeared. He decided to go away for a long, long time. He took a boat to Europe. Money was no object. He went to the very best places. In London he stayed at the Ritz, dined at the Café Royal, ate steak and kidney pie in Rules and roast beef and Yorkshire pudding in Simpson's. In Paris he went to Maxim's, watched the Folies Bergère, sat at a table outside Fouquet's and watched the world go by. He went to Geneva and Florence and Rome and Capri and Athens and Istanbul. He saw the Sphinx by moonlight and the Leaning Tower of Pisa, the snowy wastes of the Gorner glacier and the white cliffs of Dover, which weren't white at all but a scruffy grey. None of them meant a thing to him. He was that most morose of creatures, the man who can have anything he wants and doesn't want a thing.

As he travelled, he tried to write. There was no melody in the music, no emotion in the words. He went to Southampton and got a boat back to New York. Might as well be miserable at home, he thought. It was a lot cheaper, if nothing else.

'I'm through,' he told his brother Aaron. 'I can't

write any more.'

'You know what you're full of?' Aaron said, impatiently. 'It's time you snapped out of this, Iz. You want to try making what happened work for you instead of trying to forget it!'

'Aaron,' Irving said, 'You are one callous, unfeeling sonofabitch. But you're right, you know that?'

'Ain't I always?' Aaron said.

Irving took out all the photographs of her that he had hidden away. He went back to San Francisco and put flowers on her grave. He had been trying to forget her. Now he remembered, and she came alive again. Within a few days, he had written 'Why Did You Leave Me, Marie?' It wasn't a song; it was a phenomenon. It swept the country like a brush fire. Aaron simply couldn't keep up with the demand for sheet music. He sub-contracted the printing first to one, then two, and eventually six other printers.

The song sold a million copies in its first month, another million in the two weeks following. From the Barbary Coast to the Tenderloin, a thousand tenors put a catch in their voices as they sang its last, rising, impassioned lines:

> *Nobody told me how lonely I'd be*
> *Oh, why did you leave me, Marie?*

Irving had always said he could write a song every day if he wanted to; but who'd need them? There was always something you could use. The distributors clamoured for another hit. Irving gave them one. The big craze of the moment was bicycling, so he wrote a song about that. It wasn't as successful as 'Marie' – how could it have been? Give us another ballad, the stores begged. Write us another love song, entreated the ten thousand tenors. So Irving again turned to his memories of Marie, and wrote a song called 'The Day You Went Away'.

'Ev'ry little flower, ev'ry little bird,
Ev'ry little child at play,
Ev'ry little breeze, sighing in the trees
Cried, the day you went away.

It was another smash hit, and Irving followed it with another called 'When Two Became As One'. His songs made him the most sought-after writer in New York. Producers begged him for a score, and he wrote two shows for the Broadway stage before leaving for London, where the British producer, Desmond Arlington, had invited him to write a score for a new revue he was producing called *All Change*. Irving used the Atlantic crossing to good effect, landing at Southampton with six songs already written. A new dance, the two-step, was all the rage in New York. Irving's 'Boston Two-Step' made it the rage of London as well. He was fêted, interviewed, entertained. He danced with a duchess. Although his plan had been to return to America when the score was finished, he stayed in Britain for six months.

When he finally returned to America, there was a telegram waiting for him. It was from Billy Priestman. STOP WRITING SONGS ABOUT MY DAUGHTER, it said. It was a revenge Irving had not even considered.

In 1898, Witmark bought out the publishing catalogue of Weber, Fields and Stromberg. They were becoming a power-house, and Irving knew he would have to find ways of combating their octopus-like grip on the music-publishing business. He inaugurated the practice of distributing 'free' copies of his songs to performing artists. He hired orchestrators to prepare complete scores for bands to play his songs, and gave them to the bandleaders. Free sheet music: it was a bonanza for the singers and the bands. Everybody else asked for payment. Therefore Irving Strasberg's songs got all the plays, and consequently sold more copies to the public. Before long, however, Witmark and the rest followed suit: they had to. Irving knew he would have to think of something else.

He was in Tony Pastor's when the 'something else' came to him. On the stage was Ben Harney, a one-time songwriter turned entertainer from Kansas City, who'd made his name with what they called 'coon songs'. Harney's act consisted of syncopated versions of hymns and semi-classical pieces. It was foot-stomping stuff, and Irving instinctively knew he was on to something. He went backstage after the show to talk to Harney.

'That's interesting stuff you were playing,' he said. 'Have you got a publisher for it?'

'Nobody wants to know,' Harney told him. 'See, a lot of it is improvised. Ya never know where ya goin' with it.'

'What's it called?'

'What they call that down home music, Strap?' Harney yelled to his stooge, Strap Hill.

'Ragged-time, Boze,' Hill said, showing great white teeth.

Irving was fascinated by the potential of the music, but first he had to find a way of taming it. He could hardly wait to get to the piano in his apartment. The syncopation was easy enough: you just put an artificial accent on the off-beat, delaying or anticipating the real emphasis. The left hand played a steady 2/4 or 4/4 rhythm, while you used the right for syncopation. Ablaze with enthusiasm, Irving pounded away at the piano for hours. There was something in there, but what? What? You couldn't write down improvisations. A song was a song. Thirty-two bars. Da-da-da, da-da-da, doodle-doodle-doodle, da-da-da. This music refused to fit the standard mould. Yet it wanted to be a song.

A week later he played what he had written for Aaron.

'What the hell do you call that?' Aaron said. 'A song?

It sounds more like coon music!'

'It is,' Irving said. 'It's what they play the six days of the week they don't sing spirituals.'

'It stinks,' Aaron said.

'I like it.'

'What's it called?'

'"Give Me A Ragtime Song".'

'It won't sell fifty copies,' Aaron said.

In spite of Aaron's scorn, Irving was certain he was on to something big. He felt it, but he simply could not pin down what it was. He tried another tune in the same style. Again, it didn't quite make it. The big one, the one Irving knew was still waiting to be written, just wouldn't come.

He put ragtime aside for the moment. Its time would come. When it did he would be ready.

He moved into another area of the business. He produced shows featuring his own music, competing directly with Florenz Ziegfeld and Dillingham. He was seen in the company of beautiful showgirls and the daughters of society families. Witmark offered him a million dollars for his publishing interests. He turned the offer down without a second thought.

'I've got a million dollars,' he told Witmark.

'Well, sell anyway,' Witmark said, playing his only other card, 'and you'll have another million.'

'I've already got another million, too,' Irving said.

'That's a lot of money, Izzy,' Witmark observed, shaking his head. 'What are you planning to do with it?'

'Maybe I'll buy you out,' Irving smiled.

'That much money you don't have,' Witmark said. 'You should invest, Izzy. Let the money work for you.'

'I will,' Irving said, 'one of these days. When something comes along that's worth investing in.'

'What like?' Witmark asked.

'Who knows?' Irving grinned. 'Who knows?'

29

'Well?' Andrew Starr said belligerently, glaring at his wife. 'We going to let her marry this fellow?'

'Do you want to stop it?' Diana said, keeping her eyes firmly fixed upon the embroidery in her lap, sure that her husband's belligerence was a pose.

'Well,' he said. The truth of it was, he had found absolutely nothing about Solomon Bush with which to take exception. And he felt, somehow, that there ought to have been something. He felt disarmed, off-kilter.

'What did you make of him, anyway?' he said to his wife.

'I think he is a very decent man. A hard worker.'

'A junk merchant.'

'Is that your only objection?' she said impishly.

'Don't like being given a *fait accompli*,' he grumbled. 'Always the same with that girl. You never know what to expect.'

'No use expecting anything else of Sarah,' Diana said. 'She could do worse than young Mr Bush. He's a doer. He told me he wants to get out of the scrap business. He's going to buy a smelter. In New Mexico.'

'A smelter? What the devil for?'

'To make pancakes, of course,' Diana said waspishly.

'Does he know the business?'

'He says he does. And he has friends who'll help him.'

'The sons of Israel,' Andrew said. 'They stick together.'

'Ah,' Diana said. 'That.'

274

'No use trying to pretend it's not there, Di.'

'How would you feel about it,' Diana asked, 'if Sarah married him, this Bush fellow?'

'I don't know. Uneasy, I think. Marriage is hard enough, without the complication of mixed religions. And what about if they have children?'

'They can worry about children later,' Diana said. 'Right now, it's you they're worried about.'

'Me?' Andrew said, genuinely surprised.

'Yes, you, my darling. Don't you know they're a little bit scared of you?'

'Nonsense!' he said.

'They are,' she insisted. 'Everyone is. Except me.'

'Stuff and nonsense!'

Diana smiled and said no more. She knew her man well after all their years together. Andrew saw himself first and foremost as a fair and honest man, and he was. Too honest, in many ways: it was a trait that had kept him out of the high office she had always hoped he would one day occupy. She had long since become reconciled to the fact that Andrew would never realise the dream she and her father had once had for him, but she loved him no less because of that. She might have loved him less if he *had* compromised his beliefs. He was a darling man, but he had no conception of himself at all. He believed himself to be easy-going, when in fact he was ruthless. He imagined he was generous and forbearing, when any of his family and many of his friends and enemies would confirm that Andrew Starr was difficult to please, quick to criticise, slow to praise, and sometimes heartlessly cruel, especially when confronted by anyone or anything he believed to be second-rate.

'You'll think about it, though?' Diana said.

'All right, all right!' Andrew growled.

Diana could tell by the sound of his voice that Andrew was not really angry. She thought that perhaps he liked the young Bostonian rather more than he let on. Why else would he have spent so much time telling Solomon all about Belmont and the family?

It was the biggest house Sol had ever been in, with long, airy corridors lined with portraits. High-ceilinged rooms filled with fine furniture looked out through tall portes-fenêtres over terraced gardens sweeping down to the valley of the Rapidan. There was a music room with a beautiful walnut Challen grand piano; a dining-room with a Georgian table and chairs, the seats hand-embroidered; a fine library in which Sol would have been happy to lose himself for days.

On a lectern lay the family Bible. Andrew showed Sol the faded first entry that read: '*To David Starr, on his birth, from his father's father, Ezekiel Starr, the twenty-fourth day of September, in this year of grace, 1680.*'

'The picture above the fireplace is David Starr,' Andrew said. 'My great-grandfather. He's the one who originally built this house, although it's been extended a lot since his day.'

'Sarah told me it's a tradition that oldest sons serve in the armed forces,' Sol said. 'Maybe mine will, one day.'

Andrew Starr looked at him, and pursed his lips. Sol read his thoughts correctly, and met them head-on.

'Being Jewish wouldn't prevent a boy from serving his country, sir,' he said quietly.

'I don't suppose it would,' Andrew Starr said. He showed Sol the whole house, commenting – sometimes waspishly – on the background and characters of the family as he did. By the time he was through, Sol felt as if he had known them all his life.

'It's very kind of you to do all this for me, sir.'

'I'm not doing it for you, young man,' Andrew Starr said. 'I'm doing it for Sarah.'

The night before they were due to leave Sol asked to see Diana privately. She agreed, touched by his earnestness.

'You're an unusual family,' he said. 'Not what I expected.'

'What *did* you expect?'

'I don't know. Not this.' Sol waved his hand to encompass all the broad acres and sturdy buildings of Belmont.

'I suppose it must be a bit overpowering at first,' Diana said. 'I guess we all tend to take it for granted.'

'Sarah never . . . she never told me.'

'Perhaps she had her reasons,' Diana suggested, with a smile. 'Maybe she thought you were a fortune-hunter.'

'I hadn't thought of that.'

He didn't tell Diana that he had been looking after Sarah for almost two years. Through a friend in the city, he found her work in an office, so that she had her independence. With as little fuss as possible, he found her somewhere better to live, and took care of the rent until she was on her feet financially. He visited her regularly, always bringing flowers. He worked at making her like him, and then began working harder to try to make her love him.

'You know I'm Jewish,' he said.

'Yes.'

'And?'

'Being Jewish is not a sin in our eyes, Solomon,' Diana replied. 'But tell me, how do your parents feel about your marrying a Gentile?'

'My father is dead,' he said. 'There's only Momma. She met Sarah. They got along just fine.'

He thought of his mother, who never went into a room without touching the *mizzuzah*, the little box with a prayer in it which was fastened to the doorway of every room in the house; his mother, who would not serve meat and milk in the same meal, and who had a separate set of knives and forks for fish or meat dishes. He remembered how apprehensive he had been, thinking Sarah would find Momma difficult. Instead, Sarah had smiled, and told him about her aunt Louisa, who would not celebrate Christmas except with prayer

277

and churchgoing, because it was the date of a pagan festival, and who would not allow dolls in the house, because dolls were graven images proscribed by the Ten Commandments. If he could put up with her aunt Louisa, Sarah said, likely she could manage his mother. She hadn't quite done it; not yet. Manya was too much a product of the old country to change. For her it had been quite a concession to admit, albeit grudgingly, that she had met worse *shikses* than Sarah.

'I hope you and Sarah realise what you are getting into,' Diana said. 'It isn't easy to cope with two faiths within a marriage.'

'It's the same God, Mrs Starr,' Sol pointed out. 'The only difference is the way we talk to Him.'

'If anyone else but you said that to me, Solomon, I'd tell them they were dissimulating.'

'Me, you'd have to explain it to,' he smiled.

'I mean there is rather more to the Jewish religion than that, surely?'

'Yes, there is.'

'Your religion is important to you?'

'To all Jews.'

'You want Sarah to become Jewish?'

'No,' he said. 'Yes, if she wants to.'

'And children?'

'Children? There won't be any children for a while, Mrs Starr. Not till I can get on my feet. I don't plan to be a junk merchant all my life.'

'What do you want to do?'

'Scrap metal – that's small-time stuff, Mrs Starr. There's only one way to make real money in the metal business. You got to own the mine, the processing plant. You got to control the marketing of the metal. Anything else, you're just getting crumbs off the rich man's table.'

'I don't follow.'

'I got . . . I have a friend. A metallurgist. A college man, Mrs Starr, smart as you like. He knows where I can get in on a good deal. A mine, a smelter. That's where the money is. If I can put that mine into operation, it can make a fortune.'

'The mine isn't in operation now?'

'It's flooded. Abandoned.'

'Can it be got working again?'

'Yes. But it will take a lot of money.'

'How much?'

'About a quarter of a million dollars will do it.'

'You have that much?'

'I'll mortgage the Boston business. Put my brother in as manager. Use all my capital. It will be a stretch, but I think I can swing it. Just about.'

'Where is this mine?'

'New Mexico. A town called Silver City.'

That's in the south-western part of the Territory.'

'You know it?'

'Andrew's brother James is a lawyer in New Mexico. He has a ranch at Cloudcroft. That's not all that far away from Silver City. Not by New Mexico standards, anyway,' she smiled.

'Sarah told me,' Sol said. 'That would be all to the good. She would be close to her own people.'

'You're thinking of moving out there, then?'

'On my own at first. Then when I get everything going, I'll send for her. We'll buy a place, or build one.'

'It's a hard country, Solomon,' Diana said. 'Wouldn't it be better to postpone any plans to get married until — ?'

'I got to tell you, Mrs Starr,' Sol said, 'I'm scared to do that. It's going to sound dumb, especially to someone sophisticated like you. I'd be afraid to leave her. Suppose she met someone else while I was gone? She's a beautiful woman. It could happen. I couldn't bear that.'

'You're not sure if she loves you?'

Sol shook his head. 'I told you it was dumb.'

'Then why do you think she brought you here?'

'I don't know,' he said miserably. 'Maybe she

279

thought, when he sees my home, he'll forget about wanting to marry me. I think maybe she still isn't sure in her own mind what she wants. That's why I've come to you, Mrs Starr.'

'What do you think I can do, Solomon? Sarah must make up her own mind what she wants.'

'Just . . . help me,' he said. 'I'm straight. I'm honest, I'll work hard. I'll be good for her. She's been hurt. She doesn't trust anyone. I'd give that back to her. Love. Trust. More than that. I'd make her happy. But . . . I need your help. To make her see it. To make your husband see it.'

Diana was silent. She could not help but be moved by the sincerity of the young man sitting opposite her.

'Solomon,' she said, 'neither my husband nor I can tell Sarah she should love you.'

'No, no,' he said. 'I mean, couldn't you make her see that what I'm offering . . . what I want to do, makes sense? That it would be the best thing for her to do?'

Diana smiled. 'That kind of argument has never cut a lot of ice with my daughter, Solomon,' she said. 'I doubt it would now.'

'Then what do I do?'

'You have to tell her how you feel,' Diana said. 'And ask her to decide, yes or no.'

'And if she says no?'

'Then you go back to Boston and get on with your life, and forget all about Sarah.'

'I . . . couldn't do it,' he said. 'Mrs Starr, I couldn't do that.'

'Nevertheless, I think you must.'

He pinched his lower lip between his finger and thumb, shaking his head. Then he cocked his head, first to one side, then the other. He shrugged.

'Well,' he said. 'What's to lose?'

He came across and knelt in front of Diana, taking both her hands in his big, workworn paws. He kissed her hands. When he looked up she saw he had tears in his eyes.

'You won't be sorry,' he said.

I hope not, she thought.

'Well, Di, you know I respect your judgment more than most,' Andrew said to his wife when she told him all this. 'But I think you're . . .'

'Wrong?' Diana said. 'Maybe young Mr Bush will surprise us all.'

'What he has in mind takes a hell of a lot of money,' Andrew said, testily. 'Has he got it?'

'He has now,' Diana said.

He looked at her suspiciously and Diana grinned.

'Dammitall, Di!' Andrew growled. 'How much?'

'Never you mind,' she said. 'It was the money my father left me. Nothing to do with you.'

'Nothing –' He was at a loss for words for a moment, but he could not resist his wife's impish smile. Reluctantly he grinned, too.

'Think you're pretty smart, don't you?' he said.

'Yup,' Diana said, not looking at him.

'Think you can do any damned thing you like, don't you?'

She got up and planted a kiss *smack* on the end of his nose.

'Yup,' she said again.

30

'Good God!' a remembered voice drawled. 'Look what the cat dragged in!'

Lee Starr whirled abruptly around, face wreathed in a smile as he recognised 1st Lieutenant Charles Edward Gates, 6th US Cavalry. Standing beside Gates in the lobby of Manila's Hotel del Oriente was Chris Vaughan, his smile even wider than his friend's.

'Aguinaldo better watch himself, Chuck,' he said. 'Looks like General Otis sent for the heavy brigade.'

'You going to buy us a drink, *Captain*?' Gates emphasised the word so Lee would know he had noticed the insignia on his collar. 'Or don't the extra pay run to it?'

'Still on the bum, I see, Gates,' Lee said. 'As I recall it, you owe me half a bottle of whisky from Omaha Barracks.'

'Takes a mean-minded man to remember a thing like that,' Gates said. 'Wouldn't you say, Chris?'

'He always was tight-fisted,' Vaughan confirmed.

'Tighter than a hog's ass in fly time,' Gates added.

Lee shook his head, smiling.

'Of all the gin joints in the world I could have walked into,' he said, 'I have to walk into this one.'

'Told you he was glad to see us, Chuck,' Vaughan commented. 'How long have you been in Manila, Lee?'

'Came in with General Lawton. He's getting One Division come March.'

'You know Moffatt is here?' Gates asked.

'I heard,' Lee said. He did not tell them that he had requested an interview with General Moffatt, nor that it had been refused. 'How long you boys been here?'

'Too long,' Gates said.

'We shipped out of Frisco with General Anderson,' Vaughan told him. 'The first wave. Three ships, five thousand men. We came ashore and waited for the rest of the force to arrive. All it did was goddamned rain.'

It was not difficult to imagine the men coming ashore in the brown *cascos* – native boats not unlike a junk without sails – each carrying around two hundred men in dark brown trousers, blue shirts and brown slouch hats with the brims pulled down, moving slowly shorewards over a miserable, choppy sea beneath a sullen sky, battered by torrential tropical rains. General Merritt arrived on July 25 in a monsoon of such intensity that he was unable to disembark for a week. It rained non-stop for twenty-four days, while the Philippine Expeditionary Force huddled in misery under canvas at Camp Dewey, on the site of a former peanut farm south of the capital.

The siege and capture of Manila had been an exercise in chaos, Gates said. 'More like a goddamned comic opera than a war,' he added disgustedly.

The problem was Emilio Aguinaldo, the self-proclaimed president of the Philippine Republic. He had been a thorn in the side of Admiral Dewey ever since that worthy had brought him back to the islands from Hong Kong in May. By the time the first Americans arrived, Aguinaldo had practically surrounded Manila, and taken two and a half thousand Spanish prisoners.

'Wasn't a hell of a lot Dewey and Merritt could do about him proclaiming himself president,' Gates said, 'any more than he could make them recognise his authority. Sort of a Filipino stand-off.'

On August 7, Dewey gave the Spanish governor-general, Fermin Jaudenes, forty-eight hours' notice prior to bombarding the city, initiating a flurry of negotiations. The governor-general, in true Spanish style, let it be known that while he would never surrender the city, neither would he offer any serious resistance to the Americans if they marched in. From his point of view, they were a considerably lesser evil than the vengeful Filipinos. On August 13, Dewey and Merritt launched their attack on Manila. They envisaged a bloodless occupation, but they reckoned without their Filipino allies. Aguinaldo's troops attacked their old enemies vigorously. There were long hours of confused and inconclusive skirmishing before a white flag was run up and Manila fell into American hands. Thousands of Spanish troops were taken prisoner, with only token losses on the attacking side. Then, on Dewey's orders, Aguinaldo's men – to their utter disgust – were banished from the city. The following day articles of capitulation were signed and a military government installed. Its instructions from Washington were explicit: no joint occupation with the insurgents.

'Whole damned thing was a farce from beginning to end,' Gates said, disgustedly. 'The day after we took Manila, they told us the armistice had been signed before we marched in. Aguinaldo says, okay, now do I get to be president? No, says Dewey, not yet. Not yet.'

'We may have made Cuba *libre*, buddy, but it looks to us like Congress has other plans for the Philippines,' Vaughan said. 'Which explains why Aguinaldo is mad enough to kick his own dog. He believed we were going to turn the country over to him. Now, as far as he is concerned, we've just taken the place of the Spanish. And he's ready to go to war with Uncle Sam.'

'Goddamned mule-headed yuyus!' Gates muttered.

'What?' Lee said.

'He means Filipino rebels,' Vaughan explained. '*Insurrectos*.'

The waiter brought their drinks and put them on the table. Gates glared at the little Filipino as if the man had said something insulting to him. The waiter hurried away, flustered, as Gates muttered something beneath his breath.

'What did you say?' Lee asked him.

'*Sandatahan*. It's supposed to be a Filipino club. What it really is, is Aguinaldo's spies. They're all over the place. All these people sympathise with him. Goddamn rebels know what we're going to do two minutes after we make up our minds to do it.'

'They've even got a newspaper,' Vaughan said. '*La Independencia*. One of Aguinaldo's generals runs it.'

'I thought Otis closed them down.' Gates said.

'He did,' Vaughan confirmed. 'They just moved the whole operation to Malolos.'

'Tell me about Otis,' Lee said.

Gates took a quick look around and then leaned forward, his voice conspiratorial. 'He's a tedious old fart.'

'And Chuck *likes* him,' Vaughan added.

Otis was a paper-shuffler, they told Lee. A tiresome old lawyer, pathologically unable to delegate, he had become mired in a swamp of paperwork. Dockets, requisitions, troop movement orders, quartermaster recommendations, sick-lists piled up on his desk. From seven-thirty in the morning until five, and from eight through midnight, General Otis sat reading in the Malacanang Palace, a splendid Colonial-style mansion of arches, grilles and balconies on the north bank of the Pasig River, once the residence of the Spanish governor-general. His desk half-buried in paper, and large tables at each side overflowing with more, Otis vacillated, while the tension grew. Manila, Gates said, was a shit-hole. The Filipinos went out of their way to provoke trouble with patrolling American soldiers. Knifings and street fights were a nightly occurrence. Local merchants complained bitterly about soldiers who burst open their stores looking for 'concealed weapons' and then 'confiscated' whatever goods they felt like carrying away.

The Americans retaliated by saying the goddamned yuyus were all thieves, cheats, pimps and liars who sold them spiked liquor, picked their pockets and collaborated with the enemy. The whole city was seething with resentment and bitterness.

'So you listen to your Uncle Charlie, Lee,' Gates said. 'And watch your ass, especially on the side streets. As for outside the city . . .' He made a throat-slitting gesture with his forefinger.

'I knew about the curfews, and the armed patrols.' Lee frowned. 'I didn't know it was that bad. I was kind of looking forward to showing Jenny around.'

'You brought your wife out here?' Vaughan asked, astonished. 'Are you crazy or something?'

Lee smiled. 'I'm not. But she is. She joined the Red Cross. She's a nurse.'

'Her old man know about this?'

Lee looked at his watch. 'She should be telling him just about now. I'm hoping we can patch things up between us. Not for my sake, for hers.'

'Boy, you're an optimist!' Gates said.

'Damned right!' Lee grinned. 'Or what would I be doing in the Philippines? I had one war already!'

'Yeah, that's right,' Gates said. 'We heard you was in Cuba.'

'With the Rough Riders.'

'We read about it,' Vaughan said. 'You boys had a good press agent.'

'Teddy Roosevelt doesn't need a press agent,' Lee grinned. 'He'd get his name in the papers if he found a nickel in the street.'

'So how come you're RA again?' Gates said. 'That's not an easy trick when you've resigned a commission.'

'My father and General Lawton are friends. I went to see him. No sweat.'

'He gets a captaincy and he says "no sweat",' Vaughan groaned. 'How long have we been waiting, Chuck?'

'Like I said before, too long.'

'One for the road?' Lee offered.

'Not me, Mary Ann,' Gates said. 'I'm on duty tonight. You stay, Chris.'

'I'd better move out as well,' Vaughan said. 'We can do this again. If Lee doesn't mind mixing with lowly lieutenants.'

'I'll buy you both dinner on Saturday. Jenny wants to see you. How about it?'

'Where you quartered?'

'Right here,' Lee said, grinning.

'Sonofabitch!' Gates said, clamping his campaign hat on his head. He gave Vaughan an exasperated look and then marched out, shaking his head.

'Don't mind Chuck,' Vaughan said. 'We'll see you here Saturday, around eight.'

'Fine.'

Vaughan looked all around him, as if seeing the luxurious surroundings of the hotel for the first time.

'Goddamned rich kids,' he said.

Then, smiling, he followed his friend.

'Why on earth did you have to come to Manila?' Laura Moffatt asked her daughter. Her tone was one of mild exasperation. She was determined not to lose her temper. 'Of all the places on earth, why did you have to come here?'

'The same reason that you did, Mother,' Jenny said. She had decided before she went to see Laura that she would call her 'Mother'. The formality would help her not to lose her temper. At least, she hoped it would.

'Which was?'

'To be with my husband,' Jenny said. 'Wasn't that why you came?'

'If he had known about this, your father would have done everything in his power to prevent it!'

'Why? What has he got against Lee?'

'Surely you do not need to ask, so let us not go into it again.' Laura's lips set in a hard line that Jenny knew of old: I have made up my mind; don't try to change it.

'I simply can't believe this,' Jenny said. 'I'm talking to my own mother, and it's as if I were speaking to a stranger!'

'If you feel like a stranger, perhaps you should ask yourself whose fault that is, Jennifer. What did you expect?'

'I don't know what I expected,' Jenny said hotly. 'But I didn't expect hatred.'

Laura looked up, as if astonished. 'You think we could hate our own daughter?'

'You act as though you do.'

'Your father and I thought – still think – that your running away with that man was a terrible thing. A terrible way to repay our love. But we don't hate you, my dear. If we hated anyone it would be . . . him. That man.'

'His name is Lee, Mother. Lee Starr.'

'I know his name,' Laura said.

'Why do you hate him?'

'Hate is a big word, Jennifer. Too big for a man with as little honour as your husband. Your father and I do not hate him. He is simply beyond the pale.'

'Then I must also be,' Jenny said firmly. 'If you hurt Lee, you are hurting me by doing so.'

Laura laid down her embroidery and folded her hands in her lap. Her expression was that of a patient woman confronted by wearisome wilfulness.

'Jennifer,' she said levelly, 'it was you who ran away. You who rejected our values, our plans, our love.'

'I didn't reject your love!' Jenny said. 'Loving the person you are going to marry is not the same as loving your parents!'

'I didn't say it was. It was the way you went about it which showed your true feelings, Jennifer. That was the rejection.'

288

'You tried to come between us!'

'For your own good, Jennifer, that was all.'

'You had no right. You still have no right to try to come between us. I love Lee!' Jenny said. 'I want to be with him. To share his life.'

'Then I'm sorry for you,' Laura flared. 'Because you've given up everything – and for what?'

'I'm sorry for you, Mother,' Jenny said sadly. 'Because you don't seem to know.'

'What do you mean?' Laura said, her temper flaring again. 'Are you so impertinent you'd imply that I don't love your father?'

'Do you?'

'I married your father in 1864,' Laura said, tiny spots of colour glowing on her cheeks. 'Thirty-five years ago. I have been at his side every day since then. In Godforsaken Army posts where the floors were made of dirt and the walls of mud, where rats ate what little food there was in the pantry, in places where even the Indians wouldn't live. Do you think I could have done so if I didn't care for your father?'

'I'm sorry, Mother,' Jenny said, genuinely contrite. There were all kinds of love. Maybe her mother thought hers was the only kind there was. 'I shouldn't have said that.'

'You would not have,' Laura said. 'Once.'

'Before I married Lee, you mean.'

Laura sniffed. 'You might as well know that your father and I simply refuse to recognise your marriage,' she said.

'It was all quite legal, you know.' Jenny was amused at her mother's pomposity.

'I don't find any of this remotely funny, Jennifer,' Laura said.

'Neither do I,' Jenny said, her own temper bubbling up. 'In fact, I find it downright incredible that I should be here pleading with you to accept the fact that I love Lee, and that we are married, and that all we want is

289

your blessing.'

'Nobody asked you to come here,' Laura said.

'My husband is in the Army, Mother. Like yours. He goes where he is sent.'

'I'm not talking about him, I'm talking about you! What on earth possessed you to become a nurse? You have no training, no –'

'I wanted to be with Lee,' Jenny said. 'I wanted to do something more useful than just sitting at home sewing – oh, I'm sorry, I didn't mean . . .'

'You know how to wound, don't you?'

'Mother, stop it!' Jenny said. 'Stop trying to make me feel guilty for doing something I have every right to do!'

'Hmph.' Laura concentrated furiously on her embroidery. Her shoulders were set now, her manner glacial.

'Mother, please don't be like this!' Jenny said. 'I want us to be a family again. Can't you even try to meet me halfway?'

'I am trying,' Laura said stiffly.

'Try just a little bit harder,' Jenny urged her mother. 'Bring Daddy to the hotel. Have dinner with us.'

'Your father would not sit at the same table as that man!' Laura said. 'And neither would I!' Her manner softened abruptly. 'Oh, Jennifer, if only you hadn't been so impetuous! We had such wonderful plans for you!'

'You never discussed them with me,' Jenny said. 'Or was my opinion irrelevant?'

'Marriage seems to have made you impertinent,' Laura observed sharply. 'Please remember you are addressing your mother, young lady!'

'If you weren't my mother, I wouldn't be this polite!' Jenny said, equally sharply. 'Mother, listen to me. This . . . estrangement is making me very unhappy. It must be the same for you. I want you to get to know Lee. To love him, as I do.'

'I am afraid that is utterly out of the question,' Laura said, getting up from her chair. 'You, of course, are welcome here any time. Your father will be sorry to have missed you.'

'I won't be coming again,' Jenny said, looking at the floor, biting her lip to keep the tears back. 'Not without my husband.'

'That is your privilege,' Laura said. 'Personally, I think you are acting like a child.'

Jenny's eyes widened with surprise, and to Laura's intense annoyance she began to laugh.

'You think I'm still your little girl, don't you?' she said. 'You still think you can tell me what to do the way you did when I was ten years old! Well, you can't, Mother! I'm a woman now. I make my own decisions.'

'And you'll live to rue them all!' Laura said shrilly. 'You'll see, my girl! You'll see!'

'Oh, you silly woman!' Jenny said, fighting the urge to grab her mother by the shoulders and shake her. 'You silly, *silly* woman!'

She ran out of the house before her mother could see the tears. For a while Laura stood impassively in the middle of the room, the slam of the door echoing in her ears. After a while she went back to her chair and picked up her sewing. Her face was expressionless. The needle flickered up, down, up, down. *I must do something*, she thought. *I must do something about this.*

But what?

What?

The day Jennifer's letter had arrived, telling her that General Lawton was recommending Lee Starr for a commission, Laura wrote to Billy Priestman. She thought that he might somehow be able to block the appointment, but instead, his son wrote back. His father was ill, he said, without going into details. He had looked into the matter she mentioned, only to discover that the whole thing had been arranged before her letter reached San Francisco. He did not see how he could help her further. There was no point in relying on Billy any more. No use ever relying on men. She would have to handle this herself, right here in Manila.

But how?

A phrase from Willie Priestman's letter burned like fire in Laura's mind. 'My information is that there are pockets of guerilla fighting all over the Philippines. Cannot your husband arrange it so that Captain Starr sees plenty of action? Surely, if he is sent to the sharp end enough times, the inevitable tragedy must occur.'

The inevitable tragedy. With her husband dead, Jennifer would have no choice but to return to her parents' home. In time she would forget, and they would be able to make a suitable match for her. Plenty of young widows remarried. Laura nodded, her thin lips set in a straight, uncompromising line. That night, she discussed the subject with her husband for the first time. She knew how to handle Whittier.

'What are you going to do, Whittier?' she said, as her husband helped himself to more rice.

'Do?' he said, surprised. 'Do about what?'

'Oh, don't be so tiresome,' Laura said impatiently. 'I mean about Jennifer's husband.'

'Nothing I can do, my dear, except what I have done. Refuse to recognise the fellow's even on the islands. Make sure he's not welcome at the Army & Navy Club or the University. See to it he's not invited to any of the gala parties on the battleships. Show the fellow his type's not wanted here.'

'You think that will make the problem go away?'

'Laura, my dear, there's not much more I can do,' Moffatt said, frowning. 'The man is here, and that's that. Can't make him disappear, can I?' He smiled, the ever-indulgent husband showing his wife that he understood her feelings. It was all Laura could do not to shout angrily at him.

'You miss my point, Whittier,' she said. 'As always.'

'What?'

'Do you want little nigger grandchildren?'

'Laura!' he said, shocked. 'Think what you're saying.

292

If anyone heard the servants . . .'

'They'd applaud me,' Laura spat. 'No mother worth her salt would sit idly by watching her daughter's life ruined.'

'She's not . . . she isn't . . .?'

'Not yet,' Laura said. 'But it is only a matter of time. Unless we *do* something!'

'I fail to see . . .'

'Will there be war here?'

'General Otis –'

'Damn General Otis!' she snapped. 'Tell me what you think!'

'The consensus of opinion at headquarters,' he said, as if reciting a phrase he had been taught, 'is that while we should continue to negotiate with Aguinaldo, the likelihood is we'll have to fight him.'

'There have already been a lot of skirmishes, haven't there?'

'Quite a few.'

'Where are the worst areas?'

'North of Manila. Malolos. Iloilo.'

'Couldn't you send him up there?'

'What? Jennifer's –? Well, he's not under my direct command. But yes, I suppose I could arrange it. Why?'

Laura did not answer. The silence lengthened. Slowly, what she was proposing dawned on Whittier Moffatt. He paled slightly, then coughed self-consciously.

'Look here, Laura . . .' he said.

'No!' she hissed. '*You* look here. Fate has seen fit to provide us with an opportunity to turn back the clock, Whittier. I do not propose to ignore it!'

'But . . .'

'Whittier Moffatt, what is the matter with you? Can't you see this is the only way?'

'I don't like it, Laura,' he said. 'I'm a soldier. I have to go by the book. There are things I can do, things I can't do. Not even for you. Now, I can see what you mean.

293

about Jennifer's husband. You may even be right. But I still have to go by the book. Do you understand me?'

'I'm sorry, dearest.' Her manner changed abruptly. 'I'm being unreasonable, aren't I? And you're being a darling bear, not wanting to tell me so.'

'Well . . .' he said, mollified.

'I'll get you a glass of Oporto,' Laura offered. 'I know you like one after supper.'

'I'll tell you what,' he said. 'Let's sleep on it. Tomorrow is Saturday. We've got all weekend to talk.'

'You're quite right, dear,' Laura agreed. 'We mustn't be too hasty.' She had won and she knew it. If she pushed any harder, he would grow more stubborn. There was nothing to be lost, she thought, by waiting until Monday.

In the event, she was quite wrong, because the following night, Saturday, February 4, 1899, General Emilio Aguinaldo ordered his army to attack Manila.

The dirtiest war in American history had begun.

31

After seven years of marriage, Willie Priestman was bored. He was still fond of Marietta; but there was nothing between them. He set up trust funds for the boys, put their names down for good prep schools. He paid all the bills for the house, the servants, everything Marietta needed. But he went there less and less.

Marietta hated Willie's cronies and clubs and made no bones about it. All Willie lived for, she said, was to gallivant around New York with his drinking friends, 'Diamond Jim' Brady, Stanford White, the producer Florenz Ziegfeld and their like.

'What do you want me to do, for God's sake?' Willie said. 'Sit in my apartment all night looking out the window?'

'I think you ought to spend more time here with the children and me,' she said.

'I'm here as much as I can be, Marietta. But the business –'

'It's not the business!' she said. 'It's those show people you're mixing with. You use them as an excuse to stay away from me. From us!'

Marietta was confused and unhappy. She knew she was not talented or beautiful like Irene Bentley Smith, or Anna Held, or the other women Willie knew in New York. She had no bright conversation. When they married, she had been sure she could make Willie happy. But she found sex ugly and repellent, and bearing children painful in the extreme. Perhaps with a gentler, more patient man, Marietta might have slowly blossomed. Willie was hardly that. No matter how she tried to explain her feelings to him, she knew she sounded pettish. Even when she was trying hard to be sincere, it made her over-anxious, and instead of sounding reasonable, the words came out as complaints. She could actually see his patience disappearing, like smoke. Why can't I make him understand? she wondered desperately. Why won't he try? And Willie thought, why doesn't she ever stop whining?

'I'm going back to New York tomorrow,' he said.

'When will you be home?'

'I don't know.'

'I wish you'd stay, Willie. I wish –'

'I can't,' Willie said. 'I simply don't have the time.'

'You have time for your smart New York friends.'

'They could be your friends, too,' he said, letting some of his own anger show. 'If you'd only make the effort.'

'Oh, yes,' she said scornfully. 'Just get up and come to New York. Never mind about the house, never mind about the children.'

'Don't use them as an excuse!' Willie snapped. 'They have everything they need.'

'Everything except a father!' she flashed.

'Don't start that again,' he said. 'Just don't start again!'

'That's what you always say!'

'Then I'm happy not to have disappointed you!'

Oh, but you have, Marietta thought. If only you knew. If only you could hear the words I cannot say. If only you could understand that I am trapped inside myself, and that only you can rescue me, and that if you do not, or will not, then I am lost, lost, lost.

'I . . . want . . . I want so much to please you,' Marietta said hesitantly. 'But . . . I don't know how to.'

'It's too late, Marietta,' he said. 'There's no point in going on with this.'

'Oh, Willie,' she said, unable to stop the tears from filling her eyes. 'I'm so lonely. So lonely!'

'Don't you think it's a bit late to play the neglected wife?' Willie said unfeelingly. 'Dammit, Marietta, you take precious little interest in me when I am here. Especially in the bedroom.'

'Is that all you want me for?'

'Not all,' he said. 'But I am a man. A man has needs.'

'I could . . . change. I could try, Willie. If you would.'

'Don't make any promise you can't keep,' he sneered. It was cruel, but he could not stop himself from saying it. There were times when he wanted to lash out, to hurt. It was guilt sometimes. It was self-defence sometimes. He didn't know why sometimes, but he did it anyway.

'Oh, Willie,' Marietta said. She was crying, but she made no sound. The tears just ran down her face. She turned her head so that he could not see her eyes. There was a silence that might have lasted as long as a minute before she spoke again. 'You don't love me any more, do you?'

He almost said it. He almost said *I never loved you*, but he could not bring himself to be that cruel. It was not her fault. Instead of growing together they had grown apart. It happened to a lot of people. Most of them had to put up with each other because they had no alternative. That was not the case with himself and Marietta. It would be better, he decided, if he just stayed in the East. She would get used to it. She could get on with her own life in her own way. Marietta liked things to be orderly. She liked to know that the morrow would be much the same as today, with everything in its place: all the bills paid, a nice fire in the hearth, reading the children a story and tucking them up in bed. She had just married the wrong man.

Before he left for New York he went to see his father. He said nothing about himself and Marietta. No point in upsetting the old boy any sooner than was strictly necessary: he'd put two and two together soon enough.

Billy had still not properly recovered from the pneumonia that had almost killed him the preceding autumn. It was said to hit heavy drinkers harder. The doctors told Willie he ought to try to get the old man to cut down on the drinking before it killed him. Willie said he would try, knowing nothing on God's green earth would ever stop Billy hitting the bottle. He had a pretty shrewd idea now what it was that his father was trying to drown in the whisky. I might drink some myself, if I had something like that on my mind, he thought.

'You never come to see me any more,' Billy grumbled querulously. His skin was pasty and unhealthy-looking, and the sound of his breathing filled the room. His eyes were red-rimmed and rheumy. He rarely went out.

'I'm in New York most of the time, Pa,' Willie said. 'It's a long trip.'

'I read about you all the time. In the paper. Sounds to me like you're turning into a goddamned playboy. That right, Willie? You turning into a goddamned playboy?'

'I work hard, Pa,' Willie said, wondering why he should still have to defend himself. 'I play hard, too.'

'You should spend more time with your family. Hell, boy, we never see you.'

'I do the best I can,' Willie said. There was no point getting into all that again.

'What's it all for, Willie? Where are you in such an all-fired hurry to go?'

'Man can't stand still, Pa. I've got a lot of new ideas. I want to open up another paper, in Chicago. I might even run for office.'

'Can't do everything, boy,' Billy grumbled. 'Lose sight of what's important if you chase every damned rabbit that breaks cover. You remember that.'

He meant the Starrs. His hatred of them was the most

important thing in his life. Willie was no psychiatrist, but he was fairly confident that his father's bitter hatred stemmed directly from the awful guilt that made him drink so heavily.

'Had something to ask you,' Billy said, his forehead creasing into a frown. 'What the devil was it?'

Willie waited. It would come. It just took longer every time. I wonder if we would put up with what we do put up with if they weren't our parents? he thought. No, he decided. We simply wouldn't have this kind of patience with strangers. Then why do we put up with it from parents? Because they teach us to. It was all a damned stupid business, and he would make sure his own sons were taught differently. As he watched, Billy's frown cleared, and his father smiled.

'I know,' he said. 'Laura Moffatt. You hear any more from her?'

'They've got a full-scale revolution going on down there in Manila, Pa.'

'I read the papers,' Billy said, testily. 'They said Arthur MacArthur had cut them Filipinos to pieces after they attacked Manila. Otis says it will all be over by midsummer.'

'Maybe.'

'Just like to know whether –'

'Pa, you've got to quit this!' Willie said impatiently. 'You've got to think of something besides the damned Starrs. It's eating away at you like acid. Listen, why don't I arrange for you to take a vacation? You could go somewhere sunny, warm. Forget this stupid –'

'Don't say any more!' Billy growled. 'Don't ever call me stupid!'

'Pa, I –'

'I tell you, boy, if there's a life beyond the grave, I'll hate those bastards there!' Billy's pallid cheeks were flushed, and a racking cough spasmed through his once-sturdy frame.

'You've spent a lot of money trying to hurt them,

299

Pa,' Willie said. 'Where the hell has it got us? I'm telling you: money isn't the way to do it. It's their reputation we've got to go after. Their damned Starr honour. That's the pride that will bring their fall.'

'You think so?'

'Is your way working?'

'I'd like to tell you to go to hell,' Billy said.

'You can do that. It won't make any difference.'

'You mean that, boy?'

It was the nearest Willie had ever come to telling his father that he loved him. Perhaps it was the nearest he ever could come to it. Billy looked at him for long moments. Then the hatred came back into his eyes.

'You do it your way if you want to,' he wheezed. 'I'll go on doing it mine!'

The memory of the hatred in his father's eyes pursued Willie all the way back to New York, but once he got there and plunged back into his murderous work-schedule, it slowly faded. The Starrs would have to wait their turn. Willie had other priorities right now.

He called a conference of all his editors in the big suite that he kept on the top floor of the *Inquirer* building in New York. It was also his home. The windows on the west looked out over City Hall Park and the bustle of Broadway beyond it. On the east, there was a glimpse of the East River and the Brooklyn Bridge. One wall was taken up by mahogany bookshelves. In them was his growing collection of first editions and rare books. Just last week he had acquired a fine copy of Rudyard Kipling's first book, a first edition of the *Schoolboy Lyrics* privately printed in Lahore by Kipling's parents, with the red ink rules done by either Kipling or his father.

'We're going to be making a lot of changes,' he told the editors. 'The way we approach stories, the content. I may even change the style a little. Move the papers maybe one notch up the market. Nothing drastic, but definitely different.'

'You'll forgive me for saying so, Chief,' Schofield observed sardonically, 'but this isn't your style. What's behind it?'

'I'm thinking of running for office.'

'That's what you need,' Schofield said. 'More work.'

'Don't worry,' Willie told him. 'I can handle it. I can eat nails.'

'I believe you. How big do you want this to be, Chief?'

'As big as we can make it.'

'And what about the war?'

'The Philippines aren't news,' Willie said. 'Joe Public does not wish to know that the United States Army can't even control a bunch of raggedy-assed peasants.'

He was being cynical, but he was right. As far as the American public was concerned, the Philippine insurrection was the Army's problem: as such, it wasn't worth much more than a couple of columns on page ten.

With no need any longer to work an eighteen-hour day, Willie found a new love: musical comedy. Ziegfeld was always pestering him to come to a show, but Willie scoffed at such damned nonsense.

'Musicals are much more sophisticated than they used to be, Willie,' Ziggy said, in his high-pitched tenor voice. 'Look I've got first-night tickets for the new Chauncey Olcott show. Come and see it with us. We can have dinner afterwards.'

'All right,' Willie said. 'I'll come to please you. But I won't like it.'

The show was called *Romance of Athlone*, and it was, as Willie kept telling himself all the way through it, arrant tosh. Yet he could not help liking it. And when Olcott sang the show's big romantic number, 'My Wild Irish Rose', Willie was hooked.

'Well, what did you think?' Ziegfeld asked him later.

'Tosh.'

'Come on, Willie.'

'Well,' Willie said. 'Some of it was quite good.'

'Weren't you the one that said you'd rather go to a burlesque house?'

'All right, all right,' Willie said. 'So I liked it.'

'So come to another,' Ziggy said triumphantly.

Willie became an avid first-nighter. Later that year, when the opening of the new Weber and Fields musical *Whirl-i-gig* was announced, seats were in such demand – perhaps because of the fact that Lillian Russell was going to appear in it – that they had to be auctioned. Willie got his accustomed box, but at the unaccustomed price of $750. At that, he got off lightly: Jesse Lewisohn paid $1,000.

After the show there was a party at Rector's. Lillian Russell, Victor Herbert and Lew Fields were there. More importantly for Willie, he struck up a conversation with a thick-set, grave-faced man who told Willie that he was the writer of the show, Harry Smith. He had been a newspaperman in Chicago, writing a column called 'Follies of the Day'. They found they had a number of mutual acquaintances in the business. Smith told Willie he had written his first show in 1887 with Reginald de Koven.

'It was a direct lift from Gilbert and Sullivan,' he said, with a deprecating smile. 'They didn't seem to mind.'

'Which comes first? The words or the music?'

'The cheque,' Smith smiled. 'No, I'm joking. But only mildly. You see, the hardest part of putting any show on is raising the money.'

'How do you mean?'

'Have you any idea how many musicals there are each season?'

'A lot,' Willie said. 'Fifteen, twenty?'

'Twenty-five or more. Every season.'

'Who provides the money?'

'The producers. Men like Ziegfeld, Klaw and Erlanger. Charlie Frohman. Sometimes they put it up themselves. Others they go out and look for angels.'

'Angels?'

An angel, Smith explained, was someone who invested in a Broadway show. The amount was a matter between himself and the producer. His return on the investment, if the show was a hit, was a share in the profits.

'What are you working on right now?' Willie asked.

'Another show,' Harry said, with a wry grin. 'What else?'

He was the most unlikely comic writer, Willie thought. The bloodhound expression gave no hint at all of the fecundity bubbling away beneath. Nobody in his right mind would have called Harry Bache Smith a great writer, but there was no doubt he was a damned good one. You couldn't write a song like 'The Man Who Broke The Bank At Monte Carlo' and not be.

'For Ziegfeld?'

'Aye, laddie. And for the lovely Anna.'

Ziegfeld's romance with his star, Anna Held, was storybook stuff. The penniless Ziegfeld had persuaded her to come to America, mounted a lavish show around her and made her a star. Although professing to be French, Anna was in fact Polish, and had started her career as a chorus girl. She had been sketched by Toulouse-Lautrec. In 1894 she married a wealthy South American, Maximo Carrera, a man twice her age. There was a daughter, Liane. The marriage broke up; Carrera had custody of the little girl. Anna returned to the stage just as Ziegfeld came to Paris talent-hunting. The minute he set eyes on the tiny girl with her halo of light brown hair and large dark luminous eyes, he fell like a ton of bricks. He publicised her with a flair that was the envy of everyone on the Great White Way. They were living together as man and wife.

'Where's he getting the money from? He told me he was broke.'

'Ha,' Smith said. 'Ziegfeld! Living like Kubla Khan, but he's broke.'

'Seriously, Harry.'

'I don't know. Irene says Anna told her Ziggy's having trouble putting it together. That's all I know.'

Harry Smith's wife, the former Irene Bentley, had been one of the stage's most beautiful prima donnas. She was a close friend of Anna Held.

'You think he'd let me in?' Willie asked. Harry looked at him over the top of his spectacles and smiled.

'He'd let Satan in,' he said, 'if he had ten bucks.'

Fifteen days later, Willie Priestman became an angel. To his surprise and delight, being an angel seemed to confer a great many unexpected privileges. If it occurred to him that perhaps Ziegfeld, that greatest of self-publicisers, was making sure Willie got plenty of stories for his newspapers, he didn't mind. Ziggy was a past master. Anyone who had the nerve to put on, as Ziggy had done in his early days, a show called 'The Dancing Ducks of Denmark' – the ducks danced because Ziggy put them on a hotplate and then turned on some music – deserved his headlines. Besides, Willie was having far too much fun. He got to gossip with the stars, to flirt with the soubrettes. He heard all the inside-inside gossip, who was feuding with whom. It became his habit to drop into the theatre most afternoons, to watch the rehearsals. The way a show took shape fascinated him, how Harry Smith thought of new bits of 'business', how the moves onstage were mapped out by the director. Best of all, however, was the discovery that Harry Smith was also an avid book and document collector. It was not long before the pair of them were haunting auction rooms together, sometimes returning to Smith's mansion-like residence positively euphoric over some treasure they felt they'd bought at well under its true value. Irene called them her 'naughty boys'. Willie fell in love with her, almost inevitably. She told him it was just an *amitié amoureuse*. He had never heard the phrase before. Irene said it described a love affair in which the lovers never sleep together. Her frankness was thrilling. He could not wait to see her again. She did not seem to find him dull, as women often did. She encouraged his interest in the theatre. They went to shows together. Sometimes he took her to supper.

'Good for her,' Harry would say. 'She needs a change. Stuck with boring old me all the time. Go on, enjoy yourselves!' It all seemed very sophisticated to Willie, who had not thought himself altogether unsophisticated. Show people didn't go by the same rule book. He found that thrilling, too. He was a man whose life had been bound by rules. So while Harry worked on his script, or the compilation of his lyrics – 'the first time any American theatrical writer has ever been thus honoured,' he announced, with endearing pride – Irene and Willie saw all the shows, went to all the parties, and talked, and talked, and talked.

Willie was suffering from a well-known complaint, Irene told him. It might wear off: it sometimes did. In the meantime there was nothing he could do. He was stage-struck. He sat in the echoing auditorium, singing along with the rehearsal pianist, listened to de Koven and Smith working on new numbers. He never ceased to marvel at the young actors and actresses who came to audition. They all seemed so terribly vulnerable. He did not know how Ziegfeld could choose between them. How did they muster that heartbreaking confidence? How could they, time after time, walk out on to a bare stage lit by a single naked light, and perform their hearts out for a group of people they couldn't even see? So many of them were good. So few of them were chosen. Willie was never asked what he thought, nor did he ever offer his opinion. Until the day Susan Simpson came along.

He was talking to Smith when she walked on to the stage. She was not tall. Her long dark hair framed a heart-shaped face that was too pretty to be plain, but some way short of beautiful. She wore little or no make-up that he could detect. Her manner was hesitant, and her voice more than a little unsure, as though she was very nervous.

'Susan Simpson,' she said loudly into the dark auditorium. 'Singer and dancer.'

'What have you been in, Miss Simpson?'

'I was in *The Fortune Teller* last season.'

'New York, or tour?'

'Just New York.'

'Nothing else?'

'I had a small part in Mr Hammerstein's *War Bubbles*.'

'That turkey!' Harry Smith muttered. 'Oscar had to sell the Olympia to cover his losses.'

Susan Simpson said she would sing 'Daisy Bell'. She walked across to the pianist to give him her music. She turned and walked back to face them. Her expression seemed almost defiant, as though she was thinking, I don't care what you say, I'm going to sing. Willie's heart went out to her: she looked . . . forlorn. That was the word for it! When she sang, her voice, although clear and true, was only average. She started a dance routine.

'She may not be able to sing,' de Koven said with a grin, 'but she sure can't dance.'

Ziegfeld stopped her after the first eight. 'Thank you, Miss Simpson,' he called. 'We'll let you know.'

'Give her a job, Ziggy,' Willie said, speaking almost without thinking.

'That *Shloomperl*? In my show? Not on your life!' Ziegfeld snorted, watching the next girl get ready to audition. She was a tall, striking-looking blonde.

'Goodbye, Ziggy,' Willie said, rising from the seat. 'I'm pulling out of the show.'

'What?' Ziegfeld, Smith and de Koven spoke as one.

'You heard me.'

'Wait a minute, wait a minute!' Ziegfeld said. He got to his feet and turned towards the stage. 'Just hold on for a moment, please, young lady!' Then he turned angrily to face Willie. 'What the hell is this?'

306

'That girl is out, I'm out.'

'That girl? That girl who just auditioned? The one that sang —'

'That girl.'

'You crazy or something?' Ziegfeld said. 'You seen some of the girls waiting back there?'

'Yes or no, Ziggy.'

'All right, all right!' Ziegfeld said irritably. 'She's in. I don't know what the hell we can do with her, but if it means so much to you, all right.'

'You mind telling us why this is so important to you, Willie?' Harry Smith asked.

'I don't know,' Willie told them. 'I honestly don't know.'

He got up and left them as the tall blonde girl walked towards centre stage to begin her audition. Willie hardly glanced at her. He ran up the steps at the side of the stage and went backstage. Susan Simpson was standing talking to some of the other girls who had auditioned. They did not give Willie a second glance. In his dark business suit and hat, he did not look 'show business'. He didn't know how you did, but show people seemed to be able to tell.

'Miss Simpson,' he said. 'My name is Priestman. William Priestman.'

'Yes?'

'Might I have a word with you? In private?'

Susan Simpson frowned, then bobbed her head in acquiescence. They walked around behind the console. She looked at him with mild curiosity.

'I . . . wanted to tell you personally,' Willie said, 'that you have been hired to appear in the show.'

Her face lit up, a genuine and — he thought — most appealing smile. 'Oh, that's wonderful!' she said. 'I must tell the girls. Thank you, Mr Priestly!'

She really doesn't know who I am, he thought. Isn't that wonderful?

32

Manila was a shock.

Jenny had imagined it would be a sprawling city. It was little more than a fair-sized town.

'What did you expect?' Lee grinned. 'Chicago?'

The fortress town around which modern Manila spread was called Intramuros. Its massive *tufa* walls enclosed a complete city, at whose heart was the Plaza Real, with its fountains and statues and gardens. On the far side of the square, women in black dresses put on scarves and entered the cathedral with bowed heads. Beyond lay the huge stone buttresses of Fort Santiago.

The old town had the same essentially Spanish quality as Santa Fé, she thought, but an older and sterner variety. During the Spanish rule, Lee told her, no *extrañjero* was allowed within its walls. The seven gates were locked every night and the drawbridges across the surrounding moat were raised.

They crossed the river and wandered hand in hand through the narrrow, cobbled streets of Binondo. Jabbering vendors offered them papayas, mangos, pineapples, figs, coconuts. Beggars in rags held out emaciated hands. Cheek by jowl with Chinese restaurants and apothecary shops were food stores, clothes stores, vegetable shops. Each was a hutch no more than five feet wide and ten deep. Others sold garish religious prints, plaster saints, batik shirts, handkerchiefs. Gaudy theatrical posters peeled from stucco walls. Balloon sellers stood in the shadow of the massive Binondo church, next to the young painters exhibiting their work. Somewhere someone was playing a guitar. American soldiers sat on benches with their arms around giggling Filipino girls.

'I've been posted to the relief hospital behind the Malacanang,' Jenny said. 'It's quite small. Only five wards. I'm glad about that.'

'You've been over there?'

'It was like the first day of a new term at school,' she said. 'Lots of new faces, introductions to people whose names you had no hope of remembering. I did meet the senior doctor, Colonel Eames. He's lovely.'

'You think you're going to like it?'

'I'm nervous, if that's what you mean. There's so much I don't know.'

'You'll learn,' he said, confidently.

I hope so, she thought, wishing she had as much faith in herself as Lee seemed to have. He was always so positive. Be sure that you're right, he said, quoting Davy Crockett, then go ahead. Nursing wasn't quite that easy. The training they had given Jenny was not so much basic as perfunctory. The qualified nurses who instructed her apologised because there was so little time. Three years wouldn't be enough, they said. You must learn as you go along, as we do. Each of the nurses coming out to Manila had been given a book on first aid written by Clara Barton, founder of the American Red Cross. Jenny had a nightmare picture of herself thumbing frantically through it while a wounded soldier bled to death at her feet.

After the flat grey winter landscapes of New Mexico and the slushy streets of San Francisco, the colours of the Philippines were an almost physical shock. Brilliantly plumed birds flicked between the clattering fronds of the palms; exotic flowers grew in wild profusion everywhere. She caught sight of herself in the window of a shop, a small, slender, dark-haired girl. Who ever thought this could happen? she wondered. I have been to Hawaii and Guam. I am in Manila. In the Philippine Islands. Another world.

They ate lunch in a little place just off the Escolta. A smiling Chinese woman brought them a soup called *sinigang*, and *paksiw*, which was pork cooked in a tart soy sauce with vegetables, garlic and ginger.

'*Mabait*,' Lee said to the woman, who nodded eagerly, her smile growing wider.

'*Mabait, mabait*,' she enthused. Smiling children with jet-black hair and lustrous eyes peered around the kitchen door, giggling. She shooed them away with a torrent of words.

'What's ma-by-it?'

'Tagalog for "good",' Lee said.

'Tagalog!' Jenny said. 'Well, now!'

'I picked up a few phrases,' Lee said.

'I thought you said everyone spoke Spanish here.'

'Educated people do. Not everybody.'

'Why do all the men wear their shirts outside their pants?'

'It was a Spanish law. Now they do it as a sort of "to-hell-with-you" gesture of independence.'

'Independence?'

'That's what they want. They don't want us here.'

'They seem friendly enough.'

'Maybe,' he said. 'But there are still fights down here every night. The Filipinos go out of their way to provoke our boys, knowing they're under orders not to cause trouble. Our boys say the merchants try to cheat them, the girls try to rob them. The Filipinos claim our boys steal from them, or get credit with false names, or get drunk and pick fights. Both sides are probably telling the truth.'

''The scuttlebutt is that they're getting ready to fight us.'

'I heard that, too. Well, that's why we're here.'

'What will happen?'

'Aguinaldo is at Malolos with about thirty thousand

men. He'll try to kick us out.'

'Can he do it?'

'No, he hasn't got a prayer,' Lee said. 'If he comes looking for a fight, he'll get his ass whipped.'

'When will you get your company?'

'As soon as General Lawton takes over the Division. He's seeing Otis tomorrow.'

A little silence descended. Both of them knew what the other was thinking.

'I wish you'd go with me, tomorrow,' Jenny said.

'We've discussed this, Jen. You know why I can't.'

'You said it would be ignoble.'

'That's right.'

'How can you be so stubborn?'

'You say stubborn. I say certain.'

'You're putting a lot of pressure on me, Lee.'

'Only because I know you can take it.'

'Why do you have to have this stupid code of behaviour?' she said hotly. 'It's adolescent. Most people do what they have to do to get what they want.'

'I know.'

'You don't give a damn for any of that, do you? Success, popularity, praise.'

'I want them, like everybody else,' Lee said. 'But not if I can only get them by begging.'

'If it was anyone but you, I'd say you were puffed up with pride. I'm not so sure you're not.'

'It's not pride, Jen,' Lee said quietly.

'I love you, you know that?'

'Of course,' he said, kissing her, right there on the street. 'I'm irresistible!'

They walked along the riverside towards San Miguel, arms around each other's waist. Pedlars followed them, trying to sell them brassware and woven wall-hangings, baskets from Baguio, wood carvings.

'Lee . . . ?' Jenny said.

'What?'

'If they . . . if my mother and father were to meet you

311

halfway . . . would you try? At least try?'

He was silent. No matter what *rapprochement* might or might not come, he knew he could never again respect or like either of Jenny's parents. It didn't, however, alter the fact that they were still her parents.

'All right,' he said. 'I'll try.'

That night, after they had made love, Jenny lay awake for a long time, looking through the mosquito nets at the dark sky and listening to the endless movement of the palm fronds. Lee slept quietly beside her.

'It's hard to believe they ever loved each other the way we do now,' she had said to him.

'I wonder if they ever did?'

As she remembered Lee's words, Jenny realised with a small shock of surprise that she really knew very little about her parents' marriage. She had only the most general idea of how they had met. They had gone to Niagara Falls for their honeymoon. She knew that because her mother never tired of quoting Oscar Wilde's sardonic observation, that the falls were always the bride's second biggest disappointment.

You never thought about your parents as young lovers. You saw the photographs, they told you stories. It was all part of the web of security they wove around you as a child. The game of 'do you remember?'

You assumed they had been in love, even if now there was little sign they ever had been. When had Laura begun to domineer, when had her father begun to accept the domination? Had it always been like that? Had they once known the hot, blinding waves of passion that swept through Jenny when Lee held her in his arms, and she felt the solid *presence* of him inside her body? Perhaps that passionate fire was banked by the years. Perhaps it turned to something less demanding, gentler. Perhaps it just died.

No, she thought. It only dies if you let it.

Her parents did not love each other any more. Perhaps, as Lee had said, they never had. It explained a

312

lot of things. All those years, she thought, all those years without love. It was the saddest thing she had ever imagined.

Whittier Moffatt's brevet rank wasn't anything like enough to get him his own division. He was effectively back to being a colonel, and he did not like it one damned bit. Command of a regiment, active duty: the prospect was daunting. He did not know what to do; his reaction was to strut. There was a simple way to avoid having to make decisions: delegate them downwards. He saw to it that no one below the rank of colonel got to see him. Everyone else talked to Moffatt's aide, a sour-faced lieutenant-colonel from Philadelphia named Aysgill. Like Moffatt, Aysgill had studied law. He was leaf-dry and disdainful. He was referred to by everyone as the Asshole, because it was through him that all the shit came out.

Thinking it a favour, General Lawton assigned Lee Starr to Moffatt's regiment. His battalion commander was Major Tom Corcoran. Corcoran was RA, a veteran of the last Sioux War, although he hadn't been at Wounded Knee. That glory, he said, belonged to the Seventh Cavalry, and they were welcome to it. He was a burly, short, bluntly spoken man. Privately, he considered Moffatt the poorest excuse for a commanding officer that it had ever been his misfortune to draw; but he was far too good a soldier to hint, even by the raising of an eyebrow, that he thought so. He was Army. He got his orders from Aysgill, who got them from Moffatt, who got them from Lawton, who got them from Otis, who presumably got them from God. The Army was not a debating society. Corcoran's job, as he saw it, was to make his battalion hum like a well-oiled machine. The theory was that if every battalion commander did the same thing, you had one hell of an army. He gave Lee his orders in a characteristically no-nonsense fashion.

'Captain Starr,' he told Lee, 'you will take command of Fox company, 1st Battalion. You've got six days to whip them into shape.'

'I'll do my best, sir,' Lee said.

'You'll need to, Captain,' Corcoran observed. 'Fox company is full of misfits. You must have a very special place in the colonel's affections.'

'I believe I do, sir.'

'Anything you want to talk about?'

'No, sir, thank you, sir.'

'Very well.'

Something wrong there, Corcoran thought. Captain Starr was General Moffatt's son-in-law. His military record was exemplary: Corcoran had read it carefully, as he read the records of every company commander in the battalion. He liked to feel he knew his men. But there was something here he couldn't get a handle on.

'You're going to be right at the sharp end,' Corcoran said, wondering again why it had been insisted upon. 'Scouting two days ahead of the main body.'

'I expected something like that, sir.'

Did you, now? Corcoran thought.

'The main force will move out a week Wednesday. General MacArthur's plan is to push north, in three columns. We'll attack Malolos. Capture Aguinaldo if possible.'

'So I shove off Monday. A week tomorrow.'

'Correct. You will remain forward of the main force until the attack on Malolos is mounted. You will locate bivouacs, reconnoitre enemy positions, contain and pacify villages which may be sheltering rebel forces. You'll have your work cut out, Captain.'

'If I might make a suggestion, sir?'

'Go ahead?'

'I'd like to suggest putting two companies – two of the smaller ones – between mine and the main force. Then if we run into something, we can get word back to

314

regiment fast. Or whistle them up as reinforcement. From what I've heard about Aguinaldo, Major, he can be long gone in two days.'

Corcoran hesitated. *Damn it*, he thought, the lad was right. There was nothing in the orders to prevent him from putting two companies between Starr and the main force. It would make him, Corcoran, feel better, too. He didn't at all like the idea of sending so small a unit out alone, so far ahead of help. Fox company, like many of the others, was down through illness and casualties to about a quarter of its normal complement. Sixteen enlisted men, a corporal, a sergeant, and a first lieutenant who, if Corcoran remembered correctly, wouldn't know he was in Texas if you sat him in the Alamo.

'Very well,' he said. 'Anyone in mind?'

'Gates and Vaughan, sir.'

Interesting, Corcoran thought. Starr had served with them at Omaha Barracks. And resigned his commission there, too. What was it between him and Moffatt?

'Very well, Captain,' Corcoran said. 'Carry on.'

'Yes, sir,' Lee said. 'Thank you, sir.'

That was what you did. You got your orders and you did your best. You could maybe conclude from the orders that the man who had given them to you intended to put you between a rock and a hard place. But you didn't question them. Generals could, and sometimes did. Once in a navy-blue moon, colonels did. But lowly captains saluted, did a smart about-face, and got the hell out of there.

'We're shoving off next week,' he told Jenny that night. 'I'll be scouting for the regiment.'

He didn't say anything about how far ahead of it he would be, or his gut feeling that Whittier Moffatt had put him there hoping he would get his balls shot off.

'How long will you be gone?'

'Hard to tell. We'll probably be out until the rains start.'

315

'Oh,' she said, unable to conceal her disappointment. The rainy season commenced around the beginning of June. That was nearly four months away.

'Of course, we may get it done quicker,' he said, seeing her expression. 'It depends on what we run into. The word out of headquarters is that General Otis expects to suppress the rebellion by midsummer at the latest.'

'You think Aguinaldo will make a fight of it?'

'He might,' Lee said. 'But he's likelier to fall back into the jungle. He's got all of Luzon to hide in. He can hold out there for a long time.'

'That's what he'll do,' Jenny said. 'They know better than to stand and fight after the beating they took.'

Aguinaldo's attack on Manila had been successfully repelled because the Filipinos had neither method nor plan. They simply came running in scattered lines at the American positions while the *Sandatahan* created diversions inside the city. Not more than one in three of them had a rifle, and none of them was prepared for the brutal firepower of the Army Springfields, which literally tore the diminutive Filipinos apart.

On the morning of February 5 the Americans counter-attacked. The Aguinaldistas were astonished by this ungentlemanly display. Through all the years they had fought the Spanish, fighting had been confined to the cool of the night, both sides retiring at daybreak to avoid the heat of the day. Yet the *Americanos* were coming at them behind an artillery barrage that shattered their unprepared positions.

MacArthur's division pushed right on as far as Caloocan. Anderson drove the rest of the rebels into range of the Navy's guns. The bluejackets said it was like shooting fish in a barrel. General Otis was of the opinion that Aguinaldo had been squashed like a bug. The 'insurrection', he declared, was over. In fact, it had hardly begun.

Chastened by his losses in Manila, Aguinaldo

changed his tactics. His troops cut telegraph wires, ambushed supply trains, tore up American-held sections of the railroad. When the American columns came out after them, they faded back into the jungle. The best hope the Americans had now was a fitful and inconclusive skirmish. It was like a series of brush fires: as fast as one was put out, another one flared up. Outlying posts had to be guarded twenty-four hours a day. One or two small garrisons were mercilessly massacred.

The 'good old days' when there had been horse-racing at Pasay, and gala luncheons on Admiral Dewey's flagship, when there had been dinner-dances every night at the Hotel del Oriente, and tax-free champagne at the Army & Navy Club, were things of the past. In Manila, there was an 8.30 curfew; no American civilian was safe in the town without a military escort.

At Camp Dewey the men were lined up for inspection. First Lieutenant David Morley stood at attention to one side. He saluted as Lee came on to the parade ground. The sergeant shouted the men to attention.

'At ease,' Lee said. Their ease wasn't a hell of a lot different to their attention. Sloppy, he thought. Lazy. A pity. It meant he would have to kick ass right from the start.

'A short speech,' he said. A distinct groan emerged from somewhere in the twin lines. Lee ignored it; there would be time for that later. He caught a glimpse of Morley's thin, undertaker's face. Morley looked as if he would prefer to be somewhere else. Anywhere else.

'We've got a week to train,' he told the men. 'It's going to be a hard week. You're not going to like me at all. But if you can't take what I dish out, there's no way you're going to be able to take what will happen to you out there. You're going to learn to fight dirty. You're going to learn to kill dirty. So: you better learn fast. Or you'll be dead.'

'Gung-fuckn-ho,' somebody drawled.

'I see,' Lee said levelly. 'All right, we do it the hard way. Sergeant! Double time them round the parade ground. Full packs, rifles above the head. And keep them at it until the man who just spoke is ready to step forward. Move!'

First Sergeant Hummer snapped into action, and within minutes, the squad was doubling around the perimeter of the parade ground. Lieutenant Morley came across to where Lee was standing. He glanced up at the sun.

'Bit hot for this sort of thing, isn't it, sir?'

'It's hotter in the jungle,' Lee said, not looking at him.

'They're going to *love* you,' Morley murmured.

'So are you, Lieutenant,' Lee grinned.

'Fine,' Jenny said. 'Lovely.'

'Jen, I've only got a week.'

'And you're going to spend it in the jungle.'

'Try to understand.'

'I understand. I see what's important to you.'

'You know I'd rather be with you,' Lee said.

'And that's why you're going to spend a week in the jungle, training your company,' she said scornfully.

'They're raw, Jen. If I take them out untrained, they're going to get killed off real quick. Me with them.'

'Don't say that!' she said sharply.

'Then don't make it any harder for me than it is. I'm not doing it because I want to. I'm doing it because I have to.'

'I know,' she said. 'I'm just jealous. Disappointed. I wanted you all to myself.'

'We've still got tonight,' he said.

'Will it be dangerous, Lee?'

'Safe as houses,' he said. He hoped he was right. The

rebel forces were concentrated around Malolos. He was going into the jungle south-east of Manila to train his men. With any luck at all they wouldn't encounter Filipino patrols. By the time the 'bamboo telegraph' passed word that they were there, they would be out and back. It was a calculated risk. What Lee wanted to teach his men could not be taught on the parade ground.

'I don't give a damn how you march or how you shoulder arms,' he told them. 'Learn how to stay alive. Nothing else counts.'

They moved out the following morning at first light. He led them away from the suburbs and into the paddy-fields bordering them. Women working in the fields watched them go by, their faces expressionless. Children ran after them when they passed through a village. Then the jungle closed in around them. They moved in a strange, green light, the kind underwater swimmers know. Trees soared a hundred, a hundred and fifty feet above them. The undergrowth grew higher than their heads. The ground beneath their feet was spongy. Lianas strung from one tree to another like rotting ropes had to be hacked apart so they could get through. They could rarely see more than twenty yards ahead.

'The bastard is tryin' to kill us,' the men muttered, as they hacked their way through the tangled undergrowth, sweat drenching their uniforms. The ever-present jungle stink of rotting vegetation assailed their nostrils. The temperature climbed as the sun reached its zenith above the burning, hostile, dank, dangerous terrain. Stumbling and cursing, they followed where Lee led. They had no eye for the beauty around them, the showy yellow flowers of the *narra* trees, the brilliant crimson petals of the *santan*, the butterflies with fifteen-inch wing-spans which danced in the muggy air like living flowers.

Every fifty minutes Lee gave them a ten-minute break. They needed it. Panting, sweating, legs fluttering with fatigue, tongues thick with thirst, they sprawled wherever they dropped.

Each man carried his own supply of water. How he eked it out was his own concern. No man was permitted to share his water with any other.

'If you're thirsty, drink as much as you need,' Lee told them. 'Don't try to ration yourself. There's no point. If you're low on water, don't eat. A good way to save water is to put a pebble in your mouth to start the saliva. That's what the Apaches do.'

'You spent a lot of time with Apaches, Captain?'

Lomas again, Lee thought. Lomas was the man who had voiced his drawling scorn for Lee on that first day. He had taken his punishment with barely concealed contempt. Long, lank and stringy-haired, the Missourian pitched his questions just the safe side of insolence. The other men looked on with interest to see how Lee would handle Lomas's latest jibe.

'I grew up on the edge of the Mescalero Apache reservation,' Lee said, holding on to his temper. 'Apache kids were my playmates. I learned a lot of things from them, Lomas. Apaches know how to stay alive where a white man would be dead in a matter of hours. They know how to kill a man without a sound. And they taught me. I know I can do it. Now I'm going to find out if you can.'

'Hell, Captain,' Lomas said, showing bad teeth in a lopsided grin, 'likely we'll be able to.'

Now it was Lee's turn to grin. 'Soldier,' he said. 'I'm sure as hell going to enjoy watching you try.'

He was merciless with them. Hack and move on, hack and move on. It took only three or four minutes of double-timing it along a faint jungle track to drench a man in his own perspiration. Sweat seeped through their boots and sometimes even bleached rifle stocks. When he let them stop, they ripped off their clothes with wet hands to try to catch an eddy of cool air. In the evening mosquitoes came in clouds: nothing drove them away.

They were filthy dirty, hungry, thirsty. Most of all they were thirsty. The thirst was always there, no matter how many canteens they filled. They felt as if they could drink a quart of water every time they stopped for a break. Their throats contracted; when they spoke the words literally hurt. Their voices were squawks.

Leeches dropped on them out of the trees, or fastened themselves to genitals and anuses when they forded a river. They had to be taught not to panic, not to flail around in the water, not to scream.

'The best weapon we have is silence,' Lee told them, as they lay labouring for breath on the muddy detritus of the jungle floor. 'If you get wounded, don't say a word. Don't scream, don't shout. Sit still. We'll know where you are. We'll get to you. Never forget what I'm saying. If you shout or you scream, a little brown man will slit your belly open.'

He had given a bowie knife to every man in the squad, as well as buying, at his own expense, a twenty-foot rawhide rope, which he told them to wrap around their waists. In each man's pocket was a survival kit in a tobacco tin, containing waterproof matches, fish-hooks, needles and twine, a piece of candle, some permanganate of potash in a twist of grease-proof paper, and a length of flexible tubing. As the week progressed, they learned why. Needles had many uses besides sewing: removing thorns and stings, as well as repairing clothes torn by the snagging trees. Besides the obvious use for fish-hooks, they made a wicked perimeter defence when strung at eye-height between the trees. In the dank and steamy jungle, a piece of candle would get a fire started when matches simply wouldn't, especially if aided by a sprinkle of permanganate. The chemical could also be used as an antiseptic by adding a few grains to water. The same treatment would also purify brackish or suspect water; and all water, he taught them, was suspect in the jungle.

The flexible tubing made it possible to suck up water from crevices in rocks and other inaccessible places. The rawhide ropes were invaluable when there were river banks to climb down, cliffs and escarpments to negotiate.

And bowie knives?

'A knife is always loaded,' he pointed out. 'And it makes no noise.'

He taught them how to keep to high ground when it was possible, and how to avoid leaving more trail than was necessary.

'If we are attacked, scatter,' he told them. 'Don't bunch up. Your job is to stay alive: you, personally. I don't want heroic sacrifices or any of that kind of shit. Learn to fight as if you're the only man on earth.'

He taught them Apache decoy tricks: how to fight the way the Filipinos fought, stealthily, mercilessly. He taught them how to tell if a man was dead or shamming: touch his eyeball with a stick. He taught them how to live off the jungle.

'You can eat any frog, any lizard, any snake except the head. You can't eat a toad.'

'Thank Christ for that,' someone said, feelingly.

There were small animals in the jungle that could be trapped. He taught them to dip their traps in water or rub them with leaves to take away the human smells; how to find water where none seemed to exist, at the foot of dried-up waterfalls, on the curving sandy bank of a riverbed.

'You can survive for a long time if you know what to do,' he told them. 'Remember what I tell you. Or the first time you get separated from the company you'll die.'

He brought them in early on the Saturday afternoon. They were gaunt, filthy, bearded, hollow-eyed and exhausted. But as they came into the compound, they straightened up. Fox company was coming in. They put their Krags on their shoulders and raised their voices, singing to the tune of 'The Battle Hymn of the Republic':

We'll hang Aguinaldo from a eucalyptus tree
Hang the stinkin' bastard from a eucalyptus tree
And when we've hung the bastard then we'll hang his
family,
And then we'll all go home!

They were still a long way from being a tightly knit outfit, Lee thought, as he dismissed them. Unit pride took longer than a week to build. They were a hell of a sight better than when he had taken command. That was something. It could make the difference between life and death when they did it for real.

Later, bathed and wearing clean clothes, he bought Lieutenant David Morley a beer at the University Club. They took them out on the verandah, and sat in cane chairs, watching the sun go down. The beer was icy cold, delicious. It was hard not to gulp it down. He asked Morley how he felt.

'Glad it's over,' Morley said. 'I could sleep for a fortnight.'

'Think it was worth it?'

'I'm . . . surprised,' Morley replied. 'At myself. I didn't think I could hack it. There were plenty of times I just wanted to lay down and die.'

'What stopped you?'

'I didn't want to be the first one.'

'Nobody did,' Lee smiled. 'That's what kept them all going. I'll tell you something: I felt the same way.'

'You were damned hard on us. All of us.'

'Aguinaldo's men will be harder.'

Inside the clubhouse, cutlery tinkled, male voices rose and fell. The sun was below the tops of the palms fringing the compound. Somewhere a long way away some soldiers were harmonising: *I'm half crazy, all for the love of you.* Saturday night. His company would be down in the town getting drunk: he had given them a

323

till–curfew pass. He thought of the country through which they would be moving in two days' time: rice paddies and sago swamps, fronds of acacia, flaming yellow *canas*, mango trees with the purple, red and yellow fruit among the leaves, spider orchids, outrigger boats on the shore, carabao pulling hand–carved diggers through the earth, the acrid smell of a sugar–cane field being burned clear.

'How long have you been in the service, David?' he asked Morley.

'Almost a year,' Morley said. 'I wanted to go to Cuba. Instead, I damned near died of typhoid at Camp Alger.'

'You didn't miss a thing,' Lee said. 'What made you volunteer for this?'

'You'll find this hard to believe. I wanted adventure. I was teaching English in a school in upstate New York. I thought, I'm twenty-three years of age, and I've never done anything. I could see myself twenty years on, still teaching in that same school. So I applied for a commission. Boy, I should've stayed home.'

His eyes blinked frequently behind gold-rimmed spectacles. Despite his tropical tan and incipient beard, he looked defenceless and immature. They get younger every year, Lee thought.

'You got a girl back home?'

'Sort of,' Morley said. 'Her name is Mary. You want to see her picture?' He dug out a photograph and handed it to Lee.

'Pretty.'

'She sure is.'

'Do you write to her?'

'I keep a journal,' Morley said, a little defensively. 'A sort of diary.'

Lee let it go at that. He thought he could guess the rest of the story. Mary was not Morley's girl. She was the girl he wished he had. So he kept a diary, writing in it what he could not write to her. Maybe he believed that one day she would read it. Well, I hope she waits for you, kid, Lee thought. He leaned back, making the cane chair creak.

'Another beer?' Morley asked.

'No, thanks,' Lee said. 'I've got to get home.'

'Home,' Morley said, wistfully.

Jenny was waiting for him when he got back to their cottage. She kissed him and made a face.

'You stink of beer,' she said.

'I only had one,' Lee smiled. 'With young Morley.'

'He's the one from Woodstock, isn't he?'

'How did you know that?'

Jenny smiled. He never ceased to be amazed at the way she got people to tell her about themselves. Especially men. He often watched the effect she had on them: a delighted awareness of her exclusive interest. It wasn't something she worked to achieve. She really was interested, and she really did concentrate upon who she was talking to, or what she was doing. Unlike them, however, Lee knew that the effect she had on men created no sense of obligation in Jenny. She could charm, and so she did, as naturally and unaffectedly as a bird sings.

'I think half the men in Manila are in love with you,' he said.

'Only half?' she said. 'I must be slipping.'

'What's to eat?'

'Chili con carne.'

'Authentic Filipino cuisine, eh?'

They had moved to the little cottage inside the Army compound soon after their arrival. The Hotel del Oriente was plush and comfortable, but the atmosphere there was, to use Jenny's word for it, poisonous.

'I can't spend the day looking after some poor boy who's had his arm shot to pieces, or his leg blown off,' she said to Lee, 'and then sit next to some fatheaded major-general's wife over an expensive dinner, and listen to her complain about the shortage of servants.'

325

Lee had needed no urging to leave the place. A great many of the Navy, Marine Corps and Army officers who thronged its restaurants and bars seem indifferent to the realities beyond its marbled foyer. To many of them, this whole thing was a kind of jaunt, an extended vacation, an opportunity to put on the dress white uniform and pig it a little at the government's expense.

'How are things at the hospital?'

'About the same. It's quiet at the moment.'

'Make the most of it,' he said.

His words put a chill into her heart. She wondered whether he really understood the way she felt, realising he was going out into the jungle to kill or be killed. How could he understand? She wasn't too sure herself. She knew that if anything happened to him she would not want to live, but she did not permit herself to believe for a second that anything would happen to him. If I let thoughts like that take hold of my heart, she thought, it will quickly turn to stone.

'When does Division start north?' she asked.

'Wednesday.'

'You'll be a long way ahead of them.'

'Yes.'

She tried to envisage what she would be able to see if she were in a balloon high, high above the moving army. A long way to the north, Lee and his company, probing through the jungled wilderness towards Malolos. Behind him, Gates and Vaughan, with their companies. Perhaps sixty men in all. Then, in broad phalanx along the cobblestoned highway leading north, the main body of Lawton's 1st Division, marching men, rumbling wagons, clattering artillery caissons, ambulances.

'I chilled some wine,' she said.

She poured a glass for Lee, and another for herself. They clinked glasses. The wine was dry and flinty-tasting.

'Sancerre,' Jenny said. 'Your favourite.'

326

'You trying to seduce me?'

'I'm trying not to be afraid,' Jenny said.

'I know.'

'I'm afraid of losing you, Lee. I'm afraid you might be wounded, or mutilated. I'm afraid you won't come back, and I'll be without you for always. I'm afraid of being hurt, and I'm trying awfully hard not to show it.'

'You're a good brave girl,' Lee said. He put his arm around her and kissed her on the forehead. 'I'm glad you told me. I think I needed to know how you felt.'

'And you?'

'I'm not afraid,' he said. It was hard to put into words. He took it slowly, thinking it through so she would understand. 'Not of dying. Dying is all part of being a soldier.'

'You're not going to die,' she said, trying to ignore the ghost that touched her soul with its fingers.

'The stupid thing is, I get jealous,' he said.

'Jealous?'

'I think of, you know, being dead. And you. You'd find someone else. Oh, not right away. I know you better than that. But you would. Everyone does. One day, someone would come along who you would love. And he would hold you in his arms, and he would make love to you. And that's what makes me jealous. Now isn't that dumb?'

'It's dumb, all right,' Jenny said. 'But it's lovely.'

She poured two more glasses of wine and put them on the table. He reached for his and she slapped his hand.

'After,' she said.

'What about the chili?'

'I'm pretty hot stuff myself,' Jenny said. He laughed, and swept her up into his arms, kissing her. Then he picked her up and carried her into the bedroom. Her last thought as she surrendered to sensation was: *don't let them take him away from me. Don't ever let them take him.*

33

Gates and Vaughan were in their usual place at the bar of the Hotel del Oriente, drinking San Miguel beer.

'Charles,' Lee said. 'Chris. Another of those?'

'You buyin'?' Gates asked, raising one eyebrow slightly. Lee nodded, gesturing for the bartender to refill their glasses and bring him a beer.

'Look out, baby,' Gates said. 'He wants something.'

'We're shoving off Monday,' Lee told them. 'North.'

'Have a nice time,' Gates said.

'I want you both as back-up. Your companies.'

'I'll bet you do,' Vaughan said. He looked at the bottle of beer on the bar in front of him, and shrugged. He poured some, and then raised the glass in a sardonic salute.

'I need you along,' Lee repeated. 'You, too, Chuck.'

'I believe you,' Gates said.

'He always was the sincere type,' Vaughan added.

'Have another beer,' Lee said. 'And we'll talk about it.'

'I got all the medals I need,' Chuck said. 'I ain't volunteerin' for nothin'!'

'And I'm too busy,' Vaughan said. 'I got this pretty little lotus blossom over on Binondo. Be a shame to leave her, just to get my ass shot at.'

'You'll be going with Lawton anyway,' Lee argued.

'Him and five regiments,' Gates retorted. 'That ain't quite the same as takin' the point.'

'You two eaten yet?'

'Been thinkin' on it some,' Gates admitted.

'I'll buy you lunch,' Lee offered. 'I know a good place down by Rizal Park.'

'How's Jenny?'

'She's fine.'

'You could invite us to your place for dinner,' Gates said. 'Rather talk to Jenny than you, any day.'

'She's on duty. At the hospital.'

'You planning on getting us drunk?' Vaughan asked.

'Something like that.'

'What's this place called you want to take us?'

'*Churruca*.'

'You say the food's good?'

'Superb.'

'They do *alimango*?' *Alimango* was a meal of fish, shrimp and crab, served wrapped in banana leaves.

'And *balut*,' Lee grinned.

'Bleah,' Vaughan said, disgusted. *Balut* was a Filipino speciality: boiled duck egg with the partly developed embryo cooked in its own amniotic fluid.

They walked to the restaurant. A long-haired. sloe-eyed Filipino girl showed them to a table near the window, where they could look out on to the rectangle of the square with its fountains and pigeons. Vaughan watched the movement of the girl's hips as she walked away.

'I can't imagine leaving all that behind,' he said.

'All you ever think about,' Gates told him, disgustedly. 'Behind.'

'Not all,' Vaughan corrected him.

'Wonder if she's got a sister?' Gates mused.

'We could find out.'

'You might like her,' Lee said. 'You might like her sister. But you wouldn't like her twenty-six relatives.'

They fell silent. After a while Gates looked at Lee.

'That true what they say?' he asked. 'That you're training your boys to fight Apache-style?'

'It's true.'

'I heard Moffatt like to shit a brick when he found out.'

'Ben Kenton told me he thought the Asshole was going to have a haemorrhage when he heard them singing that song you taught them,' Vaughan grinned. 'How does it go?'

'Hang Aguinaldo from a eucalyptus tree,' Lee said.

'My Gawwwwd, Starr, we cawn't hev thet kaind of thing!' Vaughan said, aping the Asshole's mock-British accent.

'Can you believe it?' Lee said. 'It was like he was saying "Train them to fight, by all means, but we don't want them *hurting* anybody."'

'They don't call him the Asshole for nothin',' Gates said. 'What's the idea, Lee?'

'The way I see it,' Lee said, 'only two things can happen to you out here. You can get wounded and be sent home. Or you can die. And then you really don't give a shit, because you're just meat. I'm planning to come out of this, boys. And come out whole. I'm not going to get wounded and I'm not going to die. I believe that.'

'Yea, though I walk through the valley of the shadow of death, I will fear no evil . . .' Gates intoned.

'Because I'm the meanest sonofabitch in the valley,' Vaughan added, finishing the well-worn couplet.

'Hear tell you're going out to find Aguinaldo,' Gates said. 'That about the size of it?'

'Me and two other companies,' Lee said. 'Yours and Vaughan's.'

'What you need two more companies for?'

Lee told them his plan, which was for his own company, Fox, to be the tip of a long, narrow triangle whose other two angles would be their companies. Fox company would locate the enemy, who might engage a small unit more readily than a large one. Once they were engaged, the other two companies would move forward to reinforce Fox, hopefully keeping the rebels occupied long enough for the regiment to move up.

'What do you think?' he said as he finished.

'Three bricks shy of a full load, I'd say.' Gates looked at Vaughan.

'Sad case,' Vaughan responded, shaking his head. 'Very sad.'

'Cut it out,' Lee said. 'I need you guys with me.'

'We know you do, *capitano*,' Gates said. 'That's what scares us.'

'Only thing is . . .' Vaughan said. 'Hell, Chuck. Maybe we better go along, to make sure he don't fuck up.'

'For the honour of the regiment.'

'"O say, can you see?"'

'"My country 'tis of thee."'

'You're nuts,' Lee said. 'Both of you.'

'Ain't that the truth,' Gates said.

'You'll go, then?'

'The way we look at it is this, Lee,' Gates said. 'You're the only guy we know will buy us beer. We got to look out for you.'

'Seems to us old Fuss and Feathers wants to send you where you'll get your ass shot off,' Vaughan said. 'So I guess there's nothing for it but for me and Chuck to come along and make sure it doesn't happen.'

'I love you guys,' Lee said. 'You know that?'

'You ever going to order that food?' Gates growled.

34

Chief Surgeon Eames was a tall, thin, bespectacled man with a precise way of speaking. He had soft grey eyes and long-fingered hands. He seemed very old and very wise; Jenny was surprised to learn that he was only fifty-four.

'Feeling blue this morning, missy?' he said, as he came into the ward. 'I hear your husband's shoved off for the north.'

'Yes, sir,' she said. 'He's gone.'

'We'll have to find ways of keeping you busy,' Eames said. 'People fret when they've got time on their hands.'

'I'll be all right, sir. It's just –'

'I think I know how you feel, my dear,' he said. 'I've got a boy in the 23rd Infantry. His battalion is going to occupy Cebu.' He lifted his shoulders and let them drop, sighing. 'Going to be hot again today.'

The relief hospital to which Jenny had been assigned was in the barracks of the Spanish governor-general's guard detachment at the Malacanang Palace. It stood in a lovely park on the north bank of the Pasig River, alongside and to the rear of the imposing white building where General Otis had his headquarters.

There were ten American nurses at the hospital. They all wore the same uniform: a stiff-brimmed light straw sailor hat with a black ribbon, a white shirtwaist with full sleeves, and a soft, ankle-length grey skirt. There were five wards in all, two nurses to a ward. Jenny shared Ward A with a short, plump, motherly woman of about forty, Peggy Ames, from Wilmington, Delaware. Peggy's husband had been killed in the Puerto Rico campaign, and she had joined the Red Cross because, she said, she felt she had to do something to repay the organisation which had done so much for her man. She was jolly and pleasant, and easy to work with. Bustling about the ward, plumping up pillows, nodding and smiling, she reminded Jenny of a fat, cooing pigeon.

Jenny did not mix much with the other girls, except at mealtimes. They talked of nothing but this officer and that, the meals they had eaten, the wine they had drunk, the fun they had had. Their frivolity seemed obscene, but she did not permit herself the arrogance of condemning it.

Lee's sister Rachel sent her a cutting from the Roswell paper. The headline read: CLOUDCROFT GIRL ARRIVES IN MANILA TO HELP AMERICAN WOUNDED. The photograph looked as if it had been taken a decade earlier. I was younger then, she thought. I hadn't been seasick for a fortnight, or seen Hawaii and Guam.

All the wards were half-empty. Everyone had time on their hands. Some of the male orderlies had Filipino mistresses in the town. How they could tend wounds inflicted by Filipino men, and then go home and sleep with Filipino women, Jenny could not bring herself to understand; but she knew that they were not the only ones. Many of the officers did, too – especially the married ones.

There were eight beds occupied in Ward A. Four of them were private soldiers who had come down with fever. Wasted and jaundiced, they spent most of their time playing poker in the day room. The Knife Wound, as Peggy and Jenny referred to the man in the corner bed on the right, was a surly, ill-tempered private from the 1st Nebraska. He had been brought in after a drunken brawl in a Chinese brothel on Binondo, his entrails hanging out. The fact that they had saved his life inspired no gratitude in the man. He never thanked them for anything they did. There was an undercurrent of resentment towards them from all the enlisted men. They said the nurses had been brought out for the officers: enlisted men were forbidden to consort with nurses. That didn't prevent them lusting. She was used to that. You couldn't grow up on Army posts, as Jenny had done, and not know all the things men said to each other. They were nothing like the sweet things they said to women. With thousands of men on Luzon for every white woman, that was the least you could expect. Peggy's reaction to the Knife Wound's surliness was typical.

'Damned thug!' she said, disgustedly.

In the bed nearest the desk at which Jenny sat during night duty, was a lieutenant named Paul Baker. He was older than the other men in the ward, dark and good-looking. He read a lot. Sometimes when she looked up quickly, she found him watching her, his dark eyes grave. He had been wounded during the Filipino attack on Manila in February; a bullet from a captured Springfield smashed through his chest from one side to the other, before exiting through the bicep of his left arm. When he was asleep, she looked at the title of the book he was reading. Spinoza's *Ethics*: she did not expect a soldier to be reading philosophy.

'What *did* you expect?' he asked her with a quizzical grin, when she mentioned it. 'Elbert Hubbard?'

Hubbard, who was known as 'The Sage of Aurora' had written an essay about the war in Cuba called 'A Message to Garcia'. It had sold millions.

'It was just a surprise, that's all.'

'That's the great thing about people,' he said, with a smile. 'They always surprise you.'

He was an interesting talker. He made no concessions to her femininity. If she asked him a question, he answered it. He had made a study of the Philippines, and the causes of the revolution. He told her the story of José Rizal, whose mock trial and execution by the Spanish in 1896 had been the spark that ignited the revolution. He told her of the Spanish reprisals in the wave of terror that followed the uprising. He did not spare her the details, which were ghastly.

'The Filipinos hated the Spanish worse than the devil hates holy water,' he said. 'Till we came along.'

'We tried to help them.'

'Sure,' he said. 'We sailed in and told them to leave the Spanish to us. We promised them independence. Then when the Spanish surrendered, we said, "Hard luck, we've changed our minds. We're going to keep the Philippines. It's time America had an empire, just like the British and the Germans and the French."'

'You sound like one of those socialists,' she said.

'I see Aguinaldo's point of view,' he said. 'If I was him, I'd hate Americans, too.'

At that moment, Assistant-Surgeon John Garson came bustling in. He was a stocky, balding man of perhaps forty-five. His pate shone with sweat. Peggy Ames had pinned him with one word: 'Pushy'. According to some of the nurses, he thought of himself as a Lothario. He certainly didn't look like one, Jenny thought.

'Shouldn't you be in the day room, lieutenant?' he said to Baker.

'Just on my way there, sir,' Baker said, with the ghost of a smile. It expressed his opinion of Garson as clearly as if he had painted it on the wall in letters three feet high.

'Insolent bas . . .' Garson muttered, biting off the word when he saw Jenny watching him. He put a smile on his face the way a child puts on a mask.

'How's it going, Mrs Starr?' he said. 'Jenny, isn't it?'

Yes, and you can call me Mrs Starr, Jenny thought, but she did not say it. 'It's pretty quiet, sir.'

'Won't be for long,' he said. 'Maybe we ought to

make the most of it.'

'Sir?'

'I've been watching you,' Garson said. 'You're pretty.'

'They say you're something of a ladies' man, doctor,' Jenny said levelly. 'Don't waste your charms on me. I'm happily married.'

'Sure, sure,' he said soothingly. 'Only your husband is away at the front. And a healthy girl like you . . . you must get lonely.'

Jenny flushed at the man's directness. He took it for encouragement. 'We could go over to my place,' he said throatily. 'I've got a bottle of champagne. Been saving it for a special occasion.'

'Let me ask you a question,' Jenny said. 'How would you like me to report this conversation to Chief Surgeon Eames?'

He laughed. 'That old fool!' he said. 'He'd shake his head, and scratch his chin, and hem and haw. But he wouldn't *do* anything. Anyway, what could he do?'

He smiled at her, a man confident he could do anything he wanted to. His smugness angered Jenny so much that she wanted to slap his face.

'I'll only say this once,' she said. 'Stay away from me, you sweaty little slug!'

Garson's face darkened with anger, but he quickly concealed it beneath what he probably thought was an insouciant smile.

'You'll come round,' he said. 'They usually do.'

He sauntered silently off. He wore rubber-soled shoes. The nurses called him 'the brothel-creeper', on account of his penchant for coming up on people silently from behind. Somehow the silliness of the whole episode made Jenny smile, and her anger melted. Maybe even a repulsive creature like Garson got lonesome sometimes.

Paul Baker told her about fighting the Filipinos. He said they were ferociously brave. They did not often stand and fight, but when they did, they were prepared to fight to the last man.

'They've got something to fight for,' he said. 'Something they believe in. Which is more than we've got.'

'What about the atrocities?'

'The ear-cutting, you mean? They say we started it, we say they did. Who knows? They've learned to disregard the rules. They don't care how they kill us, just so long as we're dead. I heard of one company that was camped on a beach one night. There was a high surf. Sentries couuldn't hear the rebels. Six or eight of them sneaked into the camp, cut off the captain's head, killed half a dozen men, stole their guns. Nobody knew they were dead till reveille.'

That night she slept badly, dreaming fitfully of shadowed jungle in which darker shadows moved. Tossing and turning in the humid night, she watched the slow turning of the stars through her window and the first faint glow of dawn. *Where are you, my darling?* she thought. *Where are you?*

Lee was in a narrow defile south of Malolos. They had not seen any sign of rebel activity for days. The jungle undergrowth pressed against them. Parrots screeched in the trees. The shrill chatter of monkeys echoed in the still air. Smoke-coloured mist wreathed around mountains glimpsed through the close-packed trees. Scorpions scuttled underfoot.

The sound of the rifle shots was immense. Lee felt the air move as the bullets went by. The shots came from the hill on their right: he dived instinctively into the undergrowth on the left of the trail, knowing that the men strung out behind him would do the same without hesitation. He yanked the revolver out of its holster and worked himself around on his elbows. As he did, a Filipino came at him out of nowhere, his face contorted with hatred, a wicked-looking machete upraised. Lee shot the man off his feet and scrambled to his knees.

Ambush! He heard the solid boom of the Krags.

'Fire-fighting drill!' he yelled. 'Fire-fighting drill!'

In a jungle ambush, when you did not know from which direction the attackers would come, a good defence was for the men to form squads of four, each facing outward in a different direction, rifle at the hip set for rapid fire. They called it fire-fighting, because whichever direction the Filipinos might come from, the full force of the American rifles could be turned on them.

Lee clambered back up to the trail and ran back along it. Two Filipinos were coming the other way, rifles ported. He fell prone, firing the Colt as he hit the ground. The first bullet blew one of the two *insurrectos* aside like a leaf. The second hit the other man high on the chest, knocking him sprawling, sending the rifle spinning into the loam. Lee gave him no time to get up. He launched himself from a crouch, bowie knife ready. As the Filipino got to one knee, his face vacant with pain, Lee put the knife between his ribs. The man made a small sound: *uuurrchk*, and fell back into the undergrowth, legs kicking high. All around, Lee heard the flat slam of rifles, the yells of the rebels, the sound of men swearing hoarsely. Then silence. All at once, the rebels were gone. Lee went back along the trail warily, his pistol cocked. The silence was almost tangible.

A movement: he whirled around, gun ready. Sergeant Hummer raised a hand. Morley eased out from behind a *nipa* tree, his face chalky with tension. One by one the men came out of the jungle. With a gesture, Lee made them spread and lie prone, rifles covering both sides of the trail.

Using knees and elbows he squirmed along the track until he was next to Morley and Sergeant Hummer.

'Anyone missing?' he hissed.

'Lomas,' Hummer said.

'Anyone see him?'

'He got cut, Cap,' one of the troopers whispered. 'I seen him go down.'

'All right, Mobley,' Lee said. 'Think you could find him?'

Mobley nodded and pointed to a gap between two trees. He pointed at Lee and then indicated that Lee should take the right flank. He moved off left, crouched low. Lee edged into the undergrowth the same way. His heart was booming in his chest. The hand that held the walnut butt of the Colt .45 was slick with sweat.

'Help!'

It was Lomas's voice.

'For Christ's sake, come and get me!' he shouted. He was off to the right front of Lee's position. Keep quiet, you stupid bastard! Lee silently shouted. Keep your goddamned mouth shut! Eeling through the undergrowth, trying to make as little sound as possible, made the going slow. He had not covered ten yards when he heard a gurgling scream, maybe another ten yards in front of him. He emptied his pistol into the jungle, spacing the shots across an arc at chest height. He thought he heard someone shout in pain, but he could not be sure. He ran forward, reloading the gun as he ran. In the same moment, Mobley came out of the bushes on his left, his lugubrious face drenched with sweat. Trooper Lomas lay on his back, his sightless eyes staring at the sky. His throat had been cut from ear to ear. Flies were already swarming around the seeping blood. His rifle, ammunition and bowie knife were gone.

Lee turned the dead man over with the toe of his boot. 'You stupid sonofabitch,' he said. 'Why didn't you keep your mouth shut?'

'Jesus,' Mobley said. 'You really are a bastard, aren't you?'

'Yes,' Lee said. 'I really am.'

★

339

By the end of March, there was not so much talk of romance at the hospital. Every bed was full. The casualties came in waves. Sometimes the doctors and nurses worked a full twenty-four-hour shift, falling exhausted into cots set up for them in the admin. block, snatching a few hours' sleep before staggering grainy-eyed back to the operating theatres and the wards.

Tiredness makes you ugly, Jenny thought, as she looked in the mirror. And I'll be tired for a long time to come. She slumped in a chair and looked at her roughened hands. Her mind felt anaesthetised. This was the first time she had been in the cottage for ten days, and now that she was here she did not know what to do with herself. What *do* I think about when I'm working? she wondered. She came to the conclusion that she thought of nothing except the job at hand. Dressing wounds, changing beds, serving meals, taking temperatures, filling in charts. There was a routine to everything, and after a while all she could remember was that her feet were sore and she was unutterably weary.

Paul Baker was convalescent now. He sat outside on the verandah reading in the sunshine each day until it got too hot.

'You'll be leaving us soon,' Jenny told him.

'I know it,' he said. 'Back to the fray.'

General Lawton had captured Malolos at the end of March, but missed Aguinaldo and his rebel cabinet, who had fled into the mountains. They were rumoured to be in San Isidro, or in Tarlac, nobody knew. The fighting was still going on, north of Malolos.

Replacement troops were pouring in. The 3rd, 4th, 17th, 20th and 22nd Regular Infantry arrived to replace volunteer units going back to the States. There were parades, reviews. Every day the Army band played in Luneta Park.

'Don't you ever have time off?' Paul Baker asked

Jenny one day. 'You look like you could use a break.'

'There's too much to do,' she said. 'I –'

'Before I go back to my unit,' he said, 'how about showing me some of Manila? They say it's quite safe now with all these new units in town.'

'It's a nice thought,' Jenny said. 'But I can't.'

'Don't think of it as a date,' he said. 'Think of it as two friends going for a walk together. Nobody could object to that, could they?'

'No,' she told him.

'I wish you'd reconsider.'

He was an attractive man. She had learned a lot about him as they talked long into the night. He had joined the Army in Arizona, having drifted there from California, where he jumped the ship on which he'd come around the Horn from Boston as a deck-hand. He was saving his pay so that when his hitch was up he would be able to buy a little farm. He had no big ambitions, he said. A house of his own, a woman, some kids. A shelf with books on it, a pipe and some tobacco.

'You never married?'

'I would have done,' he said, 'if I'd met a girl like you.'

'There are plenty of girls like me.'

'So I've been told,' he said. 'How come they're so hard to find, then?'

The following night a train came in, bringing another hundred and fourteen wounded men to the already overflowing wards. Many of them were dying; there was little or nothing anyone could do for them but wash them, give them something cool to drink if their wounds permitted it, and make the going gentle. One boy told Jenny how his unit was wiped out. A Filipino soldier came towards them carrying a white flag.

'*Amigo*,' he called out as he walked. '*Amigo!*'

He explained that he was a member of a unit that had fallen behind in Aguinaldo's retreat to the mountains. He had come in under a white flag to ask if the

Americans would accept their surrender. They told him to take them to where his comrades were waiting.

'They were waiting, all right,' the boy said, his eyes filming with the memory. 'Waiting to cut us to pieces!' It was a trick the *insurrectos* would use many times on the unsuspecting American troops before they learned to shoot anyone carrying a white flag. That was the kind of dirty war it was, where even a flag of truce was worthless.

April was hotter than March. Jenny's uniform stuck to her body as she sat at her desk on the night swing. The ward was silent except for the occasional snore from one of the men. The big revolving fan turned slowly. Jenny felt the presence of someone at her shoulder, and looked up. It was Captain Garson.

'Doctor,' Jenny said quietly. 'You startled me.'

'Relax,' he said. 'I just want to talk to you.'

'What about?'

He sensed her hostility. He smiled and ran a hand across his chin. Bristles rasped. He needed a shave. 'Heard from your husband?'

'No.'

'He's with Lawton, isn't he?'

'Yes, sir.'

'They're across Laguna del Bay,' Garson said. 'Lawton is going to attack Santa Cruz.'

'I heard.'

'I'm very good,' he said. 'Ask any of the girls.'

'And so modest in spite of it,' Jenny said cuttingly. Far away, thunder rumbled. It was early for thunder, she thought inconsequentially.

'You're very attractive,' Garson said. He put his hand on her thigh. His voice had thickened slightly. Jenny flinched away from his hot hand, and stood up, putting her desk between them.

'I'd like you to leave my ward now, please, doctor,' she said briskly.

'Be nice to me,' he said, making no effort to move.

342

'Last chance,' she said.

Garson smiled lazily. 'What are you going to do, scream? Tell them I molested you? Come on, relax.'

This is insane, Jenny thought. There are twenty men sleeping within ten feet of this whispered confrontation. All I have to do is call out. Why don't I do it?

'Come on,' he said, reaching across the desk for her hand. 'You know you want it.' His eyes were hot, and Jenny felt suddenly aware of the fact that she had nothing on beneath her uniform except the briefest wisps of underwear. Garson smiled again, coming around the desk.

'Get out of my ward,' Jenny hissed, 'or I swear to God I'll hit you!'

'No,' a quiet voice intervened. 'Let me do it for you.'

Garson gasped and whirled around. Neither he nor Jenny had heard Paul Baker cross the darkened ward. Garson's heavy brows knitted with anger.

'Stay out of this, if you know what's good for you, Lieutenant!' he snapped, trying to put an authority into his voice that simply wouldn't come.

'You fat tub of lard,' Baker said contemptuously. 'I ought to break your goddamned back.'

'You are speaking to a senior officer, Lieutenant!' Garson hissed. 'Do you know who I am?'

'The label fell off,' Baker drawled, 'but at a guess, I'd say some species of pig.'

'Damn you, I'll –' Garson's fists clenched, and Jenny saw a dangerous smile touch Paul Baker's face.

'I'd sure love you to try, you chickenshit imitation,' he said. Garson's eyes flickered with fear. He looked at Jenny and back at Baker. Then he nodded.

'Want it all for yourself, eh?' he sneered. 'Well, keep it!'

He turned on his heel, the sneer still on his face. Paul Baker took a step forward, his eyes blind with anger. Jenny put her hand on his forearm, restraining him. Baker shook his head.

Garson was at the door now. When he got there he stopped, and turned to face them.

'You've made a big mistake,' he said.

'So did your mother,' Baker snarled. The door flapped shut. The ward was silent except for the noise of the fan. Baker turned to Jenny.

'You all right, Mrs Starr?'

Jenny nodded. She sat down on her hard wooden chair and dug her fingernails into the palms of her hands. After a few moments, the wave of nausea passed.

'Begging your pardon,' Baker said, looking towards the door. 'But that is one sick sonofabitch.'

Just how sick, Jenny would learn all too soon.

35

By the end of March there were only twelve of the original squad left. Lieutenant David Morley was dead. They found what was left of him spitted with a bamboo pole, like a pig. He had been doused with oil and left turning over a slow fire. First Sergeant Hummer died in a hand-to-hand fight with a juiced-up *insurrecto* near Santa Cruz. Hummer put four bullets into the man with his .38, but the Filipino stayed alive long enough to almost decapitate Hummer with a machete. Mobley was dead, too, and a tow-headed fellow from Wisconsin named Scherzinger who everyone called 'Dutchman'. Their deaths were part of the price that had to be paid, and Lee did not brood about them. He drew replacements from Gates's company and put them in harness with his own men. The rules were still the same: learn fast or die quick.

Fox company was now a closely knit group of tough, seasoned, dangerous-looking men who came out of the jungle like bandits. Their long hair was tied back with bandannas or strips of rag; they all wore beards. They had long since discarded their blue woollen shirts for khaki ones, which they took off dead rebels. Soldier blue was much too easy to see in the glistening green jungle. They were jungle-smart, adaptable, deadly. Their eyes saw everything that moved around them. Lee called them his Apaches, and that was what they looked like.

They came to a village, a straggle of A-frame huts,

surrounded on three sides by rice paddies, with steep, heavily brushed hills behind them. Chickens foraged between the huts. Old men sat cross-legged, hammering with rough stone mauls. The women sat in a circle, gossiping as they peeled the leaves from cabbage plants. Naked children ran out into the clearing at the centre of the village, hooting and pointing at the filthy, bedraggled soldiers.

The headman came out with a deputation of elders to meet them. He was stooped and white-haired, with narrow shoulders and wispy white whiskers.

'We have food,' he said, drawing a large circle with his wasted arm that encompassed all Lee's men. 'You are welcome to share it.'

'We are grateful,' Lee said. 'We will camp here tonight. We will protect you.'

The old man nodded. He bowed his head, but not before Lee caught the gleam of contempt in his eyes. He looked around, then called First Sergeant Hanna across.

'I don't like the look of this place,' he said in English. 'Take three men and check it out.'

'Gotcha, Captain,' Hanna said.

The old man watched fearfully as Hanna assembled his squad. The elders did not look at the soldiers. The women stopped talking. Their eyes were full of secrets.

It took only a little while for Hanna to complete his search. When he came back he was pulling a little old Filipino woman along by the arm. She was squalling protests, but Hanna handled her as if she were no more than a cat he had picked up by the scruff of the neck.

'Tell you what we got here, Captain,' he said, as he set the woman on her feet in front of Lee. 'We got this old lady, all by herself in a hut with two little kids. According to her, her sons have been taken away by the rebels. Ain't that so, you goddamned old gugu bitch?' He smiled beatifically at the old woman, who smiled back and nodded.

'See, Captain? A real *amigo*, this one. Ain't that right,

346

Mama? *Amigo, si? Americanista, si?*

'*Si, si!*' the old woman said vehemently, looking at Lee. '*Amigo. Todos Americanistas aqui! Si, si!*'

'And would she lie to us?' Hanna asked.

'Heaven forfend!' Lee replied.

'So there's just the old lady in the hut with two little kids,' Hanna said. 'And they've got a pot of rice big enough to feed fifty, and cooked rice don't keep, and *no way* did they know we was comin'. So – they got to be feedin' the fuckin' rebels, right?'

'Right,' Lee said. 'You know what to do, Sergeant.'

They set the old woman's house on fire, and when the flames reached the thatched roof, the ammunition that had been hidden in it began to explode. The soldiers took cover behind one of the huts while the bullets snapped and whined. When they reformed, they discovered that the entire population of the village had fled into the jungle. Official policy was to disarm and then liberate any captured rebel; the soldiers knew there was no damned point to that. As soon as they were turned loose, the little brown bastards sneaked up on some sleeping sentry, slit his throat, stole his piece and got back into the war. Same with the villages. They fed the rebels, hid them out, stored their ammunition. Maybe they had a choice, maybe not. It made no difference.

The men took what food they needed and set fire to the rest of the houses. Then they moved out.

That was the kind of war they were fighting now.

36

Whittier Moffatt stood by the window of his office in the Malacanang Palace and looked out across the river at the tropical gardens opposite. Sampans slid by on the swirling grey water of the river, their occupants huddled beneath rubber ponchos, the driving rain making a nimbus of spray on their hunched backs. The skies were the colour of slate. A discreet knock at the door turned him to face his aide, Lieutenant-Colonel Aysgill.

'Your dau – ah, Nurse Starr is here, sir.'

'Send her in,' Moffatt said. He positioned himself behind his desk. Stern but fair, he thought; that's the way. He was not looking forward to this.

'Father,' Jenny said. 'You sent for me?'

'Sit down, please,' Moffatt said, shifting uncomfortably in his chair. He picked up a pen, looked at it, put it down. Jenny took a chair. Fear filled every part of her, every corner of her mind. All she could think was *Lee is dead, Lee is dead, he's going to tell me Lee is dead*.

'I have to discuss a very serious matter with you,' Moffatt said. 'In my official capacity.'

Jenny nodded, unable to trust herself to speak.

'A complaint has been received by this department concerning . . . your conduct.'

She could not believe what he had actually said. The sense of relief that flooded through her was so enormous that she thought she had not heard correctly.

'What did you say?' she managed.

'I have received a complaint,' Moffatt said impatiently. 'About your private conduct.'

'As a nurse?' Jenny asked incredulously. 'Father, I've —'

'I think we had better keep this formal,' he said stiffly. 'Try to keep our personal relationship out of it.'

'If you wish.'

He looks ill, she thought. The watery eyes were bloodshot, and she could not help but notice the perceptible tremor of her father's hands. Somehow, he had managed to evade front-line duty. When the troops had moved out, it was Corcoran who had taken the regiment forward; Moffatt and his aide Aysgill were seconded to the Provost Marshal's department. The word on the grapevine was that Laura Moffatt had spent hours pleading with General Otis that her husband was too ill for jungle fighting. It was not a rumour calculated to make Jenny any prouder of her parents.

'Well?' he said, 'What have you to say?'

'I'm afraid I don't know what you're talking about.'

Moffat shook his head, as though to say: Don't be tiresome. 'Let us not beat about the bush, please. Your private conduct has been called into question.'

'In what way?'

'It . . . ah, it has been alleged that . . . ah, that you have entertained enlisted men. In your cottage. You have been observed.'

'By whom?' Jenny said angrily, getting up from her chair. 'Who said such things about me?'

'I am not at liberty to reveal —'

'You mean you're prepared to let someone drag my name through the mud without giving me a chance to confront my accuser?'

'I've told you, I'm not —'

'Do you believe it? Do you believe these . . . accusations?'

'I don't know what to believe,' Moffatt said. 'That's

why you are here. I'm trying to help you. Your mother –'

'You've discussed this with my mother?' Jenny blazed. 'Before you told *me* about it?'

His uncomfortable silence answered Jenny and black suspicion seeped into her mind. What had Laura Moffatt to do with this?

'I . . . I felt it my duty. As a father. To talk to you before . . . before this is taken any further.'

'Look at me!' Jenny said. 'Look me in the eyes and tell me you believe it!'

'I don't know . . .' he began. His shifty eyes refused to meet his daughter's. 'I have a certain responsibility. I must –'

'It was Garson, wasn't it?' Jenny said bitterly. 'Doctor damned Garson. *Wasn't* it?' She shouted the last words, and her father flinched as if he had been slapped.

'I cannot –'

'Don't bother,' Jenny snapped. 'It couldn't be anyone else.'

'You don't seem to understand. I have to do this. I can't ignore a complaint by a senior medical officer about the conduct of a member of his staff.'

'I didn't expect you to,' Jenny said. 'But I didn't think you'd believe it.'

Moffatt shook his head. He really doesn't know how to handle this, she thought. He doesn't know what to do. In a way, she felt sorry for him. She realised all at once that she had been sorry for him for a very long time. But it was too late to do anything about that now. She watched as he drew in his breath and picked up the pen, tapping it against the back of his left hand.

'There is simple solution to all of this,' he said. She saw the plea in his eyes: Make it easy for me.

'And what is that?'

'If you will make a full admission,' he said, 'I'll try to make sure that no . . . no further action is taken. We can say you were ill. That you had a breakdown. The

350

separation from home, from your husband. You didn't know what you were doing. I'm sure I can persuade General Otis to take a lenient view of the matter.'

'And then?'

'I would recommend that you be sent back to the States,' Moffatt said firmly. 'I think that would be the end of it. Probably the best thing all round.'

'I can't believe what I'm hearing,' Jenny said.

'I am acting in what I – and may I say, your mother also – believe to be your best interests,' he said stiffly. 'In the circumstances, that is more than you are entitled to expect.'

'You *do* believe it!' Jenny said. 'Or *she* does! And you're doing what she wants! Admit it!'

'Control yourself,' Moffatt said coldly. For once he was in complete agreement with his wife. The best thing that could possibly happen to Jenny would be that she went back to the States. This business had simply provided a convenient excuse for giving her no choice. The further away from her husband she was, the better. 'This is nothing to do with your mother. You will do as I have suggested.'

'No,' Jenny said emphatically. 'I am not going to let you brand me a whore.'

'I'll not have that kind of –'

'I want it out in the open!' she said angrily. 'I want a hearing, right here, or at the hospital! I want to see that filthy little swine stand up and swear on a Bible that what he says is true!'

'Are you insane?' Moffatt said, his voice rising. 'There will be no hearing. My reputation –'

'*Your* reputation?' Jenny laughed, almost hysterically. 'What about mine?'

'You should have thought of that,' he said. 'Before you did what you did.'

'I want a hearing.'

'I will not sanction it.'

'Then I shall go direct to General Otis.'

'You are insubordinate,' he snapped, scrambling to his feet. 'You will do as I say.'

'No, Father,' Jenny said. 'Never again.'

'I want this done with the minimum of fuss and the maximum of dispatch, Peterson,' General Otis said to his legal aide. 'It's a damned unfortunate mess.'

He was a tall man, solidly built, with a bald head and luxuriant side-whiskers. As always his desk was piled high with paper: there never seemed to be any damned end to it, he thought, shoving it aside. He looked at the huge map of the islands on the far wall of his office, the flagged pins showing the approximate position of his forces. Arthur MacArthur had taken Calumpit on May 5, and pushed across the Angat, where four thousand of Aguinaldo's *insurrectos* had brought his advance to a halt. Lawton, driving north from Santa Cruz through Norzagaray, Baluiag, and San Miguel, took San Isidro ten days later, narrowly missing Aguinaldo himself. In spite of these successes, however, they were getting nowhere against the rebel leader. Time after time, the sweating, cursing, wasted Americans fought their way through jungle where no man had ever walked, only to discover yet again that the wily *insurrecto* had eluded them. Casualties mounted; in the first few months of the campaign, VIII Corps had lost more officers and men than had been killed in the entire duration of the war with Spain. It was not a record to be proud of, and Otis knew his War Department masters were not impressed. He had confidently predicted that the rebellion would be crushed by midsummer. There was no chance of that now.

The damned rains, he thought.

This was not just rain. It was a hostile torrent of water that lashed down spitefully, drowning the ground, battering the trees and bushes. A gusting, buffeting wind whirled through the driving lines of water, bending, whipping, spreading them. It was impossible to hear the sound of a shouting man's voice right next to your ear.

The rain made the movement of troops nightmarish, protection of equipment impossible. Even Manila came to a standstill. Stalled carriages and carts slithered and slipped backwards on the slight hill near the Bridge of Spain. Word came through that the only railway line, between the capital and Dagupan, was washed out. Nothing but bad news, Otis thought. Now this damned hearing.

'Short and sweet, Peterson,' he said again, as his legal aide led the way to the room in which the hearing was to be held. 'I don't want any fancy dancing. Keep it short and sweet.'

'Yes, sir,' Major Peterson said. 'I'll keep that in mind.' He was tall, neat, and well turned out. He anticipated no problems in carrying out General Otis's instructions. It was pretty much an open-and-shut case. The hearing was to be informal, but everyone attending it knew that there was no such thing as an informal hearing in the Army. Everything was for the record. Everything.

A long trestle table with bentwood chairs stood at one end of the room, facing the double doors. To the right and left of that table, and facing it, were two small felt-covered card tables from the officers' mess, two chairs at the side of each. General Otis took his place at the centre of the long table. Whittier Moffatt sat on his right. Otis favoured him with a sour glare. He wasn't pleased with Moffatt for letting this damned business go so far. On Otis's left sat an officer from the Adjutant-General's office.

'Very well,' Otis said, in his thin treble. 'Let us begin. Major Peterson?'

Peterson got to his feet and cleared his throat nervously. 'It is alleged that Red Cross volunteer nurse Jennifer Starr, while under the jurisdiction of the United

353

States Army, Eight Corps, Division of the Philippines, did on sundry and diverse occasions consort and commit adulterous acts with the enlisted men named in the complaint, to the detriment of order and good conduct, thereby bringing the United States Army into disrepute.' He looked across the room at Jenny, who sat at the small table opposite him, Chief Surgeon Eames at her side. Peterson walked over to the long table, and handed a sheaf of papers to each of the officers. 'This is the affidavit of Captain Garson, the complainant, gentlemen,' he said. 'You will see that page two is a list of the names of the enlisted men concerned. All of them were patients in Nurse Starr's ward.'

'Have any of them been called to testify?' Otis asked.

'No, sir, that was not possible,' Peterson said. 'They are all returned to active duty.'

'Could they not have been recalled?'

'There seemed no good reason for it, sir,' Peterson said. 'Especially since Nurse Starr had not requested their appearance.'

'I see,' Otis said, frowning at Jenny. 'I assume you have your reasons, young lady?'

'I do,' Jenny said.

'The third page of the affidavit before you lists the times and places in which the alleged . . . acts took place, gentlemen. You will see that they are . . .'

'We can all read, Major,' Otis said. 'Proceed, please.'

'Captain Garson, please rise.'

Garson, who was sitting at the same table as Peterson, got to his feet. He looked across the room at Jenny and smiled. *Bastard*, she thought.

'You are Captain John Garson, Assistant Surgeon, Malacanang Relief Hospital?' Peterson said.

'I am.'

'You give this hearing your word of honour, as an officer and a gentleman, that what you say here will be the truth, the whole truth, and nothing but the truth?'

'I do.'

354

'Please tell us in your own words,' Peterson said, 'why you lodged this complaint with Corps headquarters?'

'Yes, sir,' Garson said. 'It was not an easy decision, sir. We are all adults here. We know the facts of life and we know that . . . certain irregularities of conduct are an inevitable concomitant of overseas service in wartime. I do not mean to sound as if I approve of such liaisons. But we are all aware that they happen. We turn a blind eye to them.'

Hypocrite, Jenny thought. *Slimy hypocrite.* She looked at Otis. He was nodding agreement. Fatuous old fool, she thought. What had Arthur MacArthur said? 'Like a locomotive on its back, with all its wheels going full tilt.' How did men with so little ability rise so high in the service? Was there no one who would brand them for the incompetents they were?

'. . . some things it is not possible to turn a blind eye to,' Garson was saying. 'Especially when one has responsibility for the welfare of wounded men. It was as much in their interest as for any other reason that I reported this . . . matter.'

He paused theatrically, tugging down the skirts of his uniform jacket. He looked at Jenny again, and again she thought she saw the ghost of a smile touch his lips.

'At first, I could not bring myself to do so. I thought that perhaps what I had inadvertently witnessed was an indiscretion, nothing more. But when I investigated further my suspicions were confirmed.'

'Will you tell us what you saw, Captain?' Peterson said.

'I saw Mrs Starr . . . Nurse Starr, intimately embracing an enlisted man. She was lying on his bed in the ward.'

'Did anyone else see this?'

'I don't think so. She had screens around the bed.'

'Then how did you see it?'

'I happened to come into the ward. Naturally, seeing

the screens, I was concerned that something was wrong with the man behind them. But when I . . . I stole away from there without being seen.'

'And this happened on other occasions?'

'At least half a dozen more.'

'You also state that Nurse Starr entertained men at her home.'

'I do.'

'That could have been perfectly respectable. Why did you think otherwise?'

'That was my first thought, too, Major. But . . . at night? With drawn curtains?'

'We are on the eve of the twentieth century, Captain,' Otis said ponderously. 'Drawn curtains do not of themselves signify adultery.'

'What made you think that Nurse Starr's visitors had anything other than perfectly legitimate reasons for visiting her?' Peterson asked.

'When an enlisted man calls on an officer's wife and stays with her until reveille,' Garson said venomously, looking at Jenny as he spoke, 'there is no other possible conclusion.'

'And you know for a fact that this was the case?' Peterson said. 'How?'

'Simple, sir,' Garson said. 'I checked the man's bed before reveille. It had not been slept in.'

'There was only one man involved?'

'No, sir. Over a period of some weeks I observed several. It was then I became convinced it was my duty to make a report.'

'Thank you, Captain Garson,' Peterson said. He turned towards Jenny, who was sitting alone at the other table.

'Is there anything you would like to ask Captain Garson?' he said to her.

Jenny shook her head. 'Nothing,' she said.

A murmur of surprise rose from the officers at the long table. Peterson's eyebrows rose a fraction; but he was much too self-possessed to show his surprise.

'If you have no questions, Nurse, are we then to assume you do not quarrel with the facts as outlined by Captain Garson?'

'I said I did not wish to question Captain Garson,' Jenny said. 'I did not say I have no quarrel with him.'

'Perhaps you will explain.'

'Certainly,' Jenny said. She rose and picked up the three-page affidavit which John Garson had made. She looked across the room at him. Was it hate that lit his dark eyes?

'According to Captain Garson's *evidence*,' she said, putting contempt into the word, 'he first witnessed my . . . intimacy with a soldier at the beginning of March. He then lists eight other occasions between the date my husband left Manila and the present. He gives times, places, names, everything. Everything except one important fact, gentlemen. At the beginning of March, shortly after my husband left for the front, I had an interview with Chief Surgeon Eames.'

'And?' Peterson said, frowning uneasily.

'Chief Surgeon Eames will tell you,' Jenny said, 'if I may be allowed to free him from his oath of confidentiality.'

Otis leaned forward on his elbows and looked at Major Peterson. He said nothing, but Peterson knew what he was thinking: *What the hell is this?* He turned to Chief Surgeon Eames.

'Sir?' he said, knowing what was coming.

'Since she permits me to do so, gentlemen,' Eames said, 'I can tell you that I examined Nurse Starr on March 14 and informed her that she was pregnant. Three and a half months pregnant. I also warned her that she must take great care. That she should refrain from relations with her husband until the baby was born, or perhaps she would lose it.'

'So you see, gentlemen,' Jenny said softly into the silence, 'had I done the things of which Captain Garson

357

accuses me, I might have lost my child.' She looked at Garson with all the contempt she could muster. 'Which means that this *officer*, this *gentleman*, is a liar!'

She sat down.

Otis looked at Moffatt, and then at Peterson. Last, his protuberant eyes settled on Captain John Garson.

'This hearing is terminated!' Otis said, getting clumsily, angrily to his feet. His chair clattered over backwards. Nobody moved to pick it up. Face set with anger, he barged out of the room.

Head high, Jenny watched him go, followed by Whittier Moffatt. Her father did not look at her.

37

The scouts came in and reported a large rebel force
moving down from the mountains above San Mateo
towards the town. Lee sent word for Gates and
Vaughan to bring up their companies.

'You got any idea exactly where them yuyus are at,
Lee?' Gates asked. 'I don't want to go blunderin' in
among them an' get my balls shot off.'

'And so say all of us,' Vaughan grinned.

'You remember that old Spanish blockhouse about
six miles north of town?'

'That I do.'

'They're bivouacked in the jungle up around there.'

'So close?' Gates said, whistling between his teeth.
'You figure they're going to hit us?'

'Maybe,' Lee said.

'Should we whistle the regiment up?'

'I think we can handle them.'

'You would,' Gates said. 'How many of them are
there?'

'Somewhere around the three hundred mark,' Lee
told him. 'My boys didn't stop to count heads.'

'Your boys showed good sense,' Gates observed.

'What's our strength?'

'We got about fifty men.'

'Call it seventy with my boys,' Lee said. 'That should
be enough.'

'How do you want to play it?'

'There's a defile that runs down to the Mariquina,

west of that blockhouse.'

'I know the one.'

'I'll take some of my Apaches and draw them into it,' Lee said. 'You put your men on each side, well hidden. Let them come right on in. Then you give it to them.'

'You make it all sound easy,' Vaughan said. 'What if they don't take the bait?'

'Then you better come get me, before they start cutting little bits off of my anatomy.'

He moved out with six of his men in the half-light that precedes the true dawn. They moved silently through the jungle, and found the *insurrecto* camp without difficulty. The rebels were making no attempt to hide themselves. They were eating *desayuno* when the Americans raked their campsite with rifle fire, killing half a dozen men before they knew what was happening.

'All right!' Lee shouted over the screams and shouts coming from the clearing below. 'Let's get the hell out of here!'

He led his men at a loping run through the sweating jungle, wary of the tripping creepers they called *dalakorak*, and the sharp coral outcroppings that sometimes lay beneath the trees. Cockatoos screamed in panic as the men thrashed through the screen of bamboo and ipil and eucalyptus. Crowned pigeons whooshed through the trees, wings creaking like new shoes. The Americans made a lot of noise as they moved: they wanted the rebels to know where they were. Soon, behind them, they heard the sounds of pursuit, the faint shouts of the trackers.

Ahead of them loomed the mouth of the defile running down to the Mariquina. The jungle trail widened slightly. On both sides, the ground rose steeply, trees and undergrowth forming an almost impenetrable screen. The widening trail opened up into a long glade, green-shaded by huge trees, that closed at its far end, where the trail burrowed back into the close-growing undergrowth. They crossed the three hundred yards of open ground quickly. They ran to the far side, where the rest of Fox company lay in the long alang grass, Krags ready.

'Everything set?' Lee asked his first sergeant. He was drenched with sweat, although it was still early morning.

'All set, Captain,' Sergeant Hanna reported. Lee nodded and sprawled on the floor, his breath coming in ragged gulps. He looked around. The men ranged along the sides of the defile were invisible. Prone in the long grass, he watched the far side of the defile from which he and his men had emerged. It was about ten minutes before the first Filipino appeared. He edged nervously into the wider clearing. He had an old Springfield rifle held at port, and he was tense, wary. He came forward a yard, six, ten. Then he called out to the others still hidden inside the screen of trees. Carefully, half a dozen more *insurrectos* edged into the open.

They moved across the open ground strung out in an arrowhead formation, easing along the trail towards Lee's position. When they were past the halfway mark their leader gave a shrill whistle. The arrowhead of skirmishers fanned out to make a line from one side of the clearing to the other. At the same time, behind them, the main body of the force came into view, led by an officer in a tan shirt and breeches, with leather riding boots and a sabre. He wore no insignia; his horse was the only indication of his rank. They were all out in the defile now, and moving confidently along the trail.

Lee yelled the order to fire, and death blasted down at the rebels from both sides and ahead of them. A dozen fell like dropped coats, never to move again. Others screamed as they were hit, writhing in agony on the ground. The rest fired blindly into the faceless jungle as they ran for cover at the sides of the clearing. Lee stood, waving his line of men to move up with him. The *insurrecto* officer saw him coming and shouted something, wheeling his horse around to make a run at Lee. He drew the sabre from its scabbard and kicked the horse into a run. It was one of the bravest, most foolish things Lee had ever seen. He raised his Colt, but before he could fire, half a dozen rifle bullets tore the man from his saddle, dead before he even hit the ground.

Now Gates and Vaughan moved their men down the hillside, two ragged walking lines of death closing in on the Filipinos like the jaws of a vice. Thirty or forty *insurrectos* were down, some of them screaming in agony. Leaderless, they scrambled to their feet, those with rifles firing as they ran, and fled into the jungle from which they had come, pursued by a hail of bullets that slashed and snatched branches from the trees until Lee called a halt to the firing.

The men came out of the jungle cheering. Clean as a whistle, Lee thought. Nobody hurt.

'Captain,' Sergeant Hanna said. He pointed with his chin across the clearing to where Lieutenant Gates was supporting his friend Chris Vaughan. Vaughan's uniform tunic was dark with blood. Even as Lee ran across to them, Vaughan slid down to the ground, legs askew in front of him, a bemused smile on his face.

'Sonofabitch, boys,' he said. 'Sorry.'

'Come on,' Gates said. 'I'll carry you.'

He put an arm beneath Vaughan's limp body, and then cursed. He showed his hand to Lee. It was smeared with bright red arterial blood.

'Get out of here,' Vaughan said. 'Before those damned gugus come back.'

Gates shook his head stubbornly. 'I'm not leaving him,' he told Lee. His voice was truculent: Don't try to make me, it said.

'We've got to move out, Chuck,' Lee said. 'If those rebels come back with blood in their eyes, we're in bad trouble.'

'I'm not going without him,' Gates persisted.

'Chuck,' Vaughan said weakly. 'It's no use.' He made

a gesture towards his body. 'I'm all – shot up.'

'Is this what you do, Starr?' Gates shouted. 'Is this what you do – leave your people for the fucking rebels to have fun with?'

'Chris,' Lee said. 'What do you want?'

'Sit me up,' Vaughan answered. Gates lifted him. What little colour was left in Vaughan's face drained from it; the smile he put on his face would have broken an angel's heart.

'Rifle,' he said.

'No!' Gates shouted.

'Goddamn it, Gates, it's me that's dying, not you!' Vaughan shouted back. His outburst racked his body with pain. They watched as he got to his knees, and then, agony distorting his face, to his feet.

'Help me over to that rock,' he said. A conical rock, ten feet high, stood between two big mahogany trees to the right of the trail. A V-shaped notch in the rock would conceal a man from anyone coming along the trail. Lee watched Gates help Vaughan across to the rock. Vaughan's hair was wet with sweat. The muscles along his jawline bulged like stones. Gates eased him to the ground. Another fit of coughing racked Vaughan's frame. They saw him wipe away red flecks of blood with the back of his hand. His eyes swam, and then refocused.

'Okay,' he panted. 'Okay.' Again the wrenching cough seized him. Gates lifted a hand and let it drop, as though he was going to say something and then decided not to. There was agony in his eyes, too, but a different kind, Lee thought.

'Chris?' he said tentatively.

Vaughan shook his head. 'No,' he said. 'There's no one.'

'Not even the little Chinese girl on Binondo?'

'I made that up.' His voice was lighter, breathier now. 'Will you two get out of here?' he said.

Lee raised a hand. Vaughan smiled, the old, winning,

363

boyish smile they remembered. Lee fixed it in his memory, and then turned away. He told the sergeants to start moving the men out. Gates stood irresolutely, looking down at his friend. Vaughan shook his head impatiently.

'Go on, Chuck,' he said to Gates.

Gates cast one last despairing glance at Vaughan and then plunged blindly into the jungle. Lee followed. He did not look back again.

The trees swallowed them up. It was very silent for a while. Then gradually the jungle sounds started up again. They sounded, to Vaughan's heightened awareness, much sharper, louder. The clamour of mynah birds echoed through the trees. A bird of paradise squawked on the branch of a nipa tree. How long would it be? he wondered. How many of them would come? The lower half of his body felt as it it was on fire, and sweat dripped off him like running water. Once, he lapsed into unconsciousness, rapping his forehead against the rock hard enough to draw blood, before he jerked back to utter alertness.

'Come on,' he muttered. 'Come on.'

A flash of movement caught his eye: a monkey, high in the trees. A huge atlas moth, wings ten inches across, blundered through the close set trees. The sweet perfume of samapaguita blossoms lay heavy on the humid air. The monkey looked down at where Vaughan lay.

'Wouldn't hang around here much longer, was I you,' he whispered. Almost as if it had heard his whisper, the monkey scuttled out of sight. In the same moment, Vaughan heard the movement of men through the jungle, the slight sound of murmuring Filipino voices. He tightened his grip on the Krag.

One, three, eight, twelve of them, all dressed in the ragtag clothes of the rebel army, hair tied back with bandannas, shirts with the tails outside the pants. A patrol, Vaughan thought, trying to locate Lee's party for the main avenging body of *insurrectos*. He waited until the leading rebel was no more than fifteen feet away and then he opened up.

The bullet blew the leading *insurrecto* sideways into the jungle, and after that, Vaughan fired the gun as fast as he could pull the trigger and reload, ignoring the deep bite of pain inside him and the slow, red pulse of blood that darkened the makeshift bandage Gates had put around his middle. He killed four, maybe five of them in as many seconds and then they were gone, belly down in the sweating undergrowth.

He knew what they'd do now. They'd try to pin him down from the front, while one or two of them worked their way around behind him. He shoved himself back into the notch in the rock and waited. A flurry of shots whacked chunks of stone out of the boulder. Slugs ricocheted off into the jungle. Chips of stone whirred through the air like maddened hornets.

He saw the movement in the trees and swung the rifle round. Two *insurrectos* came out of the wall of green, screaming. He shot the first one between the eyes and the second through the body. The man spun flailing to the ground. Vaughan grinned triumphantly. Pretty good shooting for somebody half-dead, he thought.

His sight began to blur. It was as if a thick mist had descended. He swung the barrel of the gun in an arc, peering into the fog for anything that moved. He never even saw the tan-clad figure with the *machete* rise out of the grass behind him. The other rebels came running at their comrade's triumphant shout, and found him holding up Vaughan's head. Even in death he was still smiling.

38

Rain, rain, rain.

Day followed day of non-stop, lashing wind and rain. Bataan and Corregidor disappeared in a grey veil of water; whitecapped waves rushed at the sheer walls of Fort Santiago, smashing upwards like explosions. The typhoon season had begun early. In July, forty-six inches of rain fell. For days on end, lightning flickered over the bay, and the cannon-bangs of thunder rolled incessantly across the city.

By midsummer Manila was full of refugees. They streamed south from the violated north, blank-faced, silent, stunned by loss. Their villages burned, their crops destroyed, their food and livestock commandeered, they had nowhere to go but south, to where the *Americanos* had set up reconcentration camps, where it was said one could get food, shelter, medical care. They swamped the facilities set up to help them. Cardboard tenements and shacks sprang up on the outskirts of the city. Homeless children wandered the streets. Twelve-year-old boys pimped for girls orphaned like themselves.

There were battles on the isthmus: Bustos, Imus, Mayacanyan. Lawton was scouting and raiding around San Mateo, not twenty miles from Manila. Lee was up there with him, someone told Jenny. Twenty miles, she thought. It might as well be twenty thousand. Every night she prayed that Lee was safe; every time the casualty trains came in she died a little. The casualties came in waves. Many times the entire hospital staff worked throughout the night. Surgeon Eames no longer allowed Jenny to do so.

'You've got to think of yourself,' he said. 'The baby. You can only do so much. It's all any of us can do.' All through the long, sweltering, humid summer months, Jenny learned what all doctors know: there is never any end. No matter how many broken bodies you mend, no matter how many awful wounds you stitch together, more will come, and more and more. She learned not to let pity move her; or love.

'If you can neither kill them nor cure them in sixty days, my dear, you might just as well let them go,' Surgeon Eames told Jenny. He had become specially protective of her since the Garson affair. He told her that Garson had been sent back to the United States, dismissed from the service with ignominy. It was as if he was talking about something which had happened a thousand years in the past. It seemed an irrelevancy, when every train brought in more young men with torn bodies and gaping wounds. Some of them were so young they didn't have enough hair on their faces to shave. Yet they had lost an arm, a leg, a foot. They would get a medal; they said it proudly. A Purple Heart. What kind of consolation to a crippled man was that? She remembered Lee's father talking about battle: it was a frequent topic of conversation at James Starr's table.

'It ain't all glory, boy,' James had told his son. 'Sometimes you hear the bugles and you feel like you could fight the entire world single-handed. But it ain't always like that. You look at me, you'll see what I mean.'

And he had touched the sleeve pinned across his chest, his face like stone, and Jenny knew he was thinking about Gettysburg again.

'What was it like, *Tio* James?' she asked. 'What kind of place is Gettysburg?'

'Little town,' he said. 'Maybe I'll take you up there,

next time we go east. Just fields, rocks, trees. A peach orchard, a wheatfield. Not much to pay so many lives for.'

Rain, rain, rain. Death, death, death.

One day they brought in a boy named Clayton. He was from Tularosa, New Mexico. Twenty, blond, good-looking. He had been on sentry duty at Dagupan. An *insurrecto* had slit his belly open with a knife. Clayton had lain out in the driving rain all night, bleeding. They had managed to keep him alive somehow, but by the time he got to the Malacanang Hospital he was dying. He knew it, and Jenny knew he knew it. She was sure now that there was no one who didn't know it was coming. Even the greenest kids knew. All you could do was be there. Maybe it helped, she did not know. She never stopped being astonished that so few of them were angry.

'They tell me you have a scholarship to go to Fulton College,' she said to Clayton.

'Yeah, but I don't think I'll ever get to use it, ma'am. I don't think I'm gonna pull through.'

Jenny was silent for a while. She no longer said those bright, sunshiny things that nurses think they are supposed to say. It felt dishonest, somehow.

'Is there anything you want me to write your folks, or your girlfriend?' she asked.

'No,' Clayton said, turning his face away. She knew he was crying, and she felt helpless, useless. What was this boy dying for? she wondered. Why had he given his life so stupidly, so futilely, so wastefully? She no longer wept for them as she once had. Tears were no use. The fighting continued. The dying went on.

She heard that Lawton had captured San Mateo, and that Lee was there. They said the *insurrectos* were more afraid of *los Raposos* – the Foxes – than any other unit in the American Army. Lawton's victory was short-lived: General Otis ordered him to immediately abandon San Mateo because he had insufficient troops to garrison it.

The rumour swept through the hospital that Lawton was coming in, that there would be leave, that the boys would be back for a few weeks. Jenny stolidly refused to think about Lee coming home. That way, she could not be disappointed.

The refugees kept pouring in. Conditions in the ramshackle shanty towns were atrocious. The civil authorities did what they could to alleviate them, but people were dying down there by the score.

One grey and cheerless Thursday, Jenny was alone in the ward when she heard a soft footfall behind her. She turned to see a Filipino woman, dressed in shapeless clothing, standing in the doorway. She was tiny, birdlike, frightened. She came into the ward and looked around with huge, pain-filled eyes.

'Hey, nurse!' one of the soldiers shouted. 'We takin' gugus in here now?'

'Yeah!' yelled another. 'Get that goddamned nigger woman outa here!'

The woman looked at Jenny, uncertainty and fear in every line of her body. She said something in Filipino.

'*No entiendo*,' Jenny told her, smiling to reassure the woman. 'I don't understand.'

The woman nodded, as if Jenny had said something encouraging. Her eyes had the look of a dog that has been punished but does not know why.

'You must leave,' Jenny explained. 'Only soldiers are allowed in here.'

'Help me,' the woman said in Spanish.

'I cannot help you,' Jenny said. 'This hospital is not for civilians.'

'Baby.' The woman touched her belly. Her eyes moved to the plump roundness of Jenny's pregnancy. She smiled shyly. 'Me baby, you baby.'

'I'm sorry,' Jenny said. 'You'll have to leave.' She took hold of the woman's arm to lead her out of the ward.

'Baby come,' the woman told her. 'Baby come now.'

All at once, sweat sheened her face, and she let out a low moan of pain. Jenny took her into the nurses's changing room and made her lie down on one of the cots. The woman was panting, her lips caught between her teeth.

'Baby . . . come,' she hissed.

Jenny looked down and there was the head. She ran out and got some sterile towels. When she got back the woman had arched her back, crablike. Jenny slipped the towels beneath her. The baby's head emerged, slick and sticky. She turned it gently on its side and the shoulders popped out, and then there he was, a little squalling bundle, face a grimace, fists clenched, legs kicking. The Filipino woman breathed stertorously, like someone who has run a long way hard. Jenny wrapped the baby in some towels and put him in the woman's arms. Her smile was radiant, like a sunrise.

'*Mabait*,' Jenny said, using the only Filipino word she could remember.

The Filipino woman nodded and smiled. '*Salamat*,' she said. '*Salamat*. Thank you, thank you.'

Jenny realised she was soaking wet with perspiration. Her hands were trembling slightly. I delivered a baby, she thought. It hardly seemed credible. I delivered a baby, a baby! Life, amidst all the dying. It was something to help keep the hope alive. Something on the plus side, a little gift to God so that He would watch over Lee. The woman nodded, as if understanding what Jenny was feeling.

'Where is your husband?' Jenny said.

The woman shook her head. '*Muerto*,' she said. Dead.

A cold hand clutched Jenny's heart. All the happiness of the moment drained out of her. *I am carrying his son*, she thought. *Don't let him die. Please, God, don't let him die*.

Then the moment was gone, like a great black bird soaring out of sight, and she got on with the things that needed to be done for the Filipino woman.

39

Near the end of August, Corcoran pulled Fox company out of the front line. Together with what was left of Gates's and Vaughan's companies – thirty-one men in all – Lee and his men were sent to the rear for six days.

'I'd like to give you longer, Captain,' Corcoran told Lee, 'but this is the best I can do.'

'There's long leave and short leave, sir,' Lee grinned. 'But there's no such thing as bad leave. The men have earned a rest.'

'So have you, son' Corcoran said. Lee was bearded and burned, hard-muscled, gaunt. There were dark circles beneath the ever-watchful eyes. The word 'brigand' came to mind when Corcoran looked at him.

'Your wife is about ready to have her baby, isn't she?'

'Any time now, sir.'

'Something keeping you here, Captain?' Corcoran said, raising his eyebrows. After Lee had gone, Corcoran shook his head and got back to his report. It was a damned shame, he thought. He had submitted three citations: twice recommending Lee Starr for a battlefield promotion, and once citing him for a decoration. All three had been vetoed by General Moffatt at the Malacanang, as had Corcoran's each and every request to pull Fox company out of the line, and give the men a well-earned break. He had even considered going over Moffatt's head to General Lawton, but – little as he respected Moffatt – he could not bring himself to do that. Well, it looked as if somebody had done so: Lee Starr's orders had come direct from Lawton himself.

Lee got back to Manila a few hours after his son was born, on the sixth day of September, 1899. He weighed six pounds and seven ounces, and there had been no complications, a smiling Chief Surgeon Eames told him. Jenny was fine, he said, although a little tired. The baby was a healthy, handsome boy with dark hair and eyes.

'He's going to look like you,' Jenny said. She was lovelier than he had ever seen her, holding the gurgling baby in her slender arms.

'Poor kid,' Lee grinned.

They were so happy to be together again. They touched each other constantly, as if to be certain that the other was real. She hardly recognised him, so swarthy and bearded was he. There were lines at the corners of his eyes and mouth that had not been there when he went into the jungle. He was harder; yet, paradoxically, gentler.

'I'm so glad you're here,' she said. 'You've been away so long.'

'I'm damned lucky, that's for sure,' he said. 'I still don't know how Corkie swung it.'

Jenny smiled. Major Corcoran had had nothing to do with it. Lieutenant Paul Baker – now serving on Otis's staff in the palace – told her how her father had blocked all Corcoran's efforts to obtain leave for Lee and his men. Jenny wrote a brief note to General Lawton, giving him the salient details. Lawton immediately ordered Lee's men to the rear. Let Whittier Moffatt try to countermand *his* orders, Jenny thought.

'The briefings are on Monday, aren't they?'

'All day,' he said. 'We'll go back Wednesday.'

'Then we'd better get His Majesty christened before you leave.'

'I want Chuck to be his godfather,' Lee said. 'Is that all right with you?'

'I can't think of anyone I'd prefer,' Jenny said.

'I'll set it up for Sunday,' Lee said. 'Will they let you out of here by then?'

'I'd like to see them try and stop me.'

Wearing a robe made of *jusi*, or banana silk, their son was christened James Andrew Charles Starr IV by the regimental chaplain, and pleased his proud parents by not crying. The tiny chapel was full: every member of Lee's company, and most of Gates's and Vaughan's, attended. The baby's grandparents were not there.

After the christening, after the troopers had said their shy goodbyes to Jenny and thanked her for the beer and the sandwiches, Lee sat on the porch of his cottage with Chuck Gates, while Jenny put the baby to bed.

'Well,' Gates said, leaning back in his chair and pulling on his cigar, 'how's it feel to be a father?'

'Damned strange, and that's the truth. But then, every damned thing feels strange.'

He was so used to carrying a weapon at all times that he felt uneasy without one. He was so used to sleeping on the ground beneath his sweating poncho, that he could not sleep at all in a bed. He was so used to being filthy and sweaty, it was strange to feel clean. He was so used to seeing only Filipinos that it was a shock to see blondes with round eyes.

'You two are very quiet,' Jenny said, coming out on to the verandah.

'Jack asleep?'

Chuck Gates had nicknamed the baby 'Jack' because of his initials. The name seemed likely to stick.

'Out like a light,' Jenny said. 'Chuck, let me get you another whisky.'

'Hey!' Lee complained, 'how about me?'

'Mmmm,' Jenny said. 'Tricky.'

'I only had a couple.'

'And you used to be so truthful,' Jenny smiled. 'I'll be back in a moment.'

She took their glasses and went inside. The two men

sat in companionable silence. The night was warm but not unpleasant, and the screens kept most of the bugs out. The lush fertile smell of the jungle came to them on the breeze.

'That's quite a girl you've got there,' Gates told him.

'Amen,' Lee said.

'You still buttin' heads with her old man?'

'Uhuh.'

'Over at the club they're sayin' he's managed to get himself posted to the rear again.'

'You hear anything about tomorrow?'

'Little bit,' Gates said. General Otis's plan was simple, he said. They would run the insurgents north and capture them in a vast, encircling movement. MacArthur would strike due north along the railway line to Dagupan and Tarlac. Meanwhile, General Wheaton would sail with his brigade to Dagupan, there to join up with Lawton, who would by that time have ascended the Rio Pampanga with three thousand five hundred men, and occupied the mountain passes to the north, cutting off Aguinaldo's retreat. With MacArthur pushing him, and Lawton and Wheaton cutting off his retreat, Aguinaldo would have to fight to a finish or surrender.

'Can't help wondering why Otis wants us to shove off at the height of the typhoon season,' Lee said. 'We'll have hell's own job moving so many men.'

'Well, he ain't too bright,' Gates pointed out. 'Don't forget he was shot in the head at Petersburg.'

'Who was that?' Jenny asked. Ice clinked in the glasses she brought out in the tray. Gates thanked her and took a good slug of his bourbon.

'I still can't get used to havin' iced drinks,' he said, 'but I'm gonna just tough it out till I do.'

'We were talking about Otis,' Lee said. 'If he waited till November to launch the offensive, we'd be able to move twice as fast.'

'I figure he's bein' leaned on by Washington,' Gates

surmised. 'There's been some talk about Lawton succeeding him. So this is pee-or time.'

'Do you boys want anything else to eat?' Jenny asked. 'There's – '

Gates groaned theatrically. 'I ain't eaten so much since I left the States.'

'Out in the jungle we were lucky if we got wild yams or palm cabbage,' Lee said.

'Hell, yes,' Gates grinned. 'Some days we had no cookies to go with our coffee.'

'Don't laugh,' Lee said. 'It's true.'

'You poor babies,' Jenny said.

'What do you think, Chuck? You think we'll catch Aguinaldo this time?'

'I sure as hell hope so,' Gates said. He fished another Alhambra out of his tunic pocket and lit it, blowing smoke into the air. 'I wouldn't mind going home.'

Home, Lee thought. It was almost an abstract concept. There had been letters waiting for him when he got in out of the jungle, from Rachel, from his uncle Andrew, from his father. They contained news of a world far away, where people made love, built homes, picked up their kids from school, visited friends.

'You'll do it,' Jenny said. 'You're going to catch Aguinaldo. I know it. Then we'll *all* go home.'

She was right. They did catch Aguinaldo. But it took them another eighteen months.

40

James put down the bottle and sighed. The damned stuff always let you down worst just when you needed it most. Booze, he thought, the crutch that kills. He got up and walked across the room. It was nearly daybreak. The first tendrils of salmon-pink sunlight were touching the sky over the mountains. Another night gone, he thought. It was a small victory, nothing more. Now he had to get through the day. And when the day was done, he would have to face the night again.

Alone.

It would be a blessing, he thought, if someone could find a way to isolate certain stretches of a man's memory and cut them out, the way you cut pictures out of a newspaper. He looked out of the window towards the blackjack oak that shaded his wife's grave. Maybe I should have taken her to the farm, he thought, and buried her there, with all the others. But he knew that this was where she would have wanted to lie, beneath the vast New Mexico skies she had always loved, on a hill overlooking the Flying J at Cloudcroft.

She had been his wife for thirty-five years, the cement that held his life together. Of her love he had never had the slightest doubt. He had been quixotic and erratic, and sometimes heartlessly cruel, but her love for him remained constant. How much he had scarred her, he never knew, for she never spoke of it.

He saw her face in memory: dark-eyed and lovely, as he had first known her, in the garden of her home in San

Antonio, almost half a century earlier; in shadowed repose, like a madonna, with young Lee at her breast; and with pain in her eyes that he had callously ignored, as he left her to go to California, to Catherine. She had even forgiven him for that.

And now she was dead, and every word he had ever spoken to her in anger came back to lacerate his soul. Long, sleepless nights in the cold, empty bed they had shared became unbearable. He had once thought he could never get over Catherine's death, but even wounds as deep as that healed. This pain, too, would ebb in time. He just had to wait. Meanwhile, whisky dulled the anguish. Enough of it, and he could forget for a while. Forget how much he hated himself.

He had always been a drinker. The stuff didn't seem to affect him the way it did other men. James believed he used it up the way these newfangled automobiles burned gasoline. From time to time, he'd take note of the amount he was drinking, and cut back. It was always under control. He knew he could quit any damned time he wanted to. But he didn't want to, and sure as hell didn't plan to. The stump of the arm, amputated at Gettysburg nearly forty years earlier, still gave him hell on days when the rain loomed in inky clouds over the Sierra Blanca. A man needed a drink on a day like that. You needed a glass in your fist if you were bellied up to the bar, talking to your cronies in the Exchange. It was good to take a drink or two upon the successful conclusion of a deal, or to round off a hard day. Hell, that wasn't really drinking.

'You're full of what the man called taurine excreta, Starr,' he told himself. He was getting through a bottle of whisky most nights, not counting what he drank during the day. That was a hell of a lot of whisky. Old John Barleycorn was a treacherous bastard. He wasn't content with the memories you wanted him to take out of your head. After he ate up your past, he came with jaws agape looking for your present, and then your future, and if you didn't fight him, he would gobble them all up with about as much compunction as a shark eats a herring.

Just one more, then.

So as not to think about Linda dying.

Pernicious anaemia, the doctors said. The bone marrow was failing to produce red corpuscles. That explained the listnessness, the weakness, the fainting attacks, the pallor. There was nothing they could do: it was incurable. They said they were very sad. He wanted to scream at them: how the hell do you think *I* feel?

'I'm dying, aren't I?' Linda said. She held his hand in hers. 'No, don't tell me it's not so. No lies about this.'

'All right,' James said hoarsely.

'I'm leaving you so many troubles, *mi alma*,' she said. The radiant smile was wan, the dark eyes full of pain. 'That awful man Billy Priestman. Our children . . . '

'Don't worry,' he said. 'I'll look out for them.'

'You always said that,' she smiled. 'And never did it.'

'I always kept meaning to.'

'They love you, you know.'

He wondered why the thought made him feel slightly uncomfortable, as though he did not deserve their love. Or did not want it. That was impossible. Wasn't it?

'We . . . it was good, Jamie, wasn't it?' she whispered.

'Yes,' he said. 'With you it was always good.'

'My poor darling, who's going to cut up your meat for you?'

He watched his daughters standing beside their mother's grave, and remembered what he had felt as he stood beside the grave of his own mother: bereft, robbed. He was just getting to know her, and they had taken her away from him. He wanted to be angry, but there was nobody to be angry with. His father had believed you didn't die: that there was more waiting for you, up there. James had long since abandoned such beliefs. He had seen too many men mangled to meat on the battlefield to have any hope that death was not the uttermost finality.

It was easier to just plain give up.

He was old, he was tired. And the truth of it was, he didn't give much of a damn about anything any more. Let Billy Priestman win. Let him have it all if it made him happy. One by one, the wounds multiply, like the torture of a thousand cuts, till the body and brain scream in unison, *finish it!*

How the hell had he reached sixty-seven?

The events of his life lay behind him, like milestones on a long and winding road. Or gravestones, he thought. A lot of life could be measured out in gravestones.

'We've got to fight back, James,' his brother had said after the funeral. 'We can't just let him walk all over us like this.'

'I wish I knew how,' James said, wearily. 'I wish I could say I cared, Bo.'

'You've *got* to care!'

'I'm too damned old to go to war again,' James said querulously.

'He won't quit, James,' Andrew said. 'You roll over and die, he'll start in on the rest of us. Diana and me, or one of the girls. Or Louisa. By God, what a field day his muck-racking son would have with her!'

'Likely she'd take a pistol and shoot the sumbitch!' James said, forcing a smile. 'Was he to upset her applecart.'

'It's good to see you smile.'

'I sure as hell don't feel much like it.'

'Come back East with me,' Andrew urged. 'We can talk. You can relax at Belmont. It would do you good to get away from here for a while.'

'Maybe later,' James said. 'I don't want to . . . leave her. Not just yet.'

It was partly true.

Mostly it was a lie.

Deep down he knew what it was. He was beaten. And there was only one way to keep that dark knowledge out of his mind.

Drown it.

When times got bad, he'd taken a mortgage on the ranch to tide him over. Slowly, inexorably, the money dribbled away. Someone had picked up the mortgage. He didn't need to be told who that someone was.

Billy Priestman.

Here's to you, Billy, you bastard.

James's daughter Portland was a miserably unhappy woman, separated from her husband, her life poisoned by his infidelity. James had tried to talk to her after the funeral, but she would not stay at Cloudcroft. She could not bear to be in the same house as her sister.

Score two for Billy Priestman.

And have another drink.

Huntington Carver, the poor, sad sonofabitch, had lost the railroad his father spent a lifetime putting together. He had had the use of millions; now he was a salaried employee of the railroad he had once controlled. And who had contemptuously put him into the office of non-executive chairman of that same railroad?

Billy Priestman again.

Bottoms up, you bastard!

And what about Rachel, sweet, gentle, soft-hearted Rachel who had fallen in love with her sister's husband, and found out the hard way that a mistress has no status except contempt, and no home but shame? Notch up another scalp for Billy Priestman.

And pour another drink.

Then there was Lee, fighting a forgotten war for a country most Americans couldn't even find on a map, commanded by an officer who hated his guts, and who would go on sending Lee out into the jungle until some Filipino rebel disembowelled him. Nothing James Starr could do about that, about any of it.

Except have another drink.

They all said the same thing to him, although they said it in different ways. It came out the same whatever they said: they expected *him* to stop Billy Priestman. They didn't ask him whether he wanted to, or whether he was strong enough to. They just told him he had to do it, and then went back to doing whatever they had been doing before. Like Sam Elkham. He came out to the ranch and saw James, to try – as he so tactfully put it – to shake some life back into him. The Santa Fé law practice was all but moribund, and things at the ranch were going to hell in a bucket. He read James the riot act. Told him Billy Priestman was gloating to his cronies that he had broken James Starr.

'All right,' James said wearily. 'All *right*, Sam!'

'James, I hate saying these things to you,' Elkham apologised. 'Especially after . . . Is there anything we can do? Would you like Sally to come out and spend a few days with you?'

Sally was Sam's wife. She and James had always been very fond of each other. James considered the idea for about ten seconds, then shook his head. He didn't want any women around. The swish of a skirt, the faint trace of perfume; he would turn his head, thinking it was *her*. And it would only be somebody else.

'Thanks, Sam,' he said gruffly. 'I'll be all right.'

'You've got to do something, James,' Elkham insisted.

'That's what everyone says.'

'I'll go see your brother,' Sam said. 'He'll want to help.'

He damned well better, Elkham thought. James looked like something a coyote would turn up its nose at. He arranged for some Mexican women to come in and clean the place up, make sure his partner ate regularly. He made James promise to pull himself together. A couple of hours after he left, James locked himself into his study and started drinking. It was no damned use, he thought. Everything was fucked up.

381

Portland, Rachel, Lee, every one of them.

Well, forget it and have another drink.

You know you're killing yourself, don't you? said the him inside his head.

'I know,' he said.

'That what you want?' it asked.

James nodded gravely. And reached for the bottle again.

41

Near the end of August, 1899, Willie Priestman bought Susan Simpson a town house on West Twenty-ninth Street, just above Madison Square. In any other town, maybe in any other circle than the one Willie moved in these days, eyebrows would have been raised, if only slightly. But not in show business. A man who knew the people Willie knew, who had the kind of money and the kind of power Willie had, could do pretty much as he liked, as long as he didn't do it in the street and frighten the horses.

That wasn't to say that nobody remarked on his affair with Susan. The kinder souls wondered why a man who could take his pick from the line at the Casino, would settle on little Miss Nobody from Nowheresville, USA. A sweet enough kid, sure. But face it, boys, she must have been a long way back in the line when the brains were handed out. Those who were less kind, and there were more than a few of those on Broadway, said it just went to show that a pig could live with a cow and be happy.

Willie knew what everyone was saying about him and Susan. It mattered less to him than a fart in a hurricane. What they didn't know about Susan, what nobody knew about her, was that she loved sex.

'Well, Billums,' she would say, greeting him at the door in a flimsy *peignoir*. 'What games would you like Popsy to play tonight?'

She was as artlessly abandoned as a child. She posed

like Venus on the rumpled bed, pouting sweetly as she beckoned him to come to her. She stuck her naked bottom in the air and watched in a mirror, giggling, as he took her from behind. She got into his bath and soaped him sensuously, and then made splashing, rubbery love to him in the tepid water. The little Cupid-bow mouth was knowing and avid: she did things that could bring a sudden flush of guilty delight to his cheeks two days later. She painted him with honey and then languidly licked it off. She put a piece of candy in her vagina and let him suck it out. She sat him on an upright chair, and then sank down slowly on his erection, wriggling her bottom and giggling. And afterwards, she would say 'Oh, Billums, isn't Popsy *naughty*!'

She made him want to be kind to her, and he felt rather good about the fact that he was. Never once did the thought even enter his head that she might be using him. Susan simply wasn't that kind of girl.

'Tell me about all those places again,' she said. 'London. Venice. Paris.'

'I'll take you there one day.'

'Oh, that would be so wonderful!'

'You wouldn't mind going with an old man like me?' he smiled.

'Oh, Billums, thirty-two's not old,' she said. 'Why, you are a man in the full flow of his strength.'

'Ten years older than you, Susan.'

'I think that's just perfect,' Susan said. 'Just the way it should be. I think the man should be more mature. Know things, the way you do. About foreign countries, and wine, and food. You're such a clever man, Billums. I wonder whatever it is you see in a girl like me.'

'You know,' he said, and touched her.

'Oh, Billums, what a naughty boy you are!' she said.

'Susan, tell me something. What made you want to be an actress?'

'I didn't really,' she said. 'It was my mother. She always wanted to go on the stage. So she did it through

384

me, kind of, instead.'

'You want to be a star?'

'Doesn't everybody?' she said.

'Then I'll make you one.'

'Oh, Billums, don't be silly,' she said.

'I mean it.'

'You can't make someone a star, just like that!'

'Ziegfeld did it, with Anna Held.'

'I'm not that good,' Susan said, with sad honesty.

'You could be. You could learn.'

'Learn? How do you learn to be a star?'

'You get stars to teach you,' he said. He felt grand. He would ask Ziegfeld to get him the very best. Voice coaches, dancing instructors, drama teachers, elocution. He would have shows written especially for her. Ziegfeld could put them on.

'Sing something,' he said.

'All right.' She went across to the Steinway he had bought for her. She played accurately, without inflection, like a well-taught child.

'Ev'ry little flower, ev'ry little bird,
Ev'ry little child at play,
Ev'ry little breeze, sighing in the trees,
Cried, the day you went — '

'No!' he said, sharply. 'Not that!'

'Why, Billums!' Susan said. 'It's such a pretty song. It's by Irving Stras — '

'I know who it's by!' he snapped, 'and I don't want you to sing it. You are never to sing any song written by that man, do you hear me?'

'Yes, Billums,' Susan said meekly. 'I hear you. But I still don't understand.'

'Never mind,' William said benevolently. 'Sing something else.'

She nodded and played the opening bars of 'Tell Me, Pretty Maiden' from the English show *Florodora* that was opening soon on Broadway. William beamed as she started to sing, tapping his feet in time with the music.

Arthur King was a neat, prim, unsmiling man who invariably wore grey suits, black shoes and a sober necktie. He sat across the table from Willie Priestman in a private dining room on the third floor of Harvey's Restaurant, in Washington, DC. He tapped his fingers on the table. He was not used to being summoned to meetings. He was an important man, a leading light in the Tapeworm Club, a dining club composed of members of the New York delegation to Congress that met regularly at this restaurant. He was a power in the Democratic Party.

'Can we get down to business, Mr Priestman?' he said, pushing away the plate heaped with empty clam shells. 'I've another appointment across town at – '

'I want to go into politics,' Willie said. 'How do I go about it?'

'Not too difficult,' King said. He took a cigar from his breast pocket and trimmed it with a gold cutter. He took his time lighting it. Such a ploy would ordinarily have irritated Willie beyond measure. Today he chose to be quietly amused by it. The little prick thought he was Somebody.

'Now,' King said, puffing on his cigar and squinting at Willie through the smoke. 'It shouldn't be too difficult, as I say. Especially with your kind of money. What did you have in mind?'

'I want to be President of the United States,' Willie said, enjoying the look his words brought to King's face.

'Ah,' King said, putting down the cigar.

'You're surprised.'

'Somewhat,' King said. 'Unusual for someone so young to be so . . . specific.' He shook his head, picked up the cigar, looked at the end of it, put it in his mouth.

'In ten years, Mr Priestman, I'd say maybe. In twenty, I'd say, possibly. Right now, I have to tell you the truth. It's not feasible.'

'Why?'

'For one thing, you're far too young. You've absolutely no political experience. The country wants a mature man in the White House. An experienced man.'

'I see,' Willie said harshly. 'What about the Senate?'

'The . . . to be frank, Mr Priestman,' King said, carefully laying down the cigar again. 'You haven't got the right . . . image.' He coughed apologetically. 'No offence.'

'None taken,' Willie said, stifling his anger. 'What exactly do you mean?'

'You're no saint, Mr Priestman. I refer particularly to your . . . friend Miss Simpson. Not to mention the horses, the clubs, the show business people you mix with. You don't have the persona of a public servant. You'll forgive me for speaking bluntly?'

'You think the public gives a damn about my persona?' Willie said. 'My experience of the public is that it doesn't give a damn about anything except its own self-gratification.'

'You're wrong, sir,' King said. 'What a newspaper owner does is one thing, Mr Priestman, but what a politician does is another entirely.'

'I'd have to change?'

'Radically.'

'Tell me how.'

'You sure you really want to hear it?'

'Let's get another bottle of champagne,' Willie said. 'I've got a feeling I'm going to need it.'

He listened carefully to what King had to say. It took almost half an hour, and it could have been boiled down to one sentence, if King had been that type. The peroration contained but one salient proposition: that before Willie could confidently run for office he would have to establish his bona-fides not only with the party,

387

but with the public.

'Let's start with the party,' Willie said. He would worry about the public later; he probably knew as much about the public as Arthur King did. If the public thought he was going to change his ways, the public could go and screw itself in A. T. Stewart's window at high noon on Christmas Eve. With Arthur King watching.

'Bryan will get the nomination in July,' King said. 'McKinley is going to be hard to shift. We'll need all the support we can get.' He steepled his fingers and pursed his lips. It made him look like a gopher, Willie decided. 'How would you feel about starting a newspaper in Chicago? An *Inquirer* boosting Bryan out there would make a big difference.'

'You're talking money now,' Willie said. 'I mean, real money.'

'That's the only kind we use.'

So he has got balls, Willie thought, even if they're only snail-sized. 'And what would be in it for me?'

'I'll propose you as president of the National Association of Democratic Clubs,' King said. 'I think you could confidently expect to be elected.'

'So I'd be president of the whatchamacallit,' Willie said. 'What would that mean?'

'It would mean, after you'd served a while, that you could count on its votes if you were to run for office.'

'Let me get this straight,' Willie said. 'You're getting a newspaper. I get this NADC thing and what – a seat in the Senate?'

'Not the Senate,' King said urbanely. 'To become a senator, you have to be selected by the state legislature and be a resident of the state you wish to represent. You don't want to move to Chicago, I take it?'

'Not damned likely,' Willie said.

'Then you'll have to run for Congress.'

Congressman. Well, you had to start somewhere, Willie thought. The office you occupied was unimportant: it was what you did while you were in it that counted.

'You've got yourself a deal,' he said.

King blinked. 'You reach your decisions quickly,' he said.

'Never found waiting made all that much difference,' Willie replied. What King didn't know was that Willie had been working for some time on plans for a Chicago newspaper. So getting the presidency of the NADC and a seat in Congress out of it was a bonus. That was the kind of deal Willie liked.

'We'll talk again,' King said. He laid his napkin on the table and stood up. 'Thanks for lunch. And give some thought to that . . . other business.'

Willie let nothing of his thoughts show on his face. He ordered a cognac and lingered over it, looking out of the window at the carriages going by on Pennsylvania Avenue. Privately, he didn't give William Jennings Bryan a snowball's chance in hell of dislodging McKinley. When he'd been in New York last, he'd seen a show with a sketch about the forthcoming election. It had made quite an impression on him: Willie was a great judge of public sentiment, and this exchange had drawn an enthusiastic roar of applause from the audience.

'Whole town seems to be for McKinley and Roosevelt,' the top banana said.

'How's that?' asked the stooge.

'Well, there's only McKinley and Roosevelt banners on Broadway. Everyplace you look, nothing but McKinley and Roosevelt banners.'

'So what? Banners can't vote.'

'No,' said the comic 'but they sure show you which way the wind's blowing!'

Private feelings about Bryan's chances were unimportant, however. Willie would support the Bryan bandwagon because it served his own purposes. So, on July 2, 1900, William Jennings Bryan pressed a switch in Indianapolis – Indianoplace, as Willie sarcastically

389

remarked, just where you'd expect Bryan to be campaigning – and started the presses rolling for the first issue of the Chicago *Inquirer*.

Like the other papers in the Priestman chain, the Chicago paper concentrated immediately on McKinley as the tool of 'the trusts'. Willie's new campaign featured himself as champion of the little man, a public-spirited citizen putting the weight of all his wealth and his newspapers fairly and squarely behind the man who would bring the trusts toppling down. He had no real expectation of Bryan's actually doing this, even if elected. It was cynical and he knew it. That didn't matter. It sold papers, and that did.

The following November, William McKinley was re-elected President, greatly exceeding his previous margin of victory over Bryan. Theodore Roosevelt, who had visited twenty-four states and made more than seven hundred speeches during the campaign, was elected Vice-President.

Bryan was finished, and Willie abandoned him with no more scruples than he would have thrown away a chicken bone. It was time, as he liked to put it, to take the bull by the balls. Using his presidency of the NADC as a platform, and its membership as his support group, he began to campaign for office. His slogan was simple and direct: power to the people. It was the kind of slogan the great unwashed loved. He spoke at party fund-raising dinners, at rallies, at women's club luncheons. He gave splendid firework parties. He laid cornerstones. He gave scholarships and endowed colleges. He instructed his editors to ensure that his name appeared with increasing prominence and frequency as a benefactor, great organiser and fearless campaigner for the rights of ordinary people. A new man for the new century.

Look out, world! he thought. Here I come.

42

They camped beside a river whose name Lee did not know. He chose the place carefully, so that the river itself guarded one flank, with open ground before the campsite to give a clear field of fire. He formed the men into a half-circle based on the river – forty men in the outside ring, thirty in the inner, the rest posted as sentries on the river bank, in case *insurrectos* tried to swim across under cover of darkness. Inside the inner rings he positioned the ammunition packs and the provisions. He gave the Maccabebe scouts permission to start the cooking fires. The *insurrectos* knew where they were. Fires would make no difference.

The men sprawled around the perimeter, prostrated by heat and exhaustion. There wasn't much talking, just the usual backchat, discussion of the day's events, guesses about the morrow's. That was about as far as any of them thought now. Nobody even discussed the future: they were too worn out. They had no energy left for anything except the vital task of staying alive.

Lee's orders were that every third man in both circles was to stay awake, each taking a shift of three hours before he was relieved. Then he gave orders for mess call. They had dried fish, rice, some taros – starchy tubers not unlike potatoes. They'd all eaten a lot worse than that.

Some time after midnight, Lee decided to get some sleep. Mosquitoes and gnats whined in ghostlike clouds above the encampment. Night creatures filled the dark with their eerie sounds. Lee slept like a dead man. The sound of falling rain awoke him. He put on his poncho and came out of his tent. It was a steady downpour, setting up a solid wall of sound as the rain thrashed the jungle foliage. All around the perimeter, Lee could hear his men cursing the rain, coughing, stamping their feet into wet boots. It was almost dawn. He saw First Sergeant Hanna striding across the clearing, his face purposeful. A good soldier, Lee thought. One of the old unit. Not many of them left. He wondered why Hanna was bareheaded.

The discovery was announced by a shout from the direction of the river. Men started running towards the sound. Hanna stopped them with a barked command. He looked across at Lee. Lee nodded, and went down with him to the river bank, where three troopers knelt beside a huddled form that lay half in and half out of the water.

'It's Dougan, Sarge,' one of them reported. 'Throat's been cut.'

'All right,' Hanna said. 'Get him out of here. You, Furillo! Get a squad down here, organise a burial detail!'

'Sarge!' Furillo said, and hurried away.

Lee turned away from the savaged trooper's empty, dead stare, trying not to hear the buzz of the flies. It was just another pointless death. There was nothing anyone could do. Whoever had killed Dougan had slid through the jungle in the night, slit his throat and escaped without a sound. Taking Dougan's Krag with him, Lee thought. It was still the ambition of every Filipino rebel to own a Krag. If he owned a Krag he could buy another wife, raise himself up in power and rank.

Bastards, he thought, without rancour.

He began to walk back to his tent. He was about halfway there when a screaming rebel came up out of the jungle beyond the perimeter, running flat out, the wicked, irregular blade of his kris glinting dully in the watery gleam of the rising sun. He disembowelled one

392

of the sentries without even breaking stride. Lee saw Sergeant Hanna running across the encampment, pistol in hand, yelling at the petrified sentries.

'Shoot that fuckn gugu!' he yelled. 'Shoot him!'

The *insurrecto* heard Hanna's shout and veered towards him. The brown face was distorted, the eyes wide and empty. *Juaramentado*, they called it. The bastard was so hopped up he would have charged a regiment of mounted cavalry single-handed.

'Shoot, damn you!' roared Hanna, still striding across the clearing. The running Filipino was no more than ten feet from him, the deadly kris raised to strike, when Hanna raised his pistol and fired it point-blank into the man's face. The rebel stopped as if he had run into a brick wall. He fell in a thrashing heap. Without even looking at the man he had killed, Hanna strode on towards the outer ring.

'Who the fuck let that juicehead through the line?' he yelled. 'I'm gonna have someone's ass for this!'

He turned towards Lee and winked, as if to say, We know it's not serious, don't we? The next moment his head exploded, and in the same instant Lee heard the whiplash crack of a rifle somewhere in the screening jungle. He shouted the bugler into action, and the shrill notes pulled the troopers to their feet as all at once, the Filipino rebels came out of the jungle. About half of them had rifles. The rest were armed with bolos. They spread across the clearing like water spilled from a bucket. For a few moments there was wild confusion. Lee ran towards his tent, pulling the Colt .45 out of its holster. He saw Chuck Gates stumbling groggily out of the tent, pawing sleep from his eyes. Gates froze with momentary disbelief, then reacted as one of the rebels ran at him, firing a rifle from the hip. Gates shot the Filipino with the regulation .38 Colt he had snatched up, and the rebel skidded in the muddy slick, rolled over, leaped up. Gates looked him in the eye. The *insurrecto* swung his rifle around.

393

'Die!' Gates yelled. 'Die, you shithead!' There was an almost insane shrillness in his voice, and it seemed to make the rebel hesitate. In that moment Gates shoved the muzzle of his pistol against the man's chest and pulled the trigger. The Filipino was slammed to the ground, his heart blown out of his back. Smoke rose from his singed shirt. Gates sank to his knees, face raised to the sky as if in prayer.

'Get on your feet, Gates!' Lee shouted. There was shooting going on all around him now. Bullets whipped through the humid air, fired in panic, aimed at nothing. Screaming men grappled, pistols cracked. Lee ran across to where two rebels were struggling with a young trooper. He shot the nearest one off the boy. Arms freed, the young soldier smashed the butt of his rifle into the dark, twisted face of the second rebel. The native fell, his face a bloody mask, and lay mewling on the churned ground. The trooper coolly levelled his rifle and shot the writhing man through the head. He grinned at Lee and touched his forehead with a finger.

''nother good Injun, sir,' he said, and ran after the retreating *insurrectos*. Lee noticed some of the other men doing the same, saw the danger, and shouted the bugler to sound recall. The boy took a moment or two to get some spit into his mouth. Then the shrill notes sang out. The noise died.

Lee looked around. Five rebels lay sprawled dead where they had fallen. They looked like bundles of washing dropped in the mud. Chuck Gates came across. There was a fine speckling of blood, like freckles, on his face.

'Two men dead, three wounded, Lee,' he reported.

'Get a burial party to work,' Lee said.

They buried only their own men now. If they buried the rebels, their comrades came back later and dug up the bodies to take them home. Lee looked up at the sky. It would rain again soon. Better move the men out as quickly as possible.

They followed the trail south. The clamour of mynah birds echoed through the trees. Kingfishers hunted by the river on wings like sapphires. That night, when they made camp, cicadas chirred endlessly, their monotone punctuated by the croak of bullfrogs. The chilling scream of the chik-chaks kept the atmosphere of the camp tense. The shrieks of the fever bird sounded like someone being tortured. The panicked noise of a startled animal in the undergrowth could stop a man's heart.

'What you broodin' about, *capitano?*'

Lee looked up. Chuck Gates loomed in the entrance to the tent. He was carrying a water flask.

'*Lambanog,*' he said, waving the flask. 'One o' them gugus was carryin' it.'

Lambanog was a rum-like concoction made from the fermented nectar of the coconut flower. It had a kick like a mule.

'Tired of life, huh?' Lee said. Gates squatted down and unstoppered the flask. He took a swig and handed it to Lee. Lee wiped the neck and took a pull. It was like drinking flaming honey.

'Good for what ails you,' Gates said.

'They haven't invented a drink for that.'

'Got the downs?'

'The all-the-way downs,' Lee said. 'What are we doing here, Chuck? Why are we fighting this shitty war?'

'Oh, *them* all-the-way downs,' Gates said. 'You better have some more of this.'

'I mean it,' Lee said. 'We're no nearer catching Aguinaldo and putting an end to this business than we were eighteen months ago. We've lost a lot of damned good men – and for what?'

'Don't ask me, *capitano,*' Gates said. 'I only work here.'

'Sorry,' Lee said.

'It's okay.'

'I was trying to put together a letter to write to

Hanna's wife. I couldn't think of what the hell to say to her, Chuck. He was with us from the start. All those fights, all those marches. I thought he was going to live forever.'

'He was a good man,' Gates said.

'Damned good.'

If only you could say that to the man's wife, he thought, say it so she would know that you were paying her man the highest compliment you could pay another soldier. He wondered whether anybody back home in the States had any conception of what it was like to fight, and maybe die, for a cause nobody any longer cared about.

Home.

It was like an abstract concept.

His sister's letters told him that his father had been drinking heavily, since the death of their mother the preceding spring. Lee felt the familiar twinge of guilt, and shook it off. No use burdening himself with that now. He had made his choice. There was a war, and that was what he was trained for: duty, honour, country. He was not the first soldier whose mother had died while he was serving abroad; but he would forever regret that it had been so, as he would always regret that Linda had never seen her grandson.

He thought of Jack and he thought of Jenny all the time. Thinking about them kept him sane. They would all be together soon. The second fall campaign was drawing to an end. It was a guerilla war now, with a more subtle kind of brigandry. The Filipinos hid their weapons in their houses or buried them in the ground. They told the soldiers they were *amigos*, going about the ordinary pursuits of a peaceful life. But if the opportunity arose for them to attack a small patrol or an Army convoy, they would arm themselves, kill without mercy and then disappear into the population, *amigos* once more. In spite of such tactics, the Army had built over four hundred posts in the islands, and many miles of road. The wry joke that there were only two kinds of road in the Philippines: bad, and very bad, was less true now, but it had cost the Americans dear. Casualties in the first year had been more than five hundred officers and men dead in action, a further two and a half thousand wounded, and a thousand more dead of diseases the doctors sometimes didn't even know the names of.

'You got any idea of the date?' Lee said to Gates.

'I dunno,' Gates said. 'November the something.'

My God, Lee thought, is it a year since Henry Lawton stormed into the Malacanang and confronted Otis? He had been brought south and returned to supply duties. Everyone knew why: Otis didn't want him to get any more glory. If Lawton actually captured Aguinaldo – and it had looked as if he was likely to do it, that November of 1899 – Otis would be recalled, and Lawton would replace him. Lawton knew it, too.

'Give me two regiments and a free hand,' he bawled at the corpulent Commander-in-Chief, 'and I'll deliver Emilio Aguinaldo to you dead or alive in sixty days!'

Otis turned him down flat. The insurrection, he said, was over. There would be no more pitched battles of any note.

'I've been kicking my heels in Manila for weeks,' Lawton said. 'For God's sake let me do something useful, General!'

After two weeks of hemming and hawing, Otis had acquiesced to an attack on a handful of *insurrectos* at San Mateo. Damned little more than a scout-in-force, Lawton had grumbled, but he was far too much the professional soldier to call it what it was, a goddamned insult.

He shoved off on December 12 with two battalions of infantry and some cavalry. Although it was December, which was usually cool and dry, rain lashed out of the sky in torrents as he led his men to the Malacanang, where General Otis was dining with his staff officers

397

and their wives. He came out to speak briefly with Lawton.

'You sure you want to go ahead, General?' he asked, with a gesture at the sky. 'This weather – '

'The men are already on the move, sir,' Lawton pointed out. 'I respectfully suggest you allow your orders to stand.'

'Very well,' Otis said, without much interest. He lumbered back into the dining-room. Lawton came stamping back through the puddles, rain streaming off his yellow slicker. He got back on his horse, and did not speak again until they were on the outskirts of Manila. Then, as if he had been holding it in check until that moment, he hit the pommel of his saddle with a clenched fist.

'God damn that fat-arsed pen-pusher!' he growled.

The column reached San Mateo at dawn. Facing it was a well-organised Filipino force, entrenched near the Mariquina River. Lawton mounted his attack: a meticulous flanking and fording operation. He supervised the building of the rafts himself, conspicuous in his white pith helmet. As the rafts were launched into the river, they came under heavy fire from General Licerio Geronimo's *Tiradores de la Muerte*, the Death Shooters. Lieutenant Breckenridge, Lawton's aide, was hit. Lawton carried him to the rear, and returned to the river bank to rally his men. As he shouted encouragement at them, his second aide, Captain King, saw Lawton make an awkward gesture in front of his face.

'What's the matter, General?' he said.

'I'm hit,' Lawton said. There was surprise in his voice.

'Where, sir?'

'Through the lungs,' Lawton said. King helped him back from the river bank. Lawton lay down on the wet ground, and coughed. Blood erupted from his mouth. He was dead in minutes.

'You remember General Lawton?' Lee asked Gates.

'Sure,' Gates said. 'Good soldier.'

'He got me my commission.'

The irony of Lawton's death had haunted him a long time. Here was a man who had come unscathed through some of the bloodiest battles in history: Shiloh, Murfreesboro, Chickamauga, the siege of Atlanta, the Apache wars, El Caney and Santiago de Cuba, not to mention a dozen fights on Luzon. Holder of America's highest award for bravery, the Medal of Honor, fearless, just and honest. Yet he died a worthless, pointless death, shot by an illiterate Filipino peasant trained by an English soldier of fortune. If there was a God, was He amused that the man who caught Geronimo died trying to capture another man with the same name?

'You want another slug of jungle juice?' Gates offered, interrupting Lee's reverie.

'No, thanks,' Lee said. 'I can't take that stuff the way you can.'

'That's because you're only a little bitty feller an' I'm big an' tough.'

'Next time the rebs attack, I'll stand behind you.'

'Don't you always?'

'Get out of here,' Lee said. 'I need some sleep.'

'You need some home,' Gates said. 'We all do.'

Lee sighed. 'Saddle them up at six, Chuck. I want an early start.'

'You got it.' Gates stood up. 'I'll go check the perimeter.'

He gave a salute of sorts and went out of the tent. Lee sighed and rolled himself into his poncho. Maybe tonight he'd get more than a couple of hours' sleep. He took out the creased and faded photograph of Jenny that he always carried in a waterproof pouch, and gazed at the familiar features.

They had last seen each other in September, before the start of the new campaign. All sorts of changes had taken place in the command structure in Manila since the preceding June. Perturbed by widespread newspaper reports of torture, looting, wanton destruction of property and summary execution of Filipinos by drumhead courts, the Administration decided upon a change of command. President McKinley sent out a five-man commission headed by a new civil governor, the elephantine Judge William Howard Taft. Taft had not wanted the appointment, but he came anyway, bringing with him a reputation for largeness of mind and heart. The mortified Otis immediately proffered his resignation, which was speedily accepted. In his place – taking the command that would have been Henry Lawton's, had he lived – was General Arthur McArthur. His appointment was greeted with great relief at every level of the Army. Arrogant he might be, but MacArthur was a no-nonsense professional soldier. Massachusetts-born, Milwaukee-raised, he had won a Medal of Honor at Missionary Ridge, rising to the rank of colonel before he was twenty. He had come to the Philippines with Wesley Merritt, and played a decisive part in the capture of Manila. Two days after Otis vacated it early in June, MacArthur walked into his office at the Malacanang. It was awash with paper.

'File this stuff,' he told his aides.

'Yes, sir!' they said. 'Where, sir?'

'Right there,' MacArthur said, pointing to the trash bins. They had the room cleared in three hours. With Judge Taft taking care of civil affairs, MacArthur had time to concentrate upon matters military. He made it one of his priorities to review very carefully the records of every officer serving in the rear echelons.

'I've got a goddamned war going on out there,' he said. 'And I'm not going to win it while half of my general officers are sitting on their arses, pushing paper around!'

It was not long before he got around to the case of Brevet Brigadier-General Whittier Moffatt, seconded to the Provost Marshal's department by his friend Otis while his regiment was out in the jungle getting cut to bits. He summoned Moffatt to his office.

'I'm making some changes, General,' he said. 'They will affect your department directly.'

'Very good, General,' Moffatt replied. 'Whatever you say.'

'I'm glad you are so enthusiastic,' MacArthur said, 'because I'm putting you back on the line.'

'I beg your pardon, sir?' Moffatt's shifty eyes were suddenly full of fearful unease.

'I think you heard me properly, General. You are relieved. Your place in the Provost Marshal's Department will be taken by Major Corcoran of your regiment. You will hand over to him as soon as possible.

'I . . . sir, I cannot leave the department without – '

'Your regiment will leave on September 10,' MacArthur said. It seemed to Whittier Moffatt that he was smiling faintly, but he could not imagine why. 'I'm sure you would be . . . disappointed if you could not go with it.'

'I . . . ' Whittier Moffatt tried to find some way to object to what was happening. MacArthur waited, as if he was hoping for some objection so that he could blow it apart. The silence lengthened.

'Do you have a question, General?'

'No, sir,' Moffatt managed.

Lee heard the story of this exchange from 'Corkie' Corcoran when he got in from the north. Corcoran took considerable pleasure in relating it. He had formed the highest opinion of Lee Starr as a soldier and a human being.

'You just keep your eye on that old bastard when you're out in front of him, Lee,' he advised. 'Don't ever let him get you in a tight, boy.'

'Thanks,' Lee said. 'Thanks for everything, Corkie.'

'Shit,' Corcoran said. 'You didn't get anything you

didn't earn twelve months ago.'

Overruling Whittier Moffatt's objections, MacArthur advanced Lee Starr to the rank of Major, replacing Corcoran, and gave him a battalion. There were now only three men left of the original unit that had become known throughout Luzon as *Los Raposos*. One of them was Gates, whom Lee immediately requested as his second in command. Gates was thus advanced to his captaincy, and the third and final member of Fox company, Harry Singleton, was upped to first lieutenant.

On September 6, four days before Lee was due to leave for the fall campaign, they celebrated Jack's first birthday with a home-made cake sporting one commissary department candle. Jack crowed with delight in his high chair, and gurgled when Chuck Gates playfully lifted him high above his head. Chuck had brought a bottle of champagne – 'so you two can celebrate' he said. After he had gone and the baby was in bed, Lee and Jenny drank it together, then made slow and languorous love in their humid room, while lightning flickered above the mountains beyond the city.

Before they left, MacArthur called his officers together to tell them he was about to issue a proclamation, which would be posted throughout the islands. It would stipulate that henceforward, whenever action was needed, the application of that action would be more drastic. Everyone knew what he meant: there were no more *amigos*.

They had been in the field ever since. Apart from a few skirmishes, nothing in the way of a fight took place. The Filipinos were beginning to get the message that turning *Americanista* was the better part of valour. Even so, after almost two years of rebellion, the Americans had not found one traitor among eight million Filipinos to tell them the whereabouts of Emilio Aguinaldo. The men fought with dogged, almost despairing courage.

They had a different marching tune now, bitterer, darker.

Damn, damn, damn the Filipino,
Goddamned Khadiak ladrone
Underneath the starry flag
Civilise him with a Krag
And return us to our own beloved home!

It seemed he had been asleep only a few minutes when he felt someone shaking him awake. He sat up and looked out of the tent. A bright, clear day, not too hot. The sound of bugles echoed in his mind. Harry Singleton, the lieutenant's bars on his collar already tarnished, saluted.

'Officer's call, sir.'

He hadn't dreamed the sound of bugles, then.

'Very good, Lieutenant,' he said. 'Any idea what it's all about?'

'Yes, sir,' Singleton replied. 'The scouts have located an insurgent force up ahead, at a place called Santa Isabela. About six miles north of here. General Moffatt plans to attack it.

Lee pulled on his boots and jammed his campaign hat on his head. He threaded his way across the camp to the headquarters tent. For no reason he could think of, Corkie Corcoran's admonition repeated itself in his mind: *Don't ever let him get you in a tight, boy.*

Whittier Moffatt sat at the head of the table in his briefing tent, surrounded by his staff. There was a look of curiosity, perhaps even suppressed surprise on some of the faces around the table. Moffatt had won few admirers among his officers; the idea that he planned to attack was something of a volte-face: he usually did exactly the opposite. Lee looked at his father-in-law, seeing him as if for the first time. Moffatt had thinned down a lot since the beginning of the campaign. His

403

skin was sallow and unhealthy-looking, his beard and moustache now almost totally grey. Like his hair, it needed trimming. His once-pristine uniform hung on him, stained and creased. Only the ponderous voice remained the same, still pleased with its own sound. A large sketch map lay on the table in front of him, and in his hand he held a stick to use as a pointer. Lee glanced at the map.

Santa Isabela was a hamlet of perhaps three hundred souls, lying close to the banks of the Rio Angat. Nipa huts with ladders, and windows of braided thatch, huddled next to stone houses, making a rough cruciform around a plaza dominated by a stuccoed church. The jungle surrounded the village like a wreath. A trail ran north and south along the river; another joined it from the west, passing between two high, conical hills covered with dense undergrowth. It was along this trail that Whittier Moffatt proposed to advance upon the village.

The scouts had established that trenches had been dug across the trail on the outskirts of the village. Whoever was in command down there knew what he was doing, Lee thought. If the trenches were overrun, the *insurrectos* could retreat from house to house through the village, inflicting heavy losses upon their pursuers as they did. After that, they had the river at their backs, and the trails east and west along which they could quickly disappear into the screening jungle. The twin hills to north and south of the trail shielded the enemy flanks. In addition, the Maccabebe scouts had spotted some caves on the slopes of the hill which would be on the regiment's left flank as they advanced upon the village.

It stank of ambush.

The hill to the north, the one with the caves in it, was designated Hill A; the one to the south, Hill B. The trail along which they would advance ran between them, then through the village to the river bank, where it split north and south. Behind the line of trenches lay open ground, where sugar cane had been burned off.

'Gentlemen,' Moffatt said, 'I propose to attack the village in force tomorrow morning. Major Starr's battalion will make a frontal and right flank attack upon the insurgent trenches. While he is engaging the enemy, I will bring the second battalion around the left flank, falling upon the enemy from the rear.'

He looked around and beamed, as though he was expecting applause. Across the table, Gates's eyes met Lee's. There was no expression on his face, but Lee knew what Gates was thinking. *He's put us right at the sharp end. Again.*

Why don't I protest? he thought.

Damn the man, I never will. And he knows it.

'If I attack on the front and right flanks, I'll have to split my command, General,' Lee said.

Moffatt nodded impatiently.

'You think it wise to split our force into three, sir?' Lee asked.

'Are you questioning my judgment, Major?' Moffatt snapped, bristling.

'Of course not, sir,' Lee said. 'It's just that we have no real indication of the enemy's strength.'

'Maybe if we whistled some artillery up and lobbed in a few dozen rounds of shrapnel, we'd have a better idea of how many gugus we got down there, General,' Gates put in lazily. 'They could hide a division in that jungle around the town, an' we wouldn't know they were there till we got in among them.'

'My scouts tell me there aren't more than a couple of hundred *insurrectos* in the place.' Moffatt said loftily. He looked directly at Lee. 'Are you telling me you can't handle them, Major?'

One or two of the officers in the tent shifted their feet uneasily. It was no secret that General Moffatt hated his son-in-law, and made him the special target of his clumsy sarcasm.

'Not at all, sir,' Lee said with a small smile. 'I've been

handling this kind of thing for quite a long time, as the general knows.'

It was Moffatt's turn to flush now; Lee's reminder that Moffatt had been in the front line only a short time was neatly done, giving him no reason to be offended, yet nonetheless being offensive.

'Very well,' Moffatt snapped. He straightened his uniform jacket and looked around. 'Are there any other questions?'

'Sir, I'd like to send a patrol out to check the caves on Hill A.' The speaker was Captain John Lafferty, aide to Major Matthew James, commanding the second battalion.

'The Maccabebes said they saw no sign of movement up there,' interposed Moffatt's aide, Colonel Aysgill, his voice pitched between annoyance and impatience.

'With respect, sir,' the young officer persisted. 'If the rebels have got just a few sharpshooters in those caves, they could give us a lot of trouble.'

'We'll send skirmishers up ahead of us tomorrow,' Moffatt said querulously. 'If there are any rebels there, we'll soon flush them out.'

'What time do we attack, sir?' Gates asked.

'Captain Starr will advance upon the enemy trenches at ten o'clock precisely, engaging the enemy as and when he encounters them. I estimate that will take between fifteen and twenty-five minutes. Meanwhile, as I said, I shall lead the rest of the regiment around the enemy's left flank, arriving in position at approximately ten thirty-five. By that time, the enemy's attention should be fully occupied by the attack on his front. We should be able to roll him up from the rear like a carpet!'

And get the glory, Lee thought sourly. It was so much out of character for Whittier Moffatt to go on the offensive, Lee could only assume the man felt quite confident that there would be no danger for him to expose himself to.

'One last question, sir,' Lee said. Moffatt favoured

406

him with a sour look. 'Does the general wish me to attack all along the enemy front? Or would he care to nominate the point he wants me to hit?'

'Use your judgment, Major!' Moffatt said impatiently. 'I don't care where, and I don't care how. Just pitch in and do it!' He looked up, his face flushed. 'Gentlemen, I think if all goes well, we'll be celebrating a fine victory tomorrow evening. I hope I need not say I expect every man to do his duty.'

You clumsy bastard, Lee thought, you just alienated every officer in your command.

They went back to their tents. One or two of the junior officers looked at Lee as though they would have liked to ask him something. His expression did not encourage them, and they left him alone. Gates sat down with Lee, looking out through the tent flap at the encampment. He was whistling something tuneless through his teeth.

'Jesus, Chuck, will you quit that?'

'Nervous, capitano?'

'Apprehensive,' Lee admitted. 'This whole thing stinks, Chuck. I don't like it one damned bit.'

'Me, either,' Gates said. 'I got the feeling we're gonna get bit in the ass.'

'Go on.'

'One thing we learned about our little brown brothers, Lee, is that they ain't stupid. They know we're here. Even if the bamboo telegraph hadn't told 'em we're around, they got eyes and ears. The *got* to be waiting for us!'

'Maybe we could surprise them,' Lee said.

'Tell me more, my captain.'

A frontal assault would be suicidal, Lee said. They had to have an edge. What he had in mind was to roll a quartermaster wagon ahead of his men, and advance on the enemy trenches using it for cover. That way they'd have a fighting chance. A slim one, but better than walking straight into a wall of lead.

'You reckon Moffatt's plan'll work?'

'If he's right about the numbers.'

'And if not?'

Lee just looked at him.

'I'll take a company,' Lee said. 'Fox. For luck. I'll go in down the trail. Behind the wagon. You take the rest of the regiment and work your way through the jungle, up the side of Hill B. While I'm keeping them busy, see if you can't get around their line. If we time it right, yóu'll hit their left rear about the same moment Moffatt hits their right. That way, we might just pull of that 'fine victory' he was talking about.'

'One company,' Gates said dubiously. 'You're gonna be in trouble if you run into any kind of numbers, Lee.'

'You heard the general,' Lee said. 'There's no more than a few half-witted Filipinos in those trenches. Probably haven't even got guns.'

'Oh, sure! All the same, I'd feel a hell of a lot better if you'd go in with at least two companies, *capitano*.'

'My God, Mother, don't you ever stop worrying?' Lee grinned.

'Kiss my ass,' Gates said, and stalked out of the tent.

Like Lee, he was going to try to get some sleep.

Like Lee, he probably wasn't going to get any.

By ten o'clock next morning the temperature was in the high seventies. The sky was brilliantly blue, with dramatic white clouds framing the conical hills above the trail through the jungle. Lee moved forward on horseback, two companies of the 33rd behind him. He had given orders for them to march in columns of two, and to sing as they came. He wanted the *insurrectos* to think the entire regiment was coming at them down the trail. The men were in good voice, bawling out a bawdy version of 'Goodbye, Dolly Gray'. Waiting in their trenches, the *insurrectos* would be smiling over the breeches of their stolen rifles, waiting for the stupid *Yanquis* to come and be killed.

Nearer the village the trail widened. Lee halted the

408

column and gave orders for them to form skirmish lines. Through his binoculars, he could see the ragged earthworks in front of the Filipino trenches, just out of rifle range.

He called an order to the bugler, and the sweet, deadly sound of the command to advance sang out in the still air. The sweating men in blue moved slowly forward. Up ahead the spiteful snap of rifle fire began. Bullets whined through the air, snicking pieces off the trees around Lee. The headquarters guidon flicked and flopped in the fitful breeze. The sound of rifle fire was now a continuous crackle. In the long grass on the open ground below the knoll on which he was standing, he could see his men inching forward. He swung his glasses to the right, searching for signs of Gates and his men, but the dense jungle screened everything. He looked at his watch. Ten twenty-five.

'All right,' he said to First Lieutenant Singleton, who was standing at his side. 'Wagons roll!'

'Sir!' Singleton said, with a grin. He shouted a command at two men, and they ran to where the big quartermaster wagon stood in the trees. Slowly, they shoved it forward till it was on the crest of the long, gentle slope that led down to the enemy position.

'Let 'er rip!'

The soldiers gave the wagon a huge heave, cheering as it began to roll down the slope, slowly at first, then gradually picking up speed as it careered towards the Filipino trenches.

'Let's go!' Lee shouted, kicking his horse into a run. The men streamed out of the screening jungle in his wake, running down the slope behind the lumbering wagon, which was passing through the skirmish line. The skirmishers rose out of the long grass and bunched behind it, covered by its bulk as they shoved it to add to its speed. The Filipinos in the trenches laid a withering hail of rifle fire on the advancing wagon; even at this distance, Lee could see great chunks of body timber

409

being whacked off it. Here and there a man slid to the ground and lay still. Then the wagon was at the edge of the trenches, bucking upwards and crashing over on its side. The blue-clad American troopers were charging in on the disorganised Filipino trenches, shouting and firing their rifles into the smoke. The *insurrectos* held for what seemed to Lee like an aeon, then he saw the line waver. The first of them turned and ran back towards the town. Lee spurred his horse forward, waving his hat.

'They're on the run!' he shouted. 'Pour it on, lads!' As he approached the trenches, an *insurrecto* leaped up and tried to grab his reins. Lee shot the man out of the way. He saw another picking up a Krag rifle from the body of a wounded American trooper, and rode his horse into the man, knocking him flying. As the Filipino scrambled to his feet, eyes glazed with panic, Lee shot him in the chest. Men were shouting, screaming, all along the line of trenches. The acrid sting of cordite mingled with the old familiar copper stink of death. All around, Lee saw *insurrectos* scrambling out of their emplacements and retreating to the village.

Now was the dangerous time. There could be rebels hidden in the town. The retreat could have been planned to suck the *Americanos* into an ambush. He shouted at the lieutenants to hold the line, and dug into his pocket for a watch. Ten twenty-four. Where was Gates?

As if in answer to his question, he heard the sound of bugles off to the right, and the stuttering crackle of rifle fire. It looked as if Gates had made it through and was attacking the Filipino flank. The noise of firing swelled and swelled, a roar that drowned the sporadic shooting going on in front of Lee. He frowned; it sounded like a lot more guns than Gates had. They had gone into battle with a complement of about two hundred men, the remnants of five companies. Lee had sixty of these, Gates the rest. Had Gates run into trouble?

Suddenly, a horde of *insurrectos* came out of the jungle

like a wave, running towards Lee's position between the scattered houses on the straggling street ahead of them. yelling and screaming, they simply ran right over the line of retreating skirmishers and cannoned into the main body of the American troops, guns firing, bolos slashing. Fighting degenerated into hand-to-hand struggles; for a moment, it looked as if it would turn into a rout.

'Fall back to the trenches!' Lee screamed at the men in front of him. 'Back into the trenches!'

The Filipino trenches lay just behind them. Fighting like tigers, the Americans managed to regroup and then form a ragged line. They poured a murderous hail of rifle fire into the packed ranks of the Filipino rebels, who stood irresolute, then ran for cover. The Americans fell back and took up positions in the trenches which they had captured only minutes earlier. Ten, a dozen of them lay where they had fallen in the straggling street beyond.

'Jesus, Major!' It was Harry Singleton. His cap was gone, his uniform torn. A trickle of blood had dried on his face, tracing a path from his hairline to his mouth. 'Where the fuck did all those yuyus come from?'

'They suckered us, Harry,' Lee gritted. 'They hid their main force, and let us come on in before they hit us.'

'What about Captain Gates, Major?'

'He'll be here,' Lee said, hoping to God he was right. The sound of firing in their right flank had slackened. Was it imagination, or had it moved further away?

Lee dug out his watch again. Ten thirty. Where the hell was Moffatt?

'Major!' Singleton shouted. Lee looked up and saw blue-clad troopers staggering out of the jungle on the right flank.

'Covering fire for those men!' he shouted. 'Singleton, take a squad – ' He didn't need to complete the order. Yelling as he went, Singleton was already running in a

411

crouch towards the battered remnants of Gates's unit as they emerged from the jungle, firing back into the dense undergrowth as they came. Lee felt his whole being shrink with an awful premonition. He watched in horror as Gates lurched out of the jungle and staggered towards the trenches. Blood pulsed from a gaping bolo slash as the base of his neck. The front of his body was a bright, glistening mess of blood and torn tissue; he was moving on will-power alone. Even as Lee watched, one of the little rebels ran at Gates and hacked at him again with one of those deadly knives. Lee emptied his pistol at the running *insurrecto*, almost tearing the man in half. Gates stood for a moment alone, rocking on his heels, totally disoriented. The men in the trenches screamed at him to come, as Singleton threw a cordon around the retreating Americans, screening them from the pursuing *insurrectos* with a devastating wall of fire that drove the rebels back into the jungle. The battered remnants of Gates's force fell gratefully into the loamy shelter of the trenches as Singleton backed his men in, firing as they came. He was an old hand, and a good one: they did not lose a single man.

Gates staggered across the ten yards separating the trenches from the jungle. During that brief interval, the rebels in the jungle put at least half a dozen bullets into his back. Yet still, somehow, miraculously, he stayed upright, moved forward, fell finally into one of the trenches.

Lee scrambled across heaving, cursing, sweating men to get to the trench where Gates had fallen. The big man lay wedged in a corner, legs asplay. His eyes were empty, as though there was no longer any intelligence behind them. He moved a hand, turned his head. His lips tried to form words, but nothing came. The bright blood bubbled on the front of his body. He was all torn up, the way a bull is after the picadors have had him. Lee slid across and put his hand on Gates's shoulder. Gates turned his head, the sightless eyes trying to focus.

The bitten lips moved again.

'Lee?'

'Hold on. For Christ's sake, Chuck, hold on!'

'Sorry . . . *capitano,*' Gates said, his voice hardly more than a sigh. 'There was . . . too damned many of the . . . bas – '

He sighed and turned his head away from Lee, like a tired child. It was a few moments before Lee realised his friend was dead. He stared at the earthen wall of the trench. His mind was as empty as a bucket.

'Major?'

It was Harry Singleton. His lantern–jawed face was full of concern. He shook Lee's shoulder. Lee did not respond.

'Major!' This time Singleton put force in the word, and he saw Lee blink, like a man coming out of a deep, deep reverie.

'You better come take a look, Major,' Singleton said. Lee frowned. Why was Singleton bothering him?

'Come on, Major!' Singleton shouted. 'We're in trouble!'

Lee stumbled to the edge of the trench and peered over the top. In the village street, well out of rifle range, the *insurrectos* were wheeling a field gun into position.

'Jesus Christ, Harry!' he hissed. 'Where the hell did they get that from?'

'Captured it, I expect.'

'Pass the word along. Tell the men to keep their heads down.'

Singleton grinned, showing tobacco–stained teeth.

'I'll pass the word, Major,' he said. 'Although I doubt they need tellin'!'

Lee nodded. Singleton hesitated for a moment. His glance flicked at the still body of Gates, then back to Lee.

'He was one of the best,' Singleton said softly.

Lee made no reply. Instead, he watched as the Filipinos loaded the field piece. From this distance, it

413

was hard to tell what it was: a 3.2-inch, maybe, Lee thought, the old non-recoil type firing unfixed ammunition with black-powder charges. More sound than fury, thank God. He flinched as white smoke bulged from the muzzle of the gun. The shell went well over their heads, *shuggashuggashugga . . . boom!* smashing down a coconut palm in a thrashing tangle.

They've got us pinned down, Lee thought.

He dug the watch out of his pocket again.

Ten-forty.

Where the hell was Moffatt?

General Moffatt's advance had been completely stalled by the twenty Filipino sharpshooters holed up in the caves on the slopes of Hill A. Three times, squads of volunteers tried to storm their position; three times they were thrown back with heavy losses. Every time an attempt was made to force the trail, the vicious enfilade from above ripped the moving line to pieces. In his command position, Whittier Moffatt raged at his company commanders, castigating them for their inability to neutralise the snipers. Finally, he ordered three companies to ascend the hill to the north and attack the Filipino position from above. They moved out at ten-twenty, while the rest of the battalion waited, deployed along the trail and below the caves. The sound of the engagement in the town below came at them loudly and clearly on the still morning air. At ten-forty, just as Moffatt's three companies engaged the snipers from above, and the remnants of the First Battalion were pinned down by the field gun in the village, General Maximiliano del Pilar threw his entire force of four hundred and fifty well-armed, well-trained soldiers against Moffatt's unprepared position.

The Americans were thrown back by the sheer weight of the attack, losing twelve dead and suffering fourteen wounded in the first five minutes' fighting.

The *insurrectos* pressed their advantage, coming at the disorganised battalion like a tidal wave. Outnumbered almost two to one, the American soldiers fell back. The officers tried desperately to get them into some kind of fighting line, but the *insurrectos* gave them no time, charging in a hacking, screaming, hate-filled phalanx. Within five minutes of attacking, the rebels had turned the uphill flank of the column. The line wavered, held, then broke. Terrified troopers fled to the rear, running like rabbits through the tearing jungle. The rebels pursued stragglers without mercy, killing them where they found them. Only when Major Matthew James planted a guidon on a knoll in a wide clearing facing the oncoming Filipinos, and rallied the men around him, did the line hold. Calmly and methodically, James formed his men into a three-line phalanx shaped like a V, with the point towards the enemy. As they came running through the jungle, he unleashed the full force of seventy Krag rifles, firing in volleys, upon them. The Filipino line was torn to ribbons. The *insurrectos* who survived scuttled back to the shelter of the dark jungle. James marched his phalanx forward a hundred yards, firing as they walked. Nothing could live in that hail of lead. The Filipino advance was stopped cold. It was at this juncture, to the astonishment of every man present, that the bugles sang recall. General Moffatt had ordered a retreat and had made his way to the rear.

Burning with anger, Major James made his way to the headquarters tent. General Moffatt sat on a camp stool, staring at the ground. His aide, Aysgill, looked uncomfortable and embarrassed.

'In God's name, General, why are you pulling us back?' Matthew James shouted, unable to contain his rage. 'We had them on the run!'

'We have to regroup,' Whittier Moffatt said, looking up. His eyes were muddy with – what? James wondered. Confusion? Panic? *Fear?*

'General, we can't leave our people down there!' he

said. 'They'll be cut to pieces!'

'We must regroup,' Moffatt said again. The normally ponderous voice was scratchy, thin. 'Major, sound officer's call!'

'Sir, there's no time for a conference!' James shouted. 'Let me go forward and see if I can get through to Major Starr and his men!'

'If Major Starr hasn't the good sense to fall back and rejoin us, Major, I'm damned if I'm going to go down there and fetch him home like a baby!' Moffatt snapped, his face rigid with petulance. The sound of small-arms fire rose and fell in the valley below, punctuated by the heavier, solid sound of the field gun.

'General, I beg you, sir!' James said, shaking Moffatt's arm. 'I'll volunteer. Let me take two companies and try to relieve them!'

'No,' Moffatt said, his eyes averted. 'Let them get out of it themselves. We've got to go by the book. You understand me, Major? We've got to go by the book.' He turned to face James. His eyes were empty, as if he had forgotten who he was.

'To hell with the book and to hell with you, General!' Matthew James shouted. 'I'm going down there to get our boys out!'

Moffatt's eyes flared with sudden anger, and he lurched to his feet. Matthew James stepped back, startled, as Whittier Moffatt levelled an arm and pointed a shaking finger at him.

'Do you presume to tell me what you will do, sir?' he screeched, spittle flecking his lips. 'I'll see you broken if you utter one more word! You hear, do you? Once more word, sir, and I'll have you placed under close arrest!'

'But, General – '

'Shut your stupid mouth!' Moffatt roared. 'Aysgill, get this insubordinate swine out of here!'

Aysgill put his hand on Matthew James's shoulder. James shook it off. 'This is all wrong, Colonel,' he said.

'You know it is.'

'You heard what the general said, Major,' Aysgill said officiously. 'Leave at once!'

'Talk to him, for God's sake!' James begged. 'Make him see he's got to do something!'

'Out,' Aysgill said.

'You bastard!' James shouted. 'You're as bad as he is.'

'You'll answer for your insubordination when we return to Manila, Major!' Aysgill snarled.

'And you'll answer for this, Colonel!' James retorted.

'For following orders, Major?' Aysgill said. 'Don't be a bigger damned fool than you already are.'

'Jesus Christ!' James spat. 'They really picked the right name for you, Colonel.'

He turned on his heel and strode angrily back to his own tent. Johnny Lafferty looked up as he came in, saw James's face, and refrained from speaking. There was no need to ask what had happened. The two men sat silently, listening to the sound of firing coming from the direction of Santa Isabela. It went on for perhaps another fifteen minutes, rising to a crescendo, then fading slowly into silence. James took a deep breath and let it out very slowly.

'They're dead,' he said. 'Those little brown bastards have killed them all.' He turned to look up the hill towards the headquarters tent, and shook his fist impotently.

'Do you hear that, you yellow-bellied sonofabitch?' he shouted at the top of his voice. 'They've killed all our boys!'

43

For a while, James Starr got a hold of his life. Having
Rachel home helped a lot. He had been drinking pretty
steadily since Linda's death, but he got a hold of that,
too. He began to think that maybe he could start putting
his life together again, although how he was going to do
it without Linda, he didn't yet know. Take it one day at
a time, like Rachel said. Everything was a lot better
with her around. She saw to it that he ate properly, and
put him to bed those nights when he passed out in the
big leather armchair with the whisky decanter in front
of him. They had a nice Christmas, just the two of
them: turkey, sweet potatoes, all the trimmings.

Then the letter from the War Department arrived.
The Secretary of War regrets. Missing, presumed dead.
James had been pretty much drunk every night since
then. Not roaring, fighting drunk; not maudlin, singing
drunk; not reeling, falling-down drunk. Just blank-
faced, mind-numb drunk. Every day he crawled out of
bed around eleven, drank some coffee, read the paper.
Took a walk as far as the corral and back. Washed when
he felt like it, shaved once in a while. Life was just
something that went on around him while he waited till
sundown, and he took out the decanter and blotted out
everything that was going on in his mind.

Was this some sort of punishment? Was this what
God had planned for him, to take the people he loved,
one by one? Wait till the scar begins to heal from the loss
of one, then take another? Who will be next, Old Man?

No answer from God. He didn't expect any answer from the old bastard. Missing, presumed dead. It could mean anything. There was still a chance that Lee was alive. Every instinct James possessed wanted to believe it; cold commonsense told him it could not be so. He went into Lee's room and stood silently, looking at the books on the shelf and the pictures on the wall. My boy, he thought. He grew up in this room. He went to school, and rode ponies, and I helped him to learn everything he knows. Everything he *knew*. All wasted, wasted.

In the mornings, James sat where he was sitting now, by the window in the big living-room of the ranch, looking out at the bare grey hills along the Peñasco. There had been a light sprinkling of snow the night before. Snow. He remembered a little boy in a red suit throwing a snowball at him, and Linda laughing. They bought him a wooden sled and towed it up the hill behind the house, and . . . You old bastard, he thought, looking up at the angry grey sky. You miserable old bastard, God.

He picked up the newspaper and stared at it. Headlines shouted the news of a big oil strike at Beaumont in Texas. He wasn't really interested. He wasn't interested in anything except getting through the day, and then getting through the night. He was still staring at the printed pages when Rachel came into the room.

'Want something to eat, Daddy?'

'No, I don't think so,' he said.

She came and sat beside him, laying a gentle hand on his arm. He did not trust himself to look at her. He was perilously close to tears a lot of the time these days. Damned stupid old man, he thought. But he was glad she was around. He hoped she knew that. Rachel had come back home for her mother's funeral and stayed on. At first she was subdued and uncommunicative, and he did not press her. She was grieving for Linda, he knew, but there was something more. Little by little he got her to tell him. It wasn't easy, but she told him, and she cried, and he tried to console her. Despite the humiliation, she was still in love with Huntington Carver. He told her time would take care of that, and he hoped he was right. He had no time for a man who could act as Carver had acted. There was no word from Portland. There never would be, he thought. She had maintained a cool apartness while she had been home, and there had been no mention of what had transpired between her and her husband. Porty was much too proud for that. She would act as though nothing had happened. She would buy new drapes, or new carpets, or new furniture. She would take a trip to some fashionable spa, stay with friends. She would never show the hurt, or even admit that it existed.

'How are you feeling this morning?'

'I've had better days.'

'I need to talk to you, Daddy,' Rachel said.

'Not now,' James said. 'I'm tired.' He wasn't tired at all. He just didn't want to talk. There was nothing to talk about. There was nothing left to say about anything at all.

'It's important,' Rachel said. 'Please?'

'So, talk,' he said. He put down the newspaper and took off his glasses. He hated the damned things, but fine print defeated him now. He could see all the way to the end of the damned world outdoors, but he couldn't read a book close to. God played some scurvy tricks on a man when he got old.

'It's about Hunt and me.'

'I don't want to hear it,' James said, turning away.

'Daddy, you've got to listen to me!' Rachel insisted.

'I said, I don't want to hear it, Rachel!'

'Damn you, do you think you're God?' she shouted. 'You just say "I don't want to hear it", and that's the end of it? This is my *life* we're talking about!'

'Your life,' James said. 'It's in fine shape, your life.'

He felt, rather than saw her flinch, and regretted the words. She was angry, and her anger had sparked his. He wanted to be kind to her. He wanted her to know he loved her. Why was it so goddamned hard to say it?

'I'm not proud of what happened,' Rachel said. 'I'm sorry because it hurt so many people. Especially you. I'm ashamed. I so wanted you to be proud of me.'

Rachel, Rachel, he thought. At twenty-seven, she had grown into a beautiful woman, dark-haired and dark-eyed like her mother. A picture of her with ribbons in her hair and a pink party dress came into his mind, and as always, he wondered where the years had gone.

'Don't cry,' he said.

'I'm not going to cry.' Rachel blinked back tears. 'I've got something to tell you and I want you to . . . to just . . . hear me out. Okay? Just let me say what I've got to say.'

'Go on,' James said gruffly.

'I love Hunt,' she said. 'In spite of what happened. In spite of everything.'

'The more fool you.'

'Fool or no, I've decided,' she said. 'Hunt and I want to be together. He's going to ask Portland for a divorce.'

'Don't hang upside down till she gives him one.'

'Then we'll live together anyway.'

'I see. Then anything I say wouldn't make much difference.'

'We would . . . prefer your blessing.'

'Not a chance,' he said, shaking his head.

'Why, Daddy?'

'Even if I could give you my blessing, I wouldn't,' he said. 'That man's no good, Ray. He's weak. Look at the way he let Willie Priestman walk all over him. How can anyone respect a man like that?'

'He didn't have any choice,' Rachel said. 'Not like you.'

'What the hell is that supposed to mean?' James barked.

'Can't you hear what you're saying, Daddy? Don't you realise you're describing yourself? "The man's no good, Ray. He's weak. He's got no guts. He let the Priestmans walk all over him." Isn't that a description of you, Daddy? Isn't that why you're trying to kill yourself with your damned whisky?'

'You don't know what you're talking about!' he said.

'Yes I do!' Rachel flared. 'I'm talking about you and Catherine Priestman, and this damned stupid feud you've been fighting ever since!'

He was silent for what seemed a long time. When he spoke, his voice was very soft. 'I didn't know you knew about that,' he said.

'We were here, Daddy. We watched you, we watched Mama. We heard her crying when you were . . . away. We could tell something was wrong. The way you talked, the way you treated us. Kids *know*, Daddy.'

'I didn't realise,' he said. 'I couldn't see anything but my own hurt.'

'We knew that, too,' Rachel said. 'We knew you loved Catherine. And that you loved Mama, too, and that it was terrible for you. We wanted to help you, but you wouldn't let us. Not any of us. Not even Mama.'

He was silent again, thinking of her, thinking of both of them. He shook his head from side to side like a baited bull, then picked up his whisky glass and emptied it. Almost defiantly, he refilled the glass from the crystal decanter.

'Is that what you're going to do every time life deals you a bad hand?' Rachel said angrily. 'Hide at the bottom of a bottle?'

'I'll do what I damned well please!' he shouted.

'Even if it kills you?'

'Who the hell cares if it does?'

'I do!' Rachel shouted back. 'I care! Don't you understand? I need you! I don't want you to die.'

'I won't die,' James said.

'You won't fight, either.'

'Fight?'

'Fight this . . . thing that has hold of you. Why won't you?'

'What the hell for?'

'For *me*, you selfish bastard!' Rachel shouted. James stared at his daughter. He had never heard her talk like this before. Ray had always been the quiet, docile one. Yet there she was now, arms akimbo, dark eyes flashing angrily, shaming him with words he'd never dreamed to hear from one of his own children.

'For you?'

'The dead are dead, Daddy!' she said. 'We're alive! We don't have to die with them! You think they'd want that – Catherine, or Mama? Or Lee?'

'Don't,' he said. 'Don't!'

'I'm not going to stop now. You've got to listen to me. Help me.'

He shook his head. 'Have I been wrong about everything, Ray? Everything?'

'You've been down a long time,' she said. 'It's time to get up now. Fight back. We'll fight with you.'

'Fight who?'

'Fight the damned Priestmans,' she said. 'They're the ones who did this to you.'

'Huntington Carver fight the Priestmans?' James snorted. 'That'll be the day!'

'He's willing to try,' Rachel said. 'The question is, are you?'

James was silent for a moment, then he smiled.

'You're a clever girl, Ray,' he murmured. 'You let me paint myself right into that corner, didn't you?'

She smiled.

'And now I got to put up or shut up.'

'Something like that,' she said.

'You really love that man, don't you?'

'Yes, Daddy, I really do,' she said.

'Maybe I misjudged him. I can't imagine you loving anyone that didn't have some redeeming features.'

'Oh, I don't know,' she said, grinning mischievously. 'I love you, for instance.'

'Get out of here!' James said, with a growl. 'Go call young Carver and tell him to get the hell out here as soon as he can!' He grinned as Rachel threw her arms around him and gave him a great big smacky kiss.

'I love you, Daddy!' she said, her big dark eyes shining. 'A mile and a half wide!'

She ran out of the room to telephone Huntington Carver, and James smiled, remembering the little girl who, when asked how much she loved her Daddy and Mama, would reply that she loved them, *oooo,* a mile and a half wide!

He reached for his glass. It was empty.

One more wouldn't hurt, he thought.

He got up and put the decanter in the cupboard, and took the glass out into the kitchen.

It was going to be a long fight.

Maybe he could win it.

Maybe.

BOOK FOUR

PEACE

44

At first, Jenny lived on hope.

He wasn't dead, she kept telling herself, he was missing. There was a big difference. Missing meant you could go on hoping. Hoping that when someone knocked on your door, it would be to tell you he was alive. Hoping that when someone called your name, it was because word had come through that they had found Lee.

She got through December by telling herself that he would be home by Christmas. She got through the novena of pre-dawn masses called *misas de gallos*, culminating in *noche buena*, or Christmas Eve, by telling herself he might turn up at any moment. She wrapped presents for the baby, and smiled when little Jack crowed with delight on Christmas morning, wishing Lee were there to see him. New Year, she told herself. Maybe he'll be home for New Year. On New Year's Eve she was invited to parties and said she would come, but never went to any of them. Mañileños celebrated with fireworks, and the traditional *media noche*, a midnight feast followed by early morning mass. As the bells rang out to welcome 1901, Jenny lay in her bed and wondered where Lee was. She never doubted that he was alive. If he had died, she would have known. Some instinct, some telepathy, would have told her.

She got through each day by hoping for news on the next day, or by the weekend. She carried on with her life. It wasn't all that different, anyway. Lee had been away a great deal of the time during their two years in Manila, and Jenny had learned how to live her own, separate life in his absence. She exchanged visits with Frances Eames, the chief surgeon's wife, with Peggy Ames, with nursing sister Jane Dawkins, and with some of the other nurses she had got to know at the hospital. There was a whist drive once a week at the club, and she sometimes made up a four at tennis. On Sundays, some of the garrison cavalry officers played polo. She kept busy, not allowing herself to think of the days slipping by.

Every Wednesday and Sunday afternoon, Paul Baker, now promoted to captain, called at the house and escorted her on a long walk. They put a canopy on the pram to shield Jack from the sun, and wandered through the city together, while Paul told Jenny gossip which didn't interest her about people she hardly knew. She was aware of the intensity of his interest in her, but she had none at all in him. He was someone who filled in certain portions of certain days. She felt sometimes as if she would never experience an emotion again. Paul always wore a sidearm, although Manila was quite safe now. The rebels had been pushed back to the far north of Luzon. Fifty prominent Filipino insurgent officers, agents, sympathisers and *Sandatahan* agitators were deported to Guam that month. It was beginning to sink into the *insurrecto* mind, Paul said, that to turn *Americanista* was the better part of valour. Everyone was sure Aguinaldo couldn't last much longer.

The days went swiftly, the nights less fast. January slipped into February. On Ongpin Street the Chinese celebrated their New Year with firecrackers and the traditional greeting: 'Kung hey fat choy!' There were street parties, and a fearsome silk and papier-mâché dragon, and laughing children in new clothes. It was seven weeks since they had brought Jenny the news that Lee was missing. Fifty days. Maybe he'd be home on the sixtieth day, she told herself. But he was not; nor on the seventieth, nor the eightieth.

She had not wept before. It was as if weeping would be an admission that Lee was never coming back. She wept now. She wept with the bitter realisation that her waiting was hopeless, her courage futile. Lee was not coming home, not soon, not ever. He was dead.

Dead.

The fact was there, and she forced herself to face it. But that was all it was, a fact. Tuesday was a fact. Weather was a fact. Troop movements were a fact. None meant more than any other. She carried on with her daily chores. She fed Jack and took him for his walk, she ate and slept and wound the clocks. Day followed day. She wept less, although sometimes something silly – dropping a cup, banging her funny-bone – could make her cry uncontrollably. People came and went. They said comforting things that gave her no comfort. None of it meant anything.

She had decided she would not believe it just yet.

Later, but not yet.

She took refuge in feelinglessness. Time swirled around her like a cocoon. She was not sad, she was not anything. She was numb.

Her mother came to see her. The regiment was back, the spring campaign was being planned, there was so much to do. She said nothing about Lee. She ignored Jack, who brought her his toy truck and showed her how he could ride his new red tricycle.

'What a sweet little fellow,' Laura said, without enthusiasm. She had never cared much for children, and her daughter's son looked far too *Spanish* for Laura's taste.

'Now dear,' she said to Jenny, 'we must talk.'

'Talk about what, Mother?'

'I've talked to your father,' Laura said. 'We think you ought to go back to the States.'

Jenny said nothing. Undaunted, Laura plunged on.

'You could stay with Aunt Maybelle in Charleston,'

429

Laura suggested. 'They'd love to have you.'

'I don't want to go back to the States, Mother.' Especially not to Charleston, she thought. I don't want to go anywhere. I want to stay here. Until I *know*.

'Give it some thought,' Laura said. 'You're a young woman, Jennifer. You have your whole life before you. We must make some plans.'

'Yes,' Jenny said. 'Soon.'

She forgot her mother's proposition five minutes after Laura left the house. She did not even bother to wonder what had prompted Laura's visit.

The chaplain called in a couple of times a week. They prayed together. It meant nothing to Jenny, but the chaplain seemed a nice man and she didn't want to hurt his feelings. Like her mother, he talked about the will of God. Jenny said nothing. If the chaplain wanted to think Lee had been killed because of God's will, let him. It didn't matter. Nothing mattered any more.

One morning, she was sitting on the porch, not reading a magazine, when a young officer came to the gate. He was tall and blond, about thirty-six or seven. The khaki jacket with its blue collar, shoulder-boards and cuffs, and the broad white stripe on the blue pants, told Jenny he was an infantryman. A major, she realised, as he opened the gate. Could it be? she thought, almost afraid to speak. Is there, finally, some news?

'Mrs Starr?'

'Yes.'

'My name is Matthew James. I wonder if I could talk to you?'

'Of course, Major,' Jenny said. 'Please come in.'

He shook hands with her, formally, almost shyly. She saw from his insignia that he was 33rd Infantry. Lee's regiment. She felt like screaming *tell me, tell me!*. Wondering at her self-control, she watched Major James place his campaign hat carefully on the seat, as though it was fragile. She sat down in the wicker chair opposite him and waited.

'Ma'am, I don't know quite how to begin,' Major James said. 'It's . . . about your husband.'

'You have some news of him?' Jenny said, torn between hope and dread. Her heart throbbed painfully in her breast. 'He's all right?'

Matthew James shook his head dumbly. 'I'm afraid I have no news, Mrs Starr,' he said, staring at the ground. 'I wish to God I had.'

'Oh,' Jenny said forlornly. Tears filled her eyes. She couldn't help it. She wanted to scream at the young officer sitting opposite her, his lower lip thrust out like a small boy, *Damn you for letting me hope again, damn you, damn you!*

'I'm truly sorry, Mrs Starr,' he said wretchedly. 'It never . . . I should have known you'd think . . . look, I'll go. I'll come back some other time.' He stood up, picking up his hat.

Jenny laid a gentle hand on his forearm. 'It's all right, Major. I was just . . . hoping. That maybe this time . . .' He hesitated, and she smiled, blinking away the tears.

'Sit down, Major,' she said. 'Tell me what you came to see me about.'

'I was at Santa Isabela, ma'am. But I wasn't with your husband. He had the First Battalion. I was in command of the Second. I take it you know what happened to us?'

'General MacArthur told me,' Jenny said. 'Lee was cut off from the main force while attacking the town. The regiment was driven back by superior forces, and was unable to relieve him.'

'That's right, ma'am,' Matthew James confirmed. 'As far as it goes.'

'I'm sorry?'

'Did General MacArthur tell you that your . . . that we were ordered not to try to relieve Major Starr?'

'I'm sorry, Major, I don't – '

'Understand? Course you don't, ma'am. That's why I came to see you. It's been bothering me ever since it happened, that you might have thought we didn't try to help your husband.'

'You think you could have reached Lee and his men?'

'I'm sure of it, ma'am.'

'But you were ordered not to. By whom?'

'By General Moffatt, ma'am.'

She sat stock still, hearing Lee wearily explaining that Moffatt had ordered him out into the jungle again. *He's going to get me killed if he can, Jen. He's going to keep on sending me up to the sharp end until one of our little brown brothers gets me.*

No, she thought.

It wasn't possible.

Was it?

'I think you had better tell me the whole story, Major,' Jenny said. 'Start at the beginning, and don't leave anything out.'

He told her the story of the engagement at Santa Isabela, as he had seen it. He told her about the caves on Hill A that Whittier Moffatt would not let them reconnoitre, and the battle rendezvous that could not be kept when the snipers held up the main column for nearly twenty minutes.

'The plan of attack was pretty simple,' he explained. 'Major Starr's battalion was to attack the enemy front. While he kept them occupied, the rest of the regiment was to hit the rebel flank. Not brilliant or clever, or anything, really. But it usually works.'

'But this time it didn't.'

'They second-guessed us all the way, ma'am,' he said. 'They held us up long enough to pin down Major Starr and his battalion under an artillery barrage. Then they hit us with everything they had. We were outnumbered maybe two to one. They were all over us. I rallied the men, and we managed to stop them. We thought we were pushing them back. It was only later I realised

432

they'd all gone back down to the town. Where Major Starr and his men were. To be – ' He stopped, embarrassed.

'In on the kill, you were going to say,' Jenny said.

Matthew James shook his head and did not answer. 'We started to go after them,' he said. 'Then General Moffatt sounded "recall". I couldn't believe it. I told him we had to go down and get our people out. He said he was damned if he was going to go down there and fetch Major Starr home like a baby. He said we had to go by the book. I was so goddamned mad, begging your pardon, ma'am, I told him I was going down there whether he liked it or not. He screamed at me, said he'd put me under close arrest if I didn't do exactly as I was ordered. I had no choice, Mrs Starr. I had to sit there. We all had to sit there. While . . . we could hear the firing. Heavy firing. It went on and on and then it sort of thinned out. Like there weren't so many guns firing any more. Then we didn't hear any more firing. Next morning, General Moffatt sent patrols down towards the town. They came back with news that the *insurrectos* were advancing on us in force. General Moffatt decided to fall back. And . . . well. That's about all I can tell you, ma'am.'

She was silent when he finished speaking. It seemed a long time to him. He coughed, apologetically.

'I'm sorry . . . I didn't mean to distress you,' he said.

'It's all right, Major,' Jenny said. 'I'm glad you told me. I'm grateful.'

'Your husband was a damned fine man, Mrs Starr. One of the best officers in this whole damned army, and there's nobody I'd – ' He stopped abruptly, as though he had said more than he planned.

'What it is, Major?'

'I don't want to bother you with my troubles, Mrs Starr,' he said. 'You've got your own to contend with.'

'Tell me.'

'General Moffatt has preferred court martial charges

433

against me, ma'am. For insubordination, disobedience, and God knows what else. He said he's going to throw the book at me.'

'Because of what happened at Santa Isabela?'

'I called him some pretty bad names, ma'am,' Matthew James said ruefully. 'In front of a witness.'

'That was . . . injudicious, Major,' Jenny said. 'My father is a vengeful man.'

'I know that now, Mrs Starr. He's going to do his best to get me busted.'

'Is there anything you want me to do?'

'No, I don't think so, ma'am. I didn't come for that. I just wanted you to know I . . . tried. And I'd do it again, if I had to!'

'I know you would, Major,' Jenny said softly.

'I'd better move along.' He stood up, turning the brim of his hat between his fingers. Jenny extended her hand, and he held it clumsily for a moment.

'You mind if I say something?' he asked.

'Go ahead.'

'I don't understand. Why wouldn't he let us go down there? It was his own son-in-law, for God's sake!'

'To my father, Lee was just another soldier, Major,' Jenny said. 'They were . . . not close.'

'He ought to have let us try,' Matthew James said, stubbornly. 'No matter who it was down there. He should have let us try. You don't know, Mrs Starr. We had to sit there and . . . listen. Every time I think about it I get so goddamned mad. I'm sorry, ma'am. I shouldn't be talking like this. It being your father and all.'

'I'm glad you came,' Jenny said. 'Glad you told me.'

Matthew James nodded. He put on his hat and saluted her. Jenny acknowledged with a nod and a smile. She watched the young officer as he closed the gate behind him and walked off towards barracks. Then she went back to her chair on the porch. A slow, slow pulse of anger began inside her head.

Was it true?
No, she thought.
But if it was?

45

'Those sonsofbitches cost me two million dollars last year, Willie!' Billy Priestman shouted down the telephone. 'I want you to do something about it! I want you to get a law passed slapping a tax on imported ore! I want those bastards stopped dead in their goddamned tracks!'

When chemists proposed that carbonate ores under the surface of played out mines could be smelted to produce silver and lead, Billy had moved quietly out of mining stocks, investing heavily to acquire a controlling interest in a dozen smelters in Nevada, Utah and Colorado. It had given him a new lease of life. He was off booze, eating well again, full of the old vigour. But Western Smelting, as his company was called, was taking a beating from what Billy called 'raggedy-ass outfits' down on the Mexican border. They were importing cheap ore from Mexico, and producing silver and lead much more cheaply than Western, which had to pay American wages to its miners. As a result, the pirate smelters could sell their metal below any price Billy set, and still make money. Every bar Western sold was selling at a loss.

'Those Messican sonsofbitches are going to put me out of business, Willie!' Billy told his son. 'You talk to Jim Stillman in New York. Get him to put up some money. Tell him I'll do the same. We'll bust the ass off those bastards down there in Silver City before they know what the hell has hit them!'

'I'll do what I can, Pa,' Willie promised. How much that would be was moot, he thought. He had damned little clout in the House. All the same, he did as his father had suggested, and got in touch with the banker in New York. Stillman agreed to help. He did not specify what form his help would take, and Willie did not ask. He took the train to Washington and introduced a bill to tax the importation of foreign ores. To his gratified surprise, it was taken up, given the support of a powerful lobby, and quickly ratified. For a little while, his victory gave him a heady sense of accomplishment; but he was not fool enough to believe the victory was his. Before long, he was as bored as ever, and as anonymous as he had been before.

He never got to like Washington: the place stubbornly refused to grow on him. It was full of mediocrities, Willie said, either human or architectural. He stayed on only because he had to; toughing it out, he called it. He hated it, because he was just another congressman, and a very junior one at that. Not even his money could alter the pecking order. Serving the mundane needs of a constituency with which he had only the most tenuous connection could not fill the slow-moving months. Willie became an absentee, leaving the running of his office to a secretary and an assistant.

Arthur King's invitation to meet him for supper at the Hoffman House in New York did not therefore come altogether as a surprise. The ornate arched mahogany bar was crowded. A waiter in tails conducted Willie to King's table. It was in a corner, and King was sitting in a chair against the wall. Like a goddamned gunfighter, Willie thought, afraid of being shot in the back.

King had changed considerably since their first meeting, Willie thought. He was thicker around the waist, altogether more solid and bulky. He still wore the same unstylish clothes, but there was a hard confidence in the eyes and the way King sat, hands

437

splayed palm down on the table.

'Fine,' King said, brusquely, in answer to Willie's greeting. 'How's Washington?'

'Also fine,' Willie said. 'As far as I know.'

'Yes,' King said. 'We must talk about that.'

'Fire ahead.'

'Let's eat first. Are you hungry? They do a damned fine porterhouse steak.'

'I'll have the sole meunière,' Willie said to the waiter who hovered at his elbow. Arthur King might be the high muckymuck of the Democratic Party now, and a lot of other things besides, but Willie was damned if he was going to dance to King's tune like a tame monkey on a barrel-organ.

King nodded. 'I'll have that, too,' he said. 'And bring us a bottle of the Gewürtztraminer.'

The waiter hurried away with their order, and Arthur King leaned back in his chair, hooking his thumbs into the armholes of his waistcoat.

'Well,' he said. 'That's that taken care of. How's the newspaper business?'

'It's been better.'

'You still planning to run for the Senate in the next election?'

'Most certainly,' Willie said.

'You haven't got much to campaign on.'

'I've got five million dollars.'

King smiled. The waiters came back with the food, and they concentrated on it for a while. The fish was very good. The wine was all right. Willie preferred champagne.

'Now,' King said, pushing his plate away. Willie noticed that he had eaten very little. 'Let's talk.'

'Fine.' Willie went on eating. Damned if he was going to let King spoil a perfectly decent meal.

'You've been giving Tammany a lot of stick lately,' King observed.

'I'm not responsible for every word that goes into

438

every one of my papers, Arthur. My editors – '

'As far as . . . certain people are concerned, William, you are your papers and your papers are you. They all dance to your tune, and there's no point pretending otherwise.'

'So?'

'Ease off on Tammany.'

'Why?'

'Good God, man, surely not even you are that näive?' King expostulated. 'You're crusading against the very interests which will ensure your election to the Senate.'

'I don't need Tammany,' Willie said. 'I've got the people on my side. The ordinary people.'

'The ordinary people?' King sneered. 'The ordinary people couldn't get you a job cleaning the Senate urinals!'

'What's that got to do with leaving those crooks alone?'

'Just do it, Willie,' King said.

'Nobody tells me what to do,' Willie growled. 'Not the party, not you, nobody!'

King shook his head sadly. 'You're not thinking, Willie,' he said. 'Let me ask you a question. Have you ever read Machiavelli's *The Prince*?'

'At Harvard.'

'Then you'll recall his advice: "The prince must avoid those things which will make him hated or despised and so contrive that his actions show grandeur, spirit, gravity and fortitude".'

'No,' Willie said. 'I'll march to no one's drummer but my own!'

'Listen to me, Willie!' King leaned forward on the table. His eyes were cold. All the mild indolence had disappeared. 'I'll only say this once!'

'I'm listening,' Willie said, still unwilling to give ground.

'You either do what I tell you to do, or you abandon once and for all any plans you have for political

439

advancement. Do you understand what I'm saying?'

For the first time Willie saw the iron fist usually concealed in the velvet glove, and realised how Arthur King had risen to the position of power he now held in the party. Beneath the diffident exterior lay a driving ruthlessness, a merciless decisiveness. He meant exactly what he said: he would ditch Willie without a second thought.

'All right, Arthur,' he said huskily.

'Good!' King snapped. 'You want to be groomed for a presidential nomination, you tell me. You want to get to the White House. Well, you can do it, Willie. You're young and you're rich. A term in the Senate, two perhaps, and you'll be ready. You can do it. If you do it our way.'

'Go on.' Willie managed to hold on to his temper. It wasn't easy. He wanted to tell the fussy, arrogant little man sitting opposite him to go to Hell, but knew it would be fatal. He needed King now. The day would come when he did not. He could wait until then.

'You'll run for the Senate in the 1902 election,' King told him. 'That gives you plenty of time to put your house in order.'

'My house – ?'

'In politics, like everything else, Willie, planning ahead is what counts. Once you're in the Senate, you can look towards the White House. But I tell you now, as I have told you before, that if you maintain your association with Susan Simpson, you have no more chance of getting there than has a dead mule.'

'Good God, man!' Willie burst out, 'hundreds of pol – '

'We're not talking about hundreds of politicians, Willie. We're talking about you. We're talking about the presidency. There has never been a president yet who wasn't a solid, reliable family man. Go back to San Francisco, Willie. Mend your fences. Given the realities of American politics, having a *wife* is a necessary

440

prerequisite for anyone bold enough to aim at the White House.'

'I see,' Willie said.

'Your term as a congressman is coming to an end. Your record has been less than brilliant, but at least you haven't alienated anybody, so I think we can take care of that. You'll get your seat on the Senate, Willie. If you are sure that it is what you want *more than anything else*.'

Well, Willie thought, was it? Was Susan Simpson worth more than the presidency of the United States? Nobody was. If he was honest with himself, the whole thing was beginning to pall, anyway. There had been more than a few times when he'd noticed acquaintances wince at Susan's gaucheness. He liked less and less the way she clung possessively to him in public, her childish tantrums when he 'neglected' her, and her extravagance. Even the sex thing wasn't what it had once been. Face it, he told himself, sex isn't that important anyway. He could do without Broadway if he had to. He could do without Susan. He could do without anybody.

'It's what I want, Arthur,' he said, hoping he sounded humble. 'And I'll work at it. I promise.'

'That's good.' King's tone was that of a man who had never doubted he would win. In the private memo-book of his memory, Willie put another mark against King's name. He'd pay. They all would. One day.

'There's something else you can do while you're in San Francisco,' King said, cutting the end off a cigar without ceremony. 'I assume you'll be seeing your father. How is he, by the way?'

'Never better. Getting back into business was the best thing that ever happened to him.'

'Something of a wild man, your father,' King said reflectively. 'Impulsive. A gambler?'

'You don't make the kind of money he made without taking chances,' Willie smiled.

'Can he afford the losses he's making?' King asked

bluntly. 'We hear he's going to drop another two million, maybe three, in this financial year.'

'He knows what he's doing.'

'How long can he keep it up?'

'As long as he wants to.'

'Nobody's got that much money,' King said drily. 'Not even old Morgan himself. We did our sums, Willie. Your father is going to go broke if he keeps on pouring money down this particular hole.'

'What makes you so sure of that?'

'These people he's fighting – Bush Exploration – they've built smelters in Mexico to get round the problem of the tax on imported ore.'

'I know that.' Willie knew all about Bush Exploration. What he was waiting to find out was how much King knew he knew.

'They've spent millions down there putting in new machinery, railroads, digging canals. Now they're producing metal at half what it costs in the States and selling it here below par. They're murdering Western and everyone else in the smelting industry.'

'Everyone else?' Willie said.

'Your father's feud – I gather that's what's behind it – doesn't matter a damn if it's only himself he hurts. But he can't take the entire damned industry down with him, Willie. He's got to stop being such a bloody maverick!'

'You tell him.'

'No,' King said softly. 'I've got a better idea. I represent certain . . . interests. You know James Stillman, I think. What about Henry Rogers? John D. Archbold?'

Willie knew them all. The men King had named were three of the most powerful financiers in America. Stillman, head of the enormous National City Bank of New York, he had met at his father's behest. He remembered watching the taciturn Texan send batch after batch of breakfast eggs back to his cook, refusing to eat anything not cooked exactly as he wanted it. Rogers was renowned as a man who created investment opportunities. Ruthless as a shark, he would stop at nothing to absorb or ruin anybody who got in his way. Archbold was another of the Standard Oil crowd, cut from the same cloth.

'I see by your expression you've guessed what comes next?' King said, with a faint smile.

'Your . . . clients own smelters. And they want to merge with Western.'

'Our . . . my clients' group, Pan–American Smelting, is about the same size as Western. We're taking as bad a beating as your father. *Because* of your father. Bush Exploration is murdering us in the world market. We want to put a stop to it, and fast. A merger makes sense. We can stop them dumping cut-price metal on the market, close them out, take them over. And move on to the next stage.'

'A trust,' Willie said.

King smiled his faint smile again, like a teacher with a bright pupil. Trust was another word for monopoly. The overlords of the all-powerful trusts were men of incredible wealth and power. No income taxes were subtracted from their enormous fortunes, no regulatory agencies interfered with their methods. Once you formed a trust you controlled the raw material, the manufacture, distribution, and often the retail outlets for your products. At each stage, you set your own prices, raking in huge profits. Trusts controlled the tobacco industry, rubber, banking, oil, lumber, railroads, gas, coke, steel. The names of their owners were household words: Carnegie and Rockefeller, Morgan and Schiff, Harriman, Swift, Armour, Duke, Biddle, Frick and McCormick. Yes, a trust made sense. Willie thought of his ace in the hole, and allowed himself a momentary glow of satisfaction.

'We'd want a controlling interest,' he said.

'I'm not sure my . . . clients would agree to that.'

'Not even if I deliver Bush Exploration to them on a platter?'

'We've tried to buy them out, Willie. They as much as told us to go to Hell.'

'You didn't answer my question.'

'All right. Suppose – just suppose, mind you – that you could do what you say. I think my clients might consider Western taking fifty-one per cent of the stock. I say might, Willie. Don't hold me to it.'

'You talk to them,' Willie said. 'I'm sure they'll agree. You see, I'm the only person in the world that can put Bush Exploration out of business. You've got to do it my way.'

'All right,' King said quietly. 'I'm listening.'

'Bush Exploration is owned by a man named Solomon Bush. He is married to Sarah Starr, the daughter of Andrew Starr.'

'Is this something to do with that damned silly vendetta of yours?'

'You won't think it silly in a moment,' Willie said, savouring what was to come. 'As I was saying, Solomon Bush owns Bush Exploration. The principal stockholders are his wife's parents. A family business. That's why you can't buy them out. Their shares are not available. So the only way to bring them down is with a Trojan Horse. And I have a Trojan Horse.'

Arthur King watched him closely, not speaking. Willie smiled and played his ace. 'Huntington Carver,' he said.

'Carver? I thought he –'

'Was working for me as a glorified office boy,' Willie said disdainfully. 'Until I remembered his affair with Rachel Starr. She –'

'She's James Starr's daughter.'

'And Carver's mistress,' Willie said. 'It seemed to me when Bush Exploration started hurting Western, that it was time I took a renewed interest in our friend Carver. To cut a long story short, there has been a

444

reconciliation. He has been accepted into the family again. And is working alongside Solomon Bush in Mexico.'

'You mean – ?'

'I know every move they make as soon as they decide to make it. I know, for instance, that they're running out of finance. If we just hang on, they'll have to sell stock to raise money, or go to the banks. Either way, we'll have them.'

'And our merger?'

'Oh, yes,' Willie said. 'Definitely. But only on the conditions I stated, Arthur. Control goes to my father. That's final.'

'If you can deliver Bush Exploration,' King said, 'I'm sure there'll be no problems about that.'

'I'm glad to hear it.' Willie signalled a waiter. 'Bring us a couple of large cognacs, right away,' he said. 'The Rémy, I think.'

'Celebrating, sir?' the waiter smiled. Arthur King looked at Willie and the nearest thing Willie had ever seen to a grin appeared on King's face.

'By God,' King said. 'I do believe we are!'

46

'Well, General,' Colonel Charles Aysgill said. 'You must be pleased.'

'Satisfied, I'd say,' Moffatt replied. 'The verdict was no more or less than I'd expected.'

'Of course, sir,' Aysgill said deferentially. 'Can I get you another of those?'

'I shouldn't,' Moffatt said, knowing he was going to. He was slightly drunk. Well, why not? He felt truculent, yet uncertain. This was the first time he'd been in the officer's mess since the James court martial. He had not missed the small silence that greeted his entrance. They'd never liked him, he thought. They'd always kept him on the outside. Everywhere. It was as if there was some special knowledge you had to have to be accepted. If you had it, you were in. If you did not, you would never be in. You could do all the right things, say all the right things, buy them all drinks, listen to their jokes, and still never be one of them. If they knew you noticed the just-discernible half-turn away as you tried to catch their eye, or the just-concealed distaste when they could not evade you, they gave no sign. He looked around as Aysgill signalled the mess-boy and told him to bring two more whiskies. The bar was little more than half full; the conversation all around them was of the approaching offensive against Aguinaldo. MacArthur was determined to bring the insurrection to an end by the summer.

'Cheers!' Aysgill said, and Whittier lifted his glass

automatically. He wasn't impressed by Aysgill's pretensions. He did not like the man at all. But he was stuck with him. For the moment, anyway, he told himself.

'MacArthur laid it on the line,' he said. 'What did you think?'

'He's absolutely right, General,' Aysgill said. 'If we don't finish Aguinaldo this summer, we'll be out here for ever.'

Twenty-five regiments of volunteers were due to be mustered out in July. They were all trained and seasoned troops. It was only their presence in the islands that kept the *insurrectos* in check. Send them home and put green, untried replacements in, and you might as well write off the last two years of guerilla warfare as if they had never happened.

'Not looking forward to it,' Whittier said. 'You?'

Aysgill shrugged and sipped his drink. Calculating bastard, Whittier thought. Another cold fish. Always the same. Never get anyone I can get to know. Someone who likes me. Laura didn't know what it was like. Only another man could know. He tried to make her see, but he could not.

'You can't *skulk*, Whittier!' she said, her fingers busy with the crochet needles. 'You've done nothing to be ashamed of.'

Tell *them* that, he thought. He knew what they were saying. Commonsense insisted that there was no possibility of their knowing he had lied. It made no difference. No matter what the verdict of the court martial had been, they *knew*. He had violated the code. Laura did not understand that. She never had understood it.

He realised Aysgill was watching him closely. He reached out and touched his shoulder.

'Charles, I want to thank you for . . .'

'No need, General,' Aysgill said deprecatingly. 'I'm glad that I had the opportunity to support you.'

447

'Could have been nasty, all the same,' Moffatt said. 'I appreciate your . . . backing me up like that.'

'Couldn't very well let the fellow get away with all those lies about us, sir,' Aysgill said.

Us, Whittier thought. Now it's *us*. Because of Matthew James's court martial, his destiny and Aysgill's had become linked. The thought repelled him, made him uneasy. Nobody ever did anything for nothing. Somehow, Aysgill had manoeuvred him into a vulnerable position.

'Damned fool,' he muttered.

'He brought it on himself, sir,' Aysgill said, obviously thinking Whittier was talking about Matthew James.

'I suppose so.'

The verdict of the court martial had been pretty much of a foregone conclusion. Although Major James's counsel had tried hard to break down the testimony given to the court by Moffatt and supported throughout by Aysgill, he had never really had a chance. The word of a general officer, endorsed by that of his senior staff officer was, to an army court, the equivalent of documented fact. That was the rock the troublemaking young bastard had perished on, Whittier thought vindictively. Tried as hard as they could to prove I was a coward. Couldn't do it. They could say it; they could think it; they could even believe it. But they couldn't prove it. And that was all that mattered.

'I wonder, General, if I could ask your advice about something?' Aysgill said, in that deferential way he had. There was something decidedly Heepish about the fellow, Whittier thought irritably. Yet he knew he dared not alienate Aysgill right now.

'What's the problem?'

'I was wondering how you'd rate my chances of getting a full colonelcy?' Aysgill said.

So there it was, Whittier thought bleakly. Aysgill wasn't letting any grass grow under his feet. There was nothing he could do. Aysgill had him.

'Very good, I'd say,' he forced himself to reply. Aysgill smiled, and Whittier wanted to strike him. He did not look into Aysgill's eyes, afraid he would see contempt in them.

'Put your papers in,' he said. 'I'll see what I can do. If there are any vacancies . . .'

'You're very kind, sir. I appreciate this very much.'

Whittier wanted to shout obscenities at the man, and he saw now in Aysgill's eyes that Aysgill knew it, and was enjoying his impotence. He thinks he's got me just where he wants me, Whittier thought. I'll show the bastard. I'll show him.

'I'd better be going,' he said, choking on the whisky as he poured it down his throat. 'Get an early night.'

'Good idea, sir,' Aysgill said. 'I'll walk across to the barracks with you, if I may?'

Whittier wanted to tell him to go to Hell.

'Of course,' he said. Aysgill smiled that smile again. Whittier recognised it. Now I've got you, it said. He stood by as Aysgill signed the mess bill. They walked towards the door together. Whittier saw General Young sitting with some of his officers at a round table near the big windows to the left of the main entrance, and lifted a hand, smiling. Young favoured him with a frigid nod, and Whittier did not, as he had intended, go across to Young's table to speak to the big Pennysylvanian. Bastards, Whittier thought, they all hate me. All because that stupid boy had to open his stupid mouth.

The sun was going down. The slender palms around the parade ground threw long, curved shadows across the dusty square. They heard some sort of commotion going on near the main gates.

'What the deuce . . . ?' Aysgill muttered.

The two military policemen at the gate were shouting at what looked like a crowd of Filipino peasants. Then Whittier saw that some of the men were carrying rifles. A cold chill of panic touched his heart. Were they

449

insurrectos? He stood stock-still for a moment, certain that the next sound he heard would be the flat bark of rifle fire.

'Jesus Christ Almighty–' he heard Charles Aysgill say disbelievingly. The milling men near the gate had formed into twin lines, like scarecrows playing soldiers. One of the men stood to one side, shouting orders. The disjointed words drifted across the parade ground on the still evening air.

'Get . . . damned head up! . . . goddamned bandits, you're soldiers! . . . in there singing! . . . the right, *harch!*'

The squad of men began to march towards them. As they came they sang a song.

> *We'll hang Anguinaldo from a eucalyptus tree*
> *Hang the stinkin' bastard from a eucalyptus tree . . .*

No, Whittier Moffatt thought.

It can't be.

But there was only one unit in the world that had ever sung that song. Whittier felt the strength going out of his legs. His mouth was suddenly dry. He thought he was going to collapse. He grabbed Charles Aysgill's arm.

'It's Starr!' Aysgill said, his voice little more than an astonished whisper. 'It's Starr!'

Oh, sweet God in Heaven, Whittier thought.

I'm finished.

47

'Don't you ever get tired?' Jenny said throatily.

'Not of this,' Lee said softly. He moved against her and then on top of her, and she felt the long flood of pleasure as his hands caressed her, the soft, slow invasion of her body by his.

'Go slow,' she whispered. 'Slow.'

'Easier said,' he breathed, 'than done.'

'Got your boots on?' she said.

Lee snorted with laughter at their private joke. She'd said they'd made love so much since he came back that he'd better wear heavy boots so he didn't float away. He had been rough at first, demanding, greedy for her body the way a man who has been lost in the desert is greedy for water. She sensed that he was finding his way back to her, trying to put the bloody months of jungle fighting out of his mind. So she waited for the greed to sate itself, waited for the healing. He told her some of what had happened, but not all of it. Maybe he would never tell her all of it, she thought. He was so thin at first that she felt she could count every bone in his body, but good food and plenty of rest were already taking care of that. And now their lovemaking was loving again, and not merely the urgent promptings of biology.

Jenny felt the rhythms of her own senses quicken to match his, felt the pulse of awareness inside her, and moved with Lee's strong thrusts, meeting his strength with her softness. She lifted herself against him, giving as she took, and soon she heard him whisper, as he had whispered so many times, 'Now, Jen,' and she relaxed, let everything rush to meet all his climax, and she said, 'Yes, now, yes, now,' and felt the long solidity of his throb inside her, and her own sweet silent engulfment of their joining. She floated, as if in limbo, almost unaware of Lee's weight on her, of their rapid breathing or their pounding hearts. Then she smiled in the pearly darkness, and kissed her man, and felt his arms tighten around her.

'I'm serious,' she said. 'You'd really better get those boots!' Their laughter was warm and sharing.

'Don't make so much noise,' Lee said. 'You'll wake Jack.'

'Fat chance,' Jenny scoffed. Jack was one of the world's great sleepers. Even the rolling fusillades of monsoon thunder failed to disturb him. 'He's like you,' she told Lee. 'He can sleep on a clothes-line if he has to.'

They lay silent for a while, hips and shoulders touching. The sky gradually paled as dawn neared. Gusts of wind threw rain against the closed shutters like handfuls of rice.

'Rain,' he said softly. 'You know, Jen, there were times we prayed for it. We were always thirsty. Always.'

Jenny remained silent. It was as if a spell had been cast that would be broken if she spoke. She knew Lee needed to talk about what he had been through, but she also knew he would never do so until he was ready. So each time he opened the door of his memory, she waited with bated breath, hoping that this time would be the one.

'We ate roots, leaves, papayas,' he said, 'monkey, if we could catch one, or wild chickens. Some days, nothing. I lost twenty-two men between Santa Isabela and Manila. Most of them just lay down and died. We'd climb a mountain, get down the other side. There'd be another mountain. We'd climb that. It was like . . .

452

nightmares. There was always another one. And after a while, some of the men just gave up. They'd lie down, and that was the end of it. The rest of us would just keep going. Hating ourselves for leaving them, knowing there was nothing we could do. Some of the time we'd be out of our heads, tongues all swollen, so it was all we could do to swallow. Some of the men went deaf. Some of them couldn't see properly. Water, you see. Lack of water.'

Every day around noon, he would stick a two-foot stick into the ground and peg the head and foot of the shadow to orient himself: the top of the shadow pointed south, the base north. Then he'd take a bearing on whatever landmark he could see, and they'd set off again. They could lose all sense of direction before they had gone fifty feet. Some days they made only a few miles. Their route was marked with the bodies of men who could not keep up.

'Enough of that!' Lee said decisively, swinging his feet out of the bed. He slapped Jenny's backside. 'Up and at 'em, kiddo!'

She was disappointed, but she did not let it show. Lee and his men had been through a hell outside the imagination. It would take a long time to exorcise those experiences.

'I'll make some coffee,' she said.

'*Bueno.*' He went across the room and opened the door of his wardrobe, taking out the dress uniform. He laid it on the rumpled bed and looked down at it, his lower lip sticking out.

'Penny for them,' she said.

'I was thinking about your father.'

'What about him?'

'I wish there was something we could do.'

'What will happen to him, Lee?' Jenny asked.

'The verdict of the court martial will be reviewed.'

'And then?'

'MacArthur will have to decide that.'

453

'Will they – ?'

'Break him? No, not a general officer. They'll just paint him grey.'

'What does that mean?'

'That's what this hearing's about in MacArthur's office, Jen. Your father, Matt James, me. We've all got to concur, for the good of the service. Cover up what your father did. They'll call it exhaustion, or a nervous breakdown. They'll ship him back to the States for observation. They'll find some way of dressing it up, and when it's all forgotten, they'll post him off somewhere to the back of beyond until he's retired. He'll never command in the field again. Or anywhere else.'

'What time are you seeing MacArthur?'

'Ten sharp.'

'Would it bother you . . . if I went over there? To see mother? I ought to, Lee.'

'It wouldn't bother me. I keep on thinking: why aren't I angry about what happened? Yet somehow all I can do is feel sorry for him. For both of them. Yes, you go. She'll probably be glad to see you.'

'Where do you think MacArthur will send them?'

'Probably Leavenworth first. Until they find somewhere to put him. Somewhere useful but harmless. Somewhere they can forget his existence.'

'It's cruel.'

'It's how the Army works, Jen. You know that.'

'I know,' she said sadly. 'Military justice is to justice as military music is to music. It's still cruel.'

'MacArthur doesn't want to rock the boat. Not with Aguinaldo ready to take the Oath of Allegiance.'

'Poor Aguinaldo,' she said. 'I hear the American papers are saying it was unsporting of that awful little man, what's his name – ?'

'Funston.'

'Funston, to have *tricked* Aguinaldo like that! Such a crazy, brave thing to do, and they say it was *unsporting*!'

454

Armed with the information Lee had captured, 'Fearless Freddie' had gone straight to MacArthur and asked for permission to mount a daring raid. Posing as captured prisoners, Funston and four other American officers would be 'taken' by the courier Segismundo, three other trustworthy renegades and eighty Maccabebe scouts, to Palanan. The Maccabebes were mercenaries from Pampanga province; the Filipinos would not suspect them. Funston's plan was just daft enough to work. They would march right into Palanan and drag Aguinaldo out, he promised MacArthur. Sure he'd never see Funston alive again, MacArthur agreed. The party was assembled, Funston kissed his bride Eda goodbye, and embarked on the gunboat *Vicksburg*, which took the expedition around the southern tip of Luzon to Casiguran, where Captain E.B. Barry landed them in driving rain.

To everyone's astonishment, Funston had done it. On March 25, he was at the prearranged rendezvous with Aguinaldo in custody. In one daring, unbelievable coup, Funston had effectively ended the Filipino rebellion. Aguinaldo would publicly declare his allegiance to the United States on April 2, and a formal declaration of the cessation of hostilities would follow. The insurrection was ended, although Lee was not naïve enough to believe – any more than the men who would have to stay on and fight it – that the war was over. The fearsome Moros on Mindanao, and other rebels on outlying islands, would take a long, long time to pacify. Meanwhile, however, MacArthur had no intention of giving them fuel for the flickering fires of their propaganda by court martialling a senior officer for dereliction of duty.

Lee chaired Jack around the room on his shoulders while Jenny got breakfast ready. The little boy giggled and chortled as they played his favourite game.

'Bumpy onna sealink,' he shouted, 'bumpy onna sealink!' And Lee would swing him down and then up and bump his head gently on the ceiling and Jack would shrick with pleasure, and Jenny chided them both and told Jack he'd be sick if he wasn't careful.

'Sickiffy int carefulled,' Jack mimicked, as Lee dumped him into his high chair and went into the bedroom to get changed into his uniform ready for his interview with General MacArthur.

'Chin up,' he grinned, tipping Jenny's head back to kiss her on the lips. 'They won't hang him.'

'Good luck,' she said. 'To both of you.'

'You're all the luck I need.'

'Ah, go on wid yez!' Jenny gave him a shove towards the door. 'I'll bet ye say dat to all de goils!'

'Alldergoils!' Jack echoed.

After she took Jack to the kindergarten, Jenny walked across to her parents' house. She knocked several times without receiving a reply. The door was unlocked. She pushed it open and went inside. Laura sat by a window, staring out. She did not turn as Jenny came into the room. Her eyes were swollen and red from crying. A little lace handkerchief was balled in her fist. The room smelled musty, as if it needed a good airing.

'Mother?' Jenny said, almost timidly.

'What do you want?' Laura said listlessly.

'I came to see you, Mother. I was worried . . .'

'Worried!' Laura sniffed. 'You expect me to believe that?'

'Lee has gone to see General MacArthur about –'

'I know what he has gone to see General MacArthur about!' Laura said angrily. 'He has gone there to ruin the career of a fine man and a good soldier. He has gone there to disgrace your father, Jennifer.'

'Mother, that's not true!' Jenny said. 'Lee has been ordered to attend a meeting. I don't know the reasons. Neither do you.'

'I know,' Laura said darkly. She shook her head. 'How could you let him do it, Jennifer?'

'Do what?'

456

'Come back to disgrace your father like this.'

'Do you think Lee ought to have died in the jungle to save Daddy embarrassment?'

'I had such wonderful plans for you,' Laura said, her voice soaked with regret. 'Such wonderful plans.'

'What has that to do – ?'

'But you had to have things your way,' Laura went on, as though there had been no interruption. 'You had to run off with that . . . You could have married a senior officer. A colonel. A general. Instead – ' She shook her head and hit her knee with the clenched fist holding the handkerchief.

'Why didn't he die?' she said, rocking to and fro.

'Mother!' Jenny said, shocked beyond belief.

Laura Moffatt rose from her chair, her face white, eyes burning with anger. 'All your fault, all of it!' she screeched. 'Your fault, your fault, your fault!'

'My God' Jenny breathed. 'You're crazy! I never realised it, but you're crazy!'

'Get out of here!' Laura hissed, pointing a trembling finger at the door. For a moment, Jenny had to struggle not to laugh, the scene was so like an over-acted Victorian melodrama. But she knew that Laura was in deadly earnest. Her own anger swelled to meet her mother's.

'I'll go, don't worry!' she said. 'I just want to say something before I do, Mother. You deserve everything that's going to happen to you.'

'And so do you! The only thing I regret is that your father was unsuccessful!'

'Unsuccessful?'

'Unsuccessful in getting that damned half-breed husband of yours killed. God knows, he tried.'

'Daddy tried to get Lee killed?'

'Ah, you'd like to get me to admit that, wouldn't you, eh? Like to make more trouble for your poor father? Well, you're not getting any more out of me, young lady. Not one word more!'

'One word more would make me vomit!' Jenny said. She turned on her heel and grabbed the door handle, yanking the door open.

'Come back here!' Laura screamed. 'Come back here! I'm not finished!'

'Yes, you are, Mother!' Jenny said sadly. 'I wonder if you realise it yet, that's all. Do you understand what life is going to be like for you from now on? Let me tell you, Mother. Wherever you go for the rest of your days this thing is going to follow you. You'll see people sniggering and you'll know it's you they're talking about. You'll see men ostentatiously leaving a room when Daddy enters, and you'll know why. You'll send invitations that won't be answered, and there'll be parties to which you'll never be asked. There is nowhere you can go that they will not know what happened here. Yes, Mother, you're finished. May God pity you!'

'Pity?' Laura screeched. 'I don't want your pity, you little bitch! I don't want your pity or your –'

Jenny slammed the door behind her, shutting off her mother's screaming imprecations. Something heavy hit the wall inside and shattered. Jenny squared her shoulders and walked away from the house. She did not look back.

Two weeks later, the steamer *City of Portland* left Manila for San Francisco, travelling via Guam and Hawaii. On board were General Whittier Moffatt and his wife, bound for supply duties at Fort Leavenworth, Kansas. On the day she sailed, a telegraph message was delivered to Brevet-Colonel David Lee Starr. It was brief and to the point:

DELIGHTED KNOW YOU ARE SAFE. AM RELIEVING YOU IMMEDIATELY.
GET ON BACK HERE AS FAST AS YOU CAN.
YOU MADE A DEAL WITH ME, REMEMBER?

It was signed 'Theodore Roosevelt'.

48

Although he hated to do it, Billy Priestman knew he had to talk to Solomon Bush. Stillman and the others had been insistent at their last, furiously outspoken meeting.

'Buy them out, Billy,' they said. 'Tie this thing up. You're seven million dollars in the hole.'

You're seven million dollars in the hole, mind, not *we*. Some of them were already letting some of their stock go. If they thought Billy didn't know, they were even dumber than he thought they were. Billy knew all about rats and sinking ships.

Bush Exploration had reacted to the merger between Pan American and Western by flooding the domestic market with cheap silver and lead, driving prices to rock-bottom. Every time Pan-Western tried to raise prices to economic levels, Bush would ship in more metal from Mexico, driving them down again. Meanwhile, Pan-Western's enormous overheads and giant dividends were eating up its working capital. The solution was simple, the financiers said to Billy. Buy the bastards out. Offer them whatever they want. It made sense, but it was not what Billy had planned. He had wanted to crush them, ruin them, finish the Starrs. Instead he was going to offer them millions. It stuck in his craw like a fishbone, and his displeasure showed on his face when his secretary, Miss Stanley, showed Solomon Bush into his office.

Bush was a big man, slab-bodied, with powerful

arms and hands. His skin was tanned and healthy, his eyes clear. He took the chair that Billy proffered, and refused a cigar.

'You don't mind if I do?' Billy smiled.

'They say every one of those things a man smokes takes fifteen minutes off his life,' Solomon said, smiling back. 'Smoke as much as you want.'

'I thought it was time we met,' Billy said, suppressing his anger. He took longer than he needed to get the cigar going. 'Time we talked. I'm obliged to you for coming in.'

'I was curious,' Solomon said.

'What about?'

'I wanted to see this man, Billy Priestman, in the flesh. For years I'm hearing about him, what a tyrant, what a terror, how ruthless. So I thought, *nu*, take a look, can it hurt you?'

'Is that what they say about me – the Starrs?'

'Some of it,' Solomon said. He took a watch out of his pocket and looked at it. 'If we could get down to business, Mr Priestman? I've got meetings uptown.'

'Of course,' Billy said, trying for a gracious smile. 'What I have to say won't take long.'

Solomon Bush nodded, folded his hands together, and waited.

'I want to buy Bush Exploration,' Billy said, plunging in. 'At any price you care to name.'

'Not interested.' Solomon started to get up. 'You're wasting your time, Mr Priestman. And mine.'

'I don't think you understood me. I said any price you care to name.'

'Bush Exploration is not for sale, Mr Priestman.'

'Please, sit down. Just for a moment. Let me tell you what I have in mind.'

'You're taking a beating and you don't like it,' Solomon said. 'So you're reacting the way people like you always react. You try to buy your way out of trouble. Well, not this time, Mr Priestman.'

'All right. You won't sell. I can understand that. I admire a man who wants to cut his own trail. But I'm talking about hard commercial sense, man! If you won't sell to Pan-Western, then merge with us. We'll control –'

'Let me give you my answer in a way you'll understand, Mr Priestman. I don't want to sell to you and I don't want to merge with you. I wouldn't piss on you if you were on fire. Do I make myself clear?'

'Very clear,' Billy said, letting the anger take hold. His instinct had been right. There had never been any chance of persuading the man to sell. 'You know what you're up against?'

'Crooks,' Solomon sneered. 'Bandits. Thieves.'

'You want war, all right!' Billy shouted. 'War you'll get! I'll bury you! All of you!'

Solomon stood up, and Billy felt the man's anger radiating from him. For a moment he thought Solomon Bush might strike him, but with a sharp shake of the head, his visitor turned on his heel, flung open the door and marched out. Miss Stanley hurried in, her face shocked.

'Is everything all – ?'

'Shut the door!' Billy snapped. She jumped visibly, and hastily did as she was bid. Billy sat hunched over his desk. After a while he jabbed the button on his desk. Miss Stanley came in again, her expression apprehensive.

'Get hold of Huntington Carver!' he said. 'Find him. Tell him I want him here immediately. I don't care where he is or what he's doing. Understand me?'

'Yes, sir,' Miss Stanley said.

'Well?'

She bolted, and Billy smiled. That was what life was all about: making people jump when you told them to. He was looking forward to doing the same thing to Huntington Carver. Solomon Bush had been altogether too confident for Billy's liking. Where were they

461

getting all their money from? The Starrs were wealthy, but they didn't have the kind of resources this fight was eating up. They hadn't gone to the banks. If they had, Stillman would have known about it before the ink was dry on the papers. Well, that was why they had a paid spy on the inside. Carver had better know, or be able to find out; otherwise, he was going to have a very trying day. Billy Priestman smiled grimly at the thought, and turned his attention to the papers piled on his desk.

It had been a disastrous year for Pan-Western. How could they hope to be profitable when those damned pirates were undercutting every price they set? He got practically no help at all from Stillman and the others. They had given him control; they expected him to run the thing and come up with dividends. So day after day, Billy attended meetings, talked to bankers, lunched with smelter managers, dined with fellow directors, listening to them all drone on and on about overheads and operating costs and prices, while his personal finances dwindled at a rate that alarmed even his son. Willie had his own problems: the newspaper business was going through a bad patch, and his political activities were taking up more and more of his time. And more and more of his money, Billy thought . . . There had been a time when six, ten, fifteen million dollars wouldn't have made a dent in what they had on deposit. Not these days: cash was tight, and the interest on overdrafts crippling. Yet still Billy continued to live and entertain lavishly, keeping up his front. He knew he dared not stop. Nothing spread faster than the word that a man had run out of money.

A timid knock interrupted his thoughts. The door opened enough for Miss Stanley to poke her angular face around it.

'Mr Carver is here,' she said.

'Send him in.'

Huntington Carver came in. He was dressed in a city suit, with a pearl waistcoat and matching Homburg hat.

The cropped beard and iron grey hair gave him a solid, prosperous look that belied his youth. He looked fit and tough, and Billy could not help but make a mental comparison between Carver and his own son. This man looked as if he took care of himself. Willie was overweight, puffy-faced, unhealthy-looking. For no reason he could identify, Carver's good looks irritated Billy, making him want to take the younger man down a peg.

'I saw Solomon Bush,' he said. 'He won't sell.'

'I could have told you that. They plan to fight you, Mr Priestman. To the end.'

'Damned fools,' Billy growled. 'They don't have the dollars. How can they fight us?'

'They've got backing, Mr Priestman. All the money they need.'

Billy frowned. This was something new. 'From a bank?'

'No, sir. They're getting the money from a man named Irving Strasberg.'

'Strasberg? The songwriter?'

'I see the name means something to you.'

'I know him,' Billy said. His mind was moving fast, covering all the possibilities. How had the Starrs formed an alliance with that little Jew bastard? What kind of money did that put at their disposal?

'You sure of this, Carver?'

'Of course I am,' Huntington Carver answered. 'You're paying me to be.'

'Is that why you do this? For money?'

'I've got a deal with your son. You remember.'

'You still want the OKC back?'

'That's right.'

'Damned thing's done nothing but lose money ever since Willie took it on,' Billy said. 'You'll need a few millions of your own if you get it back.'

'I'm working on that,' Carver told him. 'I've been picking up Northern Pacific stock. Already cleared a quarter of a million.'

'Northern Pacific? What are they up to?'

'I don't know. The insiders say the Vanderbilts are trying to get control. Stock's up fourteen points since the middle of the month.'

'How much have you got?'

'Twenty thousand. I'm waiting till it hits 120, then I'll sell.'

'That's nearly two and a half million,' Billy said. 'I didn't know you had that kind of money, Carver.'

'I haven't,' the younger man grinned. 'I'll unload before payment falls due and take my profit.'

He stood up, picking up his pearl-grey hat and gloves and putting them on.

'Back to Mexico?' Billy said.

'Silver City first. Then Aguascalientes.'

'Stay in touch,' Billy said. 'Keep me posted, Carver. We're on a damned knife edge.'

Huntington Carver did not offer to shake hands. When the door closed behind him, Billy put the man out of his mind. Irving Strasberg, he thought. That the man should have come back to haunt him after all these years! He reached for the phone and put in a call to a broker he knew.

'Dick,' he said, 'I need a favour.'

'Name it.'

'I want a net-worth report on someone, fast.'

'It will take a couple of hours.'

'Dick, I want it yesterday.'

'That bad, eh? All right, who's the party?'

'Irving Strasberg.'

'The music publisher?'

'Make it snappy, Dick.'

Billy sat silently in his chair, glowering at the pile of papers. Outside, rain pattered against the windows. He wished he was back in San Francisco. He loathed New York, with its crowded, narrow streets and its featureless office blocks, and the hurrying throngs with their harried, edgy faces. While he was waiting for Dick Douglas to call him back, he checked the price of Northern Pacific shares in the *Journal*. They were up to 117½ at yesterday's close. At a quarter to twelve, the broker called back.

'I got your information,' he said. 'Irving Strasberg. He's triple-A at Dun & Bradstreet. Estimated net worth around twenty-five, thirty mill. That what you wanted to know?'

'What's his cash position like?'

'Top-rated,' Douglas said. 'Most of his money is in over-the-counter sales in sheet music. Owns his own copyrights, his own printers. He's a little money trust all of his own.'

Billy was silent for a moment, thinking.

'Any trading in Pan-Western, Dick?'

'Nothing much. All the smart money is going after Northern Pacific stock.'

'What the Hell is going on there?'

'There are fifty different rumours. All I know is the price keeps going up.'

'You think they'll go higher?'

'Not the slightest doubt of it.'

'How high?'

'Before they top? Hard to tell: 130, 140. Who the Hell knows?'

Billy's mind was working fast. Here was a chance to recoup all his losses in one swift stroke. Never mind why the Northern Pacific stock was rising, or who was buying it. It must be heading for a fall. By selling short – selling stocks he didn't own, which he would be able to pick up at the lower price before delivery was due – Billy could make a killing. If the stock stayed at this artificially high price, he could cover enough to meet his commitments until the price came down again. It was only a matter of a few hours, finely judged.

'Go on the floor for me, Dick. I'll float fifty thousand.'

'Fifty thousand,' Douglas said. Billy sensed the hesitation in his voice. 'I'll need you to sign some papers, Mr Priestman.'

Pipsqueak, Billy thought. Douglas wanted him to sign a release so that if the short-selling backfired, he wouldn't go down the chute with Billy. I'll bet he's short-selling with me, share for share, he thought contemptuously.

'Of course,' he said urbanely, his mind still racing. Fifty thousand shares at a hundred and twenty dollars was six million. When they dropped back to a hundred, the difference, a million dollars, would be his. Not bad money for a day's work. Twenty minutes later the phone rang. It was Douglas again. He sounded breathless.

'The price is up to 125,' he said. 'People are fighting to get anything they can.'

'Sell another fifty thousand,' Billy said, without hesitation. He could imagine the scene down at the Produce Exchange, which was being used for trading until the new Stock Exchange was completed. 'And call me tomorrow. No, wait, I'll come down to the Exchange. Ten o'clock suit you?'

'I'll expect you,' Douglas said and rang off.

At ten the following morning, when Billy arrived at the Produce Exchange, the place looked like something painted by Breughel. Northern Pacific stock was still climbing: 130, 140. It seemed incredible, yet there it was on the board.

'What do you want to do, Mr Priestman?' the broker said nervously. 'Get out now, while the going's good?'

'Don't be a gutless wonder, Dickie,' Billy smiled. 'The damned stock's overpriced by more than fifty per cent. It's got to fall, and when it does, we'll make a bigger killing than ever.'

'But we've got to deliver yesterday's shares by four, Mr Priestman,' Douglas said unhappily. Little rat, Billy thought, he did short-sell. He could see the panic in the man's eyes.

'Borrow some,' Billy told him. Douglas hurried off, only to return ten minutes later with the news that there was little NP stock to be had, certainly nothing like a hundred thousand. The few blocks left on the market were held by smiling figures who offered to lend them at fifteen per cent, or sell them seventeen points above the closing price.

'Tell them to go to Hell,' Billy snapped. 'My note's good, isn't it?'

'I suppose so, Mr Priestman,' Douglas said.

That evening, it became apparent that Northern Pacific had been cornered, although by whom was still a mystery. Everyone who had sold short was trapped.

'We have no choice,' the broker said to Billy. 'We have to pay up, or fail to deliver and go broke.'

'What's the going price now?' Billy said.

'A hundred and fifty-two.'

'All right,' Billy said. 'Get everything you can. Every single share you can lay hands on. I don't care what they cost!'

'But, Mr Priestman, that will –'

'Do what I tell you!' Billy roared. He felt the fires of the old days stirring in his belly. They wanted a fight, did they? Well, by God, he'd give them one. He'd buy every damned share in the market. All the other jobbers and speculators who'd sold short would have to come to him. He'd cover his losses and even make money on top of it.

On Wednesday, May 8, the prices soared again: 155 . . . 165 . . . 175 . . . 180. When one tough operator loaned a thousand shares at 35 per cent, there were gasps of disapproval. An hour later, the going rate was 85 per cent.

Still Billy Priestman obstinately refused to concede that he was ruined. Hour after hour, drinking endless amounts of scalding black coffee, smoking cigar after cigar until his mouth felt like a sandpit, he wheeled and dealed and covered and shored up his tottering position. The exhausted Douglas simply could not get any more paper without hard cash, and the only way to raise the cash was to start unloading Billy's other holdings. All over the Exchange, the other frantic 'shorts' were doing the same. Soon everything but NP was heading down: steel off seven points, copper twelve.

Haggard, unshaven, Billy Priestman spent a sleepless night at his town house on Park Avenue, while at the Netherland Hotel, James J. Hill, the temperamental, shaggy little tyrant who dominated the Northern Pacific, urbanely told reporters from the New York papers, 'Really, I have no more to do with this than the man in the moon.'

Thursday dawned wet and grey. Long before opening time, a restless crowd milled around the doors of the Produce Exchange, spilling out into the street and around Bowling Green. Rumours flew through the crowd like starlings through a thicket. The doors opened; within minutes, Northern Pacific, which had closed at 160, moved up ten points and then shot up to 200.

At ten, Douglas staggered out of the arena and slapped a strip of paper on the desk in front of Billy Priestman. The price of Northern Pacific stock was up to six hundred and fifty dollars a share. Hollow-eyed, Billy read the figure that Douglas had extrapolated. Sixty-five million dollars. Sixty-five million dollars that he did not have.

'I don't understand,' Douglas wailed. 'I just don't understand. I thought –'

'Shut up!' Billy growled. His mind would not function. All he could see was the line of zeros in front of him.

'What are we going to do?' Douglas said, his voice trembling. 'Mr Priestman, what are we going to do?'

'Nothing,' Billy croaked, lighting another cigar. 'Get some more coffee. Wait. There's still hope, Douglas.

468

You're not dead yet.'

'I wish I was.' The broker's once-immaculate suit was wrinkled and dirty. One pocket flap was half torn off. His shoes were scuffed. His eyes were pouchy and bloodshot. Any other time Billy would have been sorry for the man, but right now he couldn't even be bothered.

'Get some coffee,' he repeated. Douglas scuttled away. Billy sat and watched the shouting, pushing, paper-waving horde on the floor, their voices a wave of sound that created a constant thunder in the huge trading area. The morning dragged on; the chaos continued: American Tobacco down twenty-one points, Standard Oil down a hundred and fifty by midmorning. The horrific climax came at noon, when the brokerage firm of Street & Norton sold three hundred shares of NP common for a thousand dollars each. The whole market was a shambles, in worse confusion that the littered floor of the exchange itself. Hundreds of 'shorts' were insolvent, with no hope of ever being able to pay off. Hundreds of thousands of stockholders had lost their entire savings as all the other stocks tumbled. At noon, Kuhn, Loeb & Co. joined with Morgan & Co. to announce a respite: no deliveries would be required that day. Another announcement quickly followed. Northern Pacific shares would be 'fixed' at 150, and 'shorts' would be allowed to settle at that figure.

'What are we in for?' Billy said to Dick Douglas.

'A hundred and eighty-five thousand shares at 150,' the grey-faced broker told him. 'Twenty-seven million, seven hundred and fifty thousand.'

Billy smiled. Douglas looked at him open-mouthed: how could anyone smile on being told such awful news?

'It's better than sixty-five million,' Billy said. He stood up and stretched.

'Mr Priestman –' Douglas began.

'Sell everything,' Billy said tonelessly. 'Do whatever

you have to do.' He got up and walked out of the Produce Exchange and into the street, rubbing his upper left arm. That damned throbbing: it had come back yesterday and now it was like a gigantic toothache, the pulse of pain dull and sullen. He felt soiled and greasy. He needed a hot bath, a shave, a change of clothes.

He decided to walk up Broadway and get a cab outside the St. Nicholas Hotel. It was already warm on the street and he breathed the fresh air gratefully. By God, he thought, I could eat some breakfast.

As he reached the corner of Morris Street, a deep unease touched him. Without warning, something that seemed to him like a huge piano being demolished by a giant sledgehammer exploded in his head. He collapsed on the sidewalk, and lay there staring at the blank wall in front of his face. He tried to command his body to rise, but it would not function. He felt angry, in a put-upon sort of way. As if he hadn't had enough this last few days! His face felt numb. He heard the clatter of running footsteps. Someone bent over him, a dark shape between his eyes and the bright sky.

'Whatsa matter?' a voice shouted. 'You sick or sumpn?'

No need to shout, Billy thought petulantly, I'm not deaf. He tried to speak but no words came. It was as if he was someone else looking down at the man lying on his back in the street, along with the roughly dressed stranger kneeling by his side. The man began to go through Billy's pockets, snatching out his watch and wallet. Billy felt a huge surge of anger – the bastard was robbing him! He half-raised himself off the sidewalk, his eyes bulging with the enormous effort, his arm extended in accusation. He had managed to sit upright when the huge, reverberating noise sounded again inside his head, and he collapsed, dead, as the thief bolted down Morris Street and disappeared.

49

It was warm for September, so they took their coffee out on the porch and sat in the soft twilight, watching the light change on the crest of Pajarito Mountain. It had been a noisy, happy meal, a party as well as a dinner. They drank more wine than usual, celebrating Lee's new job with Teddy Roosevelt, the success of Bush Exploration, and anything else they could think of. Hunt and Rachel sat in the swing seat, Jenny and Lee in the sprawling leather armchairs facing it. James sat in the Old Man's Chair, a padded rocker set at an angle to the left of the three porch steps. Faraway across the sage-stippled scrubland, a coyote yipped. James hooked his heels over the porch rail and tipped back his chair.

'Feels like old times,' he said.

It was good to have them all here. It was especially good to have Lee and Jenny back, and the grandson he had never seen wandering all around the house asking small-boy questions. That took a man back in time a long way.

'Tell us about Teddy Roosevelt, Jen,' Rachel asked. 'What's he like?'

'Stagy,' Jenny said. 'Like a mixture of St Vitus and St Paul.'

Even in his most sedate business dress, Theodore Roosevelt had a florid style. When he got excited, his voice became high-pitched and loud. His huge smile was startling, his gestures jerky and over-emphatic. He walked at a pace just short of a run, and all in all, Jenny

471

thought, acted like an overgrown schoolboy. He had come beaming towards them as they got out of the car that had brought them from the station.

'Glad you could come up!' he said, pumping Lee's hand up and down. 'Dee-lighted!' He flashed them the horsey smile that had already made him the favourite of the nation's cartoonists and ushered them towards the house.

'This is a lovely place,' Jenny said.

'Isn't it?' Roosevelt beamed. 'Built it in '84, mostly out of book royalties. Twenty-two rooms. With a family as big as mine, you need plenty of space!'

Sagamore Hill, he called it. The big fieldstone house stood at the end of a winding, sandy road that led down to Oyster Bay on Long Island, commanding a magnificent view across the sound. The sparkling blue water was speckled with the white triangles of sailboats, and for a moment, Lee felt a pulse of envy for the sailors, feet snugged under toestraps, leaning far out as the wind filled the sails and the boats cut through the chattering waves.

'We'll go inside,' Roosevelt said. 'Lunch is ready. Nothing grand, you understand. Just plain food.'.

'Suits us fine, sir,' Lee said, looking at Jenny. They went into the dining-room, where the fine oak table was laid with beautiful silver and Royal Doulton china. On the sideboard, chafing dishes steamed; bacon, liver, kidneys, scrambled egg, kedgeree, steak. There was toast and soft white rolls. Simple food, Jenny thought with a wry smile. About fifty dollars' worth.

After they had eaten, she walked in the garden while Lee and Roosevelt talked. It was quite a jump from Manila barracks to New York, and she was still having trouble adjusting. Lunch with the Vice-President of the United States was a long step from haggling over the price of fish in Binondo market.

'Why do you think he's invited us up?' Lee had said to her on the train. She smiled at his boyish nervousness.

'Relax,' she said. 'What's the worst that can happen to us? That he *doesn't* want you to work for him?'

'I don't mean why, I mean *why*-why,' Lee said.

'He wants to look us over,' Jenny said confidently. 'Make sure we're the right sort.'

'Right sort of what?'

'Chaps,' she said, in an utterly–utterly British accent.

It would have taken the hide of an elephant to be unaware of Roosevelt's scrutiny at lunch, she thought, as she walked. He could have telephoned to offer Lee whatever job he had in mind. No, he had wanted to vet her. She hoped she'd passed the test. She wandered between banks of carefully tended flowers, across smoothly rolled lawns with never a plantain in sight. It must be nice to have a big house with a beautiful garden, she thought and six kids sliding downstairs on tin trays, and a whole sub-family of cooks and nurses and nannies and maids and manservants. She looked back towards the house. Through the tall window she could see Lee leaning forward in his chair, listening to what Roosevelt was saying.

'You enjoying life, Lee?' the Vice-President said.

'Very much, sir.'

'Made any plans?'

'Not before I'd spoken with you, sir.'

'How old are you, Lee?'

'Thirty-five, sir.'

'Great age. Wonderful. Whole life ahead of you.'

Lee nodded, but said nothing. Best to let Roosevelt work up to whatever he had in mind in his own time, his own way.

'Interested in politics?'

'In a general sort of way.'

'You're honest. I remember that. It can get you in trouble sometimes. Like . . . I heard about what happened. In Manila. You did a wonderful job bringing those boys back in.'

'Thank you, sir.'

'Sorry business about your wife's father. Couldn't be avoided, I suppose?'

'General Moffatt was relieved on General MacArthur's orders, Mr Roosevelt, not mine. I don't believe he had much of a choice. General Moffatt lied under oath at a court martial.'

'Yes, yes. Damned shame, all the same. Leaves a nasty taste in the mouth.'

This was not the first time Lee had been given the impression that it might have been a lot better if he'd never come out of the jungle. The sleeping dogs would still be lying, the Army's skirts clean. He had been astonished at how quickly the Moffatt affair had been filed and forgotten.

'Well, let's hope we've heard the last of it,' Roosevelt was saying. 'Now. Want you to work for me. You interested?'

'Naturally, sir.'

'I'm putting a group of men together to manage my affairs. A team, you might say. If everything goes according to plan I intend to run for president in 1904.'

'Against President McKinley?'

'That's the general idea.'

'I don't know much about politics, Mr Roosevelt, but I know enough to know the hardest man in the world to beat is a president in office. And President McKinley's got a fine record.'

'I can win, I think,' Roosevelt said. 'McKinley's a good man, but he belongs to the old century. I belong to the new one. Anyway, I plan to give it a try. Now – want you to come in with me?'

'As what, sir?'

'I want to put some of my own ideas to work,' Roosevelt explained. 'Try a different style of campaigning. One of the things I'd like to do is have someone go ahead of me to each new town I'll be visiting. Get to the right people, make sure they're there when I'm there. Start the excitement, light the fire. It's something new. A big job. Are you interested?'

I ought to be excited, Lee thought. *Why aren't I?*

'I've no experience of work like that,' he pointed out, stalling for time to think.

'Experience comes with doing,' Roosevelt said. 'What I'm looking for are those rare birds, honest, decent men who won't let me down. Men with plenty of stamina, plenty of pluck, plenty of get-up-and-go. I thing you fit the bill, Lee. That's why I'm offering you this job.'

'It's a wonderful opportunity, sir,' Lee said. 'I don't know what to say.'

'Say, "yes",' Roosevelt grinned, showing his enormous horse teeth. 'Say "yes" and we'll shake on it!'

Still unsure, Lee nodded. How could you say no? They shook hands warmly, and Roosevelt clapped an arm around Lee's shoulders, walking with him out of the room.

'You'll want to find your wife,' Roosevelt beamed. 'Tell her the good news.'

Tell her the good news that I'm going to be a flack, Lee thought flatly. Tell her that Mr Roosevelt brought me all the way home from the Philippines because he needed an honest man to convince other honest men that he was the one they should vote for. It was only as he passed through the door into the garden that he realised how expertly Roosevelt had terminated their interview and got him out of his study. There was probably someone else in there already, being offered some other job, or being briefed on Roosevelt's plan to go climb Mount Marcy in upper New York State, or any of the thousand other things the Vice-President seemed to be involved in every waking moment of his day.

'What was it?' Jenny said, turning as he came towards her. 'He want you as his new secretary of state?'

'He wants me to be a member of his staff,' Lee said. 'His advance man, as he calls it. When he runs for president.'

'Advance man?'

He told her what Roosevelt had said, and his own reactions. She said nothing for a while. It was something he was going to have to work out for himself. They walked across the beautifully kept lawns to the bluff, where they could look down on the broad sweep of Long Island Sound and the wooded hills of Connecticut on the far shore.

'Do you like him, Lee?' Jenny asked.

'He gets things done,' Lee said. 'People find him amusing, or infuriating – even inspiring, I'm told – but he gets things done.'

'You haven't answered my question.'

'Why do I have to like him to work for him?'

'You don't,' Jenny said. 'But I seem to remember you telling me how you felt about him the very first time you saw him, in San Antonio, all those years ago.'

'It's crazy,' Lee said. 'Here I am being offered a big job by the man who wants to be the next president of the United States, and I'm not sure if I want it.'

'You could do something else.'

He shook his head. 'I told him I'd do it,' he said. 'And I won't go back on that. Anyway, it'll be nearly three years before he starts campaigning.'

'Him?' Jenny said, scornfully. 'He's been campaigning since he started talking.'

There the matter rested. They travelled back to New Mexico with the dilemma unresolved, ticking away like a time-bomb that both of them pretended did not exist.

'I take it you don't care for Teddy the Bear?' Rachel said, her face shadowed in the porch seat.

'He's just a bit *too*, oh, – masculine for me,' she replied. 'He overdoes it, and you end up thinking he's less tough rather than the opposite.'

'Well, it's quite an opportunity,' Hunt said. 'It could lead to all sorts of other things.'

'Beats the Hell out of jungle fighting, that's for sure,'

James said. 'Talking about which, when the Hell you going to tell us the story of how you got back to Manila with your boys, Lee?'

'Fellow I know was out there,' Hunt said. 'He told me those Filipino guerillas were worse than Apaches.'

'Ain't nobody worse than Apaches,' James growled. 'Take it from someone who knows.'

'Daddy, let's hear Lee's story,' Rachel reproached him mildly. 'We've heard yours plenty of times.' It was true: James never tired of relating how he had saved the life of an Apache 'princess' at Fort Defiance, and how, many years later, his life had been spared because of it.

'Let's talk about the Philippines some other time,' Lee said. 'I want to hear about the Pan-Western business.'

His evasion came as no surprise to Jenny. Lee seemed to want to forget his experiences in the Luzon jungle, bury them somewhere deep in his memory. She had tried a dozen times to get him to talk about it, so far without success.

'Sol and I formed a company,' Hunt said, smiling. 'Rachel Investments. Nice and anonymous. We're buying up Pan-Western stock. A few thousand here, hundreds there. Nothing that will make waves on the Exchange.'

'I can't figure out why there are so many for sale,' James said. 'What's wrong with them?'

'The shareholders see their directors squabbling, nothing but labour unrest and strikes, profits going down, us undercutting their prices every time they try to stabilise . . . if you were a shareholder in Pan-Western what would you do?'

'I'd get out.'

'And I'd buy your shares,' Hunt grinned. He looked like a smart, sharp, grey fox, Jenny thought, with his neat beard and cropped iron-grey hair.

'Willie Priestman finds out what you did, he's not going to be your best friend,' James observed, puffing on his cigar.

'He was paying me to be a traitor,' Hunt said harshly. 'He's hardly in a position to shout "foul".'

'That won't stop him doing it,' Lee said. 'Do you and Sol think you can get control of Pan–Western, Hunt?'

'We will. No doubt about it. Those turkeys aren't interested in running a business. They're only interested in money. They've seen millions go down the drain. They held on hoping we'd go under and they could get a monopoly. Once we've got control, they'll get out. We'll be able to pick up their stocks for par or even less.'

'And what does all this share-buying mean?' Jenny asked.

'Very simply,' Hunt said, with a smile they had all come to recognise, 'we will control the smelting industry in this country.'

A small silence followed his words. The Starr family had always had money, but never riches. They knew Hunt was talking about millions and millions of dollars.

'Hunt, you've done miracles,' Lee said. 'Billy Priestman would have wiped us out long ago if it wasn't for you.'

'That old buzzard,' James said. 'Hard to believe he's cashed in his chips.'

'That was some funeral they gave him,' Hunt remarked. 'Stopped the traffic in San Francisco for two hours. The cortège was a quarter of a mile long.'

'Proves what they've always said,' James said briskly. 'Give the public what it wants, and they'll turn out to see it.'

'Daddy, that's cruel!' protested Rachel.

'Wouldn't be surprised,' said James, unabashed. 'Don't expect me to be sorry because that old sonofabitch is dead!'

'For what it's worth, I agree with your father,' Hunt said. 'Billy Priestman hated this family. He wanted to see it ruined.'

'What did he go down for?' Lee asked.

'Something around the thirty million dollar mark, I

478

heard.'

'Whooooe,' James said softly. 'That is a lot of money.'

'Did he have that much?' Jenny asked.

'He was worth plenty,' James said. 'But not that much.'

'They say Willie is selling everything to meet his father's obligations,' Hunt added. 'There's even talk that he's using his newspapers as security to borrow money.'

'Breaks your heart, don't it?' James said. 'You know, if I wasn't on the wagon, I'd have a drink on that!'

'Tell you what, Pa, I'll have one for you. Hunt?'

'Don't mind if I do.'

'I'll get them,' Jenny said, jumping up. 'Ray, you want something?'

'Is there any wine, Daddy?' Rachel asked.

'Sure.'

'I'll bring some,' Jenny said, and went inside. She was back in a few minutes with whisky for Lee and Hunt, and glasses of wine for herself and Rachel. James grinned as they toasted each other.

'Watch out for that damned stuff,' he said. 'It can play hell with your liver!'

He was looking better now, Lee thought. Their first meeting had been a shock. His father looked so much older, as if it had been ten years instead of two. Rachel told him about the drinking, the despair, the times she thought James really would kill himself.

'I don't know how you got him on the wagon, Ray,' Lee said. 'Damned if I do. I never could have done it. You must be tougher than any of us thought!'

'We all are,' Rachel smiled. 'You look at us: Sarah. Your Jenny. Me. We're all tough, we women. It goes with the job.'

'Well, boy – you got a drink, I got a smoke. There's maybe an hour till it gets too cold to sit out here. So – start talking.'

His father's abrupt command jolted Lee's reverie, and it took him a moment to collect his thoughts. 'Talking?' he said, frowning. 'About what?'

'About the Philippines,' James said impatiently. 'Been asking you to ever since you got back, dammit!'

'Hell, Pa, it's too nice a night to talk about that,' Lee protested. Jenny sensed the tension in him, and in herself. *Tell it, Lee*! she begged him silently. *Tell it and let it die*!

'Maybe if I topped that drink up it would help,' Hunt said, sensing Lee's inner conflict. He took the glass from Lee's unresisting fingers. 'I could certainly use another one.'

No one spoke as he went inside. Jenny reached over and touched her husband's hand. It was cold and unresponsive.

'Was it awful, Lee?' Rachel asked softly. 'Was it really that bad?'

He nodded. At that moment Hunt came out with the drinks, and put one in Lee's hand. He frowned at it as if he had never seen a glass before.

'Luzon is a strange place,' he said quietly, as though to himself. 'Nothing you've ever seen prepares you for what it's like. Animals you've never heard of, flowers you didn't know existed. Colours. Everything huge, dazzling, bizarre. At first you think, this is astonishing, this is fascinating. Then you find out. The jungle is like the sea. You get no second chances. If you make a mistake, it kills you. And before long, you hate it. You hate it as you've never hated anything, as if it were a live, sentient thing that is trying to kill you. Which it is.'

He looked up and smiled, then shook his head. 'Sorry. I got carried away for a moment.'

'Don't stop,' Jenny said softly.

Lee looked at her and saw the plea in her eyes. He knew what it was, and he loved her for her concern. It was just . . . he didn't know if he was ready to go back there yet. To remember Chuck Gates bleeding to death

480

in his arms. And the grim, relentless death march south through the sweating, murderous, unforgiving jungle.

And yet . . . something in him said, *Now, tell it, tell it and let it die.* Where had that thought come from?

'All right,' he said, making a decision. He walked across the porch, hitched himself on to the porch rail, and faced them. Their faces were indistinct in the dying light. Manuela had lit the lamps inside; moths blatted against the windows. It was as if they were children, waiting breathlessly for some story of witches and hobgoblins and magic to begin.

'Luzon,' Lee said. 'Try and picture what it's like. Three ranges of mountains, like the fingers of a man's hand laid on the outline of the island. Between them, the two great rivers, Cagayan and Angat, joining way up north to empty into the ocean at Aparri. All the main settlements are on the west coast. There are only two kinds of road: *malos caminos*, and *muy malos caminos*. Bad and very bad. A few trails that the jungle will overgrow in four or five days if they're not kept clear. All the rest you have to hack through. Killing work even if you had plenty of food and water. Try and imagine it. Three degrees hotter than hell, sixty-nine of us, trying to move quietly, fighting the jungle.'

Santa Isabela was about two hundred and eighty kilometres from Manila as the crow flies. A hundred and seventy-five miles, say. Between the two places, the terrain was mostly unexplored jungle, with a few scattered villages hardly worthy of the name. Mountains six, seven thousand feet high, and below them, range after jumbled range of ever-higher hills rolling southwestward towards Balete Pass, the main gateway to the south.

'The *insurrectos* had a field gun,' Lee continued. 'They were beginning to get our range. We were pinned down in the trenches. Then we heard the rebels cheering. They were all moving up the hill. We thought it must be Moffatt coming to relieve us, but nothing happened.

481

All I could think of was something a colonel I knew had said to me about Moffatt: "Don't ever let him get you in a tight". He meant he'd abandon me. I couldn't believe it, but I wasn't going to wait to find out. I got my men up out of the trenches. There were fifteen men too badly wounded to take with us. We had to leave them behind. That was one of the hardest things I've ever had to do. A top sergeant from Arkansas named Tom Hanna took charge. He said he'd cover for us as long as he could. He knew what would happen to them. We all did. There wasn't a damned thing any of us could do about it.'

They moved warily through the deserted town, and were skirting the paddy fields north-east of the plaza when they ran into patrolling *insurrectos*. The six Filipinos killed two Americans before they were dispatched, in a fierce, almost silent struggle, with bowie knives. As the Americans moved away from the town, rifle fire rose to a crescendo behind them. Sergeant Hanna and his wounded comrades were keeping their promise.

'We travelled by night for a week,' Lee went on. 'I figured if Moffatt had fallen back, it would be to the south. As it turned out, he went east, and down the coast. We were on our own.'

He reverted to the old Apache tactics. In open areas, there was always a pair of scouts ahead of the main party, another pair alongside, and another behind it. They kept to high stony ground whenever it was possible, leaving little or no trace of their passage. Each man carried his own water. Each day, that night's assembly point would be designated, so if anyone got separated from the unit, he'd know where to aim for.

Day after day they fought the burning, seething jungle. Their food was whatever they could catch and kill. There was never enough water. Lee watched helplessly as man after man collapsed, dehydrated. At first it was a headache, dizzy spells, tingling limbs. They had difficulty speaking and walking. Then they passed to twitching, deafness, loss of vision, and numbness, and from there into delirium and death. He saw men open their own veins with knives to wet their lips with blood that merely intensified their awful thirst. He saw men tear a live monkey apart and stuff its raw, bloody flesh into their mouths. He saw men die of fevers he could not treat, snakebites for which he had no antidote, or from utter, final exhaustion. Every day they prayed for the rain they had so often cursed, but none fell. When finally they found a river, two of his men plunged over the steep, sloping mud bank, and slithered flailing into the powerful current, too weak to fight it, swept away to die in the element for which, minutes before, they had been begging.

'Sometimes we'd make five miles, or six, in a day. Other days, no more than half a mile. Sometimes we seemed to be doing nothing but climbing mountains. We'd get to the top of one, thinking, God, we've done it, and then we'd look up and see that there was another one in front of us, higher than the last one. And we'd sit down and sob with, I don't know, disappointment, exhaustion, maybe both.'

They came to a village, a tiny place where the children scurried away in terror as the Americans came out of the jungle. They no longer looked like soldiers, but like staggering, gaunt, hollow-eyed scarecrows. Most of them had some kind of fever, or dysentery, or both. The villagers gave them rice and chicken. It was a feast. Some of the men found rice wine and drank until they were unconscious. They slept under a roof for the first time in a month. They rested up for two days, then moved on. Two hours after they left, *insurrectos*, informed of their presence by the 'bamboo telegraph', fell on the advance pair of scouts and decapitated them, hardly breaking stride as they ran screaming at the column. The Americans were slow and weak. The rebels killed four more men before Lee got them into fire-fighting positions, driving the *insurrectos* back into the jungle. For the next five days and nights, the *insurrectos* shadowed them, picking off two men with sniper fire, and butchering another who collapsed, too sick to keep walking. Nerves as taut as drawn bowstrings, senses alert for any sign of the enemy, Lee's column inched forward through the green hell. The sudden whirring flight of a parrot could draw a panicked fusillade of shots. The snapping of a branch beneath a foot would send them diving for cover. The rebels were out there somewhere. Only they knew when and where they would attack. On the fifth day, one of the troopers, a man named Furillo, whom everyone called 'Joe the Wop', put his right leg into a mantrap the rebels had dug in a small clearing. At the bottom of a three-foot deep hole, sharpened stakes of bamboo, angled upwards, pierced Furillo's groin. Furillo screamed like a pig in a slaughter-house, arching his body upwards in a reflex attempt to pull himself off the spearing spikes. They ran to him and pulled him out of the trap and laid him on the ground. The lower half of his body was already slick with dark red blood. Furillo drew his knees up to his belly, still screaming. His eyes were empty, as if there was no one behind them any more. Singleton looked at Lee and shook his head.

'Shoot me!' Furillo screeched. 'In the name of God, shoot me! Jesus, Mary and Joseph, one of you men, shoot me, shoot me!'

They stood and watched, like dumb cattle, while Joe the Wop's screams turned to whimpers, then groans, and finally, silence. The faceless jungle mocked their helplessness. There was no point in even burying the man. The *insurrectos* would dig his body up and cut it to pieces anyway.

'Every time I lost a man, it was like a personal insult,' Lee said, speaking so quietly they almost had to strain to hear him. 'It was between me and the jungle, in the end. I was half-crazy, I suppose. We all were.'

He kept track of the days by tying knots in a rawhide strip he carried. It was on day eighty-two that they found Balete Pass, three thousand feet high, and saw the land sloping away from them southwards, and knew they were going to make it home. In the hills there were settlements friendly to the Americans. The villagers fed them, gave them supplies, washed their filthy clothes. No longer did they reel and stagger as they moved. They walked purposefully, soldiers again. Tatterdemalion, bearded, long-haired, jaundice-skinned, maybe, but still soldiers.

At a village above Baguio, the headman and elders brought them two *insurrectos* who had been captured by the young men of the village. They were very proud of this display of zeal.

'¡*Nosotros, Americanista*!' they said, nodding and smiling. '*Yenkee Dooal.*' The two *insurrectos* looked at Lee's men with terror in their eyes. The men returned their stares with the dispassion of butchers appraising meat.

'*Por favor, Señor Comandante,*' the younger of the two men said to Lee.

'¿*Hablas usted Español?*' Lee said, surprised. Most of the natives spoke only the singsong Tagalog dialect, of which he knew but a few words.

'We have papers of much importance, *Señor Comandante*,' the man said. He was tall and skinny, his face pockmarked, a two-day growth of beard making him look older than he was. The other one, squatter and thicker set, looked about forty. He was probably less than thirty, Lee thought. Men aged fast in the Philippines, the women even faster.

'Show them to me,' Lee commanded.

'You will see to it that we are well-treated, *Señor Comandante?*' the man asked hesitantly. He looked again at Lee's men sprawled around the compound.

'What is your name?' Lee said.

'Cecilio Segismundo.'

'Where are you from?'

'Isabela province.'

'What are these papers of which you speak?'

Segismundo gestured to the second courier, who reached inside his shirt and brought out an oilskin-wrapped pouch. It was quite thick, and filled with documents. Segismundo opened it and handed some of the documents to Lee.

'They are orders from President Aguinaldo to General Tomas,' he said.

Lee's attention sharpened. 'You received these papers from President Aguinaldo himself?' he said, putting disbelief into his voice. The older of the two men took a deep breath; his eyes flashed with insult.

'*Naturalmente,*' he said haughtily.

'I cannot believe it.'

'*Es verdad.* It is true.'

Lee shook his head. 'You are telling me Aguinaldo is near here?'

'No – ' Segismundo blurted, then stopped. The older man was glaring at him.

'Lieutenant!' Lee snapped.

Singleton jumped to his feet. 'Major?'

'You know how to do the water cure?'

Singleton grinned. 'You bet, Major!' He pulled out his pistol and gestured at the two cowering rebels. 'On your feet, you two!' he growled.

'*Señor Comandante, Señor Comandante!*' the older Filipino pleaded, grabbing Lee's arm. 'We are your prisoners. You promised we would be well-treated. You said – '

'Where is Aguinaldo?' Lee said.

'*No sé!*' the man whispered. '*No sé!*'

'All right, Singleton, carry on!' Lee said, turning away.

As he did so, the younger man shouted, 'Tell him, you stupid *hijo de puta*! Tell him or he'll do it!'

'Palanan,' the older man said, sullenly staring at the

ground. 'Aguinaldo is in Palanan.'

Taking the two *insurrectos* along as prisoner-guides, the Americans left the village and marched south. Four days later, as they approached the town of Malolos, they ran into a patrol of the 20th Kansas Volunteers. A burly non-com led Lee to the headquarters tent, where he found himself in the presence of Brigadier-General Frederick Funston.

'"Fearless Freddie", they call him,' Lee said. 'Won the Medal of Honor at Calumpit in '99 and got promotion to brigadier. Little fellow, not more than a few inches over five feet, topped off with carrot red hair. He got very excited when I told him about Aguinaldo. Said he'd take the papers in to MacArthur personally.'

Lee and his men were given transportation south from Malolos and arrived in Manila two days later. It was one of the best moments of his life, Lee said, when he formed up the remnants of his unit at the barrack gate and marched them across the parade ground.

'After that it was all downhill. I found out Funston had been given all the credit for locating Aguinaldo. That I was accused of having wilfully disobeyed my commanding officer's orders, and thereby causing the defeat at Santa Isabela. I brought what was left of my unit halfway across Luzon and they wanted to arrest me! Oh, it all got straightened out later, of course. Nothing personal, they said. You know how it is, how the Army works. I told them they could take it all and shove it where the sun never shines, along with the medal they were talking about giving me!'

There was a long silence as he finished speaking. It had grown cool now, and a soft wind was sighing over the dark land. James got up, shaking his head, and put his hand on his son's shoulder.

'Thank you, Lee,' he said softly. 'I know how hard it is to come to terms with losing good men. It's even harder to talk about it afterwards.'

Rachel stood up and kissed her brother on the cheek.

487

'I'm proud of you, Lee. We all are. Don't ever forget that.' She turned to Hunt. 'I'm going in now. It's cold.'

'I'll make some coffee,' Jenny said. 'You want some, Advance Man?'

'And maybe a nightcap,' he said. 'All of a sudden I feel absolutely wiped out.' Jenny took his hand and he smiled. She knew what he was talking about. Now that it was over, he was surprised to realise it hadn't been as much of an ordeal as he had thought it might be. Maybe the mind had its own way of healing the wounds, he thought. He would never forget any of the men who had died on that death march across Luzon. But maybe now they would cease haunting him. It was a thought worth hanging on to.

As Rachel, Jenny and Lee went inside, James touched Huntington Carver's arm to detain him a moment. The two men stood on the dark porch, not looking at each other.

'Wanted to ask you, now your business is shaping up: What about you and Ray?'

'Porty won't divorce me. I expect you know that.'

'It doesn't surprise me.'

'Ray's probably told you, we want to live together. It would make her happy if you told her you approved.'

'Can't do her, son,' James said. 'Don't misunderstand me – it's not that I'm against it. But Portland's my girl, just the same as Rachel is.'

'Portland doesn't give a damn – '

'Don't say it, Hunt,' James said quietly. 'I won't believe it, even if you do. She's my daughter. We're not seeing things quite the same way right now. That'll pass. Everything passes. She'll still be my daughter.'

'I envy you.'

'Envy me? Why?'

'For being able to do that,' Hunt said. 'You think I'll ever learn how?'

'We all get older, son. Seems a shame to do it and not learn anything worth a damn along the way.'

'I'd marry Ray tomorrow, if things were different.'

'Well, they're not,' James said. 'So the best I can offer is to say you'll have to live with the hurt you cause. Like all of us do.'

'I think I can do that, sir,' Hunt said.

'Then I envy you,' James told him. 'Because I never could.'

Buffalo *Inquirer*, September 7, 1901

PRESIDENT McKINLEY SHOT
AT THE EXPOSITION

★

ANARCHIST TRIES TO ASSASSINATE HIM
AT RECEPTION

★

TWO BULLETS FROM REVOLVER LODGED IN
STOMACH

★

MAN LOCKED UP AT
POLICE HEADQUARTERS

★

IVER-JOHNSON .32 PISTOL
UNDER A HANDKERCHIEF
AS HE SHAKES HANDS WITH THE PRESIDENT

★

DOCTORS HOPEFUL AT MIDNIGHT

★

'BOYS, DON'T HURT HIM' PLEADS McKINLEY
PRESIDENT BORNE OUT

★

TROOPS ON GUARD

★

DAY BEGAN WELL

★

SENSATION IN WASHINGTON
SCENES AT THE WHITE HOUSE
MRS McKINLEY RECEIVES THE NEWS

50

For something like four months, Willie Priestman had worked a fifteen-hour day and a six-day week; even now, he wondered whether he would ever get straight again. His father's death had flattened him in more ways than one. Despite the time that had elapsed, he still felt cheated. Death was sometimes like a betrayal.

It was as if Billy's sudden death had set off a chain reaction, and nothing Willie could do seemed even to slow it down. On Willie's instructions, a group of brokers, carefully selected by Dick Douglas – himself still recovering from the losses he'd incurred in the Northern Pacific fiasco – sold off his father's shareholdings, moving cautiously so as not to depress prices. The house on Nob Hill was auctioned, and the ranch at Santa Barbara sold outright. Yet no matter how much was sold, it was still not enough. Willie floated loans, using his own companies as surety, only to find that he was using the capital he had raised to pay the interest on his father's outstanding debts. With the newspapers themselves endangered, he had no choice. He started selling his own shares; but as he began to do so, the death of President McKinley, six days after he was shot at the Exposition in Buffalo, made the market jittery, and prices fell. Because of this, he had to go slowest when he needed speed the most: the longer he took to raise the money, the more interest he must pay on his outstanding debts.

He travelled across the country eight times in that

four months, visiting every city where one of his newspapers was published, reviewing operating procedures, reducing staff, slashing expenses, cutting down overheads. It was like attacking Hell with a bucket of water.

The newspaper industry was not as profitable as it had once been. In each major city, the *Inquirer* chain now had three or four competitors. There just weren't that many readers. Print runs were now dramatically down in comparison to the halcyon days of the war with Spain. Everywhere he went, Willie racked his brains for ways to boost circulation, but somehow the ideas didn't seem to come the way they once had. It was just that he was so damned tired all the time.

On top of all that, his personal life was in chaos. He returned to San Francisco to try to effect a reconciliation with Marietta, as Arthur King had suggested. Although she received him civilly enough, Marietta made it very clear that she wanted nothing more to do with him.

'You walked out of my life a long time ago, William,' Marietta said quietly. 'It . . . it took me a long time to get used to the idea that I was married to a man who did not love me. Who probably never had loved me.'

'Marietta, I —'

'Don't!' she said, not raising her voice. 'Don't start lying now! You don't want to come back to me because of *me*. Or because of your children. You have some other reason, one I don't know about yet. You want to use us, the way you've used people all your life. And when we've served our purpose, you'll walk out on us again.'

'You're my wife,' Willie said. 'They're my children. I have some rights in the matter, Marietta. You can't deny me them.'

'I'd never prevent you from seeing your children, William. You know that. But I'm not going to let you destroy everything I've struggled to achieve in the last few years. The children are happy. I have my own life,

492

at last. I won't put all that at risk to satisfy your whim!'

'And what if I insist?' Willie said harshly.

'That would be the rock you'd perish on. I'd fight you, William. In open court. I'd produce witnesses who'd testify about you and . . . that woman. I'm sure I don't need to tell you what your competitors would do with a story like that.'

'You really hate me that much, Marietta?'

'Oh, don't play hurt and wounded with me, William!' Marietta said, her eyes widening with anger. 'Sympathy has to be earned. You've never merited it, not in your entire life. No, I don't hate you, William. If anything, I'm sorry for you!'

'Sorry for me?' he said, his own anger kindling. 'I don't want pity.'

'What you want is totally immaterial,' Marietta retorted. 'Don't you understand that?'

'Damn you, Marietta, this is important!' Willie said, his voice rising. 'My whole future is at stake here!'

'I'm no longer interested in your future, William. Only mine, and the children's. You can do what you like. We have long since ceased believing that the sun rises and sets because you tell it to. We don't need you any more.'

'You need my damned money, though!' Willie shouted. 'What'll you do if I cut down the money tree, eh?'

'Don't waste your time, William,' Marietta snapped. 'My father saw to it that the best lawyers in California drew up our agreement. As long as you live, as long as any one of us lives, you will pay what you agreed to pay. As long as one sheet of one newspaper in one town is published under your name, the first monies resulting from its sale will come to me. And I defy you – do you hear me? I *defy* you to try to change it!'

'You may find I'm not as powerless as you think!' Willie raged. 'Don't threaten me, I warn you!'

'Go away, William,' Marietta said wearily. 'Leave me

alone. I don't want you to come here again. Go back to your mistress, if she'll have you. She's probably better than you deserve, and I tell you this: apart from your children, she's probably the only person in the world who cares a damn about you!'

'I'll go,' Willie said hoarsely. 'And don't worry – I won't be coming back. You've had your chance. There won't be another. I came out here hoping we could start again, put our lives back together. And you've thrown all my hopes in my face. All right, if that's what you want. But you'll be sorry. Mark my words, one day you'll regret what you've said here to me today.'

Marietta shook her head and smiled, the sort of fond yet exasperated smile a mother might give a wayward child.

'Poor William,' she said sadly, 'all the money you've spent on Broadway, and you haven't even learned how to act.'

Frustrated and angry, Willie left San Francisco and returned to New York. Things were no better there. Susan was touring with a Ziegfeld show, and wouldn't be back for at least another two months. Typical of the damned woman, he thought, always missing on the few occasions when he really needed her. At the office, dozens of urgent messages lay awaiting him. The first person whose call he returned was Dick Douglas. The broker sounded agitated.

'I've come across something I think you ought to know, Mr Priestman,' he said.

'Go on.'

'Huntington Carver. He's been buying up the OKC shares we released.'

'It doesn't surprise me,' Willie said. 'He's always wanted to get back control of that railroad. It's not the end of the world. I can talk – '

'There's more,' Douglas said, cutting him off. 'Carver floated a dummy corporation, Rachel Investments. They've been buying Pan–Western stocks, a little at a time. I don't know exactly how many, but it looks to me as if they might be very close to having control.'

'Control?' Willie said, astonished. 'Of the whole cartel?'

'That's what it looks like.'

'Carver hasn't got that kind of money!' Willie said emphatically. 'Someone's behind this. Find out who it is, Douglas. I want to know –'

'Carver's partner is a man named Solomon Bush. They're getting their finance from Irving Strasberg, the music publisher,' Douglas said. 'Hello? Hello? Mr Priestman, are you still there?'

'I'm here,' Willie said, his voice little more than a whisper. All at once he saw the pattern. His father had thought himself pitted against the Starrs and Irving Strasberg, never realising – any more than Willie had realised – that they had a traitor inside their own camp. Huntington Carver, that bastard, he was in with them! They'd brought his father down, and now they were trying to ruin him. Well, they were going to find out that Willie Priestman didn't break quite that easily!

'What can we do to stop them?' he asked.

'I've spoken to Mr Stillman and Mr Archbold,' Douglas said. 'Their feeling was we ought to get a bear market started if possible. Drive the prices down as far as we can. Make their holdings worthless.'

'It's risky,' Willie said, 'and it will be expensive.'

'I know,' Douglas agreed. 'If you can think of any other way, I'd be happy to –'

'No, you're probably right. How soon can you start?'

'I already have.'

'Let me know what happens,' Willie said, 'As it happens.'

He put the phone down and stared out of the window. He hadn't missed the message implicit in what Douglas had told him. The broker had spoken to Stillman and Archbold, and they had told him what to do. Willie's judgment, Willie's decisions, were irrelevant. It was good to know exactly where he stood with his partners. How quickly you found out who were your friends and enemies when times got tough! Well, they could all go to Hell along with the rest. He picked up the telephone and called Arthur King. Might as well get it all in one day, he decided. When King came on the line he told him what had happened in San Francisco.

'And there's no chance she'll reconsider?' King asked, when Willie finished speaking.

'None.'

'We'd better meet soon,' King said. 'And talk.'

'All right. When?'

'I'll call you,' King said.

I'll bet you will, you sonofabitch, Willie muttered to himself as he slammed down the phone. King was like all the rest of them; going along for what he could get out of it, and running like a rabbit at the first sign of a reverse. Well, I can do without you, too, Mr I-run-the-party King, Willie thought. The rules for getting to the White House were still the same. He knew enough people in the state legislature and at City Hall to push through a nomination for the Senate in the forthcoming elections. It would mean greasing a few more palms, but he was used to that by now. Once he was in the Senate, he'd be able to use his newspapers to propel him towards his ultimate goal, and there wouldn't be a solitary damned thing Arthur King or anyone else could do about it. Willie smiled: the thought of telling King exactly where to stick his fat cigar was one to look forward to.

He looked up at a discreet knock on his office door. It opened, and his secretary came in.

'There's a gentleman outside to see you, Mr Priestman,' she said. 'He won't give a name.'

'Tell him I don't see anybody without an appointment,' Willie said impatiently. Good God, did

496

he have to do everything?

'He . . . said to tell you it was most important, sir.'

'They always do,' Willie snapped. 'What time is my meeting with Stillman?'

'Half past four, sir.'

Willie looked at his watch. He had well over an hour. Miss Stanley hovered distractedly at the door. 'Well, what are you waiting for?' Willie said to her. 'Get rid of – '

'That would be very unwise, William,' an urbane voice interrupted. Surprised, Willie whirled round to confront an elegantly dressed man of perhaps sixty, somewhat corpulent, smiling like a confidence trickster. Which was probably what he was, Willie thought angrily.

'Sir, I'll thank you – '

'Quite probably,' the man smiled. 'You don't remember me, I see. Never mind. If you'll tell your secretary to close her mouth and take it into the other office, I'll explain why I'm here.'

'You'll get out, or be thrown out!' Willie snapped.

'Oh, don't be tiresome, William!' the man said. 'My name is Mortimer Ashby. Doesn't it mean anything to you?'

'All right, Miss Stanley,' Willie said. 'I'll take care of this. Shut the door, please.' He waited until the door was closed and then turned to face Ashby. 'I remember you now. You worked for my father. You're a lawyer. Of sorts.'

Ashby smiled. 'The famous Priestman charm,' he observed, 'as irresistible as ever.'

'I'll give you five minutes,' Willie said, pointing at the chair set in front of his desk for visitors. He went around to his own chair. Dissipated, he decided, looking at Ashby's puffy jawline, the receding hair, the shifting, pouchy eyes and thin, disdainful mouth. All the same, Ashby's manner was confident; bold, even. As if he was sure that whatever he was selling, Willie would want to buy it.

'Well, William,' Ashby was saying. 'you've been through the wringer and no mistake. My condolences on your father's death, by the way. Sorry I couldn't come to the funeral.'

'I don't recall your being invited.'

'That winning charm again,' Ashby murmured. 'How is your battle with Bush Exploration going?'

'How – What the devil are you talking about?'

'Come, come, William,' Ashby said. 'You can't keep things like that secret. You're fighting Bush Exploration for control of the smelter business, aren't you?'

'Is that what you came to see me about?'

'Your father really got caught in that Northern Pacific mess, didn't he?' Ashby ignored Willie's question. 'What's it cost you so far? Twenty million? More?'

'What's this all about, Ashby?' Willie said impatiently.

'Bear with me.' Ashby held up an elegantly manicured hand. 'I really do have a reason for asking. You're not the only one who keeps an eye on the doings of the Starr family, you know.'

'What have you got to do with them?'

'Quite a lot, as it happens. Tell me, do you know Stephen Elkham, Senator Elkham's son?'

'I know of him. He married one of Andrew Starr's girls. Joanna, was it?'

'That's the one. Runs a stud near Fredericksburg in Virginia. Something of a gambler. And a wife-beater, if the rumours are true.'

'And?'

'And he's presently very deeply in debt to some people it's very unwise to owe money to.'

'Good,' Willie said. 'I hope they break his neck.'

'My information is that Elkham has mortgaged the Rapidan stud to pay his debts, but is still in the hole for twenty-seven thousand.'

'He sounds more like an idiot than a gambler.'

'You're right, he's not too bright,' Ashby said, his shifty eyes twinkling. 'I want you to pick up his markers.'

'Let him get the money off the Starrs. They've got plenty.'

'That would be a mistake,' Ashby said. 'He doesn't want to ask them, although he would if he had to. He'll jump at an offer from you.'

'Why would I want to bail him out?'

'He has some diaries.'

'Diaries?'

'Some years ago I was involved . . . socially, with Henry Starr, who was the original owner of the Rapidan stud. He was Andrew and James Starr's cousin. He killed himself. His widow stayed on at the stud, living alone in a little cottage on the estate. She was a recluse. Drank heavily, got enormously fat. Died of dropsy in '97. Ann Beecher Starr.'

'It's taking you a long time to get to the point, Ashby.'

'It'll be worth the wait, William,' Ashby smiled. 'Here is the diary for the years 1865 to 1870. Read a few of the pages I've marked.'

He handed Willie a leather-bound octavo book, fastened with a gold clasp and embossed with the initials 'A.B.S.' Slips of paper had been inserted between the pages. Willie opened the diary and began to read. The room was silent for perhaps twenty minutes as he turned the pages. Then he laid the diary down on his desk and looked at Ashby.

'How many of these are there?'

'Seven,' Ashby said.

'Are they all like this?'

'Yes,' Ashby said. Ann Beecher Starr had written everything down, everything she knew and a lot of other things she had guessed at. She had poured all the emotions damned up inside her on to the page in

499

sloping, cramped handwriting: all the old family scandals, including the story of James Starr's love affair with Catherine Priestman. There was much, much more, Ashby told Willie. Steve Elkham's sadistic beatings of his wife were recorded, as was the back-street abortion that had nearly killed Sarah Starr, and a great deal about Henry Starr's homosexuality and the way in which Andrew and James Starr had covered it up.

'You can get the diaries?'

'For sixty thousand dollars. And a consideration.'

'What "consideration"?'

Ashby smiled. 'With those diaries you can regain control of your father's businesses. Put Bush Exploration out of business, wipe out the consortium. You can take the OKC railroad back. Break all of them: the Starrs, Solomon Bush, Irving Strasberg. You can put a stop to Lee Starr's political ambitions. You can do anything you want to do.'

'All right,' Willie breathed. 'What do you want?'

'A partnership,' Ashby said coolly. 'A million in cash, and directorships of all the main companies.'

'Is that all?' Willie said. 'You want your pound of flesh.'

'Yes,' Ashby hissed, 'by God, I do! I've waited for it long enough!'

'All right,' Willie said. 'I'll have the papers drawn up as soon as you deliver the diaries to me.' He would have promised Ashby City Hall gold-plated and wrapped with silver ribbon if he'd asked for it. Once he had his hands on the diaries, however, that would be a different matter. He had no more intention of giving Ashby a partnership and a million dollars than he had of flying to the moon, but no sign of that showed on his face. Willie had played poker with some of the best players in the business.

'I'll need a bank draft,' Ashby was saying. 'I take it you've got the money, William?'

'I've got it,' Willie said curtly.

'You're a strange one, William,' Ashby commented. 'I thought you'd at least gloat a little. You act as if this was just another business deal.'

'Oh, no,' Willie told him. 'It's a lot more than that, Ashby. I'm going to finish the Starrs now. All of them. That Jew-boy, and that treacherous bastard Huntington Carver. By God, Ashby, I'm going to enjoy this!'

'That's my William,' Ashby said.

51

Christmas at Belmont was a tradition. Each year the family would gather on the weekend preceding the holiday, and once more, as in earlier times, the house would be full of laughing, noisy people. There would be horses to ride, ponies for the children. Neighbours would come to visit and there would be return visits with hugs and kisses and squeals of delight as old beaux met old flames.

On Christmas Eve, all the servants and grooms attended the Farm Ball in the great Dutch barn, specially cleared and decorated for the occasion. Andrew Starr would make a little speech, there would be a tall Christmas tree with a present beneath it for every employee, and they would dance all the way through to Christmas Day.

This year there were even more reasons than usual to celebrate the holiday, and nearly everyone came down. There hadn't been such a gathering for a long time, Andrew thought. It pleased him immensely to see so many of those he loved gathered around the great Georgian dining-table. His wife, Diana, sitting next to her 'partner' Solomon Bush. His brother James, looking better than he had done for a long time, smiling and talking to his son's wife, pretty, dark-eyed Jenny. Even Louisa looked less formidable than usual, he thought; obviously the doctors she had seen in Washington had given her a clean bill of health. She was still underweight, but her eyes sparkled as she sipped her wine and listened to her favourite, Sarah, boasting about her new baby, Lillian.

'I like these family gatherings,' Louisa said, smiling. 'Gives a body a chance to catch up on all the hatchings, matchings and despatchings.'

Next to Louisa, Huntington Carver, clipped and neat, was listening gravely to Irving Strasberg's account of the rehearsals of his new show. Irving was a quietly spoken, self-effacing man, the last person in the world anyone would think would write such pretty songs. He had promised to play for them after dinner. Rachel, next to Strasberg, leaned forward, her chin cupped on her hand, watching both men with keen interest.

Andrew caught his brother's eye and they smiled. Something about this old room: the crystal glasses glimmering on the table, the family silver brought out of its velvet boxes and specially polished, the portraits on the walls, gave a man a sense of continuity, of belonging to something that scorned the passing of the years. He knew James felt the same way; they had talked long into the morning hours, of old times, and lost battles, and dead warriors.

'Sometimes feel out of my time altogether, Bo,' James complained. 'Everything changes so fast these days.'

Automobiles, telephones, great passenger ships that could cross the Atlantic in days, voices recorded on cylinders of wax, flickering nickelodeons in which life was projected moving on to a screen – there seemed no end to the wealth of new inventions that had emerged with the new century. Well, a man just had to adapt, Andrew thought. That was what life was all about.

'Pity Dan and Mary couldn't make it,' James said, leaning over to refill his glass with spring water.

'That damned mail-order business eats his life up,' Andrew replied. He had been unhappy about every one of his daughters' choice of husband, but Dan Hampson had made him the most uneasy of all of them at first. He

503

was footloose, Andrew told his daughter Mary, and he'd never amount to a damn. Turned out Daniel Hampson was a shrewd and inventive businessman, and his Chicago mail-order firm would be billing more than four million dollars' worth of business in the coming year.

I wish I saw them more, Andrew thought, knowing even as he framed the thought that he made no real effort to get on a train and go out to Chicago. I'll go in the spring, he promised himself. It would do Diana good to see the kids. Mary and Dan had two sons, Andrew and Grant. Drew was already a sturdy seven, Grant five. Andrew smiled, recalling Drew's answer when he asked the boy what he was going to be when he grew up.

'Gonna be a shoulder,' Drew said decisively. 'A big, brave shoulder.'

The Hampsons were doing fine. He had to admit he'd been wrong about Dan, and even wronger about young Steve Elkham. James's partner's son had turned out to be a worthless little shit who didn't even think it worth joining his wife's family at Christmastime, even though he and Joanna lived less than five miles away. Well, he wasn't going to let that spoil his Christmas, Andrew thought.

'Well, Lee,' Louisa said, her voice cutting through the murmur of conversation, 'ain't you ever going to tell us what President Roosevelt said to you?'

The question stopped all other conversation. Lee looked at Jenny and smiled. They'd been expecting this.

'He wished me luck. He told me to call on him if there was anything I needed. And he asked me to forgive him if he didn't stay to talk, but he was a touch busy right around now!'

They all laughed. Teddy Roosevelt, everyone knew, was the nearest thing yet seen to perpetual motion.

'I can't get over it,' Rachel said. 'My brother running for senator!'

'I'm not elected yet, Ray,' Lee warned.

'Fiddlededee!' Louisa said. 'You're as good as sitting in the House right now!'

'I'm relying on you all for good advice,' Lee said. 'Especially you, Uncle Andrew.'

Andrew smiled; it had been his idea that Lee run for office. James had enthusiastically seconded the suggestion.

'I feel like that monk in the joke,' Lee had said a few months earlier, when his father asked him how he felt about not working for Roosevelt.

'What monk?'

'This man joins a silent order. He's a real trier, but clumsy. Keeps tripping over the hem of his robe all the time. Every time he does he swears, *dammit*! One day the abbot calls him into his office and tells him he's got to put a hobble on his tongue, or else they're going to have to ask him to leave, can't have blasphemy in the monastery. Sorry, says the guy, I'll try harder, honest. Turns around to leave the abbot's office, trips on the hem of his robe, and comes down with a bang. "Oh, dammit!" he shouts, mad enough to kick his own dog. Then he realises what he's done. "Aw, hell, I said dammit!" he says, picking himself up. "Well, screw it, I didn't want to be a monk anyway!"'

'That how you felt when you saw T.R.?' Andrew asked.

'It was when he said he was sure he could find me *something*,' Lee said. 'The way he said "something" curdled my blood. I could see myself being head bootlace presser or some such damfool thing. I said it was very kind of him but that I'd thought it over, and decided it would be better all round if we just forgot the whole thing. "Bully for you," he said. "I want you to call on me if there's any way that I can help you. Anyway at all".'

'What will you do now? You could come in with us, work with Sol and Hunt.'

Lee shook his head. 'I'd be no good at that.'

'Have you got any idea what you'd like to do, Lee?' Andrew asked.

'I don't know anything except soldiering,' Lee said, 'and there's no damned future in that.'

'You could try something else. There are battlefields nearer home than Luzon.'

'I don't follow, Uncle Andrew.'

'What about statehood?' Andrew suggested. 'Wouldn't that be something worth fighting for?'

Bills to admit New Mexico to statehood had been introduced to every session of Congress, he said, since the Treaty of Guadalupe Hidalgo had made New Mexico a territory of the United States. Subsequently, delegates Manuel Gallegos, Miguel Antonio Otero, Colonel Jose Francisco Chavez had all introduced bills that were rejected. In 1887 Congress admitted the Dakotas, Washington and Montana but refused Arizona and New Mexico. In 1890 it was the turn of Idaho and Wyoming; New Mexico was again excluded. During his five terms in Congress, Antonio Joseph of Taos had twice secured the passage of statehood bills in Congress, only to see them die in Senate committees.

'Everyone's tried: Catron, Harvey Fergusson, Bernard Rodey, Sam Elkham. Nobody's had any success at all.'

'What makes you think I could succeed where they all failed?' Lee asked.

Andrew grinned. 'You'd have me pushing,' he said, 'and T.R. pulling. That might get you through.'

'First I'd have to get elected.'

'We might be able to get something going,' James said. 'If you were really interested.'

'The Senate,' Lee said, almost bemused. 'You really think I could do it?'

'I really think you ought to try,' Andrew said.

In the months intervening, both he and James had worked furiously to set up a climate favourable to Lee's being elected by the territorial legislature; and it looked as if it was going to happen. That was what Lee meant about relying on Andrew for good advice.

'I'll be around,' Andrew said. 'Always did think politics was more enjoyable than being a politician.'

'You'd have done a lot better if you'd tried just once,' Diana told him.

Andrew shook his head. 'Don't start that again, Di,' he said. 'She's been after me to run for office since about 1871,' he told everyone.

'You'd have made a lot better president than some of the men you helped put there, my dear,' Diana said tartly. 'Garfield, for instance. Or Chester Arthur.'

'*Anybody* would've made a better president than Chester Arthur, my love,' Andrew said, to general laughter. 'See here, I don't want to talk politics, I want to have a good time. So let's all go and listen to Irving play the piano!'

Irving ducked his head. 'I play pretty badly,' he said. 'Black notes only.'

'Wait till you hear us sing,' Rachel said, slipping her arm through his. Everyone in the family had taken a great liking to Irving, but no one more than Rachel. She liked his understated sense of humour, his wry appreciation of his good fortune. As everyone went into the music room, James hung back, touching Hunt's arm.

'You finalised the Pan-Western deal?'

'Sol will sign the papers on the first of the year,' Hunt said. 'Then it'll be ours. Lock, stock and barrel.'

They stood by the door while Irving played the songs from his new show. He sang in a husky, but not unattractive voice. When he was finished, Rachel begged him to play some of his other songs. As he sang them, Lee Starr remembered a laughing girl in a carriage, coming over a hill in San Francisco, the whole bay set out below them like a glistening painting. *Lovers is nice, but friends is better*, she said. What a strange, full circle all their lives had described!

After Irving finished playing, Diana took over at the piano, and played while Sarah sang 'Banks of the Wabash' and 'My Wild Irish Rose'. One by one, everyone was called on. James sang 'I'm a Good Old Rebel' and Andrew countered with 'Marching Through Georgia'. Then Diana played carols and they all joined in, singing 'In the Deep Mid-winter', 'Away in a Manger', and 'Hark, the Herald Angels Sing'.

Lee grinned at Solomon as they finished in a more-or-less harmonised crescendo. 'You don't sing bad for a rich Jew,' he said.

'You have to be Christian to enjoy Christmas?' Sol replied, raising his eyebrows.

When the carols were finished, Diana told the servants to bring coffee into the drawing-room. When everyone was settled, Solomon held up his hands and asked for silence.

'I'm not a speechmaker,' he said. 'I'll leave that to Lee. But I want to ask you all something. You allow it, Mrs Diana?'

'You're one of the family, Sol,' Diana said quietly.

Sol nodded in that abrupt, embarrassed way he had. Sarah thought she saw the quick shine of a tear in his eye, but perhaps it was just a trick of the light. There were still sides to her husband that surprised her.

'Tell me something, General,' Sol said to Andrew. 'You *like* the smelter industry? Iron foundries? Lead mines? Copper mines?'

'Not particularly,' Andrew replied. 'But they make lots of money.'

'What about the New Mexico branch?' Sol said.

'I'd have to say the same as Andrew,' James replied. 'The whole busines is beyond my ken.'

'Lee, Jenny? You go into politics, will you have time to be interested in ore prices, mineral rights, exploration costs?'

'None of us will, Sol,' Lee said.

'Then I want to suggest something. You let Hunt and me run the business. We can make it huge. Bigger than anything anyone's ever seen. Electricity's going to be an enormous new industry, believe me. And for that they'll need copper cable, millions of tons of it. I've already got people prospecting out in Utah and Nevada. We can build smelters where they find deposits. We can control the raw materials, production, distribution – ' He stopped, and shrugged eloquently. 'So, so, enough. What I want to say is, you Starrs, you'll pardon me, it's not your style. You're military people, you're politicians, you breed horses. What I'm saying is – all the things you know, none of them is *this* business. Me, I'm in it ever since I was a kid. It's something I know.'

'What do you propose, Sol?' Hunt said.

'We'll draw up agreements,' Sol replied. 'Every member of the family will have an equal share in the profits. That way each one can do anything he wants to do. Paint, build bridges, write books, run for president. But I'll run the company, me and Hunt. We'll do what we think needs doing. That's my proposition. What do you think?'

'It sounds fine, Sol,' James said slowly. 'But it's not something we can decide in five minutes.'

'What would a share in the profits be?' Louisa asked, her bright blue eyes sharp and inquisitive.

'Two, maybe two and a half million.'

'Each?'

'The first year. If it all goes the way we're hoping, it would be more.'

'Andrew Starr, you do what this young man says!' Louisa said. 'If he wants to pay me two million dollars a year to stay out from under his feet, I am more than willing to oblige him!'

'Di?' Andrew said. 'What do you say to all this?'

He always turned to Diana, as naturally as a flower turns to the sun. She was his strength, as she was the strength of all the family. Her sense of purpose and shining integrity was the standard by which they had all learned how to judge. And it was Diana who had financed Solomon and Hunt, right from the start.

'Sol and I have been partners for quite a while now,' she smiled. 'It's no surprise to me that he's done what he's done. But Sol, you're not going to get rid of me quite that easily. I think I'd like to stay with you, for a the ride. I want to be involved, the way we started out. What do you say?'

'I'd say it sounds fine, Mrs Diana,' Sol said, his eyes twinkling. 'But it's not something we can decide in five minutes.'

'He means "yes", Mama,' Sarah interpreted, smiling at her husband.

'That's what I thought he meant,' Diana said.

'Looks to me like this board meeting is concluded,' Louisa said. 'Andrew Starr, isn't it time we brought in that champagne you put on ice?'

'You weren't supposed to see that, Louisa,' Andrew said.

'Quite a few things around here I'm not supposed to see,' Louisa sniffed. 'Doesn't mean I don't see 'em!'

The servants brought in the ice-bucket and glasses.

'A jeroboam?' Lee said. 'I don't think I've ever seen one before. Where on earth did it come from, Uncle Andrew?'

'I've been saving it for a long time,' Andrew admitted, and Diana smiled as she caught his glance. Andrew had laid down the bottle for the birth of their first son. She had produced three daughters, and somehow they had never got around to opening the champagne. When the glasses were all filled, Andrew Starr stood to propose a toast.

'To all of us!' he said. 'May we always have love, may we always have success, may we always be happy, but most of all, may we always be together!'

He sat down to applause, and Diana took his hand and squeezed it. 'That was lovely, darling,' she said softly.

'I feel good,' he told her.

'We all do, Bo,' James said, overhearing his brother's remark. The future looked solid, safe. Wealth gave them the freedom to follow whatever star they chose. Each of them had his own dream. All they had to do now was go out and realise them.

At that moment one of the servants came into the room and spoke quietly to Andrew. James saw astonishment on his brother's face.

'What is it, Bo?' he said, quietly.

'We have a visitor,' Andrew said.

'Who the Hell would come calling at this time of night?' James said, disbelievingly.

'It's Willie Priestman,' Andrew said. They went out into the hall, the others trailing after them, astonished by the news of Willie Priestman's arrival. He was standing in the hall, looking around him as if he had come to appraise the house.

'Well, well,' he said, as they came out and stood facing him. 'How nice to find you all assembled like this!'

'What the Hell do you want, Priestman?' James said, his voice tight with anger. 'What the Hell have you come here for?'

'I've come to wish you a merry Christmas,' Willie said. 'And an unhappy New Year.'

52

'What does he want?' Andrew asked.

'He wants a piece of paper giving him complete control of all our holdings,' Solomon replied. 'Bush Exploration. The Pan-Western shares. The Ohio, Kansas and California railroad. And that's not all.'

'Go on,' James said hollowly.

'He wants an agreement of sale – at a price he will set – for Belmont,' Hunt said. 'And Rapidan stud. And the Flying J. I'm sorry, James.'

'That damned woman!' Andrew said. 'How could anybody have been that stupid?'

'That's as much our fault as hers, Bo,' James said quietly. 'We took pretty much no notice of her after Henry died. She had no one else to turn to, so she turned inwards.'

'And Steve Elkham did the rest!' Louisa said fiercely. 'I'd give something to lay my hands on him, the little bastard!'

They all looked at her, astonished. It was the first time any of them had heard Louisa swear in all the years she had lived at Belmont. She saw their stares and glared back defiantly.

'We can't just let him take everything away from us, Andrew,' Diana said. 'There must be some way we can stop him. Lawyers . . . '

'We've discussed all that, Di,' James said. 'It's not a question of legality. We have to do what he says, or Willie says he'll publish everything in Ann's diaries in the *Inquirer*.'

'You think he could?' Hunt asked. 'You think he could actually print that stuff, word for word?'

'Of course not,' Andrew said. 'Not even Willie Priestman's papers could get away with that.'

'Call Willie all the names you like, he's not stupid. He'll do it with innuendo, with phrases like "insiders say" and "many people believe". You know the way they write those stories. He'll find a way of blackening our name so badly we'd stink for a century!'

'Maybe one of us ought to get a pistol and go and shoot the sonofabitch!' Lee said angrily.

'Don't think it hadn't occurred to me,' James grinned wryly. 'But I figured if it was a choice between being slandered and being hung, it wasn't much of a choice.'

'Then what are we going to do?' Louisa demanded. 'What exactly are you men going to do?'

'Short of a miracle, Louisa, we're going to sign the paper,' Andrew said, with a sigh. The entire family, assembled in the library at Belmont, greeted his words with a chorus of disbelief. It seemed impossible that there was no other solution.

'Well, if there is,' Andrew said, 'I wish one of you would tell us. James, Hunt, Sol and I have spent the last seventy-two hours breaking our brains over it.'

'And we've come up empty,' Hunt said glumly.

'How long have we got?' Lee asked.

'Two days. He wants his answer by Friday,' James said.

'Forty-eight hours,' Louisa muttered. 'It might be enough.'

'What?' Andrew said. 'What did you say, Louisa?'

'Nothing.' Louisa said. James looked at his brother and frowned. They both knew Louisa very well, and they both knew something was hatching behind those bright blue eyes.

Louisa stood up. 'I've got some calls to make,' she said.

'You up to something, Louisa?' James asked.

'Might be,' she fenced. 'Then again, I might not. You men stall that villain until the very last minute, you hear me? Don't sign anything until there's no alternative.'

'You *are* up to something,' Andrew said.

Louisa ignored him. 'Lee, I may need you later. You hold yourself ready, hear?'

'What do you want me to do, Aunt Lou?'

'Just be ready,' Louisa repeated. 'You'll find out soon enough.'

'Mrs Starr?' Theodore Roosevelt said, a smile on his face concealing his puzzlement. 'You said a matter of life and death. Would you like to sit down and tell me what it is that brings you here so urgently?'

Louisa Starr sat down in the chair to which Roosevelt ushered her, and folded her hands primly in her lap. She was still surprised at the alacrity with which the President had acceded to her request for an immediate urgent interview. Perhaps I didn't realise how powerful the Starr name is, she thought. She realised Roosevelt was regarding her quizzically from behind his desk. He looked like a walrus wearing eye-glasses, she thought, almost giggling at the irreverent thought.

'I've come to ask you a favour, Mr President,' she said. 'Well, an act of faith might describe it better. With no questions asked.'

'What act of faith do you have in mind?' Roosevelt said. He leaned back, his expression wary. Mustn't rush my fences, Louisa thought, cross with herself for being clumsy.

'We Starrs are in trouble, Mr President,' she said. 'I won't tell you what kind of trouble, but it is the kind that could destroy everything the family is and everything it has stood for during the last hundred and fifty years.'

'I see,' Roosevelt said, although he did not. 'And how

514

can I help?'

'I want you to give me one dollar,' Louisa said.

'I beg your pardon?'

'One dollar,' she went on, 'in return for which I will sign over to you, here and now, everything the Starr family owns.'

'Why on earth would you want to do that?'

'You'll remember I said "no questions asked", Mr President. You will acquire everything we own for the sum of one dollar. At the end of, shall we say, one month, we will repay the dollar, and you will return everything to us.'

Rōosevelt nodded, his eyes bright with curiosity. 'In other words I become the nominal proprietor of all the Starr affairs, is that right?'

'Correct, sir. We will, of course, continue to manage the properties and businesses . . . on your behalf.'

'Bully!' Roosevelt said. 'Is that all?'

'I hope it will be enough,' Louisa said. 'Here is the document. I have signed it on behalf of everyone in the family.'

'Are you entitled to do that?' Roosevelt asked. He quailed as Louisa Starr glowered at him across the desk. 'I beg your pardon, that was . . . I didn't mean to imply . . . ' he stuttered, chagrined. He was President of the United States, and he was apologising to this formidable woman as if he were an errant schoolboy.

'You have a dollar?' Louisa said, waving his apology aside. Roosevelt took out his wallet and gravely handed her a dollar bill. She slid the deed across his desk.

'Mrs Starr,' Roosevelt said, 'can't you give me some idea of what this is all about?'

'I'm afraid you'll just have to trust me, Mr President,' Louisa said, with a smile. 'For the moment.'

'Is there anything else I should know?'

'I think not,' Louisa said, getting up. 'I'm very grateful to you, sir. I speak for everyone in my family.'

'If gratitude is called for, then this office, aye, and even this public servant, have much to be grateful to

515

your family for, Mrs Starr. I'm honoured to have made your acquaintance. Have you a carriage waiting?'

'Yes,' Louisa replied. 'I've got another call to make.'

'In town?'

She nodded. 'I've got to see a dog about a bitch.' She was out of the white-and-gold room before Roosevelt got his breath back.

Willie Priestman's Washington home was on Lafayette Square, within sight of the White House. He liked to boast to cronies that it would be handy to walk from in years to come. It took Lee only a few minutes to drive Louisa there. He recognised the house at once, and when he pulled up outside, he asked Louisa what she was going to say to Willie.

'Wait for me,' she said, without answering his question.

'Aunt Louisa, you sure this is wise?' he said. She had sworn him to secrecy, insisted that only he and no one else drive her to see the President, and that no word of her activities reach James or Andrew. What the hell is she up to? he wondered, as he watched her cross the wide sidewalk. She rang the ornate bell of the big house and a butler opened the door.

'Mrs Starr,' she said, sweeping into the hallway. 'To see Mr Priestman!'

'If you'll wait here, madam,' the disconcerted servant stuttered, 'I'll see if –'

'Don't *madam* me!' Louisa snapped. The man flinched visibly. 'Go tell him I want to see him!'

The butler bolted out of the hallway and went up the stairs. Louisa looked around her. Just as James had said: all Willie's money would never buy him taste. The hallway was big and airy, with a great glass skylight above it, and a broad, curving staircase leading to the first floor. The hallway narrowed to a corridor lined with bookshelves, and Louisa knew without inspecting them that the books would all be expensive, matched

516

and unread. Statuettes stood in niches, vases on pedestals; one wall was devoted entirely to paintings of what looked like Dutch barges. After a few minutes, Louisa heard a door close upstairs, and saw Willie Priestman, a frown on his face, come down the curving staircase.

'It's Louisa, isn't it?' he said, his voice unfriendly. 'What do you want?'

'Five minutes of your time, Willie. Don't make the mistake of saying no.'

'I've nothing to say to you or any of your damned family!' Willie snapped back. 'Now please leave my home!'

'Last chance, Willie,' Louisa said, 'or I take what I have with me to Joseph Pulitzer.'

'What the devil – '

'Five minutes,' Louisa repeated, putting a snap into her voice. 'Take it or leave it!'

He hesitated, and she knew she had him. He came down the stairs and lifted an arm slightly to indicate that she should follow him.

'We'll go into my study,' he said stiffly. 'It's this way.'

He led her along a hallway lined with more books. Halfway along, he pressed a button somewhere, and one of the bookcases swung aside to reveal a small room. It was furnished with comfortable leather armchairs and a chesterfield, a desk and chair, and heavy velvet drapes. On one side was a fireplace with a huge turtle shell for a firescreen. Above it hung crossed swords above the coat of arms of the Priestman family. To Louisa's surprise, the room was lit by big oil lamps on brackets.

'Well?' Willie said, when they were both seated. 'What's all the mystery about?'

'I have come to tell you that everything the Starr family owns has been sold, Willie. Every single share in every business. Every acre of land, every animal, every building. It will not, therefore, be possible for James and Andrew to sign the papers you have instructed them to sign. They own nothing any more.'

'I don't believe you!' Willie said hoarsely. 'A thing like that couldn't have been done without my hearing of it. There aren't six men in the country who've got the kind of money it would take to buy everything the Starrs own!'

'It's been done.'

'Who is the purchaser?'

'The President of the United States,' Louisa said. There was a silence. A new, wary light came into Willie's eyes. Roosevelt was wealthy, but not that rich. Therefore . . .

'I begin to understand,' he said. 'You've made an . . . arrangement. With Roosevelt?'

'Perhaps,' Louisa said. 'The main thing for you to understand is that there is no longer any means by which you can gain control of anything we own. Nor are you any longer in a position to threaten us or dictate to us. It's a new game, with a new deck. And I am the dealer!'

'You must be crazy!' Willie said, his voice rising. 'Do you think I'm going to let you get away with this?'

'I'll be interested to hear how you plan to stop us,' Louisa said.

'You'll find out soon enough!' Willie sneered. 'Now – go back and tell James Starr, since I am sure it is he who is behind this, this nonsensical plan, that he is a fool. If he were anyone else I would say that what is going to happen to him will be a lesson to him. It seems that is not enough. You are all arrogant fools, you Starrs. So I will show you no mercy!'

'You seem to be having such a good time, it's a shame to interrupt you,' Louisa said mercilessly. 'However, let me ask you a question. You are involved with a young woman. A Miss Susan Simpson. Is that correct?'

'What in the name of – ' Willie spluttered, rising from his chair.

'Sit down!' Louisa said. Her voice cracked like a whip, and something about her made Willie Priestman's jaw slacken. He sat down, eyes wide.

'That's better,' Louisa said. She opened the document case she was carrying and removed a brown manilla folder. 'Let me see. Miss Simpson is an actress. Chorus girl, I think they call it?' She made it sound like an obscenity. 'She made her debut in a show called *Over The Moon*, and appeared in Ziegfeld's – '

'All right, all right!' Willie said angrily. 'Get to the point!'

'Read it yourself, Willie,' Louisa said, handing the dossier across the desk. He started reading. When he was finished, he looked up with eyes that were sick with shock.

'Is . . . is this true?' he managed.

'Do you doubt it?'

'She . . . never . . . she told me . . . her mother was dead. She told me she'd never – '

'As you see,' Louisa said briskly, 'she was lying.'

'What are you going to do . . . with this?'

'I wanted you to see it before I take it to the New York *World*. I'm sure you can imagine what will happen when they learn the truth about your . . . lady friend?'

'Yes,' Willie said softly. 'And so do you, don't you? You know they'll crucify me. And that's what you want!'

'Not at all,' Louisa said. 'All I want are my sister-in-law's diaries.'

'All?' Willie said, with an explosive, affected laugh. 'You really think I'll let you snatch everything out of my hands, trade you those diaries for . . . this?'

'The diaries are worthless, Willie!' Louisa said sharply. 'Oh, you could publish them and blacken our name, perhaps, but that's all. They give you no power over us any more, because we own nothing. However, if you did decide to use the diaries, we would have no alternative but to take this dossier on Miss Simpson to your competitors. Between the two, they'd make an interesting circulation war, and when it was over, you'd be finished, Willie. Finished in every way. You'd have about as much chance of running for office as I have of going to Heaven.'

'And so would you,' Willie said.

'Not quite,' Louisa smiled. 'We'd still have all we are, all we have been. We'd still have our history and our pride, Willie. We'd survive. You would not. And you know it!'

'Goddamned nerve!'

They glared at each other across the desk. Willie's gaze was the first to waver. 'I won't do it,' he said, but his voice was a croak. 'I won't do it.'

'Yes, you will.'

'I've never been beaten!' Willie screeched. 'Never! Never!'

Louisa said nothing. She did not flinch as Willie kicked his chair over backwards with a banging clatter and stood up, his face dark with rage. Without another word, he flung open the door of the safe on his right and grabbed the diaries piled on the shelf inside. He hurled them across the room in Louisa's direction. They fell, thumping on the carpeted floor like broken birds. Louisa still said nothing. Willie Priestman glared at her, eyes burning.

'Get out, get out, get out!' he shouted. 'Take what you came for and get out!' Louisa got up out of her chair and knelt by the scattered pile of books. As she picked them up, Willie stood like a stone.

'There are only six diaries,' Louisa said. 'There should be seven.'

'Here, damn you!' Willie shouted. He hurled the last of the leather-bound books at Louisa. It hit her high on the forehead, knocking her reeling backwards against the leather-padded door of the study. Her trailing arm caught the big oil lamp on its wall bracket, sweeping it to the floor. It smashed, splattering coal oil across the room which ignited instantaneously. Before Willie could get round his desk and cross the room, the floor and walls were a living, leaping mass of yellow-red flame and smoke. Out of them came a terrible scream.

520

53

Lee was sitting in the coach, idly watching the people walking in the little park and the pigeons circling the head of Andrew Jackson's statue, when the front door of the Priestman house was hurled open and a servant came rushing out, shouting 'Fire! Fire!' Behind him, a great billow of smoke ballooned into the street, and through it, screaming, ran two maids and another manservant.

'Fire, fire, fire, fire!' screamed the man. Lee vaulted out of the carriage and grabbed him by the shoulders.

'The lady who went into the house, where is she?' he shouted. The man tried to shake him off, eeling to one side, screeching the same word over and over. Lee slapped him hard across the face and the man stopped screeching all at once and looked at him with shocked, empty eyes.

'The whole place!' he said. 'It's just . . . all fire. All fire!'

'Where is the lady?' Lee snapped. 'And Mr Priestman?'

'They went into the study, I think,' the man said, his eyes flickering with panic.

'Where is it?'

'Ground floor, on the left of the hallway.'

'There's an alarm on the corner,' Lee said. 'Run quickly and get the fire brigade here!'

The man dashed off, and Lee turned towards the house. As he did, the ground-floor windows bulged outwards and exploded in a leaping tongue of flame and smoke that erupted towards him. Behind him, the frightened horses lunged against the traces of the carriage, their hooves striking sparks from the pavement.

'Grab those horses!' Lee shouted at a man in the small crowd that was gathering. 'Take them across the street. Move yourself, damn it!'

The startled man ran to do his bidding as Lee dashed towards the doorway of the house. Roiling clouds of smoke came out of it, stinking and black. He wrapped his coat around his head and ran through the smoke into the burning hall. Light from the skylight above the vestibule thinned the darkness slightly, and he saw that the fire already had a terrible, gloating hold on the big house. Flames danced upwards along the banisters of the curving staircase and licked hungrily at the priceless Gobelin tapestries hanging on the walls. How could it have got so far so *quickly?* he thought. He threw himself flat. There was more air at ground level. He crawled along the hall, shouting Louisa's name. Smoke rolled ever more thickly over his body. The air was almost too hot to breathe. Flames leaped at him from open doorways. Somewhere he heard glass exploding, and the heavy crash of falling objects.

'Louisa!' he shouted, hacking and coughing as he sucked smoke into his lungs. He felt, rather than saw, a doorway on his left. Flames roared inside it like a furnace. They'll never put this out, he thought. Nothing could be living in there. Where the hell was the study?

In the blinding blackness he thought he saw a movement, and reached out to touch something solid yet yielding. A hand grabbed his like a vice, and he pulled hard. Willie Priestman lay on the floor ahead of him, his clothes smouldering, his face seared by flames.

'Die,' Willie coughed. 'Die, ease.'

Lee put his mouth next to Willie's ear and shouted

'Where? Louisa? Where? Louisa?'

Willie shook his head, his body heaving. He lifted a hand and pointed. The books on the wall were burning. Behind them, the wooden partition was already gone, and Lee saw through the smoke that there was a room behind the bookcases.

'Study? There?' he yelled in Willie's ear. He thought he saw Willie's head move Yes, and edged forward across the floor. Flames rushed at him, and he felt the quick zizz of his hair singeing. The heat was intense now, almost unbearable. He kicked at the burning bookcases with his feet, and rolled back as they disintegrated into flying, burning fragments that fell towards him like a waterfall. He closed his mind to the pain of the burns. Now in the great glare of the burning staircase he could see the lumpy shape of Louisa, lying on the floor inside what had been Willie's study. The place was already a ruin, and in the strange off-and-on flare of the fire, Lee saw a beautifully bound book ignite and burn brightly, like a match, until it was nothing but a pile of blowing ash, whirled upwards in the spiralling heat of the fire.

Grabbing hold of Louisa's clothes, Lee started working his way backwards into the hall. She seemed to weigh a ton. The smouldering carpet hampered movement; he lay, racked by sobs and coughs, exhausted in moments.

With an enormous roar like an express train going through a tunnel, the fire rushed upwards now towards the glass skylight above the hall, leaping and turning, higher and higher. Flames like the tongues of dragons reached Lee, searing his skin as he dragged Louisa along the hall to where he had left Willie Priestman. Inch by inch, choking and heaving, Lee worked his way along the scorching floor. The floorboards beneath the carpets were charring; every time he laid his hand flat it was like touching a hot stove. Lee knew he was close to collapse; he could no longer open his eyes. Bells seemed to ring constantly in his ears. His breathing was a shallow rasp.

All at once, with a terrible rumbling boom, the staircase collapsed, and towers of flame and sparks and smoke leaped upwards, as though in triumph. Dragging Louisa and pushing the half-conscious form of Willie Priestman in front of him, Lee felt the life slowly being sucked out of him by the seeking, relentless fire. He lapsed in and out of consciousness. He no longer had any idea where he was.

He was two feet from the front door when one of the firemen saw him and shouted to his comrades. They dashed into the hall and dragged him clear. The flames were burning the soles off the shoes on his feet. Reeling, vomiting, his mind almost numb, Lee was carried out into the street.

'Hold on, buddy, there's an ambulance on the way,' a fireman said, giving him a pitcher of water. Lee gulped at it greedily, then splashed some on his face, clearing the muck from his eyes. He saw Louisa lying on the pavement, her clothes still smouldering. He saw Willie Priestman kneeling on the ground, looking at the house with mad eyes, his mouth forming words.

As Lee watched helplessly, Willie got to his feet and reeled towards the burning doorway. One of the firemen blocked his way. 'You crazy, mister?' he said. 'Get the hell away from here!'

Willie shook his head angrily. 'Diaries!' he said. 'Get them!'

'There's nothing in there but ashes, mister!' the fireman said, holding Willie's arms. With a sudden surge of strength, Willie threw off the man's grip and dashed back into the burning house. Lee stared at the smoking space into which the man had disappeared, unable to believe what he had just seen. The fireman looked at the doorway and then at Lee, his mouth gaping with astonishment.

Diaries, Lee thought. That's what he was mumbling. Willie had gone back into that death-trap for Ann Starr's diaries. It was the act of a suicidal madman.

A dull, prolonged rumbling shook the street, and the firemen yelled at the gawping spectators massed along the street to get back, as the roof of the house collapsed inwards. Flames rushed forty feet into the air. The smoke climbed in a turning tower towards the sky. The thunder of the hosed water smashing against the façade of the building was like the sound of some great waterfall. Lee picked his way through the chaos of hoses and tenders and running firemen to the ambulance that had drawn up. Two men jumped out of the back with a stretcher and very gently lifted what was left of Louisa Starr on to it.

'Wait,' Lee said softly. 'A moment, please.' The two men looked at each other and shrugged. Lee knelt beside Louisa and put his mouth close to her ruined ears.

'He's dead, Louisa,' he whispered. 'It's finished.'

She stirred slightly, and something that might have been a sigh passed through the charred skin around her mouth. He bent very close as the burned lips moved. He was never sure whether he heard correctly, but he could have sworn the last word she spoke was 'Jesse'.

54

They stood together on the platform of the railroad station: James, Lee, and Jenny with young Jack in her arms. The little boy was vastly excited.

'Goan onna chain!' he kept chanting. 'Goan onna chain!'

'Well, Pa, we're off,' Lee said.

'Hard to believe,' James replied. 'Senator.'

Look at him, he thought. My son, boarding a train to go to Washington as senator for the Territory of New Mexico. Lee would do well, he knew. He was quiet, solid, dependable. He looked more like a writer or a teacher than a politician. Maybe one day, James thought, I'll see him off from some railroad depot as the first senator from the State of New Mexico. Statehood was coming, never a doubt of it. That was something to hold on for.

Lee looked well. The burns he had suffered in Willie Priestman's burning mansion had healed completely in the two months since that awful day; and there had been no after-effects from the smoke he had inhaled. The doctors told him he was lucky to be alive, and Lee grinned.

'I was in the Philippines,' he said. 'You think I don't know that?'

He turned to face his father. 'Pa, I want to thank you. For everything.'

'Hell, boy, I didn't do much,' James said. 'I just got in touch with people I know. Your Uncle Andrew too.

We got a lot of contacts between us.'

'You make it sound simple,' Lee said. 'It takes the best part of a lifetime to make contacts like those. I just want you to know . . . I'm proud of you, Pa.'

'This mean you're gonna quit bitching about all them speeches I made you write?' James grinned.

'Even that,' Lee said.

'You look after him, Jen,' James said to Jenny. 'Make sure he don't get into any worse trouble than you can handle.'

'I'll watch him,' Jenny promised. They hugged each other and said their goodbyes. Jack kissed his 'Ganpop', still chanting 'Goan onna chain, goan onna chain,' as Jenny climbed aboard the Pullman coach and found her way to their compartment.

'We'll see you in June, Pa,' Lee said. 'At the Academy.'

June would be the centennial of West Point, and it was to be marked by a three-day celebration attended by President Roosevelt and Secretary of War Elihu Root.

'Take care of yourself, boy,' James said huskily. He put his arm around his son's shoulder. Lee turned and hugged him and James felt the prickle of tears. Damned old fool, he told himself.

Lee gave his father a last hug and then got on the train as the shouts of "board!" echoed along the platform. He walked through to the compartment and opened the window so they could lean out and wave to James as the train moved out of the station.

James stood with his arm raised until the train reached the bend in the rails at the far end of the depot and they could see him no more. Lee closed the window and settled in his seat. He looked at Jenny and his son and smiled.

'So,' he said. 'Here we go.'

Jenny nodded. She knew what he meant. The fire, the inquest, the protracted business negotiations which had followed the death of Willie Priestman, and the funeral

527

of Louisa were all behind them now. It had been a hard and testing time, but it was over.

'I'm going to do things, Jen,' Lee said. 'In Washington. I'm going to make a mark. For you. For Jack. I mean it. I'm going to make you proud of me!'

Jenny felt a surge of love and pride, and reached across to take her husband's hand.

'I'm proud of you already,' she said. She put her arm around him and kissed him. Jack squirmed between them.

'Me's well,' he said. 'Me's well.'

That was how it ended.

That was how it began.